# A DARCY SWEET MYSTERY

## BOOKS ONE TO SIX

## K. J. EMRICK

SOUTH COAST
PUBLISHING

**First published in Australia by South Coast Publishing, December 2013.**
**Copyright K.J. Emrick (2012-2017)**

# BOOK 1 - DEATH COMES TO TOWN

# CHAPTER 1

*S*omething wasn't right.

As Darcy Sweet approached the front porch of the small, neat as a pin house she could feel a dark presence surrounding it. Even the cheerful window flower boxes that were brimming with an assortment of brightly colored flowers couldn't detract from the oppressive feeling emanating from the house.

Unable to stop herself from continuing she stepped carefully up onto the porch. Advancing slowly and cautiously toward the front door she could see it was open slightly, left carelessly ajar in the darkened night. Alarm jabbed her sharply in the chest. Darcy knew that it should have, would have, been closed at this time of the night. Something bad had happened here. She was certain of it.

She laid a shaky hand carefully upon the door. Feeling the cool surface of the wood beneath her palm she gently pushed on it, letting it swing inward on its own. Afraid of what she might see, Darcy cautiously peered around the edge of the door. Inside the room it was almost completely dark and she couldn't see a thing.

Nothing stirred. It was like the house was waiting for her to enter. All she could hear was the almost deafening ticking of the clock.

Tick tock, tick tock.

Why was it so loud?

Darcy could feel her heart pounding at a rapid rate as, against her better judgement, she moved through the doorway and further into the room. It felt like the house was swallowing her up whole. Something evil was here. She could feel it as it skittered down the length of her spine.

Tick tock, tick tock.

She wanted to run but she couldn't. Her feet seemed to have a mind of their own as they carried her further into the darkness. Sweat formed in little beads across her forehead and she blotted the moisture with the sleeve of her shirt. Wiping uncomfortably damp palms against her jean clad thighs Darcy took a deep breath to try and calm herself down. It didn't help.

Where was she? How did she get here? No answers came to her as she carefully navigated the darkened room.

Tick tock, tick tock.

What was with that clock? It seemed to reverberate inside of her head making it pound in pain. Where were a pair of ear plugs when you needed them?

Her eyes were beginning to adapt to the darkness and she could make out the shapes of the furniture. The room looked a little familiar but she couldn't quite place it. There was a faint hint of perfume in the air. The scent was also familiar but Darcy couldn't place where she'd smelled it before. Something was tugging at her memory. What was trying to get through to her?

A kind of shuffling noise just off to her left broke her out of her thoughts and set off a fresh feeling of alarm as she involuntarily turned toward it. She could see a dark figure bending over something. There was some sort of lump or pile that the figure was interested in. He was fussing about with it but Darcy couldn't see what he was doing.

Terror lanced through her as the figure moved out of the way and she could finally see what the lump was on the floor at his feet.

A body!

Who was it? She couldn't see. Was it somebody she knew?

An involuntary gasp escaped her lips and the dark figure swung around in her direction. Darcy couldn't make out his features but there was a strong feeling of familiarity about him. Did she know him?

There was no more time to worry about the dead body as the dark figure straightened and began to move. She could see he was tall and well-built but still his facial features remained a mystery to her. He moved toward Darcy in seemingly slow motion. Darcy needed to get out of here now but she was rooted to the spot. She tried desperately to move but her legs wouldn't obey her.

The edges of Darcy's vision blurred as the dark figure moved slowly in her direction. He didn't seem to be in a hurry. He moved like he had all the time in the world. Slowly and surely toward her.

Then without seeming to move any faster the tall dark figure was looming over her blocking out what little light there was in the room. Quicker than a flash his hands were around her neck... squeezing, squeezing ever so tightly... his fingers biting into her soft flesh... she couldn't breathe... she tried to claw at him but her arms flailed around missing her target. Her vision was beginning to fade... she was losing consciousness... she couldn't... she couldn't...

Tick tock, tick tock.

GASPING FOR BREATH, her whole body writhing in panic, Darcy Sweet tried in vain to remove the choking fingers from around her neck. It took a moment to register that she could actually breathe and the fingers were only phantom fingers, not real.

Wait. What?

Completely disoriented and not at all sure what had just happened she rubbed a still shaking hand over her face, and her neck, where the feeling of the phantom fingers choking her still lingered. She tried to relax her tense muscles and calm her breathing, hoping to clear her mind enough to work out what was going on here.

Hadn't there just been someone trying strangle her? Yes, or so she'd thought but actually no, obviously not, as she was in her bed in her own room. She flicked on the lamp that was situated on the bedside table. She felt a little better as warm light flooded the room. It had been a dream. Just a bad dream. That was all it was.

But what did it mean?

She squeaked a little as the bed dipped slightly and a blur of black and white fur passed before her, rubbing up against her in a feline hello.

"Oh for Pete's sake Smudge, you scared me half to death." It was just her big, beautiful, black and white tom cat come to find out why she was awake so early. Maybe it was time for breakfast already. Not yet buddy boy. She smiled as he rubbed up against her once again, purring loudly as was often the case with him. She could always count on Smudge to make her feel better. He was more than just a cat to her. He was family. He was her best friend.

"Hello boy." She ruffled the fur around his neck and pulled him to her for a friendly hug. She sure could do with it after that awful dream. What had it meant? Hopefully it was just a dream but she knew from previous experience that wasn't always the case.

She had a very bad feeling about it.

"*W*ell ladies, what did you think of the book?" Darcy looked expectantly at the members of the book club she hosted twice a month in her shop. She was anxious to hear their views on the latest book they were reading.

The Sweet Read book store was a quaint little shop located on the main street of Misty Hollow and every inch of it was filled with books. Old books and new books alike stood side by side on the shelves. An odd assortment of books lay around on every available surface and some were even stacked in corners. The whole shop looked like ordered chaos.

There was always a vase of colorful fresh flowers on the counter, usually Darcy's favorite combination of lilacs and daisies, and their fragrance would permeate all corners of the store. Pretty pale blue curtains with little flower motifs hung in the windows giving the store a real homey feel.

It was late afternoon and the members of the book club, eight in all including Darcy, had just settled down to discuss their latest book choice. They were sitting in a circle of comfortable overstuffed armchairs on one side of the store, each with a cup of something warm to drink. As Darcy looked from one face to the next she felt a sinking sensation in the pit of her stomach.

The book club had been reading Agatha Christie's "And Then There Were None." Darcy had known that the other women probably wouldn't enjoy it but she had been getting so sick of reading the usual sappy romances that the group favored and had decided that a change was in order.

The ladies looked at each other, eyes darting anywhere but in Darcy's direction. She sighed inwardly. Finally, Anna Louis, Darcy's neighbor, was the first to speak up.

"Honestly Darcy?" The small dark haired woman, who was older than Darcy by ten years or more, paused, her bright blue eyes wide and earnest. Darcy nodded for her to go on. "I didn't love the book. A bit too suspenseful for me. Kept me up all night long."

As she spoke Anna fiddled nervously with the front cover of the book, which had a long crease worn down into it. Probably caused by the nervous worrying of Anna's slim fingers, Darcy thought. Anna had always been a little on the skittish side for as long as Darcy had known her. The other women in the group murmured their agreement as Anna continued, "Sorry Darcy, I know you love mysteries and all those ghost tales. They're just not for me." She softened the remarks with a small smile.

Darcy wasn't offended. She had a reputation in the town of Misty Hollow as a bit of an odd duck because she was often involved in strange occurrences that sometimes happened about town. It wasn't that she sought these odd events out, but ever since she was little she had been able to tap into another world, the world beyond the grave. In this tiny town everything was gossip and Darcy was quite often at the center of it, even if no one but her sister knew the entirety of her secret.

"That's fine Anna," Darcy said in a soothing tone. "I realize that not everyone is going to like the same books. That's a good thing. It gives us something interesting to discuss." She smiled at the older woman, and Anna visibly relaxed.

Darcy didn't try to fight it when the ladies started up a conversation about the latest romance novel by Debbie Macomber. In fact, she quite enjoyed it. The ladies could be very high-spirited when they were talking about a subject they all loved. Two hours slipped by very quickly.

"It was a great meeting today Darcy. I really enjoy these book club sessions." Anna gently patted Darcy on the arm as she was preparing to leave after the meeting had ended.

"I'm glad you enjoyed it, Anna." Darcy smiled at the older woman and walked with her to the door as Anna shrugged on her coat and gathered up her bag. Anna stopped, brow furrowed, and pointed out of the window. "The mists are starting to rise again. I'd better hurry home. Bye Darcy."

Darcy pulled the door open for Anna to leave and watched her friend wave as she quickly rushed away into the gathering darkness.

Darcy let the door swing shut and stood looking out of the window. The bad dream she'd had made its way into her mind again. She hadn't been able to shake it and it had left her feeling odd all day. A shiver ran through her at the thought of it. The mist was getting heavier by the moment as she gazed outside. It gave everything such an eerie feeling.

That same odd sensation was settling inside of her once again, like something was going to happen but she just didn't know what. She never knew what. She shivered again and absentmindedly started to twirl the delicate antique ring on her finger. It was a habit that she had whenever she got stressed or anxious. It had been her great-aunt's ring and Darcy wore it to feel closer to her.

The lighting was dim inside the shop and she could see her image reflected in the glass of the window as she stared outside. She took a good look at herself and wondered why she was blessed, or perhaps cursed, with these odd feelings and visions.

She looked pretty ordinary on the outside with dark hair framing a heart shaped face, green eyes and petite figure. Ordinary.

She sighed. As she was about to turn away from her reflection she felt Smudge rub up against her leg causing her to startle a little. Shaking her head at herself Darcy absentmindedly bent down to scratch his ears and hoped that the mist wouldn't last too long.

~

DARCY FLIPPED the sign from 'OPEN a good book today' sign to 'CLOSED, THE END' and pulled the front door of the book shop closed behind her. She locked up for the night and started for home. Not owning a car meant that she had to walk everywhere she needed to go. In fact, there weren't that many cars in Misty Hollow as the town was small enough that you could walk from one side to the other in about fifteen minutes.

Darcy didn't mind the lack of a car though. The exercise did her good. She had contemplated, more than once, getting a bicycle to use as transport, but hadn't gotten around to it yet.

Pulling her coat tighter around her to keep the damp mist out she set off along the main street with Smudge following along behind her, occasionally darting in between her feet and nearly tripping her up.

The sun was slowly setting and Darcy liked this time of day when the main street was quieter. She loved this town with its quaint shops and lovely town square complete with a gazebo in the center. Beautifully trimmed grass flanked the gazebo on all sides and several regal red maple trees stood tall and proud. Darcy loved those trees. They brought glorious color to the town center all year round. She loved to spend time in the town square and often ate her lunch there when the weather was fine. Tonight as she walked past, the mist gave it an almost other-worldly quality. She shivered again. That odd feeling settling like a stone in her stomach. She tried her best to just ignore it though.

As she walked she imagined that everyone was home already in their cozy houses. On her way she strolled slowly along Main Street with its lovely evenly paved sidewalks. She even did some leisurely window shopping as she passed the lit windows of those shops still open at this hour.

As she came to where the town Library stood on the other side of the street she saw her friend Linda come out through the double glass front doors. Poor Linda, it looked like she had scored the closing shift again. Her boss, Marla, was always making her work the odd hours of the day and usually Saturdays as well.

Linda looked up and when she spotted Darcy she smiled and lifted her hand in a happy wave. Darcy smiled and waved but wasn't about to stop to chat. She was anxious to get home and Linda could be very hard to get away from when she got started.

She turned to continue her trek home and hadn't taken two steps when she heard Linda calling her.

"Darcy, Darcy wait up a minute." Darcy sighed as she turned toward her friend who was just stepping up onto the pavement. "Oh Darcy, how are you? I haven't seen you in simply ages."

"I'm good Linda. Just heading home to get some dinner now actually." Darcy tried to get the message across that she wasn't interested in conversation but it didn't seem to register with Linda.

"Oh good, good. Actually I wanted to ask you if you've seen my cat?" Linda's face was eager, eyes wide.

"Your cat? No, I can't say that I have."

Linda's face fell, her eyebrows drooping down. "Oh darn, I was hoping you would have seen her. Persephone has been missing for about a week now. I've looked everywhere but I can't find her. I'm getting so worried about her."

Darcy was concerned. It wasn't like Linda's cat to wander.

The beautiful, fluffy, snowy white Persian was a mostly indoor cat and usually never ventured far from home.

"That's too bad Linda. I'm sorry I can't help you. I will keep an eye out for her though, she can't be too far away surely."

"Oh thanks Darcy. I don't know what could have happened to her. She's been acting odd for a while now. I was thinking of taking her to the vet over in Meadowood as she's gotten a little overweight. I haven't changed her diet so it seemed strange to me. But then she just upped and disappeared. Maybe she has a tumor or something. Maybe she's run away to die." Linda was working herself up into a right state, tears running down her cheeks.

Darcy felt bad for the woman and pulled her in for a comforting hug, patting her on the back like one might do to comfort an upset child. "It will be okay Linda. We'll find her."

Linda sniffed loudly and pulled away to look at Darcy. "Thank you, thank you so much Darcy. I knew I could count on you to help."

"Anything I can do Linda, I will."

"Linda!" Darcy saw Linda jump when the voice of her angry boss Marla rang out across the square.

Linda sighed. "I thought she'd gone home. I'd better get back to work. Thanks again Darcy." She ran across the road with a final wave.

Darcy stood for a moment thinking about where Persephone could have gotten to. It was a mystery. One she was surely going to try to work out for Linda. She knew how she would feel if anything happened to Smudge.

As Darcy left Main Street and stepped onto the path that would take her home she stopped and turned to look back on the town. The sun was settling below the horizon now and there were lights twinkling in all of the windows. The beautiful scene spread out in front of her somehow made her feel melancholy.

She turned away and continued walking, hands in her pockets, feet dragging slightly.

As she walked along the path to her home, she thought about her life, as she so often did. She didn't think she was doing too badly for a twenty-nine-year-old woman. She owned her own business and house. She had inherited both of them from her great-aunt Millicent Carlisle or Millie as she was known about town, when she'd passed away eight years ago, but she had made them her own.

Darcy's home life hadn't been that great when she was younger. Her 'sixth sense,' as she liked to call it, had been somewhat of an embarrassment to her upper class mother. Darcy always felt like her mother wished she would disappear. So eventually she had, kind of. Darcy had left home at fifteen to come here to Misty Hollow and live with her aunt.

Millie had been more of a mother to her than her real mother had ever been. So much so that Darcy was still connected to her now, even after her death. Of course, she hadn't told anyone that little detail. Not even her sister Grace, who now lived in Misty Hollow also, with her husband Aaron, and worked for the Misty Hollow police force. She hadn't told her friends either, who already thought she was a little nuts. She didn't need to give them any cause to think she was completely mad.

She sighed at the sudden thought of going home to an empty house once again. She shook herself. This wouldn't do. Just because she was alone didn't make her lonely, and she did have Smudge after all. She looked around for her cat but couldn't see him anywhere. There was only so much comfort a cat could give, she supposed. He was probably home by now wondering where she had got to. He would be demanding his dinner as soon as she got to the house. She smiled at the mental picture. "I love you too," he would say if he could talk. "Now where's my food?"

The melancholy mood refused to budge, though. She figured it was probably partly because she lived further away from the town than most people. The only neighbor she had was Anna and there was quite a big pasture between their two houses. It wasn't like they could talk over the fence or anything.

As she rounded a bend in the path and could see her house she felt a little better. She loved this house. She loved how it sat among the tall pine trees that gave wonderful shade when it was hot. She loved the big porch and the big lawn. She sighed. It did feel like she was a little isolated sometimes. Though most of the time she enjoyed the solitude.

But sometimes she wished for something more. It would be nice if there was someone waiting at home for her on nights like this. Someone she could talk to and take comfort in. Someone she could have children with, a family. She laughed at herself then. She didn't need those things. Most of the time she actually preferred to come home to an empty house. Those things would maybe be nice but she was okay as she was right now.

When Darcy reached her front porch she stopped short. Her front door was slightly ajar. That was odd. She could have sworn that she'd shut it properly when she'd left for the book shop that morning. Her dream popped into her head again. But it hadn't been her house in the dream. Still, it unsettled her a little seeing the door open.

She pushed on the door carefully and stuck her head around to have a quick look inside. She couldn't see anyone. She could usually sense when something was off and she wasn't really getting anything right now. Only that squirmy feeling from the dream that she couldn't shake. Deciding it had nothing to do with her home she entered the house. It was as she was taking off her coat that she heard a kind of rustling noise coming from the living room. Alarm shot through her as she remembered the dream again.

That feeling might have been trying to warn her about something after all. Could the dream be coming true here in her own house? There was definitely someone, or something, in here.

Settling her coat on her shoulders again she grabbed the nearest heavy object, which happened to be an old umbrella of her aunt's that had been hanging from one of the coat hooks in the entryway, the one with the heavy plastic end shaped like a diamond.

Not much of a weapon, but it wasn't like she kept a shotgun by the door. Foolish perhaps to try to defend herself but she didn't see any other alternative right now. She couldn't call her sister because the phone was in the room with the intruder. And unlike most everyone else she knew, Darcy didn't own a cell phone. Long story.

Darcy carefully tiptoed along the passageway to the living room doorway. Craning her neck, she looked around the edge of the doorjamb. She could just make out the figure of a man riffling through the drawers of the computer desk that sat flush against the far wall. Was it the man from her dream?

Her heart was pounding so loud she was sure he would hear it and it would give her away. She tried to calm it down and then entered the room as quietly as possible. She raised the umbrella with the heavy end up over her head in a defensive pose. Then she screamed as loudly as she could to hide her fear, "What do you think you are doing?!"

The man jumped back and dropped the papers he had been holding. He turned to face Darcy with his hands held in the air.

Then he saw what she was holding, and his eyes popped. He started laughing loudly. "What were you going to do with that thing? You Mary Poppins or something?" He pointed to the makeshift weapon she was holding with a sneer on his lips.

Now that was an expression she'd seen him wear any number of times.

"Jeff! What on earth are you doing in my house?" She was shocked to see her ex-husband standing there in her living room. They didn't associate anymore. They really didn't have anything to talk about. He definitely didn't have any right to be in her house going through her things.

And he was the reason that she preferred to come home to an empty house every night. She had momentarily forgotten that little detail when she'd been wishing for more on her walk home. Their marriage had been at best rocky. No, once was quite enough and she had no intention of ever doing it again. Jeff had cured her of that.

He began laughing so hard at her that he was bent over double. Reluctantly she dropped the umbrella with a clatter to the floor. She would much rather have hit him over the head with it. Repeatedly.

"Oh for Pete's sake!" She rolled her eyes and crossed her arms under her breasts. "Will you stop laughing and tell me why you are skulking around inside my house? My house, Jeff! And why are you going through my personal things?"

Jeff calmed himself down enough to be able to talk to her. "Stop assuming the worst, will you? I came here to get an old box of photos that my mom wants." He was wiping the tears away from his eyes as he spoke. "Not get hit in the head with a stupid umbrella."

"So, what, you just decided to come on in and help yourself?" Darcy considered calling her sister at the police station. Maybe she could talk some sense into Jeff.

His laughter evaporating, Jeff set his face in a scowl. "Always hospitable, aren't you?" He stood up straighter and crossed his arms over his chest. "Anyway you weren't here and I was in a hurry."

Darcy felt her blood start to boil. Jeff always brought out this reaction from her. No matter how she told herself she wouldn't rise to his bait, rise she did. That was one of the reasons they were now divorced and had been for three years. Divorced that long, and still he thought he could come and go in her life just as he pleased.

She bit her tongue to prevent herself from retaliating how she would like to. Taking a deep breath, she said, "I don't want to argue with you Jeff. I want you gone. That's why I divorced you."

"Excuse me," he said to her with that same sneer, "but I think you've got that backwards. I divorced you."

Taking another deep breath to settle her nerves she said, "Whatever Jeff. You believe that if it makes you happy. Spin it however you want. I think those photos are in the basement. I'll get them. Then you'll leave. Okay?"

She didn't wait for him to answer as she turned and headed for the door to the basement steps off the kitchen. He followed behind her, grumbling under his breath as he did. Served him right, she thought to herself.

She kept the basement of her aunt's house clean and organized. The ceiling was low and most of one corner was taken up by the furnace, leaving little space for storage anyway. There were metal shelves set up along one wall where she kept bits and pieces of her life that she didn't have much use for anymore. It didn't take long for them to locate the box of pictures belonging to Jeff that he'd stored down there when they were married. The box was among everything else that was leftover from another life.

"There you go, Jeff," she said to him in a stiff voice, shoving the box into his hands. "Now if you wouldn't mind leaving? I want to get my dinner and relax a bit."

"Aww Darcy. You're always trying to get rid of me." His smile was full of ideas she had no interest in. "I could stay and have dinner with you."

Was he for real?

Darcy gave him a dark look. "Why on earth would you want to do that? You can't stand me and I can't stand you. Why don't we just leave it that way?"

He grinned at her and winked. "Yeah, you do have a point there. Well, I'll be going then."

She followed him all the way to the front door to make sure he actually left. As he opened the door she said, "Oh and Jeff…"

He stopped and looked back at her. "What?"

"Don't ever come in my house uninvited again. Got it!"

He screwed up his face as he slammed the door shut dramatically. She made sure to lock it and throw the deadbolt as well.

Darcy grinned as she went into the kitchen to start getting her dinner ready. Smudge startled her when he jumped up onto the counter to demand that she get his dinner first.

"Where have you been? You couldn't have warned me about Jeff? Hm?" He looked at her with his big green kitty cat eyes and she smiled at him. "It's okay, I don't blame you for keeping a low profile while he was around. I should have done that myself instead of agreeing to marry him."

She watched as Smudge seemed to nod his head at her words. His tail twitched as if he was in complete agreement with her.

Smart cat.

# CHAPTER 3

*D*arcy could feel her heart pounding in her chest as the dark figure walked slowly towards her. She was standing on the sidewalk of Main Street as the apparition moved closer and closer to her. He was surrounded by mist, wearing a dark overcoat and a wide brimmed hat, making it impossible for her to see his face. But there was something so familiar about him…

He approached her menacingly and she stepped back a few paces as he came closer. She tried to speak, to tell him to stop, but she found that no words would leave her mouth. Her heart nearly leapt from her chest as he reached into his coat with his right hand and…

Pain blossomed in her chest. She'd been shot. Wait. Disoriented, struggling to find reality, she realized that she wasn't in the street. Hadn't she just been there? No. She was in her bed. Smudge had jumped on her, landing on her chest. That was all it was. She tried to calm her breathing and pushed at the cat gently as she tried to relax her tense muscles. It had been a dream once again. Just another bad dream.

Right?

She hoped that was all it was. Two similar dreams about the same man trying to kill her two nights running made it a little harder to dismiss. She was seriously worried now that the dreams meant something but tried to push it away. She didn't want them to mean anything at all but she feared that they did.

Smudge mewled at her from where she had pushed him aside onto the mattress. Patting her cat, she said, "I'm sorry, Smudge. Thank you for waking me up. I was having another very bad dream. You wouldn't believe it. I wonder who that man is that's invading my dreams and trying to kill me. I hope it was just another stupid dream and not some premonition. What do you think?"

She was in the habit of talking to Smudge as if he would answer her, as if he could understand her. He looked at her now with those wide eyes of his and shook his head, as if to say "how would I know?"

"Well you're a big help." She laughed at herself and rolled over into a comfortable position where Smudge could crawl in between her feet where they were tangled in the comforter. "Goodnight good boy, I'll see you in the morning."

It took a little while for her to fall asleep again. All Darcy could see when she closed her eyes was the dark figure. She wondered who he was and what it all meant. She'd like nothing more than to just ignore it all as a fantasy of her tired mind. But unfortunately, things rarely worked that way for Darcy. When she saw things, when she had dreams, she knew she had to pay attention to them.

That thought rolled around in her tired brain before she finally drifted off to sleep again.

THE NEXT MORNING Darcy was feeling a little on edge from her dream. It had repeated itself just before she had woken this morning. The same dark figure, the same menace, the same gesture of reaching inside of his coat for... something. Three dreams in twenty-four hours made it very difficult to ignore them. She was so agitated and couldn't settle to anything so she decided to get ready and go to work early. Smudge just rolled over and yawned at her when she asked if he was ready to head into town with her. Apparently, he was still too tired to join her.

Usually she enjoyed the walk into town but this morning her mind was once again filled with the images from her dreams. By the time she reached the town center she was totally out of sorts. Wondering what she could do to settle her nerves, she decided that maybe some coffee and perhaps something sweet would help. She headed towards the Bean There Bakery and Café, Misty Hollow's one and only café-slash-bakery.

Thoughts of her strange dreams buzzed in her head and kept her from paying attention as she made her way through the door of the bakery. She found herself bumping into someone on their way out.

"Oh, sorry! Sorry," she tried to apologize.

"Darcy! Where is your head? You almost made me drop these coffees." Darcy was embarrassed to hear the familiar female voice admonishing her. Her sister stood there now, scowling at her, the dark blue pantsuit she always wore for work pressed and perfect. Her long, dark hair pulled back in to a tidy pony tail.

"Grace, what on earth are you doing here?" Darcy cringed as the words left her mouth. She realized how stupid that sounded.

"Well, I don't know Darcy. Maybe I was digging for gold or working on my car or something." Grace tilted her head to one side. "What do you think I'm doing here? It's a coffee shop. I'm getting coffee." She lifted the Styrofoam coffee cups she held in a cardboard tray up to Darcy's eye level.

Darcy shrugged. What could she say? She bit her lip and wished she hadn't decided to get breakfast this morning.

"What's up with you today?" Grace leaned closer to Darcy and continued, "Has it got anything to do with... you know?" Grace wiggled the fingers of her free hand, indicating that she was talking about Darcy's tendency to get mixed up in weird stuff.

Darcy looked at her sister for a beat, deciding whether or not to tell her about her strange dream. Grace knew more than anyone about the dark secrets of Darcy's life, but not even her sister knew it all. And Darcy wanted to keep it that way.

"I just had a couple of strange dreams, that's all. It's probably nothing." She left it at that. At least she hoped the dreams had been nothing.

Grace looked at her watch. "Okay then. If you say so. Are you getting a coffee?" Darcy nodded. "Go ahead. I'll wait for you. You can come and meet my new partner. He just started at the police department a few days ago."

Darcy knew that the police department had recently gotten a new detective. She didn't know much about the man. Grace's old partner had recently left Misty Hollow to marry a girl from another state.

Darcy knew she had no choice now. Not that she minded spending time with Grace. She just wanted to get to the book store and spend some time quietly thinking on those dreams. She needed to figure it out or put it out of her mind. She went up to the counter and placed her order, chatting with Helen Nelson, the owner of the bakery, while she waited for her coffee and Danish. Helen was the Mayor's wife, and always full of news.

As she and Grace walked toward the black and white patrol car that was parked just down the street, Darcy saw the tall, dark haired, very good looking man slouched against the driver's door.

He had his arms folded across a muscular chest and he oozed indifference to the world around him. His suit was a similar color to Grace's, and just as stiff-looking. As they moved closer to him he turned to them with a shadow of a smile and Darcy's breath caught in her throat. She was mesmerized by the most gorgeous pair of blue eyes she'd ever seen.

Grace handed the coffees to him then held a hand out towards Darcy. "Jon, this is my sister, Darcy Sweet."

He inclined his head ever so slightly in her direction and she felt her face heat. It was an intense something that rose up in her with each breath as his eyes pinned her. She hadn't had a reaction like that to a man since she couldn't remember when. Probably never. For his part, he looked her up, and down, and if she'd been standing there naked in front of him she couldn't have felt more exposed. She bit her lip and told herself to just breathe.

"Darcy," Grace continued, "this is my new partner, Jon Tinker."

She felt Grace nudge her as she stood there, still mute. Gathering herself she placed her cup and pastry bag onto the car roof and held out her hand to him. "Hi, um... Jon. How are you?"

She figured it was her day to put her foot in her mouth.

He took hold of her offered hand and little electric currents ran along her fingers and then up her arm. The tingling settled in her spine, and she knew she was in trouble.

He looked at her like he'd just found something distasteful on the bottom of his shoe. Then he dropped her hand like he'd just found out she was infectious and turned away from her to take a coffee from the tray where he'd set it on the roof of the car. He thanked Grace in single syllable words and then took a sip of the hot drink. Darcy was a bit let down by his curt attitude but decided to try again. Sometimes she couldn't help being a woman.

"So Jon," she said to him, determined to make a better second first impression, "what do you think of our town? How are you handling all of the mist?"

"The town's okay," he said, and then added with a twist of sarcasm, "And all this mist doesn't bother me at all." He turned away from her and took another sip of his coffee.

Her mouth hung open. What a rude man! Had she really been attracted to this jerk? Angry at herself, she twisted the ring around her finger over and over. "Well, I guess that's great then that you love the mist so much. I'll see you later Grace, I've got to get to the book shop."

She grabbed her coffee and pastry and wondered as she stalked off if it had been her. Something she said? Then she realized that unless Jon was the type of guy to be insulted by someone saying hi, then the problem wasn't her. It was him.

God help her sister if that was her new partner.

"I THINK it will be great fun. I simply can't wait." Sue Fisher, Darcy's only employee at the book store, was chatting excitedly about Misty Hollow's anniversary festival that was going to be held the next day. "This is the biggest thing to happen here for ages. I can't wait for the fireworks." She was swinging her blonde head from side to side as she twirled on her stool in her excitement making Darcy feel a little seasick.

Darcy couldn't help but grin. Sue was just twenty, working at the book store while on a break from college for a year while she decided whether she wanted to get that law degree or not. That kind of energy could only belong to someone so young.

Sue stopped swinging around and looked through her lashes at Darcy. "Randy's coming into town tomorrow to go to the festival with me." She had a little flush on her cheeks as she spoke. Randy was her on again, off again boyfriend that she had met at college. "I'm so excited to see him, it's been ages."

Darcy sighed, such was young love. She admitted to herself that she was a little envious of Sue's relationship with Randy, even if it wasn't perfect, what relationship was? That melancholy mood threatened to settle over Darcy once again.

Changing the subject before it could Darcy said, "What about the Mayor's speech? I suppose you can't wait for that either."

Sue screwed up her face and shuddered. "Oh, God no. Once Steve Nelson gets started nothing can shut him up."

Darcy laughed and silently agreed with Sue. Sue started to go on about what she was going to wear to the festival and Darcy completely zoned her out. She and Sue were very different but they still got along well. Sue was a bit of an airhead and was mad about fashion. She loved wearing the latest cute dresses, at least the ones she could afford. She talked endlessly about clothes and shoes and makeup and, well, everything to do with fashion. That stuff bored Darcy to no end. Darcy was happy to wear a comfortable pair of jeans with her worn sneakers and a nice T-shirt. No fancy dresses or high heel shoes for her.

Darcy shivered as a sudden cold draft blew over her. She knew what to expect when this happened. It was her special talent coming in tune with something out of sorts with the world around her. She looked around to see where the draft may have come from. It had to be nearby…

A very faint image of her great-aunt Millie stood by one of the book shelves. The apparition's shading was at odds with the soft lighting cast by the hanging lights. Darcy wasn't alarmed at the sight. It wasn't Millie's first time visiting. The book store used to belong to Millie, after all, and she would appear at odd times. Often to cause mischief.

Keeping an eye on Millie as she pretended to listen to Sue she could see that Millie was floating towards one particular book shelf. Sue couldn't see Darcy's Great-Aunt standing there, of course. No one else would be able to. Darcy watched intently as the flickering ghostly image put out an ethereal hand to knock a book to the floor before quickly disappearing.

Sue jumped and turned her stool in the direction of the sound. Darcy let her go over and pick the book off the floor, acting like she hadn't even noticed. Her gift had led her to many wonderful discoveries. It had also made her the object of ridicule on more than one occasion. Sometimes the play-acting made things easier.

"How odd." Sue turned the book over in her hands. "Say isn't this the book you were reading in the book club?" She held the book out for Darcy to see. It was, indeed, a copy of "And Then There Were None." Darcy couldn't hold back another shiver. Definitely odd. Was Millie being playful… or was there a message here?

"What made this book fall to the floor I wonder?" Sue said as she looked all around her before shoving the book back into its slot on the shelf. "Oh well. Gravity's working, I guess." She shrugged, then came back over to where Darcy was without giving the book another thought and went back to gushing on about the festival.

Maybe that story deserved a closer look.

# CHAPTER 4

The next afternoon Darcy walked into town to attend the anniversary festival that was being held in the town square. She was looking forward to getting out and mingling with the other townsfolk. The weather was mainly fine with the sun warm on her shoulders as she walked. The mist still clung to the shadows and the tops of the trees but even that couldn't dampen Darcy's enjoyment of the day.

As she walked along Main Street she admired the myriad colorful streamers that were hanging between the buildings in decoration. The townsfolk had gone all out to make this the most spectacular, colorful anniversary festival the town had ever experienced.

She hadn't gotten around to perusing the book Great-Aunt Millie had practically tossed at her feet. There hadn't been a good time while Sue was there and then it was time to go home and, well, time got away from her as it all too often did. There had been no dreams last night, either. For now, everything in her life was normal. She was determined to enjoy it while it lasted.

Darcy spotted her sister Grace just up ahead and hurried to catch up with her. "Hi Sis. Doesn't the town look great?"

Grace smiled at her. "Yes, they really outdid themselves this year. How are you feeling? You, uh, kind of snapped at Jon yesterday. Still having bad dreams?"

Darcy smiled back at her and shrugged. Grace thought she'd been rude to Jon? Had she not been listening to the man at all? "No, no more dreams," she said, leaving it at that.

Grace nodded. She was dressed down today, taking a rare day off from her job. Jeans and a dark red blousy top. Darcy was wearing jeans, too, but somehow Grace's backside always looked better in jeans than Darcy's did. It wasn't fair.

As they walked along together weaving in and out of revellers they waved and said hello to several people. Many of the shop-keepers had stalls out in front of their shops along Main Street, displaying their wares for all to see.

Darcy had a couple of high school girls working the book store's stall so that she was free to attend the festival. She didn't think it would be very busy there. Business had slacked off with the growing popularity of e-readers. She didn't want to tell Grace, but it was getting harder and harder to make ends meet with the store's dwindling revenue. There might come a time when she'd have to consider selling the shop. She didn't know what Great-Aunt Millie would think of that.

Darcy and Grace walked around and looked at all of the stalls and the afternoon passed fairly swiftly. "My feet are killing me," Grace said. "Why don't we go and sit in the Gazebo for a while?"

"Okay, I could do with a rest," Darcy said with a laugh. But before they could make it to their destination they came upon the Mayor and his wife as they walked, and stopped to say hello. "Hi Steve, Helen, how are you both today?" Darcy thought that Steve looked a little tense. Of course, she thought, his speech that he had to give.

He pulled a crisp white handkerchief from his pocket and dabbed at his forehead with it. She noticed his hand wasn't quite steady. "Well Darcy I have to say I am doing quite well. Unless you count a bad case of stage fright."

"Oh now dear, just calm yourself," Helen patted his arm. "What do you have to be worried about? You give this same speech all the time. Darcy and Grace don't want to hear your woes." Just then Roland Baskin, the town grump, demanded the Mayor's attention, probably to complain about the festival as he always did when something was being held in the town. That gave Darcy and Grace the perfect opportunity to move on.

"Oh there's Jon." Grace turned to face Darcy as her partner spotted them and raised a hand in greeting. She laid a hand on Darcy's arm to get her to stop walking. "I don't understand what the problem was between you two the other day. He's a very kind and nice man."

"And good looking," Darcy had to admit, even though she was miffed at Grace laying the blame for the encounter on her.

"Well. He is easy on the eyes," Grace agreed with a lopsided smile.

"Grace! You're a married woman. What about Aaron?" Darcy said with a hint of humor in her voice.

"I may be married, but I'm not dead. I can appreciate a good looking guy. I can look but not touch." Grace smiled. "Aaron knows he has nothing to worry about. He knows he's the only one for me." Grace paused for a moment looking over in Jon's direction. "I'll admit I was a bit worried about getting a new partner when Jimmy left to marry his girlfriend. We'd been working together so long that we almost knew each other's thoughts but I didn't need to worry. Jon's a great guy and a great cop. We get along well."

"It's fine, Grace. He doesn't have to be nice to me as long as he's okay for you to work with." Darcy tried to ignore the way her heart sped up as she looked at Jon. She sighed. She could still appreciate his looks even if he was a jerk, couldn't she?

"Will you excuse me for a moment?" Grace asked her. "There's something I need to talk to him about."

"Sure go ahead. I'll just wander around here for a bit." Darcy watched as her sister hurried away through the crowd. She wandered along the sidewalk going from stall to stall, just taking her time and catching up with people she saw.

"Darcy! Darcy!" she suddenly heard. "Oh thank goodness I found you."

Darcy turned to find her neighbor Anna frantically weaving her way through the crowd, waving her hand in the air to catch Darcy's attention. As Anna reached her she grabbed her arm and held on tight.

"Anna, what's the matter?" She tried to guide the older woman away from the busy sidewalk to one of the park benches so that they could talk more privately. The whole time Anna was shaking her head. Her face was very pale. Whatever had upset her must be bad.

Giving up on getting to a bench she just led them away from the crowd a little way. "Anna what is it? If you don't tell me I can't help you." Anna looked at her with frightened eyes and Darcy felt that familiar odd feeling run through her again. Did she really want to know what it was that Anna knew?

"I... I found out something horrible earlier and..."

Darcy waited with impatience for Anna to continue but the woman looked at something over Darcy's shoulder instead. She shook all over just as Darcy saw her sister Grace heading their way, with Jon in tow. "I'm sorry, Darcy. I was mistaken. I'm sure I was mistaken. I'm just going to go home."

Darcy could hear Grace and Jon's voices now. They seemed to be talking heatedly about something. She was more worried about Anna, though. "Are you sure? You seemed so upset."

Anna smiled in a way that did nothing to erase the fear from her eyes. "Yes. I'm sure. The crowd. Yes. The crowd is too much for me today. That's all it is."

Darcy could tell there was something more to it. She didn't want to press Anna and spook her more, though. "Okay, if you're sure that's what you want to do?"

"Yes it is. Definitely. I'll talk to you later on." She nodded to herself and then scurried away. Rushing home as if the devil was on her tail, Darcy thought. How odd.

"...and I hear that Darcy is always causing trouble." Darcy tuned into the conversation Grace and Jon were having behind her when she heard Jon say her name. Now she was all ears. Trouble? What was he saying about her always causing trouble?

She swung around and faced him with a glare. "I don't cause the trouble. Trouble just happens to find me."

Jon opened his mouth to say something at the same time that Grace opened her mouth to say something else but the screeching of the microphone as the Mayor was about to make his speech cut them both off. Jon snapped his mouth shut with a hard stare at Darcy. Everybody in the crowd quieted down and faced the podium where Steve Nelson was now smiling nervously.

"Can you all hear me?" The crowd shouted a resounding "Yes!"

The ceremony began with the Mayor making his speech about the town of Misty Hollow's history. A glorious history, he said, starting back in the Revolutionary War and continuing through a series of remarkable events that led to the wonderful town they all knew and loved today.

Darcy knew all of this. She had researched the town's history and probably knew it better than anyone else. Plus, Steve gave this same speech, or some variation of it, at just about every town event he had ever spoken at.

After what seemed like an eternity the Mayor's speech ended. Then the celebrations got into full swing. As night fell the fog also started to descend upon them once again. The fog got thicker the later it got and Darcy wondered if they would be able to see the fireworks when it was time. As she listened to the music playing Darcy reflected that even the thick fog couldn't dampen the town's enthusiasm for their festival.

When nine o'clock rolled around and it was time for the fireworks the fog seemed to miraculously part over the center of town for the ten minutes it took for the fireworks to light up the sky. Oddly, as soon as they were done the fog soon descended upon them once again. Darcy shivered as the fog seemed to penetrate her clothing.

When the fireworks were over the festivities continued on with music and dancing. Darcy stayed for another hour or so but when it looked like the other townsfolk were dispersing she decided to head home also.

As she did her thoughts kept returning to Anna, though, and why she had suddenly stopped talking just as her sister had shown up.

DARCY WALKED HOME ALONE after the festival thinking about how lovely the town had looked all decorated and how beautiful the fireworks had been. It was difficult to see where she was going as the beam from her flashlight was bouncing off the curtain of fog in front of her. She was going on instinct alone as she walked this path everyday of her life and could do it with her eyes closed.

Despite the fog she felt great and the good feelings from such a wonderful day had succeeded in pushing those silly dreams she'd had and Millie's appearance right out of her head. Anna and her actions at the festival kept coming to mind, but she figured that would work itself out. And on top of that thoughts of Linda's missing cat weaved their way in and out of her head. It was getting very busy in there.

As she reached her porch she could see that Smudge was waiting for her. He was such a good cat. As she got closer to him and reached out to pet him he meowed very loudly at her. Instantly Darcy was on edge. Smudge was a good cat and he was trying to tell her something now.

There was something wrong.

Smudge bolted off the porch and quickly sprinted part way across the pasture that separated Darcy's property from Anna's. When he got to the edge of the flashlight's beam he stopped and looked back at her. "Lassie's got nothing on you, huh Smudge?"

Darcy followed him through the fog to Anna's house. He was a black and white shadow moving just at the furthest reach of her light. When she got to Anna's front door it was open. That wasn't right. Not this late at night. A sense of déjà vu hit her. Strains of her first dream filtered through her mind. She now realized why the house in her dream had seemed so familiar. She was standing in front of it right now.

Darcy hesitantly pushed the door open a little wider. She really didn't want to see what was on the other side. Her instincts were screaming at her. She knew it wouldn't be good. If it went just like her dream she knew it would be very bad.

As the door swung inward, seemingly in slow motion, her searching flashlight fell across Anna, lying on the floor. Darcy raced over to her and carefully felt for a pulse in her neck. There wasn't one. Behind her, Smudge meowed again.

He was right. Anna was dead. And she hadn't been dead for very long. Her skin was still warm.

Was the killer still in the house? Was he about to jump out and pounce on her like he did in the dream?

# CHAPTER 5

$\mathcal{D}$arcy tugged the police jacket tighter around her body. The night had turned cold, and not just from the mist settling in like a thick blanket. Inside Anna's cozy little home, death had visited. Even though she'd been scared that there might be a killer still lurking about she had waited there for the police, for the rescue squad personnel who were too late to do anything, for her sister to come and hold her as the reality of it set in and then tell her she had to come down to the station.

She sat now in a hard wooden chair off to the side in Misty Hollow's police department and watched as her sister went about the professional efficiency of death.

Darcy had to blink a few times to try and remove the fuzzy edges of tears from her vision. She could see her sister talking on the telephone and knew she was talking to someone from Anna's family, breaking the news of her death to them. How awful for them all. Darcy knew that Anna had been particularly close to her brother and wondered how he would cope with the news. Poor man.

Taking a couple of deep breaths Darcy closed her eyes for a moment and tried to calm herself. Instead, she found herself remembering the moment she had found Anna lying on the floor and the sheer horror of realizing that Anna was dead. And then images began flashing through her mind, like scenes from a movie, of herself running to the phone and calling the police. She could see the police arriving and Anna's body being taken away. She remembered how her body had looked...

Darcy jumped and her eyes popped open when she felt a hand on her arm. She was surprised to see Jon bending over her with a concerned look on his face.

"Here," he said. "I thought you could probably do with some coffee." He held a cup out to her. In slow motion, she took the cup from him and took a sip. It tasted awful but she felt the warmth seep through her body and chase some of the chill away. Jon sat down on the chair beside her.

"Thanks. I needed that." She gave Jon a half smile. He was still gorgeous, and she still noticed. "Do you want your jacket back?"

"No you keep it for a while." There was a small pause as he cleared his throat. "I'm really sorry for your loss. Grace told me how close you were to Anna."

"Thank you." She didn't understand his change in attitude, his suddenly being nice to her like this. They sat in silence then and waited.

Grace soon came over to where they were sitting. "I was finally able to reach Anna's brother. He's going to inform the rest of the family."

Darcy saw the look that passed between her sister and Jon before Grace looked back at her. She knew something was up. "What?" It came out sharper than Darcy meant. She blamed it on how frayed her nerves were at the moment.

Grace put a hand on her shoulder and said, "It's nothing to worry about Sis. We just need to ask you a few questions about what happened. Um, where were you before you found Anna?"

Darcy sighed. She knew this was just another part of the process, like the endless paperwork had been when they first got to the station. So she went on to tell them how she had been at the festival and Anna had come up to her saying that there was something important she should know about. How Anna had suddenly looked spooked right when Grace had found Darcy again, and then rushed off to go home.

Darcy frowned. It hadn't just been Grace that walked up to her at that moment. It had been Grace and Jon, both.

Before she could mention that tidbit her sister sat down on the other side of her and prompted her, "What happened then?"

What happened then was my cat told me something was wrong, Darcy thought to herself. Aloud, she said, "When I got home I had a funny feeling that something wasn't right so I went to Anna's house and, well, you know the rest."

"What do you mean, you had a funny feeling?" Jon asked.

Grace put a hand up with a knowing look at Darcy and said, "That's fine, we have all we need right now. Thanks, Sis. I have a few more calls to make." Smiling, she turned to include Jon. "Maybe you could walk Darcy home?"

Jon looked at them both, knowing he was missing something, but not knowing what. "Sure. If it keeps me from doing the paperwork."

Grace turned back to Darcy and said, "I'll call you later."

Darcy nodded and took the hand that Jon offered to help her up. Home sounded good right now.

AN AWKWARD SILENCE descended upon Darcy and Jon as they walked along the path off Main Street to Darcy's house. Jon had offered to drive her but she had insisted she wanted to walk. There was too much on her mind. She needed the air. Jon had shrugged and said he'd walk with her.

Halfway to her house Darcy realized she was still wearing Jon's police jacket. Even though the mist seemed to be letting up as dawn approached, she felt chilled and pulled the jacket around her body tighter. She saw Jon notice but he didn't say anything. Not long afterward they reached Darcy's front porch.

"Are you going to be alright alone?" Jon looked at her with concern and she wondered again why he was being so nice to her.

"I'll be fine," she said to him, standing on the porch with her arms crossed, shifting her weight from foot to foot.

"I can stay with you if you need someone to be here with you," he said. "I think it'd be quite understandable after the ordeal you've just had. I mean, it's not every day that you see a dead body. Right?"

Right. Who sees dead people all the time? "No, no you go. I'll be fine on my own. Thanks for the offer though." She quickly pulled off his jacket and handed it back to him. "Here. You'll want this back, I'm guessing."

"Thanks. You're sure you'll be all right? We'll have extra patrols in the area, and you can always call your sister if you need to, I suppose."

He smiled at her. She caught her breath at the way his eyes lit up when he smiled.

She was so caught off guard that she almost missed the implication in what he had said. "Extra patrols? Why? Anna just died, it's not like…" The police hadn't officially told her that Anna had been killed and she had begun to hope that her dream had been wrong and Anna's death hadn't been murder after all.

She felt her eyes get wide. She asked Jon the question that she already knew the answer to because she'd seen it happen in her dream. "You don't think this was an accident, do you?" Part of her hadn't wanted to believe that someone had deliberately ended Anna's life. Darcy had seen no obvious cause of death when checking Anna's pulse and was hoping that her dream was wrong and was just the fantasy of an over active mind.

Obviously not.

His smile locked in place, he shook his head. "I'm sorry. I really can't talk about that."

That cinched it. They really thought there might be more to this than just Anna dying. And she did, too. Why had Smudge felt the need to bring her to find Anna? Why had Anna's door been open? What was it that had made Anna so upset at the festival? And her dream had been very vivid. She'd learned not to ignore those dreams, this time should have been no different.

She stood there now, eyes downcast, her mind trying to lock onto any one of these questions and answer them. When Jon cleared his throat, she realized how foolish she must look.

Jon looked at her intently for a moment. His scrutiny made her feel uncomfortable. "Are you sure you don't know anything else about this, Darcy? It's very odd that you just had a feeling and went to check on her and then she ends up dead."

Oh, so that was what all the being nice was about. Buttering her up so that he could squeeze information out of her. She should have known. Darcy's meter went from annoyed to angry in a split second. "Are you serious? I can't believe what you are implying. Anna was my friend. My friend!" She turned her back on him and threw the door open, slamming it shut behind her.

Without turning on the light she pulled back the corner of the window curtain to make sure he was leaving. She saw him still on the porch, staring at the closed door, the expression on his face concealed in shadows. She shrunk back away from the window when she saw him take a step and lift his hand as if he was going to knock on the door. At the last minute he shook his head, turned, and walked away.

Feeling completely drained Darcy went into the kitchen. Dirty dishes were set in the sink. She had planned on getting to them later. Well. It was later. Trying to keep her mind busy and off what had happened she filled the sink with hot, sudsy water and set to doing the menial task. She didn't realize she was crying until she felt the tears running down her cheeks. Sensing her distress Smudge appeared from wherever he'd been hiding to rub up against her leg.

"Hey there, Smudge. Want some dinner?" He meowed and she imagined she could hear a question in it. "Oh I'm fine. I'm just so upset about Anna. I just don't know how something like this could have happened. And I just let her go home when she told me she was upset. If only I'd made Anna talk to me. Maybe she might still be alive. You know?"

Smudge meowed again and shook his head energetically. It made her laugh. "Yeah. You know."

Darcy finished washing the dishes and went up to bed. As she got comfortable under the covers Smudge jumped up onto the foot of the bed. He sat there looking at the bedroom door like he was on guard, protecting her.

# CHAPTER 6

*S*he should have stayed home from work the next day. She said it to herself over, and over, every time a customer asked the same question.

"Oh Darcy, isn't it awful about Anna? And I heard you found her. Poor you. Oh my, the whole town is talking about what happened to Anna. They're saying she was murdered. Is that true?"

It figured that the whole town was talking about what had happened. The town was filled with people ready to gossip about any little thing. Something this horrifying would never go undiscussed.

The bell over the door jingled to announce the arrival of a customer so Darcy left Sue with the unpacking of their shipment of new books and went over to the counter. Mark Cameron, who worked just down the street at the bank, was standing there jumping from foot to foot.

"Oh D-Darcy. I-Isn't it awful about A-Anna?" He peered at Darcy, taking a second to concentrate. Mark had been a stutterer since he was a little boy. Excitement made it worse. "I-I heard that y-you were th-the one to f-find her. Th-that must have b-been awful f-for you. W-what d-did you s-see?"

"Yes it was awful, Mark." That was all she gave him. She wasn't going to help turn her friend's death into gossip. She avoided answering any more of his questions by changing the subject. "Um. Did you want to buy a book today?" He nodded and when it looked like he was going to keep going on about Anna, Darcy called for Sue to come and help him choose a book.

Darcy went back to unpacking the boxes and making a mark in pencil on the inside cover of each new book to show they belonged to her store. As she was doing that, she could hear Mark chattering on to Sue, who was a willing participant in the conversation. Darcy could tell he was getting more excited by the minute as his stutter got worse and worse. Shaking her head with annoyance she ripped another box open with more force than was needed. It did make her feel better though.

Mark and Sue finally came back to the counter with a book that Mark had chosen. He was still going on about the murder of Anna and Darcy snapped, "Really, Mark. Can't you think of anything better to do today than gossip about someone we all knew?"

Sue raised her eyebrows in surprise. Darcy suspected that Sue was a little scared of her when she got like this. She knew she was being rude but at that moment she really didn't care, she just wanted Mark to shut up.

Sue rang up Mark's purchase herself on the cash register and he paid for his book and walked away with a sheepish look. As he was about to leave another customer came in to the sound of the bell over the door ringing. Darcy looked up to see Jess O'Conner, who worked at the bank with Mark, entering the shop. Great another person come to gossip about the events of the previous evening.

Sue quickly greeted Jess, probably sensing that Darcy didn't want to deal with anyone else today. "Hi Jess, what can I help you with today?"

"Oh, I'm not here to buy a book. I've come in to get Mark. There's a customer who will only deal with him so he's needed back at the bank." She looked at each of them curiously. Okay so I was wrong, Darcy thought.

Mark looked like he was about to launch into the whole discussion of Anna's death. Darcy quickly said, "Mark was just leaving, weren't you Mark?"

Mark looked a little sheepish again. "Uh yes, I g-guess I was. M-my b-break is over anyway. Um. R-right."

Darcy watched the pair of them leave the book shop with relief. Out the window, she could see Jess animatedly talking with Mark, grilling him about what he had learned about Anna's death, no doubt. Jess was a tall woman with bright red hair and a quick temper. Mark was a shorter man, even more so next to her. Darcy almost felt sorry for him.

Sue sighed and went back to their stack of new books. "I wish I had Jess's job."

Darcy looked at her employee, a bit surprised by what she had just heard. "What makes you say that?"

The young woman shrugged. "I don't mean that I don't like working here. I love my job. But Jess's job must pay so much more. Did you see those expensive high heels she was wearing?"

Darcy rolled her eyes. Sue was always talking about the latest and greatest fashion. It must be nice to have enough time in your life to worry about things like that.

DESPERATELY IN NEED of a break that afternoon Darcy headed to the Bean There Bakery and Café. She was looking forward to having a leisurely coffee by herself. She should have known better.

"Oh Darcy, my goodness, are you alright?" Helen was working at the bakery like she always did even though she was the owner. She had rushed over to Darcy as soon as she entered the shop. "I heard you were the one to find poor Anna. That must have been simply awful for you. I hope you're okay."

Helen pulled her in for a comforting, motherly hug that Darcy wanted nothing to do with but suffered through just the same. "Come on, dear," Helen said to her, "sit down and I'll get you a coffee."

"Thanks, Helen. But I'm alright, really." Helen made a tut-tut noise and pushed Darcy into one of the booths along the bakery walls. Darcy sunk down into the plush cushioned seat and sighed. Helen was loved by everyone in town. Sometimes, though, she was a bit overbearing. Why fight it, Darcy figured.

Helen came back with a steaming cup of dark, aromatic coffee and set it down in front of her. As Darcy went to pay for it Helen tapped Darcy's hands with her fingers and said, "No it's on the house."

"Thanks Helen." She was honestly appreciative, even if she'd had her fill of well-intentioned concern from her neighbors and friends.

Helen sat down on the other side of the booth and they chatted for a little while about this and that. About anything, really, other than Anna. Helen was always a font of information about the goings on in Misty Hollow. But eventually she got around to the subject that Darcy was trying to avoid. "Everyone who has come into the bakery today has been so upset and devastated by the death of Anna. Steve couldn't sleep last night. He was so upset that he was pacing around…"

Before she could finish what she was saying Helen was interrupted by a customer coming into the shop. She hurried away to serve them and Darcy took the opportunity to go and put some milk into her coffee.

As she was standing at the little counter of sugar and milk and other condiments she could hear two women talking. She hadn't realized that her friend Linda was sitting at one of the other tables on the other side of the shop. She was with one of her co-workers, Dianne Chamberlain, and they seemed to be having a good old gossip session. Darcy tried not to listen but when she heard Anna's name she couldn't help herself.

"I heard that her family is going to have the funeral in their home town in some state down south," Dianne was saying to Linda. Linda made a scoffing noise and Dianne continued to talk. "That's such a bad idea. What about all of her friends here? None of us will be able to attend."

"Well I just can't believe that anyone would hurt Anna." Linda sounded perplexed. "She was so nice and led such a quiet life."

"Well, it might not have been all that uneventful. I overheard Grace Wentworth and another police officer talking when I went to pay a parking ticket this morning." Darcy was all ears now. What had her sister said? "Apparently the police found something suspicious in Anna's house."

Linda again. "Really? Do you know what they found?"

Dianne said, "No. No I don't. They didn't elaborate and by then my ticket was paid and I had to leave."

Darcy was intrigued now. Grace hadn't said anything to her about that. Linda and Dianne saw her then, and they smiled at her. Linda waved her over. Darcy grimaced inwardly. She wasn't in the mood for more questions or sympathy. She really just wanted to be left alone right now.

She smiled stiffly as she moved over to their booth and sat down next to Linda.

"Hi Darcy, it's terrible about Anna. Poor you, finding her. That must have been awful."

Darcy nodded and made some non-committal comment and then sat quietly sipping her coffee. She had no intention of talking about Anna to them and the other two women soon got the message.

"I still haven't found my Persephone Darcy," Linda said by way of changing the subject. "I've looked everywhere and I have 'Lost' posters stuck up all over town. I've spoken to everyone about town, nothing. It's like she's disappeared into thin air." Linda looked frantic. Darcy felt for her friend. She would be beside herself if Smudge was missing. But to be honest the mystery of the missing cat had flown out of her head since Anna had been murdered.

"I'm sorry Linda. I wish there was something I could do."

Linda gave her a measured look. "Well... I thought maybe you could... you know... use that special talent that you have." Linda looked extremely uncomfortable and Darcy knew exactly what she was asking. People around town knew that she had some sort of special ability but they didn't know what it was exactly and for that reason she could make the townsfolk feel very uncomfortable when the subject came up.

Darcy smiled. "It doesn't really work like that." Linda's face fell in disappointment. "But that doesn't mean I won't help. I'll do everything I can to find Persephone and bring her home to you."

"Oh thank you so much Darcy." Linda looked relieved and much happier. Darcy was glad. If only she could work out who had killed Anna, then maybe she could feel better too.

AFTER SHE FINISHED dinner that night Darcy settled down on her sofa with Smudge. She had begun feeling nostalgic and had brought out some of her old photos to look through.

She sifted through the photo's she held in her hand. There were a lot of her and Grace when they were younger. She smiled at their innocent faces goofing off for the camera. There were a few of Aunt Millie and some of Smudge when he was a kitten.

"Look Smudge. You were so cute when you were a kitten." She held the picture in front of his face so he could see it. He looked at it a moment then shook his head and let out a little sneeze noise. Darcy laughed. "Okay, you're still cute."

She sifted through some more photo's. "Oh look. Here's a photo of the first book club meeting we ever had. It was only five years ago but don't we all look so much younger?" She laughed as she held the photo up once again for her cat to look at. He yawned before going back to cleaning his paws, not interested in the photo at all.

Choosing not to notice her cat's disinterest she flipped through a few more photos. "Aww, look. There's Anna." She ran her finger over Anna's face in the picture and felt a chill run through her. A sensation crept over her skin and she pulled her finger away quickly. Smudge looked up at her curiously.

"Don't look at me like that. What am I supposed to do?" Smudge continued to stare at her, until Darcy finally relented. She didn't know if it had been her idea or Smudge's, but either way it felt like the right thing to do. "Fine, I guess it won't hurt to check." Grabbing up the phone she dialled Grace's number.

"Hey Darcy how are you?" her sister asked. "Are you okay?"

"I'm fine. Everyone in town has asked me that today, Grace. There's nothing to worry about. I just felt like talking to you. That's all."

"Uh-huh." Grace sounded unconvinced. "Well. I'm glad you're okay. After what happened last night you could be forgiven if you weren't. One thing they teach us in the academy is that a shock like that can eat away at you if you don't talk about it."

Darcy smiled at her sisters concern. It was nice to know that her big sis was still there for her, even now. Pushing Grace's worry away again, Darcy directed the conversation onto other topics until she could bring it back around to ask her question.

"So there's been a lot of speculation around town today about why Anna was killed. Do you have any idea why yet?" Darcy spoke very casually, trying to make it sound like a simple question so she could find out what she needed to know without tipping Grace off.

She was disappointed by her sister's answer. "No we don't. I know what you're doing Darcy and it won't work. You know I shouldn't be talking about this with you."

"Aww, come on Grace. I heard that you found something suspicious in Anna's house last night, can you at least tell me if that's right?"

Darcy heard Grace sigh on the other end of the line and knew that she'd hooked her. "Okay, fine. Just let me get in the other room. Aaron's taking a nap." There was the faint sound of a door closing and then Grace said in a whisper, "You didn't hear it from me, alright Sis?"

"You got it." Darcy scratched behind Smudge's ears and waited impatiently on the edge of the couch.

"We found an envelope," Grace confided, "with seven thousand dollars in it, all in twenties, on Anna's kitchen table."

Darcy was stunned. "Wow."

"Exactly. Now look, Sis, I'm not saying any more. I've said too much already. I have to get going. I'll talk to you tomorrow okay?"

"Sure. Goodnight, Grace." Darcy hung up the phone, still unsure what to make of this little fact. She didn't think that Anna even had that much money. Especially not to just leave it lying around on her kitchen table.

Maybe this really was a murder. And maybe there was a lot more going on here than anyone knew about.

# CHAPTER 7

*T*he next day Darcy and Sue were busy rearranging some books when the handsome Detective Jon Tinker stopped by. Darcy felt a funny little flutter in the pit of her stomach when she saw him coming through the door. Not her normal something's-wrong-flutter. This was a very intimate sensation and she was hard pressed to call it anything other than what it was. Attraction.

Her fingers immediately went to twirl the ring anxiously but she stopped them when she realized what she was doing. She was finding herself playing with the ring more and more recently.

Jon was holding a cup of coffee and as he walked toward the counter the thought came to her that he always looked like he could have just stepped out of the pages of a fashion magazine. Today he had on a different dark blue suit with a lighter blue shirt underneath and a gray tie. She licked her suddenly dry lips. His blue eyes were stormy and his lids narrowed while he studied her. Her fingers itched with a sudden desire to feel along the outlines of his muscles in his chest and arms and instead went to her ring as a substitute. She mentally shrugged. She would break herself of the habit another day.

When he reached the counter Darcy became aware that Sue had gone suspiciously quiet. Looking at the younger woman Darcy found her standing, just staring at Jon. For some reason her reaction annoyed Darcy.

Jon smiled at them and then said to Sue, "I wonder if I might speak to Darcy alone for a few minutes." He placed the cup of coffee he was holding down onto the counter and rubbed his hands together. Darcy thought he looked a little nervous.

Sue smiled back at him. "Sure, I can go for a walk. Um. Yeah."

Darcy was sure she saw Sue's cheeks turn red as she nodded and quickly left the shop. Jon waited for the bell to ring and the door to close before turning back to Darcy. His gaze was intense. She felt uncomfortable under his scrutiny.

"Look, Darcy, I just wanted to apologize for the way I treated you the other night. I was rude to you when you had been through a very rough ordeal."

This was what he came here for? Seriously? "Thank you, Jon. I appreciate it but you don't need to apologize."

He nodded like he didn't believe her. "So how are you anyway? Are you okay now?"

"Yes, I'm fine." She just wanted one day when someone didn't ask her that.

"It must have been so hard for you to find Anna's body the way you did. You know, sometimes we can think we're okay and then all of a sudden things catch up to us. Before you know it you're an emotional mess." He was still smiling but Darcy caught the hint of something behind his words. What was he up to?

Darcy tilted her head up at him and narrowed her eyes. It finally sunk in what he is up to. He was on a fishing expedition. He was trying to subtly question her for information. Bastard.

"Get out!" She was satisfied to see his startled look. Did he think she was stupid? Without trying to justify himself Jon turned and started to walk away from her.

Six feet away from her his cup of coffee lifted off the counter and flew across the room, hitting him squarely in the back of the head. Brown coffee splattered all over him.

Jon spun around to spear Darcy with an angry glare. "What the hell did you do that for? I was already leaving!" He sputtered and swiped coffee from the backs of his shoulders, waiting for her to say something. When she didn't, he turned toward the door and stalked out of the shop.

Darcy grabbed a handful of paper towels to clean up the coffee spill. She hadn't thrown it, of course, but he never would have believed her if she'd told him that Great-Aunt Millie had taken a dislike to him. With a little smirk she watched out the window as Jon stalked down the street. He was very angry with her right now. Good.

As she bent down to clean up the mess she wondered what it was that Millie was trying to tell her. She wondered if perhaps Jon was the dark figure from her dream. Could he be the one who killed Anna? Why would he have killed her?

Deciding that she couldn't let this go, couldn't just wait for the police and her sister and that cold hard fish Jon to figure out this mystery, Darcy made her decision. She needed to find out who murdered Anna herself.

Sue came back twenty minutes later.

"I need to step out for an hour or so," Darcy said to her. "Can you take care of things for a while?"

"Sure Darcy. No problem."

Darcy headed straight for the police station. The desk sergeant let her through with a nod and a wave. She found Grace sitting at her desk engrossed in paperwork. "Hey," she said by way of greeting.

"Oh. Hi Darcy, I didn't see you there." She pushed her paperwork aside and leaned back in her chair with a smile.

"Interesting reading?" Darcy pointed to the report.

Grace picked it up and shoved it in her desk drawer. "Nope. Not really. What can I do for you, Sis?"

Darcy looked all around the room. "I was hoping that we could talk. Away from here. Maybe go for a walk?"

Grace frowned. "Why? What's wrong?"

Darcy shook her head. "Not here."

They walked in silence for a bit until they were away from the center of town, on a side street that had a few houses on it and no people around to hear them. "Okay," Grace said to her then. "Are you going to tell me what's wrong?"

Darcy took a deep breath. "You have to help me, Grace."

"That doesn't sound too good. What's happened? Are you in trouble? Has it got anything to do with Anna's murder?"

Darcy put a hand up to stop the questions. "Nothing's happened, yet. Well, nothing tangible anyway." She paused for a moment. "I'm getting signs from my sixth sense that I need to solve Anna's death."

"Really? That's what you need my help with? No way. Look sis. I don't understand everything that happens to you or what you can do. But I do know that you've gotten into trouble too many times before playing around with... whatever it is you play around with. You should just stay out of it this time."

Darcy should have known that she would get this reaction from Grace. Her sister had buried her head in the sand more often than not when it came to matters of the supernatural.

They stopped, and Grace put a finger up to accentuate her point. "And if you do find out anything that relates to Anna's death, with your sixth sense or your sense of style or whatever, then you need to tell me. Got it?"

Darcy watched as her sister stalked away back towards the town center. She had expected this would happen, but it was worth a shot at least. Now she knew she wouldn't get any more help from Grace. Well then she'd just have to take matters into her own hands.

∾

DARCY WALKED SLOWLY BACK to her store with her mind on what she would need to do. She needed the information that the police obviously had. Her sister had never been a good liar. She knew something. And it would be in that report she had seen on Grace's desk.

She needed to break into the police department. That much was obvious. So what would she need? Time. She'd need to be there when hardly anyone else was. Most importantly, she would need Grace's keys, but how to get them?

The day got darker as she saw Jeff coming towards her down the street. She wasn't in the mood for a confrontation with him today. Or ever. It just seemed that they couldn't even look at each other these days without it turning into a fight.

"Darcy." Jeff's voice was clipped as he stopped in front of her. What had she done to get up his nose this time? "I know you're probably riding high on all of the attention you're getting right now for being in the wrong place at the wrong time. Again. But that doesn't give you the right to steal what's mine."

Irritated, she crossed her arms under her breasts and stared him down. "For Pete's sake Jeff, what are you talking about now?"

"Photos. I'm talking about photos. The ones you stole from me. The ones from in the box you gave me the other day. Some of the photos are missing. Where are they?"

"Seriously? That's what's got you so upset? I have no idea where they are, Jeff. Why would I want your lousy photos?" She'd had enough. Sidestepping him she stormed past without looking back.

"This isn't over Darcy!" he called after her. She rolled her eyes as she kept walking. What was up with Jeff and his quest to find those photo's. She sure didn't know why he was so fixated on finding them.

Shrugging her shoulders, she sighed. There wasn't much she could do about it if she had no clue where they were.

When she got back to the shop Sue met her with a wink and a half-smile.

"Where did you go to?" Sue asked her. "Were you off talking to Jon?"

"No. Of course not." Darcy sat down at one of the three reading tables in the store and rubbed her temple where a small headache was forming.

"I think that he's cute," Sue went on about Jon. "Everyone thinks so. It's really nice to have a new guy around this town. I mean, he's a little old for me, and I do have Randy, but he'd be perfect for you. Don't you think he's cute?"

"No, I don't." Just then Smudge jumped up onto the table and meowed loudly in her face. She hadn't realized that her cat was in the store. She shook her head at him and said, "What? I do not think he's cute."

Sue chuckled nervously when Darcy spoke to Smudge. Darcy was well aware of how Sue thought it was kind of odd the way she talked to him. She laughed, trying to put Sue at ease. They got back to work and Darcy went back to making her plans for getting into the police station.

# CHAPTER 8

That night Darcy went over to Grace's house. She was nervous knowing that she was about to lie to Grace. It was for a good cause, she kept telling herself, and if she ever found out what Darcy had done her sister would understand. Eventually. Grace lived in a very nice upmarket apartment in Seelander Court which was close to the center of town with her husband Aaron. Darcy timed her visit for just after dinner time. Timing was crucial to her plan.

"Uh, hi Darcy. What are you doing here?" Grace said at the door with an uncertain smile.

Oh no, that hadn't been too friendly. Darcy smiled and said something about just wanting to visit with her sister and then stood there uncertain what to do next. When she hesitated Grace said, "Are you coming in or not?"

She turned away from the door and walked back into her apartment. Darcy quickly stepped inside and shut the door.

She followed Grace into the dining room. Grace's husband was clearing dinner dishes away. "Hi Darcy." Aaron smiled at her over his shoulder as he balanced plates and bowls in one hand. They had just finished dinner. Perfect timing.

"Hi Aaron." She looked from one to the other of them. "Sorry, is this a bad time?" Grace speared her with a narrow-eyed look and then went back to wiping the table clean. Aaron picked up the last of the plates and carried the stack of them into the kitchen leaving Darcy and Grace alone. Grace was very quiet and Darcy felt a bit awkward.

"Um," she started. "I wanted to say, about this morning, I'm sorry I pushed you. I understand that you're bound by law and can't share information with me."

"Thank you," Grace said slowly, while eyeing Darcy a little suspiciously. With a sigh she finally came around the table to pull her into a hug. "It's alright Sis. You are who you are. I know that you can't stop yourself from wanting to help."

For just a moment Darcy let herself enjoy the comfort of her sister's embrace. Then she stepped back from Grace, careful to keep her smile in place. It just didn't feel right, lying to her sister this way. "I'm glad you understand. I'm alright, really. I want you to know that. I, um, I have to run now. I can see myself out."

She began to walk out of the dining room and then stopped. She turned back to Grace. This was the part of her plan that would be tricky. "Um… I haven't eaten dinner yet. Could you maybe spare me some leftovers before I go?"

Grace rolled her eyes at Darcy. When Grace walked into the kitchen Darcy bolted for the front hall in search of the police department keys. A small row of key hooks was attached to the wall just inside the door, with car keys and house keys and there next to them, the keys she needed. Quietly, she grasped them and slid them off the hook and into her pocket. Her throat was dry and her pulse pounded in her ears. She'd done it, though. No turning back

She waited in the living room until Grace came out from the dining room, a plastic container of something in one hand. She shook her head as she handed the food to Darcy. "Come earlier next time. We'll set a place for you. You know I love you, right Sis?"

Darcy could only nod as tears threatened to spill from her eyes. She gave Grace a one armed hug and quickly left. She knew Grace would be furious if she ever found out what Darcy had just done. It was the only way, though. She had to know what had happened to Anna.

MISTY HOLLOW WAS A SMALL TOWN, and the police department building was only staffed by two officers from seven at night until eleven, when the midnight patrols came on duty. During those hours the place was locked up and anyone needing assistance had to either call the emergency cell phone that one of the officer's carried, or push a big yellow call button at the front of the building. It was the only window of opportunity she was going to have.

Darcy had some time to kill before she would be able to get into the police department undetected. At least a couple of hours she figured. She didn't want to go all the way back home so she headed to the book store. Might as well eat the dinner Grace had provided and do some brainstorming on Linda's missing cat mystery while she had some time. She had made a promise and meant to keep it. Darcy knew she would be frantic if it was Smudge that was missing.

But before she could get to the store, it was as if her thoughts had conjured him up, she spotted Smudge up ahead in the distance. He was just sitting there in the middle of the sidewalk with his head held up sniffing the air. What on earth was he up to?

She watched him for a few moments more before he darted off in the direction of the industrial end of town. Where was he going? Without thinking, holding the plastic container tightly in one hand, Darcy scurried after him.

She hadn't realized before this that it was surprisingly difficult to keep up with a cat when he was on a mission of some sort. And Smudge was definitely on a mission. What was that cat up to?

She followed him as he raced off across lawns and sidewalks until he got to the narrow street that led away from town toward the section comprised of large warehouses and storage facilities. Out of breath and suffering from a painful stitch in her side, Darcy lost him around about there. He could certainly move and Darcy was no slouch in the fitness department but still couldn't keep up with him.

She took a few minutes to catch her breath. Looking all around her she tried to see if she could catch a glimpse of Smudge but it was now too dark, the sun having set completely while she was on her mad dash through town.

Darcy could hear a dog barking madly in the distance. Did that have something to do with Smudge? She hoped not. The dog sounded really mad but she knew her cat could take care of himself. There wasn't much she could do about it anyway. She didn't see where Smudge went and it was too dark to see anything anyway. Even if she knew which way he went she probably wouldn't find him now.

She turned around in the direction of the center of town and wandered along at a leisurely pace, letting her thoughts churn in her mind. Where did Smudge get to? Where was he going? He'd looked like a cat on a mission. Darcy guessed that she didn't know the half of what that cat got up to when she wasn't looking. He was always getting out of the house somehow and she had no idea how he was doing it.

As she entered the main town square she could see a patrol car parked up the street a little way. She couldn't see who was actually in the car as the face was in shadow. But the way her senses went into full alert she knew without a doubt it was Detective Jon Tinker. She debated whether or not to turn around and walk back in the direction she'd just come from when she told herself not to be so silly.

She would just walk right on past without acknowledging him at all. Taking a deep breath, she put one foot in front of the other and soon she was level with the patrol car. Darcy couldn't seem to help herself as she drew level with the car. A quick glance sideways to see if she was actually right had her inhaling sharply.

Sure enough.

Jon Tinker was sitting there behind the wheel spearing her with such an intense stare that she felt it all the way down to her toes. She almost stopped, mesmerized by his eyes that in the lighting from the street lamp looked almost black. He looked like some sort of God sitting there unmoving, just staring at her.

Breathtaking. She silently scolded herself for her fanciful meanderings. The fight or flight instinct finally kicked in and she scurried away from the car as quickly as she could and didn't stop until she was inside the bookstore. She leaned against the door for support as she sucked in air.

He had the most peculiar effect on her.

AT JUST AFTER eleven pm Darcy went straight to the police department. She couldn't see any lights on and the place certainly looked deserted.

At the back she tried one key after another in the lock. The third one worked, and checking left and right just to make sure no one had seen her, she slowly opened the door and quickly stepped inside. She pulled a small flashlight from her pocket and switched it on.

Something jumped at her from the shadows. Hand over her

mouth she only just managed to stifle a scream. She followed the darting shape with the beam of her light until it came to rest on the impassive black and white face she knew so well.

"Smudge!" she gasped at him, her heart rate ratcheting up a notch, and then laughed silently at herself. It was just her cat. Where had he come from? She hadn't seen him since he'd given her the slip earlier. She wagged a finger in his face. "You and I need to have a serious chat later boyo. Where did you get to earlier?" He just looked at her blankly. "Oh, don't pretend like you don't know what I'm saying." He shook his head and sniffed.

She calmed her racing heart and went over to the row of filing cabinets. Using the smaller key on Grace's key chain she undid the lock at the top of the set marked "Current Investigations" and opened it up. At the front of the drawer was a brown accordion folder marked with Anna's name.

The file contained a brief report on the fog, which had been so bad that night that the main roads going in and out of the town had been closed for safety. Interesting. A few pages back she located the coroner's report which said that Anna's time of death was nine o'clock. That would have been right when the fireworks were going off. The report also said that she had died of two gunshot wounds to the chest. Small caliber. Almost no blood.

That explained why Darcy hadn't realized in the beginning that Anna had been killed. At first she'd thought, that Anna had just died as she hadn't seen any evidence of blood on Anna's body. She remembered hoping that the dream she'd had was just a dream and not a premonition.

Oh, poor Anna.

Darcy wiped a few tears away from her eyes. She then set the file down on a nearby table and read the report on Anna's house. There had been no sign of a struggle, which indicated that Anna probably knew her attacker well. There were also two cups of tea on the table, which would indicate that she had been with someone she knew when she died. Darcy shuddered at the thought that someone she probably saw every day right here in town had killed Anna.

There was also the envelope of money on the table, which hadn't been taken out of Anna's bank account. There was also a list of people's names in the report, all of Anna's friends in the town. Darcy's name was on the list as well. The list had hand-written notations after each name. A list of alibis, she realized. It seemed that practically everyone was at the ceremony at the time of Anna's murder.

Darcy ran a hand through her dark hair. She'd been sure that this report would tell her something important. Something she needed to know to solve this mystery. This was all just confusing facts and notes. Angrily she slapped the report closed. Who had done this to Anna?

The sound of keys rattling in the front door startled her.

She quickly shoved the file back into the cabinet and pushed it closed as she shut off her flashlight. There was no time to get to the back door again. Racing across the room she slid under Grace's desk, hoping that she would be able to hide there without being seen. For one panicked moment she thought maybe it was Grace coming to find her but then she remembered she had Grace's keys. Whoever this was had used a key to open the door.

And then Smudge rubbed up against her. She nearly jumped out of her skin as he silently curled into her body, hiding just like she was.

The lights flickered on and she saw a pair of men's feet and legs walk past her hiding place. Blue slacks, shiny shoes.

She heard the man walk over to the filing cabinets and she poked her head out just enough to see who it was. Jon. It was Jon. He was taking out the file on Anna. Then she pulled back quickly when he turned around. She held her breath and listened to him walk over to his desk. Her mind flashed to their encounter earlier that night when she'd seen him in the patrol car. An involuntary shiver shook her body at the memory. What if he found her here, somewhere she wasn't supposed to be? What would he do?

She relaxed when she heard him turning the pages of the report. She really hoped he wasn't going to be long, she didn't want be stuck under the desk all night.

He began humming to himself. It was some tune she could almost identify but not quite. A little while later she heard him finally stand up and put the file away again. He crossed the room, passing her hiding spot, and flipped the lights off. She heard the door close and lock again. He was gone.

Darcy sighed with relief. Now she just had to get out of there.

She threw the keys she had stolen onto Grace's desk hoping that Grace would assume that she just left her keys at work the day before. She went out the back door the same way she had come in. She didn't feel like she'd accomplished a thing.

Smudge followed her, rubbing at her legs like he was trying to encourage her. "Easy for you to say," she told him.

# CHAPTER 9

The ticking of the clock was lulling Darcy into a light sleep.

Tick, tock. Tick, tock.

She was so warm and comfortable. Sighing deeply, she relished the feel of the warm sunshine on her face. Snuggling down deeper into the soft wool blanket beneath her, she could feel herself falling further asleep. A gentle breeze was ruffling her hair. It was so nice here.

"You should be careful you don't burn dear."

The gentle female voice brought her back from the brink. Darcy cracked an eye open and turned to her left to see her Aunt Millie sitting in a white wicker garden chair gently rocking backwards and forwards in time with the ticking clock.

Today she wasn't wearing the black dress that was her usual attire when her spirit presented herself. Instead she had on an old fashioned vivid white silk dress with ruffles all around the bottom and on the edges of the sleeves. Though her steel gray hair was up in its tight bun, like usual.

No chance of her burning in the warm sun as shading her was

a hand held parasol sporting all of the colors of the rainbow. She looked relaxed and glorious as the colors intensified and seemed to swirl about her. She looked like she didn't have a care in the world. And Darcy supposed that she didn't.

Tick, tock. Tick, tock.

Stretching, Darcy yawned. Sitting up she opened her eyes properly and looked all around to see the where that annoying clock that was ticking so loud was situated. That was odd. She couldn't see one anywhere. But she could hear it.

Tick, tock. Tick, tock.

"What is up with that clock!" Annoyance tinged her voice as she looked all around once again.

"Oh come now dear. You know what it means."

Darcy shook her head. "No I don't Aunt Millie."

"Time flies over us but leaves it shadow behind." Darcy whirled around to her right. Smudge was lounging back on the blanket leaning nonchalantly on a front leg and was casually picking at his claws.

"Where did you come from?" Darcy was perplexed. He hadn't been there a moment ago.

"Nowhere, somewhere, around."

"Around?"

"I'm always around Darcy, you should know that by now."

That was true enough. He seemed to appear from nowhere sometimes like he did at the police station.

Darcy knew now that she was in the midst of a dream. Smudge could only ever talk to her in a dream state. Aunt Millie for the most part too.

"Why don't you just relax while you can dear?" Aunt Millie's voice was soothing and Darcy laid back on the blanket once again to stare at the brilliant, clear blue sky. Colors were always so much more vibrant in this dream state. She sighed.

"You sound troubled child."

"I am Aunt Millie. Anna was murdered."

"Yes, I know dear."

"You can't turn back the clock. The clock will only turn forwards into the future."

"What does that even mean Smudge?" Darcy was met with silence. She sat up impatiently turning toward her cat. But he was no longer there. That was a short visit.

"Aunt Millie…" Darcy back turned toward her aunt but she was gone also. So was the chair and parasol. Darcy was now completely alone.

The sky turned dark and the wind whipped up. Darcy wrapped her arms around herself to try and keep warm. Lightning split the sky followed almost immediately by the deafening boom of thunder.

The beautiful spring day was gone. Fat raindrops started pelting down and Darcy got to her feet looking all around her for some sort of shelter. There was nothing. Only miles and miles of grass all around. Where was she? It looked like the middle of nowhere. Soon she was soaked to the skin and shivering uncontrollably.

In the distance she saw a dark figure walking toward her. She couldn't see who it was, couldn't see his face, but recognized him from her previous dreams. He walked closer and closer. Darcy tried to move but was rooted to the spot and couldn't. He was advancing on her now and as he got closer she watched in petrified fascination as he slid his hand into his coat pocket.

Darcy watched as he drew his hand out so slowly. She tried to move, to run away but still couldn't. All she could do was watch helplessly as he pulled his hand out and in it she saw…

A clock.

What?

Tick, tock. Tick, tock.

～

65

THE NEXT MORNING, with the odd dream still weighing on her mind, Darcy made her way into town to the book store to begin her work day. Before she got there though she saw the mayor, Steve Nelson, talking to Pete Underwood. Pete and Anna had dated a long while ago, and had broken it off at least a year ago. She wondered what the two men had to talk about.

Darcy tried to make out what they were saying but they were too far away for her to hear them. She saw Pete shake the Mayor's hand and then Steve walked briskly away towards town ahead of her. Darcy quickened her pace trying to catch up to him.

"Steve!" she called out to him. He stopped and waited for her to reach him. "Uh. How are you doing today?"

"Hi Darcy. I'm okay. Thanks." Steve ran a hand through his short dark hair as his eyes darted about looking anywhere but at Darcy. She used to think that he was up to something, whenever she saw him do that, but it was just a nervous tic he had. "I'm so very sorry for your loss. I know that you and Anna were very good friends. So many people have told me how sad they are that she's gone."

"Thanks, I appreciate it." Darcy studied the mayor for a few moments. Steve was such a quiet man. In fact, it seemed like an odd sort of profession for him to choose, what with the speeches and personal interactions he had to do. He was so different from his wife. Helen was such an outgoing person.

He looked down at his watch and Darcy realized she'd better find out what he was up to quick before he made some excuse to walk away. "How is Pete doing?"

"Pete? Oh. Right. Saw us talking, did you?"

He smiled and nodded and didn't offer anything else. She found that strange. Before she could figure out a way to ask him more without being obvious, he said goodbye to her and hurried off. Darcy watched him walk briskly away.

There were all these little things happening around town that she probably wouldn't have paid any mind to before Anna's death. Now, they all seemed to be pieces of the same puzzle, scattered across a table and ready to be put together if only she knew what the picture was supposed to look like.

She slowly walked toward her store, deep in thought. Not sure what she was going to do but knowing that she needed to do something. The vivid dreams she was having had to have something to do with all of this. If only she could decipher their meaning.

As she was busy working around the store later her sixth sense began to percolate. Her skin tingled and her vision sharpened as a blurred, barely there figure appeared in front of her. It was Millie. Her great-aunt floated over to the book shelf and knocked a book off onto the floor, just like the other day. She quickly disappeared.

More confused than she was annoyed, Darcy walked over to where the book lay on the floor. The cover showed a picture of an island with a castle shrouded in mists. "And Then There Were None," by Agatha Christie. The same book that Millie had knocked down before. How strange.

Darcy bent down and picked the book up. She was immediately catapulted into a vision.

She found herself suddenly in Anna's house. Everything was blurred and moving way too fast, a whirlwind of colors. She couldn't tell what was happening but she heard a scream and saw a shifting image of Anna falling to the floor.

Darcy opened her eyes to find herself sprawled on the floor of the book store, panting. She looked up to find Smudge watching her. "Well. That was strange."

Smudge meowed in agreement.

"Like you would know," she muttered as she got up to her knees. She tentatively touched the book again and when nothing happened she picked it up and shelved it. She thought about it for a moment, then took it down again to bring home with her. If Millie thought this book was important enough to drop not once but twice, maybe there were even more clues within its pages.

She knew this was only the beginning. There would be more visions. In a way she almost welcomed them. Maybe they could give her the missing pieces to this puzzle.

# CHAPTER 10

That night Darcy sat on her couch, her feet curled up under her, a cup of cocoa steaming hot on the coffee table. She was no closer to finding out who killed Anna. She had written everything down that she found out in the police department file and anything else she found relevant and now she studied it all as she cozied into her thick cotton pajamas.

It didn't make any sense to her. Every person in town that she tried to consider as a suspect was someone she at least knew of, even if she didn't know them well. Maybe she could make her ex-husband the prime suspect. Even if it weren't true, it would at least make her feel good.

She smiled at that thought. If this was all the police had come up with, though, then it was obvious that she would have to do some investigating on her own. The little scene she had witnessed with the Mayor and Pete came to mind. Maybe that was a place to start.

The Agatha Christie book sat upside down and open on the couch next to her. She had finished the first four chapters again, not seeing any relevance to Anna's death. She'd read the book three times before. She knew the plot, knew who the killer was. She wished she could say the same thing here. Maybe Millie hadn't dropped the book for any particular reason after all. She'd just bring it back to the bookstore and put it back in its place. Millie could drop it all she wanted to after that.

She decided that she would go and question Pete tomorrow. Yawning widely, she stretched her arms up above her head to try and get the kinks out of her aching back and shoulders. She was terribly stiff from bending over the papers in front of her for hours.

She looked at the square clock up on her wall and was surprised to see how late it was. She packed up the papers and put them away in the drawer before going up to bed.

~

DARCY DECIDED to take the next day off work. She could hear the surprise in Sue's voice over the phone when she was told she'd be left in charge. "Are you sure everything is okay? You never take time off from work."

Darcy smiled. She knew that Sue could be a bit of an airhead sometimes but her heart was in the right place. "Sure, Sue, everything is fine. I just need to take care of a few things and I won't have time to come into work today."

"All right. You can count on me." Darcy was sure she could.

It wasn't exactly a lie that she had some things to take care of. She just didn't think Sue would understand if she told her exactly what.

Darcy planned to spend the day following Pete around to see what he got up to. She needed to know whether he was a viable suspect or not. She wanted to think not, but at this point she felt like anything was possible. Pete was an author and worked from home so that was where she headed first thing. He lived with his brother, Blake, who worked at the post office. Darcy figured she would wait until Blake had left for work before starting her stakeout.

Not to say Blake couldn't be a suspect too, she supposed. But Blake hadn't been the one to date Anna. Pete had.

Darcy and Smudge headed for Pete's house just before eight o'clock giving them plenty of time to walk into town and get to the other side where Pete's house was located. After a rather lengthy walk, the pair arrived on the street where Pete and his brother lived. Only one car in the driveway, perfect. Darcy knew they both had a car each, so Blake had already left for work. Walking farther down the street, she looked over the house. Very normal, plain even. Could this really be the house of a killer?

Darcy was able to sneak up behind his house and peer through his windows without being seen by anybody. She saw him working in the living room tapping away on his computer. It looked like he was on a bit of a roll. He had one break where he made a couple of phone calls. Darcy wasn't able to hear what he said as the window was inconveniently closed. When he hung up he went back to work.

He typed for what seemed like forever and Darcy was getting a bit bored when nothing happened. Then around eleven o'clock he stopped typing. He got up and grabbed his coat before leaving the house. She snuck up the side of the house and peered around the corner to watch him walk down the street.

Darcy followed Pete through the town. He never looked back once and she stayed well back so that he wouldn't see her. When he went into the Bean There Bakery and Café Darcy decided to follow him. She sat down at a table in the corner and opened up one of the complementary newspapers to keep herself out of Pete's eye range. She was glad that Helen was busy in the back and hadn't seen her sitting there yet. The lunch crowd was starting to come in. There was so much going on that no one noticed her.

She watched surreptitiously like a detective in one of those old movies as Doctor Sandal, Misty Hollow's local doctor, came into the bakery and nervously looked all around. When he saw Pete he went and sat down next to him. Doctor Sandal leaned in close to Pete and started talking to him. Darcy couldn't hear what they were saying but after a few minutes she saw the doctor hand Pete a plain, brown package. Pete then shook the doctor's hand and left the bakery.

Darcy thought that this behavior definitely counted as suspicious. Was Pete taking drugs? Was he not in his right mind? Did that lead him to hurt Anna? Her mind raced with all of the possibilities. Each one sounded more outlandish than the last.

After counting to thirty Darcy left the bakery and followed Pete again. He went right back to his house. She took up her post outside the window once again to watch him. She was disappointed to see that he just went back to writing on his computer.

Frustrated, feeling stupid for having wasted her whole day standing outside this man's house, she decided to take matters into her own hands. Taking a deep breath, she went around to the front of the house and knocked on the door.

Darcy was surprised when Blake opened the door. She hadn't seen him all morning and his car wasn't in the driveway so she had just assumed he'd gone to work. Now she had to think fast. She needed a reason for being here. "Uh, hi Blake. I was just passing by and..."

She trailed off, the half-formed excuse dying on her tongue. She took a better look at Blake. His face was terribly flushed and he looked feverish. He tried to speak but went into a bad coughing fit. She took a step back on the porch, realizing how sick he was. He looked awful.

"Oh, Darcy. What are you... are you..." he had to stop as another coughing fit racked him. Darcy hoped that she wouldn't get infected with whatever it was that he had. "Sorry, Darcy. Can't stay and talk." Cough, cough. "Listen, as long as you're here, Pete is in the other room. Maybe you can cheer him up a bit? He is having a hard time over Anna's death." Cough, hack, cough.

Pete came into the entryway at that moment. "Blake, get back into bed. I can take care of Darcy."

They watched as Blake shuffled away towards his bedroom. Pete closed the door behind her and Darcy followed him into the living room. "Would you like some tea?" he offered.

"Oh yes please, that would be lovely." She was relieved not to have to explain herself now. She was here to check on Pete. It was the neighborly thing to do. That was all.

It didn't take any time at all for Pete to start talking about Anna and how close they once were. "You know I never stopped loving her. She always laughed and shrugged me off when I tried to tell her, but that didn't change my feelings for her."

He looked so sad that Darcy just couldn't see him as Anna's killer. "It's a terrible thing, Pete. I miss her too."

"I know. It was worse for you, Darcy. You had to find her. I can't... I can't imagine."

"Yes, that was hard. I didn't see you at the festival that night, Pete. Where were you?" There. That was subtle, wasn't it?

She hadn't been prepared for him to start crying. "I was here, taking care of Blake. He's had this flu for weeks now. I must look like a wreck. I'm so sorry for crying Darcy. I've been so depressed since hearing the news about Anna that I haven't been able to sleep. I can't eat. I cry at every little thing. I even had my doctor write me an emergency prescription for a sleep aid." He held up the package that she had seen Doctor Sandal give him. "I really need to get some sleep."

Darcy felt horrible that she had ever suspected Pete. He wasn't the one to do this horrible thing. Now that she'd talked to him face to face, she was sure of it. She stayed with him for a while, comforting him as best she could, and then after some time had passed, got up to leave. Pete walked her to the front door. As they were about to say goodbye, Darcy had a thought.

"You know, I really liked Blake's car, did he sell it?" She asked, attempting subtlety.

"Huh? No... it's in the shop. Why do you ask?"

"Oh, just curious." Darcy could see by the look on Pete's face that he wasn't entirely convinced, but was too tired to press it any further. They both said their goodbyes one last time and Darcy started the long journey home. A few minutes later, a furry black and white something brushed against her leg.

"Now where on earth did you get to Smudge?" She asked, now realizing that her tom cat had abandoned her sometime this morning.

All he said in response was a cheery "meow". Darcy sighed, today had been a waste. She was no closer to solving Anna's death. Hopefully tomorrow would be more fruitful.

## CHAPTER 11

The next day didn't get any better.

In the book store, the bell over the door jingled and in walked the last man on Earth that Darcy wanted to see. Jeff smiled in that arrogant way he had and sauntered up to the counter. Sue rolled her eyes before going off into the back. She had her own opinion of Darcy's ex-husband. It more or less mirrored Darcy's own opinion.

"Jeff, I'm so not in the mood for you today. Just go." She hoped that would be the end of it. It wasn't.

He held up his hands, palms facing out to her. "I come in peace."

Darcy didn't believe him and folded her arms across her chest. "Then what do you want?"

"You're being awfully tough on someone who is here to help. I have news about Anna. I was going to tell the police but then I changed my mind. I figured, why not tell you first?"

Darcy stood up straighter and let her arms fall to her sides. She did not trust him, but Jeff had gotten her interest. He'd always known how to do that. "Well, keep talking."

His smile got wider. "On the night Anna was killed I saw her at the festival. She seemed really upset. She seemed to be talking to herself so I went over to her to see if she was alright."

"You?" She snorted. "You were never the helpful type."

"See, right there is why I divorced you," he complained. "You never had any faith in me. None." He ran a hand through his hair and started to pace back and forth.

"I broke it off with you, Jeff. I thought you had something to tell me?"

He stopped his pacing and looked at her. "Fine. Be like that. Anna wasn't making much sense, but I asked her if there was anything I could do for her just like I always do for a friend," he made sure to add. "She told me that she had seen something but was practically talking over herself and I'm not sure exactly what she said. Something about someone new in town."

Darcy stared at him for a moment. "That's it? That's your big news? What do you think she meant?"

Jeff shrugged. "I only know of one new person in town. That's your sister's new partner, this Jon Tinker character. That's why I didn't take this to the police, see?"

Darcy shook her head. "You must have misunderstood. Besides I was with Grace and Jon when it happened." Although she remembered the way Anna had run off when she'd spotted Grace and Jon heading for them. Maybe there was something to what Jeff was saying. Maybe it was worth investigating on her own later.

"Sure, Darcy. You're always right, after all." He waited a moment and when Darcy didn't rise to his bait he said, "Guess I'll see you later then." He turned away and headed towards the door.

When he got to the door she shook her head at herself for treating him so badly. He came to her, after all. "Why do you care anyway Jeff? You were never close to Anna."

He shrugged again. "You and me might have fallen apart, and I still want those photos you stole from me, Darcy. But I always liked Anna. She didn't deserve this."

Then he turned and left the store leaving Darcy standing there, wondering about Jeff's sudden unselfish gesture. And what was it with him and those photos?

THAT NIGHT DARCY was pacing back and forth in her kitchen. She was out of options and knew what she had to do next. She'd put it off long enough. Now, for Anna's sake, she needed to do it. She had to turn to the spirit world. She looked at Smudge and sighed. The cat blinked at her. "Yeah. I know," she answered his unspoken encouragement.

She grabbed a flashlight from off the counter in the kitchen and pulled on her jacket. Closing the front door behind her she walked slowly down the path towards Anna's house.

As she cut through the mist, she couldn't help but think about the last time she took this walk, the night she'd found Anna's dead body. Anger coursed through her and she knew that she had to bring the murderer down.

That resolve carried her to Anna's front steps.

When she reached Anna's house she turned the flashlight on and ducked under the yellow police tape that was stretched across the front door. She cautiously entered, her nerves on edge, and went to the spot where she had found Anna's body the other night.

The spot wasn't marked. Not even any blood on the floor. She remembered exactly where it had been, though. Sitting down on that spot she closed her eyes and told herself to relax. She created a picture of the mist in her mind. It was a method she employed to clear her mind. Concentrating on the haze allowed her to center herself and connect with the other side.

It was sudden, when it happened. With a jolt she was transported to another place. Everything came to her in flashes once again. This wasn't accidental, though. She was intentionally seeking it out. This time, she saw more.

She saw Anna opening the door, then her visions flashed to Anna pouring the tea, then to Anna running into the living room, then her on the floor. Darcy could see a clock in the background in that instant. It read ten o'clock.

Abruptly she was thrown out of the vision. She fell forward onto her hands and knees, panting like she had run a marathon. Her head was spinning. Now those dreams with the ticking clock all made sense.

She scrubbed a hand over her face as she tried to settle down. Although the vision was painful to watch she was glad she had seen it. She'd seen something. Something no one else knew.

She now knew what those dreams had been trying to tell her. The coroner got the time of death wrong by a full hour. That meant everyone's alibis were off. The entire town was now filled with suspects.

FEELING EXTREMELY SHAKEN by her vision, Darcy returned home as fast as her legs would carry her. She fell into the rocking chair on her front porch and tried to calm down. Breathing deeply, she closed her eyes in the darkness and just sat there. Smudge jumped into her lap, startling her. He curled into her lap and purred. It was reassuring to have him there with her. She could feel her muscles starting to loosen a bit.

She jumped when someone called her name. Jon Tinker. What was he doing here? It was almost midnight, for crying out loud! She was twirling the ring on her finger before he was even within the reach of the porch light. Smudge jumped off her lap and ran away into the house. Maybe she should have followed him. There was something about Jon that made her very uncomfortable.

As he got closer to her she could see that he was carrying an envelope in his hand. His hair was damp as if he had just showered. It curled slightly. At the porch he leaned one elbow casually against the railing.

Her eyes were drawn to his muscled chest and the way the shadows fell across his handsome face. She did not like this man, did not trust him, but she couldn't help but be attracted to him. Her hands itched to reach out and touch him. She licked her lips and stopped trying to keep her mind from wandering over his body. She was just too tired to fight it.

He looked her directly in her eyes. "Is this a bad time?"

No, she thought to herself. Come inside and let me run my hands through your hair... Darcy cleared her throat and made sure to keep her eyes away from his face. "It's very late, Jon. What are you doing here?"

She heard him sigh before he quietly said, "I'm breaking all sorts of rules coming here to talk to you. That's why I'm here so late. I took a chance that you would still be up and I'm really glad that you are."

"Really?" Dear God, woman, she said to herself, get yourself together.

"There's just something that I can't figure out." He pulled a small tape recorder from the package he was holding.

Darcy watched as he pressed play. She was surprised to hear Jeff's voice coming from the small device. "Hi Anna, we need to talk. I don't know what to do. I need to talk to you about Darcy."

Jon clicked the recording off. He looked expectantly at her. "Do you know anything about this?"

"I have no idea," Darcy answered truthfully. "Did you ask Jeff?"

"Not yet. I came to you with it first."

"Does... does my sister know?" Jon and Grace were partners. If this recording was evidence in the case, then she had to know about it, too. Didn't she?

"Grace knows I pulled the messages off Anna's machine," Jon said. "She doesn't know the contents. Yet."

"Yet?" She narrowed her eyes at him. Was that a threat? "You can tell her about it. Tell her you asked me about it, and I don't know a thing about it because that's the truth. Now, thank you for sharing this with me but I think you should leave."

Jon stared at her for a moment and she found herself hypnotized by his eyes. He nodded and turned away without another word. When he was gone, she let out a breath she hadn't realized she was holding.

*A*s Darcy walked to work the next morning she saw people she had looked at as friends and neighbors, and now she saw them as potential murderers. Pete was walking down the street toward the bank. He waved and smiled at her. She waved half-heartedly back to him.

Darcy kept walking until she got to the bakery. A good, strong coffee was just what she needed today. Going inside she found Helen frosting donuts fresh from the oven. Her husband Steve was pouring a cup of coffee for himself.

"Hi Helen. Hi Steve." She smiled, putting on a front even as thoughts and worries and theories spun themselves like spiders' webs in her mind.

Both Helen and Steve said hi back to her. "Now what can I get you Darcy?" Helen said to her.

"Just a coffee thanks, Helen." Darcy fielded a few questions from Helen that didn't stop after a pointed look from Steve. She made the excuse of needing to get to work and left the bakery. She passed more people on the way there. Everyone looked different. No one was who they seemed anymore.

Darcy kept herself busy at the book store to give her mind a chance to unplug and maybe work over the information she knew so far in her subconscious. She had just finished unnecessarily rearranging the last book shelf when Jess O'Connor from the bank entered the store.

"Hello Darcy, Sue," Jess said in greeting. She looked very dressed up in a stunning green dress that Darcy could tell was expensive even without Sue's help. Her shoes didn't look too shabby either.

Darcy smiled at her and said, "Hi, Jess. How are things with you?"

Jess's face broke out into a huge smile. "Oh, things are absolutely fantastic with me."

Darcy kept herself from being irritated with Jess's banter, but just barely. There was a murderer in town. Why wasn't anyone else concerned about that? "Great Jess. And what can I help you with today?"

"Well, I would really like to learn how to speak French."

"French. That's wonderful. Well, I have the perfect book with a companion CD for you." Darcy moved over to another book shelf and ran her finger along the spines of the books there. "Ah, here it is." She pulled the book and CD out of the shelf and held it out for Jess to see. "Are you planning on traveling?"

Jess took the book and flipped through it. "Yes, I am." She giggled loudly, twirling a strand of her red hair. "You know, I've always wanted to go to France."

Sue had come into the main room of the shop during this conversation. She sighed now and said, "Oh you lucky thing. I wish I could go too. I'm so jealous."

Jess smiled like she was very proud of herself, bought the book and left the store.

"Did you see what she was wearing?" Sue's eyes were wide. "I wish I could afford designer labels like that."

"That was never really my taste," Darcy said to her. The

banking business must be doing really well, she thought. Expensive clothes, trips to France. Good for Jess, she guessed.

She heard a small meow at her feet and looked down. Smudge was sitting there with something in his mouth. Darcy reached down and picked it up as Smudge dropped it. It was a key. "What's this, Smudge?"

Smudge's answer was to run outside. Darcy raced to the window to see what he was up to. She watched as he ran up the street, right up to Jeff who was just outside of the bakery. Smudge rubbed himself against Jeff's leg and then took off down the street and disappeared. She looked at Jeff, looked at the key. Obviously it was a key to a door. She looked at Jeff, looked at the key.

Then it dawned on her. Smudge had brought her a key to Jeff's place.

"I'll talk to you about how you got this later, Smudge," she murmured to herself. Then out loud she quickly said, "Sue I have an urgent errand to run. I'll be back later." She didn't wait for an answer.

Darcy arrived at Jeff's place, a small unit in Briers Place, one of the more upscale areas of town. She quickly opened the door and slipped inside. There was no telling how long Jeff would be gone. She needed to do this quickly.

She scoffed at how messy the place was. Piles of clothes littered the room and dirty dishes overflowed in the sink. She was so glad that Jeff was out of her life. She briefly wondered what Jon's house looked like, and where he piled his clothes... She quickly pushed the idea out of her head, or at least to the back of her mind.

Getting to work she looked around Jeff's apartment for clues. Where to start? What was she even looking for? Her eyes fell upon the answering machine hooked up to his phone. She pressed play to listen to his voicemails. She was disappointed to find that of the two he had saved, one was from the bank and the other was from his brother. Both sounded mundane. There was nothing of interest there.

She went into his bedroom but came up empty after another fruitless search. She had never felt so dirty as she had after rifling through his underwear drawer. His taste in clothing hadn't changed one bit. She came out of the bedroom and froze in her tracks. Jeff was standing there in the doorway.

# CHAPTER 13

"*W*hat the hell are doing in my apartment, Darcy!" Jeff was red in the face and Darcy shrank back away from him, just a little scared. She had only seen him this angry once before. It had been a bad night for everyone involved.

She thought about lying, of making up some excuse. She sighed and decided that it was probably best to be totally honest with him. Especially after her tirade when she caught him in her house. She told him all about the recording that Jon had played for her. She left out the part about going through his boxers.

"Yeah, so?" he said to her, his anger only defrosting a little. "Did you hear the whole thing? I was calling Anna about the pictures you had in your basement. I'm sure that you still have some of them and I wanted Anna to talk to you for me." She would need to ask Jeff at some point what was so important and special about those photos he kept harping on about but right now she had other things to worry about.

Darcy realized then that Jon must have turned off the recording before the end. Why would he have done something like that? Was it to throw suspicion onto Jeff? Or her?

As long as she was on a roll she decided to throw all her cards on the table. "The coroner got the time of death wrong, Jeff. It was an hour later than what he said."

He blinked. "How do you know that?"

"That's not really the point. What matters is that not only might Jon be the new person in town that you think you heard Anna talking about, but maybe he played that voicemail for me to get me off his scent." She looked at Jeff sadly and said, "He must have done it."

"Off his scent?" Jeff sneered. "Do you even hear yourself?"

"Yes, I hear myself, you big idiot. Now you listen to me, please. Jon must be the one who did this. You know I sense things. I know things that are true. So stop being dense and listen. Based on what you know, and what I know, I'm telling you that Jon must be the one who killed Anna."

Jeff's face slowly changed from angry to stunned. His eyes went off to the side for a moment before they came back to her. "So now what?"

DARCY AND JEFF were sitting at his kitchen table trying to work out a possible next move.

"Okay, Darcy. So let's say you're right about this Jon fellow being the one who killed Anna. I can't argue with you. It all makes sense." Jeff was biting his thumbnail like he always did when he got excited about anything.

Darcy was at odds with herself. Now that she'd convinced Jeff of her theory, her gut was telling her that something wasn't right about all of this. "It all fits. But why? What motive would he have had to kill her? As far as I know, he didn't even know her." She was frantically twirling the ring around her finger now. She saw herself doing it, and didn't even try to stop herself.

"I have no idea why he would have done it. Does it matter? We don't need to know the why. Maybe he's unstable. Maybe he didn't like Anna. Maybe he's just plain crazy. I don't know, and I don't care. We have to tell the police what we know."

Darcy was shocked. "How can we tell the police? He is the police!"

He looked at her like she was the stupidest person in the world. "So's your sister."

Darcy conceded that he was right. "Okay. We'll tell Grace."

She really didn't like the idea of involving her sister. But Grace was a police officer, after all. It was her job. And she knew, at least, that in this whole town of potential suspects she could trust her sister. Maybe she couldn't trust anyone else, but she could trust Grace.

"WHAT ON EARTH are you two doing together? Do you both have concussions?" Grace's shocked expression would have been comical to Darcy if the situation wasn't so serious. They had walked into the police station together, and Jeff had muttered something about how Hell must have frozen over.

Jeff ignored Grace's attempt at humor. "Is Jon around?"

Grace shook her head. "Jon? No. He said he had to go home early today."

"Good," Darcy said to her. "Grace, we need to talk to you."

"Well, I'll mark this one on my calendar. Why don't you sit down and tell me what's important enough to bring the two of you together?"

Darcy looked around the room. There were two other officers working in there, and the desk Sergeant at the front, and God alone knew who else. Maybe even the Chief. "Not here," she said as Jeff was about to speak. "Can we go into one of the interview rooms?"

Grace caught on to how serious Darcy was being. "Sure, Sis. Follow me."

The interview room was small, with a metal table bolted to the floor in the middle of it and two chairs on both sides. Grace sat down on one side, and Darcy and Jeff sat side by side on the other. A wall-length mirror showed Darcy her expression. When was the last time she'd gotten a full night's sleep, she wondered? She sure looked like she needed it.

At Grace's prompting, Darcy explained to her what they had found out about Jon. About the time of death, about what Jeff had heard Anna saying, about the whole voicemail thing and how Jon had cut it off so that Darcy would get the wrong idea. How they thought he might be Anna's killer.

Grace shook her head. "No, that's not possible. Darcy, the coroner is sure about the time of death. Nine o'clock."

"The time of death is off by an hour. It was ten P.M., Grace."

"And you know this because…" Grace's eyebrows shot up. "Of course. Look, I can't just arrest Jon. We don't have any proof." She held a hand up as Jeff started to argue. "We have what you two know, or think you know, but that is not proof. I can keep a close eye on him but I'm going to tell you, I don't think it's in his personality to do something like this."

Grace's cell phone rang. She took it off her belt and looked at the display, running a hand through her dark hair she grimaced. "Sorry but I need to take this call."

When she walked out of the room to take the call, Jeff grabbed Darcy's arm. "We should leave."

"What?" Darcy asked him. "Why?"

"Because your sister isn't going to do anything about this. And she was our best hope. I don't want to give up on this just because Grace is going to 'keep an eye' on her new partner. We should do some research into Jon's past. That's something we can do now. Come on."

～

DISAPPOINTED with their conversation with Grace, Darcy and Jeff headed back to her house to regroup.

"I thought your sister would have been more helpful but I should have known better." Jeff paced the living room like a caged tiger.

Irritation crawled under her skin at his tone. She had to admit that he did have kind of a point but she knew her sister wasn't being deliberately unhelpful either. "I know, but I can understand her reluctance to believe that a fellow cop might be a killer." Darcy fiddled with the ring on her finger trying to work out their next step.

Jeff stopped in the middle of the room and turned toward her his face contorting into a sneer. "Figures you'd defend her. So what should we do now, genius?" She bristled at his words and bit her tongue. Getting into an argument with him wouldn't help them work this out. Much better to stay focused and do what Jeff had suggested. Find out more about the police officer known as Jon Tinker.

She knew the first place to start. "I guess we could use my laptop to search the internet for information on Jon. We might come up with something useful."

Jeff shrugged and plopped down next to her on the couch. "It's as good a plan as anything I guess."

They decided to look into anything they could find out about him but there was nothing to find. All of his past jobs, records, his schools, everything was normal. There was nothing that pointed to anything dark in his past.

"Take your feet off the coffee table," she snapped at Jeff. "You know that it leaves marks on the woodwork."

Jeff sneered at her. "Stop acting like my mother. I already have one of those."

"You had a wife at one point, too. This is why you don't have one anymore." Darcy sent him a scathing look and he rolled his eyes, but he took his feet off her table. She got up and put one hand to her temple while the other fisted into her hip. "I need a break. Do you want a coffee?" She didn't wait for Jeff to answer before she left the room.

She was having trouble not letting all of her old attitudes toward him come out again. He always got under her skin, even though she knew most of the trouble was her, not him. The menial task of making coffee might help her calm down. She grabbed the container with the coffee beans down from the cupboard and pulled the lid off. She growled at herself. The container was empty. This was why she'd been buying her coffee at the bakery. She'd forgotten.

She had to make a choice. Go without coffee, or risk leaving Jeff alone in her house and having him tear it apart looking for the imaginary photographs that he thought she was keeping from him. Coffee won out. "Jeff, I'm just going to get some coffee from the bakery. Stay out of my things!"

Once again she didn't wait for his response. She just shut the door solidly behind her as she left. She stomped just about all the way into town. The fresh air and the sunshine and the way she was trying to drive her foot through the ground with each step finally did the trick. By the time she reached the bakery she was feeling much better.

The bakery was empty of customers when Darcy stepped inside. She could see Helen sitting behind the counter reading a book. She must have been totally engrossed in it because she didn't notice Darcy at the counter.

Darcy was surprised to see that Helen was reading "And Then There Were None." She was very engrossed in it and kept fiddling with the front cover of the book, folding a deep crease into it. Darcy smiled and cleared her throat to let Helen know she was there. Helen jumped as she looked up. Seeing it was Darcy she smiled back at her and put the book down.

"Oh. I'm sorry to keep you waiting, Darcy. What can I get for you today?"

"That's fine Helen, Just two coffees please. I saw the book you're reading. That's the one we've been reading in the book club."

"Oh? Really?" Helen quickly got the coffees ready for her. "I want to join. I really love this book."

The door to the bakery opened and Linda walked inside. She smiled at Helen and Darcy as she came up to the counter.

"Do I have a juicy piece of gossip to share with the two of you!" Linda was practically buzzing with the need to tell them. "My neighbor told me that she overheard Jess O'Connor talking on the phone over in the grocery store."

Darcy and Helen exchanged a meaningful look. Linda was well known for retelling questionable stories, and adding her own flair to them on top of that.

"Anyway," she continued when they didn't say anything, "apparently Jess is dating somebody new and wants to keep it a secret. She was telling her friend that she really likes this new guy and loves that he buys her all these nice new things. But she told her friend that she hates having to keep it a secret." Linda looked from Darcy to Helen and then back to Darcy again with an eager look on her face. "Can you believe it?"

Darcy just smiled at her while Helen said, "Linda you shouldn't spread gossip."

"Oh, come on now. If my life can't be exciting I might as well be happy for someone else, right?"

Helen just shook her head. Changing the subject Darcy said, "Have you found your Persephone yet Linda?"

Linda's face fell and all hint of humor left her. "No I haven't, and there's been no sign of her anywhere. No one has seen her in days. I am so worried about her." Darcy saw Linda tense. "Say, you don't think that Persephone going missing has anything to do with Anna's murder do you?"

Darcy thought about it for a moment. Could there be a connection? What could it be if there was?

"No I don't think so Linda. It's just a coincidence I think."
Linda visibly relaxed.

"Perhaps you should spend more time looking for your cat
and less time gossiping Linda. Maybe you would find her then,"
Helen said, not a little unkindly Darcy thought.

Linda looked a little shocked at Helen harshness and sighed.
"Yes, perhaps you're right Helen, although I'm not sure what else
I can do." Darcy could see tears beginning to well up in her eyes.

"It's okay Linda, we will find her I'm sure. She has to be
around here somewhere surely." Darcy patted her friend on the
arm comfortingly. "You know I am looking out for her don't you?
We're bound to find her sooner or later."

"I hope it's sooner. Thank you Darcy, you're a good friend."
Linda shot a sharp look in Helen's direction before quickly
looking at her watch. "I must get back to work. Marla's on the
warpath today." She grimaced as she rushed out of the shop.

"Poor Linda," Darcy said. Helen scoffed.

"I'm sure that girl has her head in the clouds most of the time."

Darcy wondered what Linda had done to cause Helen to have
such a low opinion of her. Never mind, it wasn't any of her business anyway she thought as she thanked Helen for the coffees
and said goodbye before heading back to her house. The inter-
lude at the bakery had made her feel better. She was even able to
look forward to working with Jeff when she got back.

As soon as Darcy entered her house through the front door Jeff
started yelling excitedly. "Get in here quick."

"What's gotten into you?" she asked. She could see the serious
look on Jeff's face.

"Look at what I found. Here's a newspaper article about the
wonderful Detective Tinker and the police department in Pequot
Lakes where he used to work at before." Jeff's voice was thick

with sarcasm. Darcy set down the coffee cups on the table and sat down next to Jeff to look at the laptop screen.

The article was brief but she could see why Jeff was excited about it. Apparently, Jon had been investigated for a murder at his last agency. Darcy's heart stuttered when she read that. So much for Grace saying Jon wasn't the killer type. She continued reading, and the wind went out of her sails. Jon had been accused of the murder, but then he'd solved the crime himself. In the end the murder hadn't actually been a murder but a suicide. Jon had been cleared of all wrongdoing.

"You read this last part, right?" she asked him. "Where it says he didn't do it?"

"Yeah, I read it. But I wonder if that's the real story," Jeff said.

Darcy handed the laptop back to him and grabbed one of the coffee cups off the table in disgust. She took a sip of the rapidly cooling liquid while she contemplated what Jeff had said. It had seemed stupid, at first, but the more she thought about it the more she had to wonder, too. She pictured Jon on her front porch the other night, his face a mix of moonlight and shadows, and couldn't help the smile on her face.

There was no way to make the pieces fit. No matter how she tried, they always refused to make a complete picture.

# CHAPTER 14

*D*arcy could see the dark figure walking through the streets of Misty Hollow again. She was dreaming. The same dream that she'd had several times before. Only with more clarity. She was there as it happened. It was happening to her.

The figure was surrounded by the fog. His wide brimmed hat and the shadows hid his face and rendered him unrecognizable. She knew him, though. In the dream she couldn't say his name. But she knew him.

He was walking closer and closer to her. He reached into his coat with his right hand. He pulled out a gun and he fired it.

She felt the bullet hit her chest.

Darcy sat bolt upright in bed, panting. Smudge was suddenly there purring against her chest, trying to calm her. She patted the cat absentmindedly while she wiped perspiration from her forehead and tried to remember every detail of the dream. Darcy knew that the figure from her dream must have been the murderer. But Anna had been killed in her house, not on a street. Why was the dream set in the street?

And was it her dream self who knew this man, or was he someone that she, Darcy Sweet, knew from her own life?

JEFF RANG the next morning as she was busy getting ready to go to work at the bookstore. "Do you want to continue digging into Jon's past today. I thought we made good progress yesterday and it's a good bet that there will be other incidents involving him that we can uncover."

"I'm sorry, I wish I could Jeff but I've already been away from the shop too much lately. I need to catch up with some work."

"Typical," Jeff sulked. "It's always about what you want isn't it Darcy?"

"That's not fair Jeff. I have a business to run. It doesn't run itself. I will catch up with you later today after work and we can continue then, okay?" Darcy was trying to be as patient as possible with him but he could try the patience of a saint when he got started.

"Don't worry yourself about it Darcy. Later will be too late for today, I have other plans. Oh, and by the way I haven't forgotten about those photo's you stole from me. I want them back."

"What is with you and those photo's Jeff?" Darcy wanted to know once and for all what it was but she was met with silence. "Come on Jeff, I really want to know."

More silence and just when she thought he'd hung up on her he said very quietly, "My mom wants them back because there is a photo of my dad in among them. It's the only one she has left of him as all of the others got destroyed in that house fire years ago. She loved him a lot you know."

Darcy felt herself soften toward him. She knew that his parents had loved each other very much. She often wondered how two wonderful people had managed to produce such an ornery son. She heard him sniff. "Are you crying Jeff?" It was really kind of sweet that he cared so much.

"No I'm Not!" He grumbled something else that she couldn't make out and hung up on her. Guess she'd hit a nerve. It was no crime to care about your parents and to be upset when one or both of them were no longer around. She never knew that about Jeff. And the funny thing was, she found she didn't hate him so much anymore.

~

SHE SPENT the whole day doing menial tasks and turning over the bits and pieces of what she knew in her mind. It was almost closing time when Darcy found herself standing in the middle of the store, staring out the window. She was watching the small town wind down for the day and watching the fog roll in. Darcy really disliked the fog. It only seemed to be around when everything in her life was troubled. There was a lot of fog in Misty Hollow.

Reminding herself that life had to go on even for her, Darcy turned away from the window and began to clean the counter just as the bell over the door dinged. She looked up and was startled to see Jon coming into the store. Without saying a word, he walked right up to Darcy, getting in very close to her, holding her gaze with his own. Her heart started pounding. Why was he here? What did he want?

He whispered, his lips barely moving. "Grace told me what you and Jeff found out. You think I'm capable of murder? Do you?" They were standing close enough for her to smell his cologne, earthy and dark, and she knew the heat that rose in her had nothing to do with whether this man was a murderer.

No one should be this gorgeous.

She shook herself and looked around for Sue. She really needed someone else here right now. "I don't know, Jon. A lot of things are, um, confusing right now." Really? She could have kicked herself. That was the best she could come up with?

Darcy shook herself and pulled herself away from his vivid blue eyes. "But you aren't guiltless. I know that much. Why did you stop the recording of that voicemail before it was over? Huh? Why try to get me to turn on Jeff?"

"I wasn't aware I had to do anything for you to turn on him," he said. Then he took a step back from her, and actually looked abashed as he said, "I wanted to fish for information. It's a standard police tactic. I can tell you what, though, your sister was none too happy with me when she found out what I'd done. I didn't think that you were involved in the murder but I know you're keeping something from me. I wanted to make you think that I had evidence against Jeff so that you would tell me the truth to save him."

Darcy couldn't help the laugh that escaped her. "Well, that was stupid, wasn't it? Me, save Jeff. There were a few moments when I actually believed that it was him that murdered Anna. I'm just... I'm so confused. I just don't know who to trust."

Jon returned his intense gaze on her. "You can trust me."

"Can I?" She tried to pull up the anger she had felt at him before. It evaporated in those eyes.

He stepped into her again, and she was frozen in place looking up at him as his breath played over her cheeks. There was electricity between them and her sixth sense was squirming in the pit of her belly... or maybe those were butterflies. She wondered, no she knew, that he was going to kiss her. He leaned forward, a barely noticeable movement that increased the heat between them and she found herself doing the same...

The bell over the door dinged impatiently as someone rushed through it.

Darcy jumped backward from Jon and then grimaced and tried to act naturally which made it worse. It was Grace who rushed in, looking at the two of them oddly as she stood there panting, out of breath.

"What's happened?" Jon asked in a calm voice. Darcy noticed that he didn't have any problem pretending nothing had happened between them.

"There's been another murder." Grace ran a hand through her hair and pursed her lips tightly. Darcy wondered why she was telling Jon this in front of her. Then her heart sank. There could only be one reason.

Grace turned to her with sad eyes. "I'm so, so sorry Darcy but Jeff is dead."

## CHAPTER 15

*H*ere we are again, Darcy thought to herself.

She sat on the same hard chair inside the police station. She was holding a cup of coffee to warm her hands. She felt cold down to her core. She couldn't believe she was here again, just like before, except this time it was Jeff that was gone. As much as she had really hated Jeff, most of the time anyway, there had been a time in their past when she had loved him.

She really thought there would be tears. There weren't, though. There was only an anger directed at a shadowy figure in her dreams that was killing the people she knew.

Jon came over and sat beside her in the next chair, just like last time. She turned her cup in her hands as a way to keep her fingers off her ring. "I have to find the killer, Jon. You have the time of death wrong on Anna's murder. All of your suspect's alibies are incorrect. You need to redo the investigation."

"How do you know that?" he asked, his eyebrows scrunching up.

"I can't answer that. You're just going to have to trust me. You said I could trust you. Now I need you to trust me." Sighing, she set the coffee cup down on the empty seat on the other side of her and held out her hands to Jon. "Let me do this."

She could tell he was confused, but he gave her his hands, and she took them as she closed her eyes. He started to say something that she didn't hear. She was hoping that she could channel her sixth sense to read him, to learn something about this man and about this murder. She concentrated on that gray mist in her mental image and was able to call it forth easily this time in her mind. From it a figure emerged. It was an older woman that had some of Jon's facial features, his striking blue eyes. It looked like she was holding a small baby.

Darcy opened her eyes and said to him, "You lost your mother when you were young."

Jon's eyes widened with shock and then narrowed. "You could have heard that anywhere," he said. "I don't really go in for this Ouija board stuff, Darcy. Let it go."

Darcy closed her eyes again and concentrated on the connection she had forged between her and Jon. Something else came through. This one she knew Jon had never shared with anyone.

She opened her eyes just as Jon pulled his hands away. "You and your dad used to collect frogs. Every summer. You'd make little terrariums for them and then you would let them go in the Fall. Your dad said it was so they wouldn't die. He was the one who taught you that life is precious. That it needed to be protected."

She felt exhausted. Feeling someone's memories like that always took something out of her. She was gratified though when she saw how wide his eyes got. "How did you know that?"

Darcy shrugged. "I just know some things. It's something I've always been able to do. So, please, when I tell you that I know the time of death is off, believe me."

It didn't happen all at once, but Darcy saw the moment when Jon decided to accept her for real. "Okay, I'll trust you."

When Jon stood up, Darcy did as well. The feel of his hands in hers was still tingling against her skin.

～

JON TOOK Darcy to his place from the police station. It was a simple apartment, clean and spartan, with a couch and a chair in the living room arranged around a low coffee table. They stayed up late that night working on the case together. He muttered to himself over and over about how he shouldn't be sharing this stuff with her, but then he would do it anyway. Jeff was killed at home, just like Anna, with a gun, just like Anna. There was no sign of a struggle. Going on the theory that both Anna and Jeff knew their killer, Darcy and Jon created a list of everyone that the victims were close to or friendly with.

There were a number of options for Anna. Less so for Jeff. He really had burned most of his bridges here in town. Mixing those names in with people whose alibis might not check out now with the correct time for Anna's death, they could come up with a list of solid suspects. Pete, Blake, Sue, Aaron, Doctor Sandal, Jess, Mark, Linda, Steve and Helen.

She didn't like seeing so many of her friends on the list, but she knew they had to suspect everyone. There were a few they could eliminate, though. "We can take out the women. I'm sure that the killer is a man."

Jon looked at her funny, but did like she asked. Her demonstration earlier had obviously convinced him.

"Blake was sick," Darcy went on, leaning closer to Jon to look at the list, "and Pete said he was home taking care of him. They alibi each other out. Plus, Pete was way too shaken up. I'm sure it wasn't him. I don't know Mark very well, but he did seem upset by Anna's murder when I saw him the day after at the bookstore. He has a pronounced stutter that gets worse when he's upset."

"So he could have been upset that he'd just killed someone,"

Jon offered. "I don't know these people very well either. Not yet. But we can't eliminate someone just because they're upset."

Darcy had to agree. She sat in silence for a moment thinking. "Fine. But Aaron had no reason to harm Anna. And he's too kind."

"We can't go by emotions we have to go by the facts," Jon said to her. "But, saying he has no reason to kill her is something I can understand. No motive. Fine. I'll put him in the 'maybe' pile."

"We have a maybe pile?"

He smiled at her. "We do now."

She couldn't help but stare at that smile. He had such perfect lips.

He tapped his pen against their written notes a few times. They really hadn't narrowed it down all that much. "All right. That's what we have. Now tomorrow I can get new alibies from everyone. You should go around and talk to more of Anna's friends." He sighed. "It's getting late."

Darcy nodded. As she went to get up their hands brushed each other. Darcy felt something akin to electricity scorch along her skin. She gasped in a breath and saw him do the same. Their eyes met and she felt like she was falling.

In a panic she rushed for the door, mumbling excuses. "Oh my, I didn't realize exactly how late it is I should be getting home."

The cool air outside helped clear her mind, but not the feel of his skin against hers.

# CHAPTER 16

*D*arcy went to work the next day all ready to ask her friends about Anna and Jeff. She was a bit nervous about all the questions she would have to ask them, but she knew that so many people in town loved to gossip that it wouldn't seem unusual for her to ask. Well. The killer might be upset with her, she reminded herself.

The first logical place to start was at the bookstore. So while they were busy working, she slipped a few questions here and there to Sue. She was quite certain that Sue was innocent and Sue confirmed it for her when she told Darcy that she had been with her family when both Anna and Jeff had been killed.

Darcy decided to visit the bakery before lunch and talk to Helen. She found her friend with her nose in "And Then There Were None" once again. Darcy smiled to see someone else enjoying the book. Helen would be a welcome addition to the book club if she ever decided to join.

"It's a good book isn't it Helen?" The other woman jumped a little at Darcy's voice. She must have been so engrossed in Agatha Christie's tale that she hadn't noticed Darcy was there.

"Oh, hi Darcy. Yes, it's a great book. I'm almost done reading it and I can't seem to put it down." She set the book aside and frowned. "I'm so sorry about Jeff." She sent Darcy a sympathetic look. "Did you want something, dear? Coffee?"

Darcy nodded and as Helen got it ready she said, "I'm really upset about all this. First Anna, now Jeff. I can't seem to set my mind at ease. Can I ask you some questions?"

"What kind of questions?" Helen placed a cup of coffee on the counter for her in a brown Styrofoam cup. Darcy noticed that she had made one for herself also. That was good. It helped her pretend her inquiries were just an informal chat.

"Did you hear," Darcy started, "that the coroner got the time of death wrong for Anna? She was actually murdered at ten o'clock."

"Really?" Helen said, her eyebrows raising. "How interesting. Did you hear that from Grace?"

"Yes," Darcy lied. Her sister was as good an excuse as any for her knowing the things she did. "So now the police are trying to find out where everyone was at ten."

Helen tilted her head to one side as thought about that. "Ten o'clock you say? How odd. That means I was all alone in my house when Anna died. I suppose I don't have an alibi at all then, do I?" She laughed at the thought.

Darcy knew it couldn't have been Helen, anyway, but she'd been hoping maybe Helen had been with someone, or knew something else. She took a sip of her coffee and tried to keep the conversation going. "This is such delicious coffee, Helen."

Helen smiled in a pleased way. "I'm glad you enjoy it." Then her smile slipped and she looked a little sad. "But I don't know how much longer it will be around. Steve and I aren't making enough money to justify keeping the bakery open. I may have to close the shop."

Darcy was shocked. The Bean There Bakery and Café had

been operating in Misty Hollow for as long as she could remember. "Oh no. I'm so sad to hear that, Helen. Is there anything I can do?"

Helen laughed. "Not unless you can turn back time or make me rich, dear."

They drank their coffees in silence for a little while. While they drank, Darcy said, "Have you heard anything else unusual around town?"

"Unusual?" Helen shook her head. "You mean other than two good people getting killed? No I haven't."

Darcy reflected on Helen calling Jeff a 'good person.' Maybe those two had been friendly, after all. "Well, thanks for the coffee and the chat, Helen. I have to run now."

Darcy walked slowly back to the bookstore, wondering what to do next. How did you solve a jigsaw puzzle that kept adding new pieces as you went?

∾

DARCY not only had the jigsaw puzzle of the murders to think about but there was also the missing cat mystery that needed her attention. Not having made any more headway on the murders she decided to spend the afternoon trying to work out what had happened to Persephone.

Cats don't just disappear into thin air. She had to be somewhere.

"Sue, I'm just heading out to see Linda at the Library for a while. Look after the shop, okay?" She heard Sue answer affirmatively from in between the book shelves somewhere and taking advantage of a lull in customer traffic she quickly darted out of the shop.

It was a nice afternoon with the sun shining down on her face and a soft breeze ruffling her dark hair. She took a deep breath as she walked toward the Library and tried to relax the tension that had built up in her body over the last few days. By the time she reached the Library steps she felt a little better and was ready to tackle the missing cat mystery.

Walking through the swinging double glass doors she spotted Linda toward the back and quickly made her way to her. Linda was very engrossed in her task and jumped a little when she saw Darcy standing behind her.

"Oh Darcy you gave me a little fright."

"Sorry, didn't mean to startle you Linda."

"Oh it's fine. I've been a bit on edge since the murders in town. It's enough to make you feel very unsafe."

"Yes it is unsettling." Darcy couldn't help agree with her. "I'm not here to discuss that though, I just wanted to ask you some questions about Persephone. See if I can't work out what happened to her."

"Oh, Darcy I'm so grateful you're taking the time to help me. I thought you may have forgotten, what with all that's been going on."

"No. I haven't forgotten although I will admit that it hasn't been my number one priority in the last few days. But I did promise to help look for her and I meant it."

Darcy was taken slightly aback when Linda suddenly threw her arms around Darcy's shoulders and squeezed for a moment. "You are such a good friend Darcy. I won't ever forget this. What do you want to know?"

Darcy let out a little laugh. "You're welcome Linda." She patted her friend on her back. Linda let go and stepped back with a little smile. Darcy asked her a few basic questions about the day her cat disappeared. Things like when was the last time Linda saw Persephone, what was the cat doing when she last saw her and nothing really jumped out at Darcy. The cat seemed like she was doing pretty normal cat things. So Darcy was none the wiser as to what had happened to Persephone. But she vowed to find out if it was at all possible.

She chatted to Linda a little longer about mundane things and then realizing that time had gotten away from her rushed back to the book store to help Sue close up for the day.

～

DARCY AND JON met up at her house that night. She had done a whirlwind cleaning, knowing he was coming, and wondered why she was trying so hard.

"Everyone has a gray alibi." Jon stopped when he noticed Darcy's perplexed look. "That means that it doesn't completely check out. There are only a few who have solid alibies." He paused for a moment and consulted his notes. "Pete and Blake only have each other as alibies. Jess was home alone when Anna was killed and was at work helping the mayor when Jeff was killed. So again, those two are each other's alibies. And Aaron was at home on his own each time."

He sighed loudly and tossed the notepad down on her living room table. "This is useless. I think we should go and have a look in Jeff's apartment. Maybe he found out something new since he last talked to you."

"Didn't you search there already?"

"Of course we did," he said, standing up. "But we didn't have you with us when we did."

The short ride to Jeff's apartment was a mostly silent one. When they arrived Darcy found all of the paper's she and Jeff had been working on. They were scattered on the kitchen table.

"We saw those already," Jon explained to her. "Your sister Grace recognized your handwriting right away. So how far did you and he get?"

"Wait," Darcy said, leafing through the pages. "There's some missing."

"Missing?" Jon looked over her shoulder. "You mean, like gone? Taken?"

"Looks like."

"Maybe you were on the right track," Jon said to her. Darcy sorted through the papers, looking for any new ones. Mixed in with them she found several bank statements for the town.

"Look here," Darcy said as she turned and handed them to Jon. Jeff must have kept working on it after she'd left to go home as there was a name highlighted on the papers. Aaron, Grace's husband. "You said he didn't have an alibi, right?"

Jon nodded. "What are you thinking?" he said. "Was he stealing money from the town? Maybe Anna and Jeff found out somehow?"

Darcy didn't want to say anything. She didn't want to believe that Aaron could be the killer, for her sister as much for Aaron. But she reminded herself about what Jon had said before about sticking to the facts and not relying on your emotions. They had to run down every possibility, until there were none left.

DARCY AND JON walked to Grace and Aaron's house. They just spent the last couple of hours going over the bank statements, which proved that money was indeed being stolen from the town and put into another, nameless account. It wasn't clear if Aaron actually had anything to do with it or not but it certainly warranted investigating.

Jon needed to ask Aaron some questions about it all so they headed over to the Wentworth's apartment.

When they arrived Jon knocked loudly on the door. Aaron opened it to them with a smile. "Hi guys. What's up? Grace isn't home at the moment." He must have seen something on Darcy's face, because his smile slipped a bit. "What's going on?" he said as he looked back and forth between the two of them.

Without hesitation Jon stepped forward and grabbed Aaron by the upper arm. Darcy had to look away as Jon took out his handcuffs.

"You're under arrest," she heard Jon say.

*G*race did not take the news well. "I just don't understand what's going on! How could you do this? Why would you arrest my husband?!"

Grace was crying. Darcy couldn't remember ever seeing her this upset. She had been out doing an errand when Jon and Darcy had brought Aaron in but she'd come screaming into the police station not long after. Anger had quickly turned to frustration for her.

Jon laid a calming hand on Grace's shoulder that she shrugged away. "Grace, listen to me. We found some papers in Jeff's apartment that seem to incriminate Aaron."

"In the murders? Are you insane?" Her voice echoed around the police department as several other officers looked on. They had heard about the arrest and come to watch. Darcy imagined everyone in town had heard about the arrest by now.

"I don't know what he's into, Grace. But you need to talk to him." Jon went to his desk and came back with photocopies of the documents that Darcy had helped him find in Jeff's apartment. "I've questioned him. He won't talk to me. Maybe you can talk to him like a wife and get something out of him."

She ripped the papers away from him, her fist wrinkling creases into them. "Screw that. You have nothing to hold my husband on. Let him go."

Jon nodded as if he'd expected that answer. Quietly, he left the room to go and get Aaron. Grace glared at Darcy the whole time he was gone.

Aaron came flying out of the back of the building where the holding area was. He fell into Grace's arms. "Come on," he said to her, "let's go home before your new partner changes his mind." He gave Jon a dirty look and then turned it towards Darcy. Without another word he and Grace left the police station.

"He wouldn't give me anything, Darcy. I'm not sure what we should do now," Jon said, running a hand through his hair in frustration.

"Well, I know." Darcy shook her head and crossed her arms over her stomach. "I know what to do, but you're not going to like it."

∼

In the bookstore Darcy went around lighting candles as Jon looked on nervously.

"Uh, Darcy? I know I said I'd trust you and all, but what are you doing?"

This was the part he wasn't going to like. She wasn't wild about it, either. "We are going to have communicate with the other side to try and channel the spirit of Anna. Maybe she can shed some light on this whole situation."

Darcy saw the look that Jon gave her. She was used to the scepticism of others. She just smiled and finished preparing the space. "Come on," she said. "Let's sit and hold hands."

They sank to the floor, cross legged, and Jon gave her his hands. She bit her lip at the warm sensation that flowed through her at his touch. She had to concentrate for this to work. She swallowed and pushed aside thoughts of the gorgeous man she was holding hands with by candlelight, and instead pictured the fog in her mind.

Nearby, within the circle of candles, mist coalesced in ethereal tendrils. She watched it, wondering if Jon could see it too. She let it happen, let the bridge between this world and the next solidify until the mist became a spirit, became the form of a figure. A woman's form, tall and shimmering dark.

But it wasn't Anna, it was Millie. Great-Aunt Millie once again floated over to the book shelf and took Agatha Christie's thriller from the shelf and sent it flying at Jon. The book hit him squarely in the head. He yelped loudly and jumped up and as he did it broke the connection the communication had created and Millie disappeared.

Darcy sighed. Millie's obsession with that book was becoming annoying. And what did she have against Jon? Darcy no longer believed that Jon had anything to do with either of the murders. So why did Millie dislike him so much?

Knowing they weren't going to be able to connect to the other side for a while she pulled Jon into the employee area of the shop where there was a small refrigerator and freezer unit.

"I'm so sorry about that. I don't know what's gotten into Aunt Millie." Jon looked uncomfortable but didn't say anything. Using a plastic bag, she dropped ice into it and handed it to Jon. "Here. This will help with that knot that's forming on the back of your head." She gently laid the ice pack to his skull. His hand slipped over hers and she pulled back at the touch of it. Once again, she looked up into his face.

"I, uh, didn't realize that you were quite so tall." She heard the breathlessness in her own voice. She'd been right. He was very distracting.

He smiled at her. "I'm glad to have you on my side, Darcy. Only, no more flying books, okay?" His voice was quiet when he spoke.

"Yes, I agree." She laughed softly. "And I'm glad you're on my side, too. I couldn't do this without you."

Standing this close she could see flecks of silver around the pupil of his deep blue eyes. And those cute freckles across his nose were begging for her to kiss them.

Her breath stalled as he moved in closer until their bodies were just touching. She watched in fascination as his head lowered towards hers. The first touch of his lips to hers felt so right. The kiss was soft and sweet and electrifying and everything a first kiss should be.

Darcy couldn't remember the last time she had felt like this, or if she had ever felt like it before. For a moment she was able to forget about all of the doom and gloom that had been hanging around her lately. There was nothing but this moment.

When they broke apart Darcy laid her head on Jon's chest for a moment. This was perfect. Like a story from a book. Then she suddenly gasped.

Jon leaned back and held her by her upper arms. "What's wrong?"

"I know what Millie has been trying to tell us. That book. The only person I know who is reading that book right now is Helen."

"But... you said the killer was a man. Remember?"

That was right. Darcy didn't know where Great-Aunt Millie was leading them, but she was sure it had something to do with that book. Helen was the key.

Jon and Darcy headed to the police station to see if they could find any information on Helen. She still didn't know where Millie was guiding them. Darcy just couldn't believe that Helen would have killed two people. She was the nicest person that Darcy knew. There was no motive.

Wait. Yes there was.

She sat with Jon at his desk. "Helen told me she was having trouble with the rent on her shop. She didn't know if she and

Steve would be able to keep it open. Maybe she stole money from the town and then Anna and Jeff somehow found out."

Jon scratched his head. "Maybe. It's as solid a theory as anything else we have. I'll trail Helen about for a while and see if I can get any hard evidence on her.

## CHAPTER 18

*D*arcy was distracted at work the next day. She wanted to know what Jon was finding out. As she put some new books on display she dropped an entire rack. Sue came over to help her with an odd glance but no comments. Darcy couldn't help it. She really didn't want Helen to be guilty.

The bell over the door jingled to announce the arrival of a customer. Darcy watched a very serious looking Linda come in and walk right up to the counter.

"What can I do for you today Linda?" Sue asked in her usual bubbly voice. Darcy moved over to stand behind the counter with Sue.

Linda shook her head and leaned up against the counter. "Oh I'm not in here to buy anything. I just wanted to ask both of you to a little last minute memorial at my place tonight. I know that everyone has been so on edge lately, but I really want to honor the memory of Anna and Jeff."

"Sure I'll be there," Sue said with a small smile as she went back to her job sorting old book stock into piles.

"I'll be there too," Darcy said hesitantly, not sure she really wanted to go.

"Great," Linda said. "I'll see you both there tonight." She pushed away from the counter and turned toward the door.

"Linda wait up a minute." Linda stopped and turned back to Darcy. "I just wanted to ask if you have found your cat yet?"

Linda's face fell and Darcy could see tears welling up. "No I haven't. She seems to have disappeared without a trace. I think I need to face the fact that she is gone for good. What with her gone and the murders in town I have been so depressed about it all."

"I'm so sorry Linda. But don't give up hope yet." Darcy felt bad for her friend. She knew that Linda thought the world of her cat just like Darcy did with Smudge. "She may turn up yet."

"I hope you're right Darcy but I'm losing hope of ever seeing her again." Linda swiped a hand across her wet eyes and sniffed. "I'll see you tonight then." And she left the store quickly.

Darcy was dreading going to it, especially since Helen would be there also. But on the other hand it would be a good opportunity for her to observe all of the suspects in one place.

Kind of like in "And Then There Was None."

~

DARCY HAD GOTTEN to the memorial at Linda's house early so that she could observe everyone as they arrived and mingled. She was hovering with Linda, who seemed a little happier now, and Sue when Mark walked in, eyes darting one way and then the other. He looked really unsettled.

"Mark looks really nervous doesn't he?" Sue noticed.

Linda nodded. "Yes, he does." Darcy agreed with them but then reminded herself that he did have a firm alibi.

As she watched the crowd, Darcy saw Jess making her way towards them.

"Hello all," she greeted them. Jess was once again dressed very fashionably with another lovely designer dress and matching expensive shoes. Darcy saw the look Sue gave to the outfit.

Darcy decided to do a little digging. "Jess, can you confirm a rumor for me?"

Jess shrugged. "I will if I can."

"I heard you have a new fellow. I wanted to know who it was."

Jess flushed and shook her head, her red locks bouncing. "You must be mistaken, Darcy. There's no one new in my life."

Darcy thought that was strange. Jess was usually a huge gossip who had no trouble telling everything, even about her own life. Had the rumors been wrong?

There was a moment of silence while the women tried to pick up the conversation. "So, Darcy," Linda finally asked. "Are there any updates on the case?" She seemed more calm now than she had that afternoon in the book store.

Now was the time to strike, Darcy knew. "Actually we have a very strong suspect. Jon and Grace think we're close to solving the case."

"Oh? Is that why they arrested Grace's husband?" Jess pressed.

"Well." What could she say about that? "That would be police business, I guess. Grace doesn't tell me everything."

They all hushed as Pete walked behind where they were standing. He looked very upset. Pointing discreetly at him Sue said, "I heard a new rumor about him. Apparently he's been going to that acting studio in Meadowood every week to take acting lessons." Meadowood was the next town over from Misty Hollow and was quite a bit bigger than their little town. It was actually more like a small city than a town.

Acting lessons? Darcy considered that. Depending on how good he was at acting...

She needed to tell Jon this piece of information right away so she excused herself from the other women. She found Jon standing alone beside the makeshift bar that Linda had set up in one corner of her living room. She could see he was scanning the crowd, checking out all of the suspects, much more obvious about it than she had been. She hurried over to him. When she got to him he took hold of her hand and she couldn't control the shiver she felt at his touch.

"Have you found anything out?" he asked her.

"I think so. I just saw Pete and he looked really upset, but maybe it was all an act." She went on to tell him what she had learned about Pete taking acting lessons.

"That's interesting. Well, I haven't been able to find anything on Helen yet. Maybe there just isn't anything to find out. Maybe she isn't the one."

Darcy didn't know how much longer she could take this. Suspecting everyone she knew of murder was taking its toll on her.

"Hey, you look upset." Jon ran a finger across her cheek, then stepped back, both of them conscious of how almost the entire town was at the memorial.

She smiled at him. "I really just want to go home. I'm too tired to be at a party. Even one for the dead."

DARCY SIGHED as she shut the door. Home at last. Although a rather solitary person by nature she didn't mind socializing at times when the mood took her. But not tonight. The memorial had been the last thing she'd felt like going to but out of respect for Anna... she shrugged, oh, alright, and Jeff, she'd felt that she'd had no other choice than to attend.

And she'd had an another reason for going anyway. She'd hoped that she might see something or would get some sort of a clue as to who was going around killing the good people of Misty Hollow.

No such luck, aside from Pete's acting lessons, if that was even true. It had been a very disappointing evening. She had really been expecting some big revelation like in Agatha Christie's novel. It hadn't materialized. Now she wasn't sure what the next move was.

Smudge was waiting by his empty bowl in the kitchen. She felt a pang of guilt that she'd forgotten to feed him today. She quickly filled his bowl and he tucked into like he hadn't been fed for weeks. She smiled at him.

Darcy got ready for bed quickly, throwing on an old pair of pajamas, and then climbing under the covers. Smudge curled up next to her as she drifted off to sleep. Thoughts of the evening chasing each other through her mind. She was no closer to working this out.

She was awoken by a loud yowl from her cat, to find a figure standing over her, wearing dark, baggy clothing. This wasn't a dream. This figure was real, the gun he held was real. She was about to be shot. The next victim of the killer.

Darcy had to think quickly so she grabbed hold of a book on her bedside table and threw it as hard as she could at the person. The figure dodged the book and ran out of the door.

Darcy gulped in great lungsful of air trying to calm herself as Smudge rubbed up against her in a gesture that said "It's okay, I'm here with you." She absentmindedly smoothed his fur with one hand as, shaking uncontrollably, she reached for her phone with the other hand to call the police.

# CHAPTER 19

*D*arcy was very shaken up after what had happened and was sitting stiffly on her couch with Smudge. She had her legs drawn up to her chest and her arms were hugging her knees as she tried to stop the shaking.

She had been watching her front door for minutes that felt like hours, terrified that the intruder was going to come back. When the handle of the front door rattled as if someone was trying to get in she hesitantly moved over to the door and checked the peep hole. Relief flooded through her as she opened it.

Jon rushed into the house and drew her into a tight hug. "Are you okay? Are you sure they're gone?"

"I'm fine, Jon. I scared him away. I threw a book at him."

He looked at her like she was crazy and she felt a smile come over her face. "What can I say? Books have been my saving grace more than once in my life."

"You really should stop investigating." He led her back to the couch and they sat down together. "We're obviously close to something, why else would you be attacked?"

Darcy was suddenly very aware that she was only wearing her

pair of yellow pajamas, and aware of how low the buttons were on the front, and aware that he was very, very close to her. Jon looked at her intently and then lowered his head to kiss her. It was a quick, hard kiss that let her know just how shook up he was by this. "I'm not going to let anything bad happen to you," he said to her. "Now. Tell me exactly what happened."

So she told him how Smudge's yowling had woken her up and she had found a figure standing over her. When she was done telling the tale, she realized how silly it sounded. "Jon, I'm sure that Anna and Jeff fought back in some way before they were shot. I mean, he had a gun. Why would the murderer change his mind after having a book thrown at him?"

Jon shrugged. She could see his mind turning. "Maybe they only meant to scare you. Listen. We need to fill out a report on this. This is big. It's the first fresh clue we've gotten."

Darcy nodded but she just didn't feel up to going down to the station. "I'm really tired. Can't we do it tomorrow? I really just want to go to sleep now."

He frowned, but nodded. "All right. I'll call another officer in and we'll do a check through your house for anything the guy left behind. A footprint or a fingerprint would be great. We'll check for prints in your room in the morning, just don't go touching too much in there, okay. Go up to bed. I'll take care of it."

She smiled at his thoughtfulness before pecking him on the cheek. Fighting the urge to stay with Jon, or ask him to stay with her, she quickly made her way upstairs to bed.

THE NEXT MORNING Darcy woke up to the smell of breakfast cooking. Suddenly realizing she was starving, she wandered downstairs to find Jon in the kitchen.

"I didn't know you could cook," she teased him.

"My grandmother made sure I knew how to." He impressed

her by flipping a frying egg in the air and catching it deftly with the pan. "She used to worry that I would starve when I left home. Because my mother was already gone she took me in and brought me up when I lost my father."

Darcy smiled at him as she sat down to a plate of eggs and pancakes. "I'll never eat all this," she said, but she was so hungry that she managed to scarf the lot down.

"Did you guys find anything last night?" she asked him.

"No. Nothing. Not a footprint or anything. The guy was either good, or lucky. Either way it leaves us with nothing."

After they'd eaten and cleaned up, and after Darcy had taken a quick shower and dressed, and Jon had dusted for prints in her room and come up with nothing again, they sat down to work out exactly what they knew.

"We need to talk to Pete," Darcy said. After she had found out that he might have gained the ability to lie to her, his alibi needed to be investigated. "After all, Pete did date Anna at one time. And his alibi is his sick brother."

"Okay, so let me ask you. Do you think that Pete fits the build of the person who broke into your house last night?"

She remembered the image of that dark form in her bedroom all too well. "I think so, but I can't be completely sure. It all happened so fast. I didn't really have a lot of time to take in too many details about the person. But I know he was tall."

Jon nodded. "What do you say I go and ask him then?"

She felt so much more confident with Jon on her side. She was very glad she had decided to trust him.

JON AND DARCY walked into town together that morning. "I'm going to talk to Pete, Blake and Doctor Sandal," Jon said. "I want to nail down Pete's alibi. You be extra careful today." He stroked her cheek before walking towards the police station. As that now familiar warm feeling zinged through her from the touch of his hand, Darcy watched him walk away, enjoying the way he moved. Then she headed towards the bookstore. At the last minute she decided to detour to the bakery to get coffee.

She felt better about seeing Helen today. Every man in town might freak her out after what happened last night, but now she was as sure as ever that Helen was not the person behind these events. "Good morning Helen, how are you today?" Darcy could see that Helen was still reading "And Then There Were None."

It took Helen a second to realize that Darcy had spoken to her. "Oh, Darcy. I'm sorry. I'm on the last few pages of this book and I just want to get it finished to find out what happens in the end." She put the book on the counter while she got Darcy coffee.

Darcy picked the book up and said, "Well, I won't ruin it for you. Where did you get this copy?"

"That? I, uh, found it lying around the house."

Helen hadn't sounded very convincing. She wondered why it would be such a secret. Darcy absently thumbed through the pages of the book and then realized that this copy was from her store. It even had the little pencil number in the front that Darcy made in every book she inventoried. Had she sold this to Helen? She didn't remember doing so. Maybe Sue had sold it to her. She made a mental note to ask her assistant next time she saw her.

She held the cover and folded it back and forth along the crease. Something was very familiar about it and she had a feeling that she was very close to something, akin to a word being on the tip of her tongue and not being able to recall it.

She turned the book over and saw a small, dark red splotch. The novel slipped from her hand to thump quietly against the floor. "Millie," she whispered.

"What did you say Darcy?" Helen came back with a coffee in her hand, an eyebrow raised when she saw her book on the floor.

Darcy shook her head and said, "I have to go." She ran out of the bakery without her coffee. She had just realized what Millie was trying to tell her by throwing around the copy of Agatha Christie's novel all over the bookstore. No need to ask Sue if she'd sold the book to Helen. The copy of Helen's book had belonged to Anna. Darcy had finally recognized that deep crease down the front cover. She thought that the red splotch on the back of the book might be blood. She raced to the police station, hoping Jon was there.

# CHAPTER 20

*J*on lifted his head up when he saw her rush in.

She was out of breath, needing a moment to gather herself.

"What's happened?" Jon asked, picking up on her anxiety.

Darcy went on to tell him all about the book with the crease on the front cover, the blood on the back. Anna's book, in Helen's hands. "And she acted so odd when she was explaining how she came to have the book," she finished.

"And you just left the book there?" Jon said to her.

Darcy could have smacked a hand to her forehead she felt so foolish. Of course. The one hard piece of evidence that could prove who had killed Anna, and then Jeff, and she had left it in the hands of the prime suspect. She called herself all kinds of stupid.

He rubbed his fingers along his eyebrows. "Don't worry about it, Darcy. I will go and bring Helen in for questioning. You should know that Doctor Sandal vouched for Blake being sick, at least. So that's that with Blake and probably his brother Pete, too."

Jon left Darcy at the station and went to collect Helen. Grace was nowhere to be seen, and Darcy was glad for that little blessing. Her sister was still mad at her, and that part of the investigation was still a loose puzzle piece.

When Jon returned he brought Helen in wearing handcuffs. It looked as if she had been crying. Jon led her to a holding cell and then returned to Darcy.

Darcy immediately snapped at him. "Really? Did you have to handcuff her? Come on, Jon."

He shook his head. "She refused to come with me. That's why she was wearing the handcuffs. I think her exact words were 'I had nothing to do with this so you can't arrest me.'" He flopped down into his chair and wiped a weary hand over his face. Then he looked at Darcy and said, "She was adamant that she loved Anna and would never hurt her or Jeff."

Jon held up the book, the one Helen had been reading, for Darcy to see. It was in a sealed evidence bag. "It does look like blood on the back. I think you were right about that. I'm going to send it to the lab to get it tested. But she gave it to me without any hesitation. She didn't even try to deny that she had it."

Darcy sighed. She still had so many questions. It didn't seem like they'd solved anything. It just felt like they'd found more pieces to fit into the puzzle. And most of all, she was just so tired. She put a hand over her mouth as she yawned widely.

"You should go home and rest," Jon said to her. He came around the desk and held out his hand. When she took it he pulled her in for a quick hug and then risked a kiss on her forehead. She didn't know what was going to happen between them, but he was right to keep it private, for now. At least in public.

BACK AT HER house Darcy found she couldn't sleep even though she was exhausted. She was sitting at her table trying to read a book, tapping her foot rhythmically against the table leg. She was so jittery and couldn't settle her mind. She kept reading the same sentence over and over.

She could feel Smudge looking at her. "I can't help it," she said to him. "We're just going to have to wait."

Finally, she tossed her book down on the table. She sighed loudly. What to do? She got up and went to the phone, punching in the number for the police station. Jon answered on the second ring. It hadn't been all that long, but in spite of how she had told Smudge to be patient, she had to know if anything had happened.

When he said hello she jumped right into it. She was too agitated for pleasantries. "How's it going?"

"Well, hello to you too," Jon said with a hint of laughter in his voice. "I've got nothing new, Darcy. Helen just keeps saying she doesn't know anything. Oh, I have to go. The mayor just arrived and I need to explain what's happening. I'll see you later, okay?"

"Hmm. I'd like that. Bye." She hung up the phone, surprised at herself for being so forward with him. She had finally accepted that not only was there something going on between them, but she wanted there to be something.

Smudge meowed and went to the door. He started scratching at it, wanting to get out. "You know what? That's a great idea. It won't do either of us any good to just sit around waiting for something to happen."

Darcy grabbed her coat and pulled it on. Then she and Smudge slipped out into the foggy night.

# CHAPTER 21

 hen she left her house Darcy didn't really have a destination in mind but soon she found herself heading towards Helen's house. It was one of the larger houses in town, a sprawling two story white mansion at the end of one of the side streets. She made it there quicker than she had expected. All the lights were off and she was certain that Helen's husband, the mayor, would still be at the police station. She wasn't even sure why she was here, except that she still didn't feel right about what had happened to Helen.

She tried the door but it was locked. She went round to the back of the house and found one of the windows opened just a bit. With a bit of leverage, she managed to get through with nothing more serious than a scrape to her left wrist. She had been in the house a few times before to visit Helen and knew her way around pretty well.

She headed for Helen and Steve's bedroom first, turning lights on and off as she needed. She wasn't certain what she was looking for. Tapping into her sixth sense and extending it out she tried to let it guide her. It didn't help. She still didn't feel anything.

She continued to walk through the house, looking for anything that was out of place. She went into the study and looked over Helen's desk. It was very neat. Everything tidy and in place.

Then she walked over to the mayor's desk, a huge oak thing that looked like it belonged in a room much bigger and grander than this one. His was much messier than Helen's. She pawed through some of the papers on top of the desk but couldn't see anything that shouldn't have been there. She opened up one of the drawers. Inside it she found a plain manila envelope. It was filled with cash, a passport and a ticket to Paris.

She didn't need her sixth sense to know this was out of place. Why would Steve Nelson, mayor of Misty Hollow and by all accounts a stand-up kind of guy, have money and the means to get out of town stashed in a drawer of his desk?

She moved the pieces around in her head. Everything was there, she felt. The picture was fuzzy, but the edges of what she knew started to line up and fall into place...

Then it hit her. The man in her dreams. Jeff circling figures in the financial statements. Helen saying they needed money. Even Steve being so nervous on the day of the festival when Anna was killed. It was the mayor! She realized that Helen's book had belonged to Anna, but Helen wasn't the one that had taken it from her. Steve had.

Oh, dear God, she thought to herself. She'd made a terrible mistake. She raced out of the room, knowing she had to get to Jon, but as she stepped into the living room she heard the front door close and someone walk into the house.

Darcy slid to a halt on the carpeted floor and took precious seconds to right herself before she tiptoed back into the office with the desks hoping to avoid detection. It was only then that she realized she had left the light on in that room. Retreating further into the house, she hugged the wall in the hallway that led from the bedroom.

She could just see Steve as he entered the office. She didn't know what to do now. Run? Hide? She felt frozen with terror. In her panic to get away she backed up into the corner of a table. Whirling, hoping Steve hadn't heard the muted sound, she tried desperately to keep the box of tissues and picture frames from falling to the floor.

Steve appeared at the end of the hallway, flipping on the light switch. "Darcy?" He sounded confused. "What are you doing here?"

"I, uh, hi Steve. Hi. I, um, I was looking for Helen."

She hardly had the words out before Steve said, "Helen is at the police station. You know that. You're the reason she got arrested, after all."

"I uh... I uh..." Darcy had no idea what to say. The thought crossed her mind that if she was going to continue getting into trouble like this then she needed to learn how to sneak in and out of people's homes better. She needed to get out of here, away from Steve. Fear gripped her heart. This man had killed two people.

She needed to get away from him.

"Wait here," Steve said. He stepped out of the hallway and back into the office and Darcy knew she had to take this chance if she wanted to stay alive. She ran for the back room and its open window but before she had hardly moved Steve grabbed her by the arm. He threw her to the floor and towered over her. He held a gun in his hand. "You have always been trouble Darcy," he said with a cold smile, "always meddling in things that don't concern you."

"You're the one who killed Anna and Jeff." She raised an arm defensively and pushed her way backward along the hallway. "I think that concerns me."

Steve shook his head and said, "You don't understand. I had to do it. What choice did I have?" He took a step toward her as she continued to scoot away. "I'm not going to justify myself to you, though. I've got no reason to talk to a dead woman. Goodbye, Darcy."

She was sure the loud noise that echoed through the house then was the gun going off but she found herself still miraculously alive as Steve looked up and away from her in surprise.

It was the front door breaking in, she realized. Suddenly she could hear Jon's voice as he burst into the hallway, followed by Smudge the cat, who landed protectively beside Darcy. His fur was on end with his back arched up and his teeth bared as he hissed menacingly at Steve.

Jon reacted quickly to the situation and tackled Steve. In mere seconds he had Steve disarmed and in cuffs. It was over. Just like that.

Smudge spit one last time and then settled himself, pushing his face into Darcy's. "I'm okay, boy," she said as she patted the cat. "I take it I have you to thank for my rescue?"

"No, actually I think you have me to thank for that," Jon said. Smudge mewled at him and looked away as if to argue the point. When he knew that Steve was subdued, Jon picked her up off the floor and pulled her into his arms, hugging her to him tightly. "Are you alright?"

She nodded into his shoulder. "How did you know I was here?"

Jon smiled. "Smudge came and got me. He wouldn't leave me alone until I followed him." Jon kissed her quickly. "I have to take care of Steve right now. Follow me out of here, okay?"

She waited for him to pick Steve up and, holding him by his shirt and his bound hands, walk him out of the house. "Steve Nelson you are under arrest for the murder of Anna Louis and Jeff Thomas..." Darcy picked Smudge up and held him in her arms as she followed Jon.

The picture was almost complete. She was just happy she hadn't ended up as part of it herself.

~

AT THE POLICE station Jon released Helen. What should have been a happy moment for her was colored black, though. "I had no idea about any of this, Darcy. You have to believe me. Steve and I have been leading almost separate lives lately."

Jon, Darcy, and Grace sat around Grace's desk with Helen and listened to the woman tell her story. "He was acting so strange the night Anna was killed." Darcy remembered that Helen had said that once before. At the time, she had thought that Helen meant after he found out about Anna's death.

Grace said, "Steve has admitted to Anna and Jeff's murders but not the attack on Darcy. He won't talk about his motive, either. Anything you can tell us about that, Helen?"

Helen shook her head as tears fell. "No. I'm sorry. I guess I didn't know him at all."

Jon turned to Darcy and she felt safe when she looked into his eyes. He was looking at her so protectively and he said, "I want to make sure that you're not in any more danger."

Grace cleared her throat and looked pointedly at Jon. "I'll look into the town's financial statements," she said, "and talk to Mark from the bank to see if we can find the mayor's motive within that."

"So," Darcy ventured, "am I forgiven for suspecting Aaron?"

Grace rolled her eyes. "You were wrong about him. There was a perfectly innocent reason that his name was on those papers and I already knew about it. We've cleared his name. You really should check your facts before you have an innocent man arrested. Just go home, Sis. I think we've all had enough excitement in our lives recently."

# CHAPTER 22

$\mathcal{J}$on walked Darcy home. "That's odd," she said. "It's still so foggy."

"What do you mean?"

Darcy laughed and said, "It always seems to be foggy when there's trouble. I just figured with everything over, it would clear away."

She expected Jon to laugh along with her but instead he looked serious and upset. "Hey. What's wrong?" she asked him.

He stopped at the steps leading up to her porch and turned to face her. "I almost lost you, again. Do you make a habit of putting yourself into danger like this? That was damned foolish what you did tonight." He paused for a moment and she braced herself for what might come next. "I have very strong feelings for you, Darcy. I couldn't stand to lose you."

Her heart rate skipped a beat with his confession. "You won't have to," she said, and then she stepped up onto the first step of the porch to put herself even with him, and kissed him. His lips were soft and warm and she felt the electricity course through her at his touch. They pulled apart and she grabbed his hand to lead him into the house. She knew, now, that this was something she wanted.

The phone started ringing as her hand rested on the doorknob.

She swore under her breath as Jon pulled her back. "We should just ignore it."

"We can't just ignore it, Jon. What if it's Grace with news?" She looked around at the tendrils of fog in the moonlight. "What if it's something else that's happened?"

She left him on the porch and went in to grab the phone before the machine could pick it up. Grace was on the other end.

"Darcy, is Jon with you?"

She looked over to see Jon stepping slowly inside and mouthed to him that it was Grace. "Yes, he's right here."

"Listen to me," her sister said, her tone serious and rushed, "I went to Mark's house to talk to him but his wife said that he was at the bank. So I went there and there was smoke coming out of one of the windows."

"What?" Darcy couldn't believe this. Would this never end?

"It was Jess, believe it or not. I know I'm having trouble believing it. She'd knocked Mark unconscious and she was trying to burn the bank's records."

"Is Mark okay?" Darcy asked her, all the while praying there hadn't been another murder.

"Yes, he's fine. Tell Jon to meet me down here, okay?"

"We'll be right there," Darcy told her.

BACK AT THE police station Jess was sitting at Jon's desk in hand-cuffs. "I'm innocent. I didn't kill anyone, it's all just a misunder-standing."

Jess was dishevelled, her red hair loose around her face, her dark blue dress torn at one shoulder. Obviously she'd been in a struggle of some kind.

Darcy walked over and sat in the chair next to her at Jon's desk. "Stop talking and just listen to me." When she was sure she had Jess's attention she continued. "Are you having an affair with the mayor, with Steve?"

Jess was silent for so long that Darcy thought maybe she wouldn't answer. Finally, though, she nodded.

Darcy pressed her lips together. There was the final piece, put in its place. She guessed the gossip around town had finally gotten something right.

Grace was shocked. "How did you know, Darcy?"

Darcy turned to face her sister. "Jess came into the bookstore and bought a book on how to speak French. I found a ticket to Paris in the mayor's desk. I'm betting that they were going to run away together." She turned back to Jess who was sitting with a blank expression on her face, just staring out of the window. It was like she was shutting down. Her dream had fallen to ashes.

Darcy shook her head and looked back at Grace. "We know that the mayor has been taking money from the town. You know Sue, who works for me? Well she's been commenting recently on how expensive Jess's clothes and shoes are, way more than she should be able to afford. I'm guessing that the mayor has been showering her with expensive gifts. That's why he needed the money. To afford his affair."

"If you cooperate," Jon said to Jess, "things will be easier for you. You may not even have to go to trial." When she didn't answer right away he added, "He killed two people, Jess. That's not a man to lie for."

Jess seemed to think that over for a few minutes and then she nodded. "We weren't running away together, Steve and I, we were just going on a trip. Steve would never leave his wife. That was something I was okay with."

Darcy would never understand that. She hoped she'd never

have to be in the position that Jess had put herself in. "You were the one who broke into my house, weren't you Jess? It wasn't the killer. Steve wouldn't have been scared off so easily."

Jess looked at her with wide, sad eyes. "I overheard you at the party saying that you were close to solving the case. I didn't want you to find out that the murderer was Steve. I just wanted to scare you off."

"So you knew what Steve had done." Darcy didn't say it as a question.

Slumping into her chair, Jess nodded miserably.

It made sense to Darcy. "You're not a killer, Jess. I know that. But you can't be okay with what happened. Where did you get the gun that you used to scare me?"

Jess couldn't look at her as she said, "It was just a toy gun, totally harmless."

Darcy shook her head. "Why did you try to burn down the bank?"

"I wasn't trying to burn down the bank." Jess said. Her voice had gotten so quiet. "I just meant to burn the financial records in a trash can, but it got out of control."

Jon nodded to Grace as he jotted down the last of his notes from what Jess had said. Then Grace led Jess back out to the holding cells. The woman didn't even try to resist.

Darcy turned to Jon, sitting at his desk, tapping his pen against the paper like he did. "I want to talk to Steve," she said.

"That's not a good idea," Jon argued. "Thank you, for helping us with Jess. But like you said, she's not a killer. Steve is."

"I know. But I need to talk to him. You have to trust me one more time, Jon."

She could tell he didn't like it. He didn't have to like it, Darcy figured. She didn't like it herself, but she had to do this. Finally, Jon threw his hands up in the air and led her to the holding cell where Steve was sitting with his head in his hands. Grace stood nearby. She nodded silent encouragement to Darcy.

When Steve saw Darcy he leaned back against the cell wall. "Hi, Darcy. I'm, um, sorry. I guess."

"You're sorry?" Jon said, his voice rising. Darcy held up a hand to hold him off.

Darcy spoke directly to Steve. "They arrested Jess. She told us everything. We know that you and she were having an affair." Steve was quiet. He looked like a broken man. "So we know everything, Steve. But there's still one thing I can't figure out, and I need to hear it from you. Why did you kill Anna in the first place?"

Steve started to cry then. Heavy tears ran down his face and he tried in vain to blink them away. "I never wanted to hurt anyone. Certainly not Anna. She had come to the house that afternoon to see Helen before going to the festival but Helen wasn't there. Instead she walked in on Jess and me together. We were... well it was obvious what we were doing. I never had a chance to explain because she just fled the moment she saw us."

He sniffed loudly and swiped a hand across his eyes. "It would have ruined me. Everything would have come out then. The affair, the money I'd stolen, everything. I went to her house after the ceremony to try and talk to her. I brought money with me to encourage Anna to stay silent. At first we just talked, but when Anna made it clear that she was going to tell my wife everything, I got upset."

They waited for the rest of it. Now that he'd started talking, he couldn't stop. Getting up, he began to pace the length of the cell getting more agitated as he spoke. "I just meant to scare her, but Anna fought back and it got out of control. The gun was Anna's. She grabbed it when she felt threatened. It made such a tiny noise when it went off..."

"Then why did you take Anna's book?" Jon asked him.

Still crying, Steve said, "I needed to get rid of the body. The evidence. All of it. The book had blood on it so I picked it up with the gun, but then I heard someone outside. I had to leave. I even left the money behind. I found out later that it was you that I'd heard, Darcy."

He stopped his pacing abruptly and stood still with his head hanging down.

They weren't done, though. "Why Jeff?" Darcy asked. She needed to know all of it.

"He got too close," Steve explained, gesturing helplessly with his hands. "I had heard that Jeff had talked to Mark, asking for the town's financial records. Like Anna, I just meant to talk to him. I had brought the gun for protection, but once again it got out of hand." Steve started to pace again, frantically.

He stopped and turned to face them, yelling, "I didn't mean to!" He lunged and grabbed the bars of the cell and Jon pulled Darcy back. "I love Jess so much. I'd do anything for her."

"Even kill good people," Darcy pointed out. Grace looked at her oddly, and she realized that she'd included her ex-husband with Anna as "good people." "Why not just get a divorce Steve? That seems so much easier than killing people surely?"

"I couldn't do that. I have a position to uphold in this town. A divorce would have ruined me."

Darcy shook her head. "Why would a divorce have ruined you Steve? You would have still been Mayor."

"Because Jess is not the kind of woman that a respectable Mayor has by his side. Helen has so much more respect in this town and was the perfect wife for me, except in the bedroom." Steve screwed up his face in disgust and Darcy recoiled, saddened for her good friend whose only crime had been to stand by a man that didn't love her.

"Come on, Darcy," Jon said to her. "We've heard enough."

Darcy was about to walk away with Jon and Grace when she had a thought. Turning back to the pathetic former Mayor Darcy said, "I know this is a longshot but do you know anything about Linda's missing cat?"

Steve looked at her for a beat. "What?" Darcy could tell he was confused by the question.

"Didn't think so but it was worth asking just in case." With that she turned away from him for the last time and left him alone. She hoped he rotted jail for the rest of his life.

# CHAPTER 23

*I*t took several days for life to get back to normal. Misty Hollow was big news for a while as the media descended upon them to break the story of the town's murdering Mayor.

Darcy was at work in her bookstore one morning after the news people had finally left town when she looked up and saw Smudge dashing across the square. He looked to be heading in the same direction as she'd seen him going that other time a few weeks ago.

"Watch the store for me will you Sue? I have a quick errand to run." She didn't wait for Sue's answer and was out the door and following her cat in double quick time.

He was dashing down the sidewalk heading in the direction of the industrial district again and Darcy wondered what on earth he was up to? What was out this way that would be of interest to her cat? She really didn't know what he got up to when he wasn't with her.

She carefully followed him as he raced across the lawns and sidewalks making sure to keep up with him this time. She was still close behind as he got to the narrow street that led away from town toward the section comprised of large warehouses and storage facilities. She had been pacing herself better this time and didn't have the painful stitch that had ended her pursuit of him last time.

She followed him down the narrow street and emerged onto a wider road. There was barely any traffic about and it was easy to keep track of him as he raced down the sidewalk. He stopped in front of one of the larger buildings and he slipped in through a hole in the fence. Out of nowhere came a huge, black dog, barking madly with slobber flying from his mouth. Smudge didn't miss a beat as he bounded up the side of one of the buildings inside the fence perimeter. The dog skidded to a stop down below barking furiously. Smudge just looked down on him with a haughty expression.

His gaze then turned back in Darcy's direction like he'd known she was there watching him. For a moment he looked straight at her and she knew then that he had known she was following him all along. She could see he had something in his mouth but couldn't work out what it was. Then she watched as he slipped easily inside the building through a broken window.

What was he up to? Did he want her to follow him? It seemed like he might. She wasn't sure what to do about the dog who was still standing at attention waiting for Smudge to come back. The dog was a problem but she needed to get into the building so see what Smudge was up to.

As she was debating what to do a shiny black Cadillac Escalade with dark tinted windows pulled up across the road and the passenger door flung open. Darcy couldn't see who was driving but heard someone whistle and call out in a deep gruff voice.

"C'mon, you mutt!" Recognizing the voice, the dog instantly left his post, slipped through the hole in the fence and up into the vehicle. The door slammed and the huge SUV powered away.

Darcy breathed a sigh of relief. One problem taken care of.

Now she needed to find her cat. She ran across the road and checked the spot in the fence that Smudge had entered and the dog had exited through. She found that it was just big enough for her to squeeze through.

Now how was she going to get inside the building? She couldn't very well climb up and get in the way Smudge had. It was too high and there were no hand or foot holds that she could see. There must be another way in.

She was worried about her cat. Why would he be coming all the way out here? She couldn't think of one reason but he was a cat after all and who knew what they got up to when their owners weren't looking.

She worked her way around the entire outside of the building trying every door to see if one may have been left unlocked.

No luck.

Just as she was about to give up and find somewhere to wait for Smudge to emerge she found a little flap of sheet metal that was bent slightly backwards like someone else had used it as a way in at some time.

Darcy wasn't sure that she would be able to fit. It looked more like a space for a child than an adult. She didn't think that the dog would have even been able to fit through.

She inspected the opening to make sure that there were no sharp edges. She didn't want to take the chance that she might injure herself in the process of going through the opening.

It looked pretty safe. The edges were mostly smooth with only a couple of sharp points. She pushed the flap of sheet metal up as far as she could. She was sure to keep well away from the sharp points as she carefully squeezed her way through the opening but still managed to snag her sleeve on one of the rough edges. After a brief struggle, she was able to free herself without too much difficulty.

It was darker inside here. She took a couple of moments to let her eyesight adjust and thought that it might have been smart to let someone know where she had gone. But she didn't really have time and now there was no way to let anyone know.

She shrugged. Too late now to go back. This was one situation that it would have been handy to have a cell phone but there were valid reasons she didn't have one. She hoped that everything would be okay and she wouldn't have the need to call for help anyway.

She needed to see what her cat was up to. She carefully made her way further into the building. It was mostly empty thank goodness. There were some large cardboard boxes throwing dark shadows across the floor and some odds and ends of wood and metal strewn about. She was careful where she put her feet though just in case.

Now where was Smudge?

She listened carefully for any sound that might give her some idea of what direction to go. Apart from the wind blowing through the eaves it was silent. She moved quietly further into the building all the time listening for any sound.

Hearing a rustling noise behind her she stopped still and listened. For a few moments it was silent and then she heard it again. It was definitely coming from behind her and it sounded like a kind of rustling noise. She was no longer alone. Something or someone was definitely coming her way. Heart rate accelerating in her chest she took a deep breath and debated whether to go back the way she'd just come and check it out.

She was sure that Smudge was further in and her goal was to find him. But the rustling noise was disturbing. Of course, it could just be another cat, or a mouse or rat, but she couldn't be sure of that. Her instincts were screaming at her that it was the two legged variety of animal that was stalking her.

She hadn't seen anyone else about when she had been outside but that didn't mean there hadn't been someone hiding in the shadows, watching her.

She decided to wait the person out. She armed herself with a nice solid piece of wood about the size of a baseball bat and then found a little niche in among the stacked cardboard boxes and settled down to watch and wait. It didn't take long before a dark figure crept past her hiding place. She'd thought she was done with dark figures stalking her.

Slowly and quietly she worked her way out of her hiding spot and crept up behind the figure. She lifted the makeshift baseball bat up and back ready to strike a hard blow to his head when he, before she could blink, swiftly turned toward her and grab one of her arms holding the bat away from him so she couldn't club him over the head with it. He wrestled the bat out of her hands and bent one of her arms up behind her back. He was strong and tall and she didn't have a hope of getting away from him.

She panicked and started to struggle violently against him.

"Darcy, Darcy stop, it's me. It's Jon." It took a moment for his voice and words to penetrate her panic. "It's okay love, it's me. You're safe."

All of the fight went out of her for a moment and he loosened his grip on her arm. Panic was replaced with anger. Turning around quickly she pounded her fists against his chest. "For Pete's sake Jon, what are you doing? You just about gave me a heart attack, especially after all that's gone on over the last few weeks and with Steve trying to kill me. Did you not think that perhaps it would have been wise to let me know you were here?"

She moved away from him then breathing deeply, trying to calm down.

"I'm sorry Darcy. I guess I didn't think. I was on patrol in the area when I saw you heading into the building and was worried about you. I decided to follow you just in case you needed help."

Darcy sighed. It was kind of sweet of him to worry about her. She just wasn't used to someone being concerned about her. She looked at him and he seemed so earnest. It was impossible to remain mad at him.

She smiled and he visibly relaxed. "It's okay Jon. I'm not mad at you. When I heard someone coming I was just scared I guess. I appreciate you looking out for me. I'm not used to someone caring."

Jon pulled her into his arms and squeezed for a moment. Letting her go he said, "What are you doing here anyway?" He looked up and down and all around. "It's not really structurally sound."

"I followed Smudge in here. I don't know what he is up to coming into a place like this. I don't want him to get hurt." Just then a blur of black and white fur scampered up to them and wound himself around Darcy's ankles.

"Smudge!" She scooped her big tom cat up into her arms. "Where have you been? What have you been getting up to?"

Smudge struggled in her arms and pushed his way out, dropping to floor. He scurried away but stopped a little way away from them, looking back at them, his eyes wide and intense.

"If I didn't know any better I would think he wants us to follow him," Jon said slowly.

"It certainly looks that way doesn't it?" Darcy smiled. "Okay boy, what is it? Show us."

Smudge looked at them for a moment more and then took off further into the building. Jon and Darcy followed him as quickly as they could but they weren't as adept at getting over the debris littering the floor as the cat was and he had to wait for them a couple of times.

It wasn't long before Smudge stopped and Darcy and Jon caught up to him. He was sitting next to a hole in the floor about three feet by three feet. He let out a heart rending meow, followed by another. Darcy was instantly concerned. Her cat just didn't meow like that, ever.

"What on earth…" Darcy was about to pick him up when Jon held her back.

"Hang on a minute." He carefully lowered himself to the floor on his stomach and wriggled his way closer to the hole. "Oh wow…"

"What is it?"

"Come look for yourself, but be careful."

Darcy copied what Jon had done and as she looked over the edge of the hole she couldn't believe it. Down below in what must have been the basement of the building was a big ball of snowy white fur surrounded by four smaller balls of snowy white fur with little black faces and black tipped ears.

"Persephone!" Darcy was overjoyed to see Linda's cat alive and… mostly well. And she'd had kittens. How on earth had she gotten herself trapped down there. Darcy guessed it had something to do with that big dog from before. More importantly how had she been surviving all of this time? It was weeks since she'd gone missing. Darcy had a sneaking suspicion that Smudge had been feeding her so that she would survive. He was such a good cat. Linda would be ecstatic.

Jon stood up and began dialling on his cell phone. "We're going to need some help." he replied to Darcy's puzzled look.

About ten minutes later, a couple of men from the local fire brigade had arrived and rescued the poor cat and her kittens. Jon had called Linda as well, and she arrived shortly after the firemen did. As expected, Linda was thrilled to see her friend safe and sound, if a bit dirty.

Darcy watched it all unfold with a big smile on her face, and a black and white cat by her side.

"Well, Smudge." She knelt down to pat him. "It seems we've both had a couple of busy weeks."

Smudge meowed in agreement.

$\mathcal{A}$ few days later after the excitement of solving the missing cat mystery had died down Darcy was working in the book store while Sue was out on an errand. She was tidying up, rearranging some books and generally getting rid of the dust that had accumulated.

It felt good to have nothing more important than this to worry about. Everything was good now. Two mysteries had been solved and even the fog had cleared out over the past few days. Misty Hollow was just a sleepy little town again.

Smudge was lying in a patch of sunlight up on top of the nearest bookshelf. He had spent a considerable amount of time cleaning himself this morning and she wondered if he had plans for later. Maybe he had a girlfriend at one of those places he visits when he disappears. She laughed at her train of thought. Sometimes she fancied that Smudge was more human than cat.

She jumped when she heard the bell over the door ring. She looked up and smiled when she saw Jon walking toward her.

He came right up to her and with no hesitation pulled her into his arms. His kiss was warm and familiar. They'd had a lot of practice over the last few days. The faint image of her great-aunt materialized just to the left behind Jon. The old woman's spirit was smiling indulgently at Darcy. Then she nodded her head and dissipated in a puff of mist. Darcy took it to mean that Millie now approved of her relationship with Jon. She felt comforted by the knowledge.

"Well, hello yourself," she said when Jon let her go. "What are you doing here? Shouldn't you be at work?"

"I am. But I missed you."

She smiled at him. It felt good, being this happy. Smudge jumped up on the counter between them and purred. He was a bit of a hero around town now after finding Persephone and helping to bring her safely home to Linda. She had promised to keep him in cat treats for life as a reward for his bravery.

Jon laughed at him and scratched the cat's ears. "I guess we'll have to share Darcy," he said to Smudge. "How does that sound to you?"

Smudge meowed and pressed his head into Jon's hand.

Apparently, Darcy thought with a smile, Smudge was fine with that arrangement.

**-End-**

# CHAPTER 25

**Bonus - The Missing Cat Mystery
(Smudges Point of View)**

It's a common human misconception that cats spend all of their time sleeping.

Not true.

We may look like we're sleeping but what we're really doing is continuously scanning our territory for any abnormality.

Like now.

I may look like I'm sleeping at the end of Darcy's bed all snuggled up in the blankets. But what I'm really doing is monitoring my human's sleep pattern. She is thrashing about, making little noises and I can tell she is having a nightmare.

It's not a pleasant one and is probably more than a dream. Darcy is different than most humans. She is so much more sensitive to the atmosphere around us.

Darcy's thrashing is getting more violent so it's time for me to remove myself before I get kicked off. It's happened before and it's not pleasant believe me.

I'm never sure what's the best thing to do in this situation. Should I wake her up? Or is it better to let her sleep through it? If I wake her up now she may miss some piece of vital information that could mean life or death.

Better to let her sleep through it.

I wait patiently by the side of the bed. I don't have to wait too long. There's more violent thrashing as she wakes up with a long wrenching gasp. It scares me a bit I'm not afraid to admit. This was a bad one. Not your ordinary dream.

She squeaks as I jump up onto the bed again. I rub up against her so that she knows it's me and that she's not alone.

"Oh for Pete's sake Smudge, you scared me." Her voice is not quite steady so I rub up against her again purring my loudest purr. That usually is enough to calm her down.

I can feel her relax as she ruffles the scruff of my neck. I love how she does that. It feels so nice.

"Hello boy." She pulled me to her for a friendly hug.

I DON'T ENJOY days when Darcy hosts the book club in the Sweet Read Bookstore. The women are always too loud and the noise interferes with my sleeping pattern.

I look down at them now from my perch on top of the book shelf and can't believe the noise they are making over some silly romance book. Although I'm not averse to some romance in my life. I smile as an image of Twistypaws, a certain girl cat with sleek gray fur and white-tipped ears and eyes the color of clear blue water, comes to mind. She's not my girlfriend. Although, don't tell anyone, I wish she was.

I stretch out my body in the warm afternoon sunshine that is streaming through the front window of the bookstore and try to ignore the noise.

But it's impossible to get back to sleep. I decide now is a good time for a grooming session. I enjoy grooming and I take my time with it. There's nowhere else I need to be right now.

By the time I finish my grooming session the book club is breaking up and the ladies are leaving. I hear my stomach rumble and can't remember if I've eaten since breakfast time. Whatever, it's time to eat now. I shake my head to wake myself up. I sure have spent a lazy day in the sun today.

"It was a great meeting today Darcy. I really enjoy these book club sessions." From high up on my perch on the bookshelf I see Anna gently pat Darcy on the arm as she's preparing to leave. She is a good friend to Darcy, and to me. Often times I'll pop by her house and she'll have some little titbit that she's saved for me.

"I'm glad you enjoyed it, Anna." Darcy is walking Anna toward the door. That's my cue to make a move.

"The mists are starting to rise again. I'd better hurry home. Bye Darcy." I see Darcy open the door for Anna. I hear the door shut as I jump down onto the floor. Rounding the end of the bookshelf I see Darcy just standing, staring out the window. She looks sad. I just know that she is thinking about that dream again.

I hear her sigh and as she is about to turn away I rub up against her leg to let her know that I'm here for her. Just as she is for me. She jumps a little which shows me just how rattled she is feeling. She bends down to absentmindedly scratch between my ears before moving into the back of the store to shrug on her jacket and grab her bag.

Time to go home. I love this time of the day. Darcy flipped the sign and we were out the door. I scamper ahead of her, glad to be out in the fresh air. I'd spent too long that afternoon just sleeping in the sunshine. I needed to run.

"Psst... Hey Smudge!"

I recognize that voice. It's Tony. Tony the tiger. I see him in the alley next to the café. Not sure where he lives but he's usually here in the alley at this time of night. He's a cat with orange stripes and flashing green eyes, hence the tiger part of his name. Sometimes I stop and we shoot the breeze, but not tonight. I'm a cat on a mission.

"Hey Tony. Can't stop tonight. On my way home for dinner." He gives me a look that can only be described as envious. Perhaps he doesn't have an owner at all and has to scrounge for all of his meals. I make a mental note to ask him some time.

I hurry away but find that Darcy has got ahead of me so I speed up and as I catch up to her I hear a voice calling out "Darcy, Darcy wait up a minute." I heard Darcy sigh as her friend Linda ran up to her. "Oh Darcy, how are you? I haven't seen you in simply ages."

Now it was my turn to sigh. You may not have noticed but cats can actually sigh. This will delay my dinner I just know it. Linda can talk the arm of a statue when she gets started. I know. I've been witness to it more than once.

"I'm good Linda. Just heading home to get some dinner now actually." Yes, that's good Darcy. Dinner now!

"Oh good, good. Actually I wanted to ask you if you've seen my cat?"

My ears pricked up at that. Linda's cat was missing. This was news. Cats rarely went missing in Misty Hollow. Persephone was a fluffy, snowy white Persian with the greenest eyes and...

What?

So... I'd noticed her alright... so what!

Please don't tell Twistypaws. She would be mad that I'd even noticed even though we're not technically a couple... yet.

Persephone's a very pretty cat but the nervous type. One of those mostly indoor cats that usually never venture too far from home. I like the more outgoing type of cat. Just like Twistypaws.

"Your cat? No, I can't say that I have." Darcy was saying.

"Oh darn, I was hoping you would have seen her. Persephone has been missing for about a week now. I've looked everywhere but I can't find her. I'm getting so worried about her."

"That's too bad Linda. I'm sorry I can't help you. I will keep an eye out for her though, she can't be too far away surely."

The humans kept talking but I tuned them out.

Smudge to the rescue. I have a mystery to solve.

I WATCHED Darcy head for home and then I doubled back the way I had come. I hoped that Tony would still be in the alley. I sprinted all the way and skidded to a halt at the alley entry way. Sure enough Tony was still there chowing down on scraps thrown out from the café.

"Hey Tony."

"Hey Smudge. I thought you couldn't stop tonight?" Tony said with his mouth full. It looked like he was dining on turkey tonight.

"Had a change of plans." My stomach rumbled loudly letting me know once again that I hadn't eaten all day. The things I sacrifice for my friends. I didn't waste any more time on pleasantries. "Have you seen Persephone lately?"

Tony stopped mid chew and spoke around the mound of food in his mouth. "Oh, that cute little Persian. She's a real looker. No, can't say I've seen her but then that's not unusual. She doesn't get out much."

"Darn it."

"What's up Smudge?"

"She's missing. I felt sure that you would have seen her about or would have heard something."

"No sorry. I haven't. Missing you say. That's strange. It's odd for a cat to go missing in this town. Can't be a good sign."

"That's what I was thinking. Thanks Tony. Gotta go."

"See ya around Smudge."

What was my next move? My stomach rumbled so loudly I thought it might wake the dead. And that was no joke in a town like Misty Hollow. I needed food if I was going to be able to think clearly. So I headed toward home and dinner.

I squirmed my way into the house through my secret entrance. Even Darcy didn't know about this one. I could hear raised voices and alarm pierced through me. Half way up the basement steps I stopped to listen. Darcy was arguing with someone.

I recognized that voice. It was Jeff. My fur instantly stood on end. Not my favorite person. Okay, time to keep a low profile until he's gone.

I heard the front door slam and knew it was safe to come out of hiding. I heard Darcy moving about in the kitchen and my stomach rumbled again. I needed food now.

I startled her when I jumped up onto the counter to demand that she get my dinner first before she gets hers.

"Where have you been? You couldn't have warned me about Jeff? Hm?" I just looked at her with my big green kitty cat eyes, looking all cute, and she smiled at me. "It's okay, I don't blame you for keeping a low profile while he was around. I should have done that myself instead of agreeing to marry him."

I nodded my head in my kitty cat way at her words and twitched my tail as if in complete agreement with her.

I know Darcy thinks I am a smart cat.

DARCY'S HAVING that dream again. Enough is enough. I get up from my warm and cozy spot on the bed and watch as she thrashes about. I can't let this continue. I lean on my back legs and spring forward, landing on her chest. Next thing I know I'm thrown to one side. Disorientated, I don't know what happened exactly.

Darcy's sitting up and gasping. At least she's awake and out of the dream. I let out a pathetic little mewl to let her know that I don't appreciate being pushed aside when all I'm trying to do is help her.

She patted me gently and said, "I'm sorry, Smudge. Thank you for waking me up. I was having another very bad dream. You wouldn't believe it. I wonder who that man is that invading my dreams and trying to kill me. I hope it was just another stupid dream and not some premonition. What do you think?"

How should I know what's going on here? It's just weird that she keeps having these bad dreams. All I can do is shake my head.

"Well you're a big help." She laughed and rolled over getting comfortable. I carefully crawled in between her feet and settled down again. I sure hope she doesn't kick me. "Goodnight good boy, I'll see you in the morning."

THE NEXT MORNING, I was just too tired to go with Darcy to the bookstore so I stayed in bed. Keeping watch over my troubled owner sure was taking it out of me. I also had another reason for not wanting to go with her today. I had work to do.

A couple of hours after Darcy left I finally got up and went in search of my breakfast. I had Darcy trained really well and found my bowl full. After my meal I was ready to tackle my job.

What job is that, you might ask? The missing cat mystery, of course. Yes, I have taken it upon myself to find out what has happened to the beautiful Persephone.

Misty Hollow Cat Detective to the rescue again.

I slipped out of the house and into the bright sunshine of a beautiful day. I wish I had nothing more to do than lie about and bask in the warmth but alas a great cats work is never done.

The first place to start was at the beginning. I needed to take a trip out to Persephone's home that she shared with Linda. I knew that Linda lived in an older area of the town out near the industrial area.

It didn't take me long to travel the distance as I cut right across town, over roads and fences and through yards. Soon I was sitting in front of a small cottage with yellow painted wood siding. I climbed up the front stone steps and entered the porch through an archway. I sat for a moment to catch my breath. This would be a nice spot to curl up for nap. It was then that I noticed the unoccupied cat bed. It was brown and made of some soft, plush material.

I sniffed all around it but there was nothing out of the ordinary. Nothing there that shouldn't have been. I was tempted to test it out but I reminded myself that there was a cat missing that needed my help.

The surrounding neighbourhood was quiet at this time of day. I wasn't sure what my next move should be when I spotted a sleek, jet black cat watching me from across the road.

I sauntered across in my usual unfazed manner. Didn't want him to think I was some sort of pushover. We came face to face and there was some subtle sniffing going on.

I detected tuna and my stomach rumbled. How could I be hungry already. My appetite never ceased to amaze me.

He had huge green eyes that seemed to penetrate my cool outer shell. Neither of us said a word, just stood and sized the other up.

"You don't belong here... who are you?" He finally broke the silence.

"I'm Smudge," I said, trying to sound as friendly as possible. It's likely that this aloof cat might know something about the missing Persephone. "Who are you?"

He shook his head and his jet black fur swung around his

head like a huge spiky collar. "I know that name. You are the one who is revered."

This cat talked weird. But I liked what he was saying. "Don't know where you heard that from, I'm just a regular cat."

"No! You are special, I have heard. I am honored to meet you Smudge. I am Onyx. Why are you here?"

"Hey Onyx. I'm looking for Persephone. I heard she's missing and I want to help find her. She's a friend of mine."

I jumped back, fur on end, when the cat called Onyx let out the loudest, most mournful mrowl I had ever heard in my entire life. He sounded like he was dying.

"Hey buddy, are you okay?"

"Oh Smudge. Poor Persephone. I have serious misgivings about her being still alive." Sounded like old Onyx here knew something about this.

"Why do you say that? Do you know something about her disappearance?"

"Mariel told me that she didn't think that Persephone would be back." He spoke in a flat tone and hung his head in despair.

"Sorry... Mariel?"

"Mariel is the ginger tabby that lives next door to Persephone. She has been very upset, telling the whole neighborhood she thinks Persephone is dead."

"How would she know a thing like that?"

"I... don't know. She seemed convinced so I never thought to question it."

"Okay. So where will I find this Mariel?" Onyx just flicked his head in the direction across the road. I turned to look that way and my eyes locked on to a petite ginger tabby sitting on the porch steps of the house next door to Persephone's. She was quite pretty in her own way. Her tail was gently flicking from side to side as her clever green eyes sized me up. "I take it that is Mariel?"

Onyx nodded his head once. "Thanks buddy. You hang in there okay. I'm going to find Persephone and bring her home."

With a flick of my tail I ran down the path and sprinted across the road. I skidded to a stop in front of Mariel and she didn't even flinch. A tough cookie hey, we'll see about that.

"Hi, you Mariel?" The ginger cat just looked at me with narrowed eyes, still sizing me up. "I'm Smudge..."

"I know who you are." Her voice held a hint of disdain and her eyes narrowed even more.

The silence stretched tautly between us. I didn't have time for this. "Onyx tells me that you know something about Persephone's disappearance."

I waited for her to answer. She took her time, still staring at me.

"What's it to you," she said finally.

"I'm going to find her and bring her home."

"Really?" She laughed. "You?" She laughed harder. "You think you're Columbo or something?" Now she was laughing uncontrollably, rolling around on her back with her legs kicking in the air.

I sighed. She thought I was a joke. I really didn't have time for this. I waited her out and when she settled down enough I said, "Can we please continue?"

She looked at me for a moment and must have seen something in my eyes. "You're serious, aren't you?" I nodded. She tilted her head to one side. I could see the change come over her when she decided to help me. "Okay then, ask your questions."

"Thank you." I was relieved to be getting somewhere at last. I asked her what she knew about Persephone's disappearance and why she thought Persephone wasn't coming home.

"Ernesto told me he thinks she's dead and I believe him. Persephone hasn't been home for such a long time now. I don't think she's coming back." She sniffed and I was surprised by the show of emotion considering the tough act she'd put on for me earlier.

"Ernesto?" I wasn't getting very far. All I had so far was hearsay.

"Ernesto is Persephone's boyfriend. He's her other neighbor." She gestured with her nose at a huge light brown cat sitting on the porch steps of the house on the other side of Persephone's house. He had a little bit of black fur around his eyes and nose and a tiny bit on the tips of his ears. And his startling yellow-green eyes were fixed on me.

"You'll find her won't you? She's my best friend and I miss her." I assured her I would do my best.

I bid farewell to Mariel and sprinted over the cool green lawn. I skidded to a stop just a little way from Ernesto. I didn't want to take the chance of upsetting him. This close he was even bigger. I thought I was big but he dwarfed me.

We sized each other up for a few moments. "Hey, I'm Smudge..."

"I'a know who you are. You'a big shot'a detective cat." He had a thick Italian accent and it threw me for a moment. Not that he was particularly hard to understand, it was just so unexpected. But with a name like Ernesto maybe I should have guessed.

"Whadyua want?"

"I'm looking for Persephone."

"You and'a me both. She's'a been missing for a long'a time."

"Well, I'm going to find her."

"That'a fact. You'a think you'a that good?"

"Yes." I straightened my back. I was good and I would find her. "So what do you know about her disappearance?"

"I see'a that'a brute Kujo chase her all'a the way outa the neighborhood. Haven't seen her since."

"Kujo?"

"Big'a mutt dog. Lives on the end'a the street." He lowered his head. "I bet he'a eat her. Huge'a jaws. Big'a teeth. Scary."

Oh no that didn't sound too good. "I'm going to need to talk to this Kujo…"

Ernesto's head popped up, his eyes wide. "No'a you can't. He's'a bad dog. Not'a nice. You'a need to stay away from him or you will end up'a like my Bella Persephone."

"It's okay buddy, I'll be careful. I really need to talk to him to find out what happened to Persephone."

Ernesto just shook his head. "You be'a careful."

"I will. Now which house was it?"

ERNESTO WAS RIGHT. Kujo was a big brute of a dog. I watched from my hidden vantage point as he harassed a young pup that was wandering the neighborhood. He was mean and foul and I knew that I'd used good sense to approach him with caution.

I watched as he came back to his base and plopped down into his overstuffed bed. He looked pretty pleased with himself. He was just a big bully. How was I going to find out what I needed to know from him? I did have a plan but I wasn't sure how safe I would be. No time like the present to find out I guess.

"Kujo! Oh Kujo!" I yelled at the top of my lungs. The huge black beast's head shot up. He sniffed the air. He sniffed the air more furiously and shot up out of his bed. Still sniffing madly, he ran one way and then another.

I knew the exact moment he locked on to me. His huge head turned in my direction and those big, dark eyes of his looked straight at me. He hurled himself in my direction making the most awful racket. Slobber flew from his mouth as he launched himself at me only to be thrown backwards by the wire mesh fence that was between us.

I thought he would be smart enough to realize that he couldn't get me through the fence but I underestimated his stupidity. He kept ramming the fence desperately trying to get to me. I waited for him to calm down but the fence was only serving to enrage him all the more. He bashed against it repeatedly with his head and I watched as the fence began to pull away at the top.

This was not good. He would be through in a matter of minutes. I needed another plan... and fast. I looked all around and about fifteen feet away was a large, sturdy tree. In the time it had taken me to look for somewhere safe to escape to Kujo had gotten his head through the fence. His huge teeth were just inches away from my face. Time to get out of here.

I sprinted as fast as my legs would go toward the tree. I heard him breach the last part of the fence and he was on my tail, literally. I could feel his hot breath scorching my rear end as I reached the bottom of the tree. Not pausing I leaped as high as I could and dug my claws securely into the trunk so as not to slip and give him the advantage. I scampered up the tree to the first branch that was out of his reach.

I took a few moments to get my breath back and get my heart rate under control. Then I looked down. The beast was jumping up the trunk in a mad frenzy trying desperately to get me. No way Kujo. That's not going to happen. Even if I have to sit here for the rest of the day.

SO I SAT THERE for the rest of the day and most of the evening. Kujo had kept watch at the bottom of the tree all of that time. The mad dog is singled minded it seems. By the time his owner showed up, the sun had already set. Boy was he mad when he saw the fence. That dog was in big trouble.

There was a lot of activity and noise as the owner of the tree I was in came home at the same time. Lots of raised voices. Glad I wasn't that dog. He sure wouldn't forget me in a hurry.

I hid among the dense leaves and waited. The commotion eventually died down and everyone went back in to their respective houses. Then it was safe for me to leave. I raced home as fast as my legs would take me. I was exhausted and felt like I could sleep for a week. The search for Persephone would have to wait until tomorrow.

I DIDN'T MAKE any headway on the case the next day either. It was the day of the Misty Hollow festival and there was just too much activity going on for me to be able to concentrate.

I did a bit of digging in the morning but came up empty so I decided to spend the rest of the day up on the bookstore roof where I could watch all of the comings and goings. In the end I fell asleep in the sunshine and missed most of it. I needed the rest as I was still recovering from my time up the tree yesterday.

It was the loud squawking that eventually woke me up. I opened my bleary eyes I realized two things. Firstly, it was already night time and secondly there was a long black beak and two beady black eyes in my line of vision.

"Corvin! What are you doing?" I was annoyed that the aggravating crow had woken me up from a fantastic dream. Twistypaws and I had been running free through fields of brightly colored flowers. I felt alive and Twist was giving me that look that she sometimes does. You know, the one where she's making gooey eyes at me and I feel like jelly all over.

"Sorry, sorry. Need to talk to Smudge now. Gotta show Smudge now."

Corvin was a very excitable fellow. I'd known him a long time and he had never been any different. Nervous energy radiated off him.

"What are you talking about." Just then there was a loud boom and the sky lit up with all of the colors of the rainbow. The boom made Corvin jump but I knew what it was and it didn't bother me.

Fireworks.

I sure had slept a long time. Corvin waited impatiently, hopping from one foot to the other. It was getting on my nerves but as soon as the fireworks finished he said, "Bad is coming, bad is coming."

I had no idea what he was talking about. He was making no sense. "Smudge has to help. Bad is coming."

"Corvin, what on earth are you talking about?"

"Smudge has to stop it. Bad is coming."

"Calm down and tell me what it is going on."

"Bad is coming."

"Yeah, I got that part. What do I have to stop."

"Show Smudge. Have to stop it."

"Okay, show me then." He waited for me to wind my way down to the street level. Flapping madly about making me lose my footing more than once. As soon as I reached the bottom he flew off. I followed him as quickly as I could but he was flying too fast. It was really foggy and I lost sight of him several times. He had to double back a few times to wait for me to catch up.

He was taking me in the direction of home but at the last minute a flew across the open space between my house and Anna's house. I followed him and when we were close to Anna's house he flew down next to me.

"Need to be quiet. Don't want him to see us."

Who? What was going on here? Corvin flew up onto the front porch and landed on the window sill. I climbed up and sat next to him wondering what I was supposed to be seeing.

"Look Smudge." He tapped his beak lightly against the window. It made a tiny tap tap sound. I looked through the window and could see Anna bustling around inside. She was getting cups out of the cupboard and placing them on the table. Two cups.

So Anna had a visitor. Not so strange. But she did seem to be agitated. That was not so strange either. For as long as I'd known Anna she had always seemed a bit of a nervous type.

I could hear her voice raise and watched as a man came into view. I couldn't see his face, he had his back to me. But his voice sounded angry. Anna and this man were arguing. This was unexpected.

I couldn't hear what they were saying but the conversation was heated. The man seemed to be pleading with her about something. This isn't good, I have a feeling something bad is going to happen.

The arguing went on for a long time. The man was becoming more and more agitated when Anna kept shaking her head and saying "No" to whatever it was that he wanted. Suddenly he grabbed her and was holding her by the arms and shaking her.

Then he pushed her away and something flashed in Anna's hand. I could see she was holding a gun on the man.

Definitely not good.

He stepped back a couple of paces and anger flared up in him again. He was yelling but I still couldn't make out the words.

I knew something bad was going to happen just like Corvin had said. How had he known? Didn't matter.

What could I do to stop this?

I jumped as the man rushed Anna and grabbed her hand with the gun. They struggled and as he pulled the gun away from her hand it slipped. As he lunged to grab it he must have pulled the trigger. Anna fell to the floor.

I didn't wait to see any more. I needed Darcy.

Now!

I raced home but the house was still in darkness. Darcy wasn't home yet. I was about to go and get her when I heard the crunching of gravel in the distance. I knew it was Darcy walking along the road toward home. Waiting impatiently for her, she came into view. She smiled when she saw me on the porch waiting for her. This was not going to be easy for her.

She put out a hand to pat me and I let out the loudest meow I had. She was instantly on alert. I bolted off the porch and headed for Anna's house. I could hear Darcy following behind and she mumbled something about Lassie, whoever that was. Sometimes humans don't make much sense.

She was slow to enter Anna's house when we got there. It was like she already knew what was waiting for her on the other side of the door. I watched as she ran to Anna and did that thing that humans do on the side of the neck.

But I knew that it was already too late.

I HAD BEEN HOPING that Darcy would be able to help me find Persephone. Now that Anna had been murdered I knew that Darcy would be involved with finding out who did that. I had my suspicions. I had seen it happen and the man involved looked very much like our own Mayor of Misty Hollow. I was finding it very hard to believe though. He didn't seem like the murdering type. But who knew.

So I guess it was up to me to find the missing cat. I needed to talk to Kujo but as I found out the other day he is very unstable. And dogs aren't really my favorite kind of animal to hang with anyway.

Give me another cat, or guinea pig or even a crow, any day.

After another disastrous aborted attempt to talk to him I gave up. I decided to inconspicuously follow him around instead. See what he got up to and if he would lead me to Persephone. I was sure he knew where she was.

In the end it was another wasted day. Kujo led a pretty boring life. He didn't do anything that led me to find Persephone. I pondered what to do about the missing cat mystery all evening as I relaxed on the sofa with Darcy that night.

She was busy going through a bunch of old photos, getting

misty eyed over them. Especially the ones of me, but who could blame her. I was cute. Still am.

And there was that one of Anna that made her act a bit weird.

I think she is as perplexed about her mystery as I am about mine. She ended up calling Grace while she scratched behind my ears. I just love it when she does that and hoped she would talk on the phone all night if it meant she would keep doing it.

The next day I continued to follow Kujo around. I was convinced he had something to do with Persephone's disappearance. All morning I followed him and watched him bully and taunt one frightened animal after another. It was like a sport with him. Didn't he have a conscience at all?

Around lunchtime I was just about to admit defeat and give up when Kujo began acting kind of furtive. I kept watching as he sauntered down the sidewalk looking one way and then the other. Then he took off… bounding out of the neighborhood. I had to be quick to catch up with him. For such a large dog he could really move.

I followed him through a couple of small back streets and alleyways. Soon we were into the industrial district. Where was he going? There was nothing but warehouses and storage sheds out this way.

I watched as he stealthily slipped through a slit in a fence that surrounded one of the buildings. He stopped and looked all around, checking to see if he had been followed. The big mutt didn't see me though, when a cat doesn't want to be found he can be very hard to spot.

Satisfied that he was alone, he quickly ran around the side of the building. I wasted no time in following him. I caught up just as he was wriggling his way through a small opening. If it was any smaller he would get stuck.

I followed him very quietly, almost on my tippy toes. I had to be really careful. One whiff of my scent and he'd be on me like white on rice. I was in a very dangerous situation right now and needed all of my wits about me.

I listened to his movements and then I heard him talking. Who was he talking to? I crept closer until I was able to work out what he was saying.

"So howya doin' today?" He laughed with a really nasty tone to it.

I heard another voice answer. I couldn't work out what it was saying as it seemed to be coming from a long way away. Definitely a female though. Could it be Persephone? Did Kujo have her locked away in here somewhere? But why?

I needed to get closer but then I risked him being able to smell my scent. I couldn't have him knowing I was here. I decided to take a chance anyway and crept closer to him.

"You gonna die down there you know? You and those little runts of yours."

"Why are you doing this? Please tell someone we're down here. Do you want to have the deaths of myself and my children on your conscience forever?"

I was convinced now that is was Persephone. It looked like she was down a hole in the floor. How far down was she I wondered?

"I don't give a damn about you or your runts. I'm having a good time watching you die. And you are gonna die lady, make no mistake about that. You's is slowly starving to death right now. This's gonna be such fun to watch."

"You're sick."

Kujo laughed. "I'll be back later." He flicked his head and turned around casually walking away. I moved as fast as I could to find a hiding spot. I wriggled my way into a pile of boxes and then froze.

He shuffled past my hiding spot and suddenly stopped. Lifting his head and turning it one way and then the other he sniffed. I held my breath. He was close, too close. I was sure he would sniff me out. Time seemed to slow down and drag as he stood there sniffing the air. I had nowhere to go if he found me. It would be curtains for me.

After what seemed like an eternity he dropped his head and sauntered off. That had been really close. I don't like getting into these sorts of situations. I'm a peace loving cat and I don't like to fight if I don't have to. After a couple of minutes, I was fairly confident he was gone. With some difficulty, I wriggled out of my hiding place.

I crept over to the hole, looking all around just to be sure Kujo wouldn't spring out. I peeked over the edge and my suspicions were confirmed. Down about twenty feet I could see in the dim light of this old warehouse, lay Persephone.

And snuggled up next to her were four little balls of fur. She'd had kittens and they were the cutest little things. I melted. I am a sucker for a fluffy baby. I could see that they were pure white and fluffy like their mother except for the little bit of black on their faces and on the tips of their ears. That would be their father's genes. Ernesto. He would be so happy.

"Persephone," I said quietly. I didn't want to startle her.

She looked up. "Smudge! Oh, thank goodness."

I smiled at her. "Are you okay?"

"I'm fine, although I'm starving and so are the little ones. My milk is running out as I haven't eaten in... I don't know how long."

"Okay. First order of business. I will get you some food and then we'll work out how to get you out of there."

"Oh, thank you Smudge. You're a life saver."

Indeed.

I ROUNDED up all the cats in town that I knew along with all of the new friends I'd made during this investigation.

Tony the Tiger and Twistypaws, my cat friends Rolo, Samson, Enzo, Paolo and Omar, and Onyx, Mariel, Ernesto and I gathered together all of the food we could find and headed for the warehouse building where Persephone was stuck.

She seemed relieved to see so many of us but the one she was most excited to see was Ernesto and he was relieved to see her also.

We made a plan that at least one of us would be with her at all times until we could find a way to get her out.

"I'm going to get Darcy," I told them. "She will know what to do." I left the others to work out the roster for staying with Persephone while I headed to the bookstore to get Darcy. I only hoped that she would understand what I needed her to do.

I raced into the town center as fast as my legs would carry me and entered the bookstore through the roof. Darcy would be mad if she knew that there was a small hole in the corner of the ceiling that I use for emergencies to get in and out of the store. Right now I was glad for it.

I jumped down onto the nearest book shelf and then onto the floor. I could hear Darcy and Sue talking up front so I made my way up there. Darcy was sitting at one of the reading tables. Good, it looked as though she wasn't busy. I really needed her help.

"No, I don't," Darcy was saying to Sue. I'm not sure what they were talking about. I jumped up onto the table and meowed as loud as I could in Darcy's face. I needed to get her to realize the urgency of what I was trying to tell her. She shook her head at me and said, "What? I do not think he's cute."

What on earth was she talking about? Who was cute? I'll bet they're talking about that Jon person. It hadn't escaped my notice the way he looked at Darcy. He'd better keep his distance though. I didn't want him hanging around making a nuisance of himself.

I needed her to come with me. Sue chuckled nervously. She was kind of weird sometimes. She really didn't get that Darcy and I have such a close relationship. Just because I'm a cat and she's a person doesn't mean we don't communicate.

Darcy patted me and then got up. Good, she got the message and is coming with me. She laughed at Sue and then walked away.

Wait! I need your help. I jumped off the table and ran after her but she just ignored me and went back to work. The rest of the afternoon was spent trying to get her attention in vain. She could be so oblivious sometimes. If only humans could speak cat, life would be so much simpler.

In the end I gave up. I knew it was a lost cause. It seemed that whatever was on her mind was more important. With a sigh, I found a comfortable spot to lay down and rest. Being a cat is exhausting work you know. I vowed to get her attention as soon as possible though. This was something that couldn't wait.

THE SUN WAS SETTING on Misty Hollow once again, and I had failed to get Darcy's attention all day. Whatever she had on her mind must be very important.

I thought that maybe after dinner when she was relaxing on the sofa would be a good time to try again. But that didn't go according to plan. She left the house and I had to scramble to catch up with her.

Where was she going? I followed her to Grace's house. What was she up to? I waited for an eternity for her to come out again and when she did she headed in the direction of the bookstore.

I sprinted along a short cut I knew to get ahead of her. By the time she entered the town center I was sitting on the sidewalk waiting for her acting all mysterious-like with my head up sniffing the air.

She finally took notice. Before she could get distracted yet again, I dashed off in the direction of the warehouse where

Persephone was trapped. I knew she wouldn't be able to resist following me. As I thought, she chased after me.

I took the longer way as I knew she wouldn't be able to cut through a lot of the places that I can. It only took a few minutes to reach the slit in the fence at the old warehouse. I turned to see if Darcy was there and saw nothing, just an empty street. I must have gone too fast for her. I should have known better; humans aren't very fast without their wheeled metal box things that they call cars.

About to double back and find her I heard something that made my blood freeze. I turned my head slowly to look behind me and there was Kujo just about breathing down my neck.

He stood still like a huge black statue, his midnight black eyes locked onto me. My life flashed before my eyes. I was sure I was done for. He was too close and there was nowhere for me to run.

He started rocking backwards and forwards and an almighty racket issued from his mouth as he started barking furiously at me. I closed my eyes for a moment trying to center myself, hoping that Darcy would work out where I was and come rescue me.

The barking got louder and I could tell he was just toying with me. He knew he had me and I was a goner. Just as I sensed he was about to issue the death pounce headlights swung into the street and blinded me. The vehicle was in a hurry as it surged along the street but as it got near it slowed and pulled up with a screech of tires.

None of this registered with the dog. He was still barking furiously and I wondered why he hadn't made the kill yet. I was afraid to look away from the dog as the door of the vehicle opened and I heard footsteps.

"Kujo!" The dog shut up almost instantly and cowered. "What have I told you about chasing cats?" The dog shrunk even further and I took this as a good time to scamper. Last I saw the dog was getting into the huge black machine that the man had gotten out of.

I took a quick detour into the building to check on Persephone and found Ernesto there with her. She seemed okay and I spent some time with them both getting to know them better. Then it was time for me to regroup and go find Darcy.

Before heading home, I decided to check the book store first. Darcy was heading there when I distracted her, so I figured she would have probably gone back there. When I arrived, I found her closing up and leaving the store. I guessed she must be on her way home then and followed her. But I was wrong. Instead of going straight home she turned down into an alley just up from the police station.

What was she up to now? And why wasn't she worried about me? Hadn't she heard that awful racket Kujo had been making? Wasn't she worried he had eaten me?

She was skulking around behind the police station now fiddling with the door. What was she up to? I'd better go find out.

Just as she opened the door I slipped through unseen. She pulled out a small flashlight from her pocket and turned it on. I figured this was a good time to let her know I was with her so I jumped at her and then darted across the room.

"Smudge!" Uh oh, she sounded annoyed.

I REALIZED that I wasn't going to be able to get Darcy to do what I wanted until she'd solved Anna's murder. She was just too preoccupied to see any of my signs.

So I figured that meant I needed to help her. I already knew who the culprit was I just needed to fast track Darcy's investigation in that direction.

This meant that I would need to keep close tabs on what she

was doing and lead her in the appropriate direction until she got to the conclusion.

A cat's work is never done.

So that is why I am now sitting here watching Darcy who is spying on Pete Underwood through his living room window. It's kind of embarrassing actually and I hope no one I know sees us.

We've been here for hours and nothing has happened. I'm so bored. I can't take it. I have to move. It's not natural for a cat to be still for so long.

Okay, I know what you're thinking. Cat's sleep a lot and they don't move then but I've already told you that is a common human misconception. Really.

I sneak away while Darcy is still glued to the window. Not sure what is so fascinating about watching a man type. This would be a good time for me to go and check on Persephone.

I spend the rest of the day just hanging out with the gang and Persephone, keeping her company and her spirits high. I head back to Pete's house in the late afternoon and find Darcy has already left.

I catch her scent on the breeze and know that she's not too far ahead of me. I sprint in the direction of home and catch up with her quickly brushing up against her to let her know I'm there.

"Now where on earth did you get to Smudge?"

I answer with a cheery "meow" as we head home.

The next day I was kept busy with co-ordinating the roster for who stays with Persephone and when. I also needed to see how her stash of food was holding up and had Tony and Enzo go out and find food to replenish her stocks.

I was pretty exhausted by the time I got home that night and was looking forward to just chilling out with Darcy.

Of course, things don't always go according to plan.

Darcy was very agitated and was pacing the length of her kitchen. She finally decided that she needed to go to Anna's house and do a communication. I was worried about her. Whenever she does these communications she loses a little piece of herself.

But she feels that it's the only option left for her to do and I don't stop her. I go with her for support and I watch while she is in that other world state just to protect her and make sure she is safe.

Sometimes it takes a long time for her to come out of it but this time it didn't take that long at all. It seemed like it may have been a success because she was mumbling something about them getting the time wrong. I hoped this was the piece of the puzzle she needed to solve it.

We headed back to our house and she collapsed into the rocking chair on the porch. I jumped up into her lap and purred to try and sooth her. But that didn't last long because that annoying Jon person turned up.

I don't like the man and I didn't hang around. I did listen to their conversation though from the safety of the house. It seemed that Jon was trying to incriminate Jeff in the murder. I knew that was wrong but I also knew that Darcy would not be able to help herself. She would investigate Jeff.

So that's why the next day when I saw Jeff at the café I had an opportunity to help. I watched as his keys fell from his pocket when he pulled out that money thing that men carry around with them. I sprinted over and scooped them up into my mouth.

I wasted no time in getting them to Darcy.

"What's this, Smudge?"

I ran outside again. Making sure Darcy was watching me I ran right up to Jeff who was outside of the bakery and rubbed myself against his legs and then took off down the street secure in the knowledge that Darcy would know what to do with it. The sooner she proved Jeff's innocence, the sooner she would move onto the real murderer, and the sooner she would finally help me.

I spent the day doing my shift keeping Persephone company

only to come home and find Darcy and Jeff working together. Well that was quick. I'm not sure how much I like them working together though. But, I guess Darcy will solve it faster with help. Even if that help was Jeff.

That night Darcy had another of those dreams. Things were getting pretty tense around home. I did my best to try and keep things calm for her. But then things got even worse.

Jeff was also murdered.

AFTER JEFF WAS KILLED Darcy started spending a lot of time with that Jon person. I don't know what happened to change their relationship but I still don't like him. I even saw them kissing in the bookstore after Darcy had tried to do a communication. It feels like she doesn't need me anymore.

But at least he was helping her solve these two murders instead of accusing her of being involved, so I guess that's a good thing. This was becoming very complicated and I didn't feel at all well enough equipped to help her on my own.

I knew who the murderer was of course but not being able to talk sure limited me in what I could do to help. I could only keep an eye on Darcy and try to steer her in the right direction whenever I could.

I still had my own problems to deal with. Persephone couldn't stay down the hole forever. We'd each been taking it in turns to sit with her and I'd done a couple of shifts.

We needed a solution and it didn't look like I was going to be able to get Darcy to help so we needed another plan. I just wasn't sure what it was. We had a meeting at Persephone's hole to try and work out what to do.

"We'a need to do something," Ernesto said. I could see that the strain of not being able to rescue Persephone was getting to him.

"Yes we do. So do you have any ideas?"

"I've been'a wrackin' my brain for something, anything... but nothing is a'comin' to me."

I looked at the others sitting in a circle around the hole in the floor. We were all here. With me was Twistypaws, Tony the Tiger, Rolo, Samson, Enzo, Paolo and Omar, Onyx, Mariel and of course Ernesto. They all had the same sort of perplexed expression that I was sure I had.

I knew we couldn't keep sitting around doing nothing but I had no ideas. We decided to break for the day. It was Tony's turn to sit with Persephone. I got home and found the house empty. I vaguely remembered Linda coming into the shop sometime today and she was talking about some memorial or something. I guessed that Darcy was at that.

I checked my bowl but it was still empty. Darcy had gotten a little absentminded about it over the last few days. Stomach rumbling, I settled down next to the bowl to rest for a while and waited for her to come home. I wanted to be sure to get the message across that I needed food.

How on earth was I supposed to think on an empty stomach?

I didn't have to wait that long before I heard the key turn in the lock and Darcy was entering the house. She looked worn out, poor thing. She looked at me sitting beside my bowl and said, "Oh Smudge I'm so sorry." She quickly filled the bowl for me and I was tucking in before she'd even finished.

Stomach full and feeling much better I followed her up to her bedroom and curled up next to her for a good night's sleep.

Only I couldn't get to sleep now. I felt agitated like something was going to happen.

What was that?

I pricked my ears up when I heard a faint noise downstairs. It sounded like there was someone in the house. I lay very still as I could hear someone creeping up the stairs.

There was definitely someone in the house.

The bedroom door slowly creaked open and I tensed, ready to

pounce. Someone was here to harm Darcy and I wasn't about to let that happen. The figure crept closer to the bed and I lunged upwards toward him yowling as loud as I possibly could.

Darcy woke up with a gasp and seeing the intruder beside her bed grabbed the first thing she could, a book, and hurled it at him. He ran away like a mangy dog with his tail between his legs. That was easy.

Yeah, too easy. What was up with that.

Shaking, Darcy grabbed her phone and dialled. I assumed she was calling the police. I rubbed up against her to let her know I was there and she smoothed a hand along my back.

As she talked to whoever it was on the phone I jumped off the bed and headed downstairs. I found the kitchen window open. Looked like the intruder was gone.

Darcy came downstairs and sat on the couch with her legs drawn up to her chest and her arms were hugging her knees. I could see she was shaking like a leaf so I jumped next to her to lend her some of my warmth.

A little bit later there was a knock at the door and Darcy jumped. She went over to open the door and that Jon person entered. I watched as he grabbed her and dragged her into his arms. My fur bristled. She was my human. He needed to go away. But I knew that with him by her side Darcy had a better chance of working this out so I kept my opinion to myself. I just headed back upstairs to try and get some more sleep.

AFTER THE EXCITEMENT of the night before I decided I'd better keep tabs on Darcy. But I wasn't the only one. Mister super detective man slept on the couch overnight. I could tell that he was going to be trouble. He got this look in his eye when he was turned in Darcy's direction and I knew what that meant.

It had been me and Darcy for years now and we didn't need

177

anyone else. He had better not be getting any ideas about moving in on my territory.

I'd found out that they'd wrongly arrested Aaron while I was off dealing with the Persephone in the hole issue. How had they gotten so far off track?

Poor Aaron had nothing to do with any of this. How was I going to get Darcy on the right track? Steve Nelson needed to be stopped before he ended up killing my human.

I watched Jon and Darcy chasing their tails. And then they arrested Helen. Of all people. How could Darcy think that Helen was a killer? I just kept shaking my head. Of course, the book "And Then There Were None" that Helen was reading was a vital piece of evidence. It had been Anna's book. So I suppose they could be forgiven for getting it wrong. But still... Helen. Really.

I watched Darcy now as she sat at the kitchen table fidgeting. She was trying to read a book but I could tell she wasn't being very successful. The rhythmic tapping of her foot against the leg of the table was lulling me into a kind of trance.

When I suggested a walk by scratching on the door she was all for it. I needed fresh air to wake up. I wasn't sure where we were headed when we left the house but I soon worked out we were walking in the direction of Helen's house. Darcy must have worked out that her agitation had something to do with having the wrong suspect.

Great!

But Helen's house was also Steve's house and Steve was the murderer. I sure hoped he wasn't home. As luck would have it the house was all in darkness indicating that there was nobody home. Darcy tried the door but it was locked.

I watched Darcy climb through one of the back windows. I was going to follow her in but my intuition told me to stay outside and watch the front. I'm glad I did because not long after Darcy had entered, a luxury sedan pulled into the driveway and

Steve Nelson got out. I watched in horror as he went to the front door and opened it, slipping inside.

With Darcy.

I didn't think, I just raced for the center of town and the police station. I hoped that Jon would be there and then realized that he was probably still interrogating Helen. I don't think I've ever run so fast in my life, even when Kujo was chasing me the other day. I had images in my head of what was happening to Darcy that spurred me on even quicker.

I was out of breath by the time I got to the police station. Just as I skidded up to the door it opened and a young officer exited. I didn't stop I just kept going right through the open door.

"Hey!" The young officer yelled but I kept going. I sprinted over to the counter and leapt up and over. Running deeper into the police station I found Jon in an office, hunched over some papers on his desk. Without breaking stride, I leapt from the floor and skidded across his desk sending the papers flying in all directions.

"What the... Smudge! What do you think you're doing?"

I didn't have time for useless questions and I nudged him hard. "Hey... stop that." I kept doing it until he jumped out of his chair. I leapt from the desk and ran to the door, skidded to a halt and looked back at him. I sent him my most intense stare and then I let out the loudest and most mournful yowl I could summon up.

He frowned at me and I could see the exact moment it registered that something was wrong. He followed me without any more hesitation.

When we got to the Mayor's house Jon wasted no time in smashing in the door. It looked like we only made it just in time. Darcy was on the floor and the mayor was standing over her with a gun. I figure he was seconds away from pulling that trigger and killing my Darcy.

I raced over to her and skidded to a stop. I arched my back

and bared my teeth hissing at Steve to get away from her. Just then Jon tackled him and I knew she was safe.

~

IT TOOK several more days for all of the excitement to die down. Misty Hollow had become a media circus as the story of our murdering mayor broke across the country. It also came to light that Jess O'Connor had been the shadowy intruder in our house the other night. She had been having an affair with Steve and wanted to scare Darcy off his trail. No such luck for her.

Poor Persephone was still down the hole but was doing well and in good spirits. Now that all of the excitement was over I figured it might be a good time to try and get Darcy's attention again.

But just in case I couldn't I hunted and killed a rodent for Persephone's lunch. I waited for the perfect moment just hanging around in the town center. I knew that Darcy would look out of the window sooner or later and then I could put my plan into action.

This time I was determined not to fail.

I didn't have to wait too long and when I saw her look out I made sure she saw me acting suspicious. I needed to get her attention so that she would follow me.

I could see it was working when she left the bookstore and started to come in my direction. That's when I sprang into action. I raced away toward the industrial end of town and I knew she would follow. I paced myself today though as I didn't want to lose her like I had that other time.

Of course, the best laid plans don't always run smoothly. As I turned into the street where Persephone was, I saw Kujo hanging around further down the street. I knew the exact moment he spotted me as he started up that awful racket again.

I could see him speeding toward me and I knew I wasn't

going to make the hole in the wall. I sprinted through the slit in the fence and straight up the sloping wall of the building. I'd had to use the route a couple times before because of Kujo but it wasn't the safest way to get in.

I stopped just before the broken window and looked down. Sure enough the dog was going ballistic down there. I shook my head. He's such a dumb dog. Think he would have given up by now. I'm just too good for him.

Then I lifted my head up and around to look across the road. Darcy was standing there watching. The dog was a problem. I wasn't sure how she would be able to get into the building with Kujo hanging around. And I knew from experience that the dumb dog would not give up. He would eventually come into the building through the other entrance and then we'd have an even bigger issue.

I considered for a moment chucking the rodent I had in my mouth at Kujo to distract him but then gave up that idea. A dog of Kujo's size could probably eat this morsel in one bite, it would hardly be a distraction. Besides, Persephone would need it if Darcy couldn't get past Kujo.

In the end I decided to head on inside and rally the troops. We'd figure something out to get rid of the dog like we'd done on a few previous occasions. Maybe Darcy would be able to scare him off. I was truly annoyed at Kujo for messing up my plan to get Darcy to help save Persephone.

I climbed through the broken window with care and then stopped on the other side. I was still thinking about what I could do about the Kujo problem. Just then I heard it. A familiar rumble coming down the street outside.

I heard it stop and then a whistle and a voice said, "C'mon, you mutt!" I chanced a quick look out the window just in time to see the dog running toward the vehicle. He jumped in and the door slammed. The big black machine powered away.

I could still see Darcy across the road and knew she now had a clear path into the building. It wouldn't be long now and Persephone would be saved. I guess I won't need this rodent after all, though I'm sure one of the others will be more than happy to have it.

It was decided that the other cats would disperse and I would lead Darcy to Persephone.

Of course, nothing is ever smooth sailing. In the end the hero Jon had to turn up like a white knight on his steed saving the day. I really do not like that man but I guess he has his uses.

When I heard them coming I scampered up to them and wound myself around Darcy's ankles.

"Smudge!" She scooped me up into her arms. "Where have you been? What have you been getting up to?"

As much as I loved the attention I didn't have time for it right now. I struggled in her arms and pushed my way out, dropping to floor. I scurried away but stopped a little way away from them, looking back at them, my eyes wide and intense.

They finally got the message and followed me. It wasn't long before they discovered Persephone down the hole. After that there was a mad dash of activity as the fire brigade came and rescued Persephone and her kittens. I couldn't believe that it had taken me this long to get Darcy to see what I was trying to tell her.

Humans. Who'd have 'em.

I guess I would. I'd hate to be without Darcy.

Linda was very happy to see her cat and her... I suppose they're her grand kittens.

"Well, Smudge." Darcy knelt down to pat me. "It seems we've both had a busy couple of weeks."

I meowed in agreement.

# CHAPTER 24

A few days later after the excitement of rescuing Persephone had died down I was lying in a patch of sunlight up on top of one of the bookshelves when that hero wannabe Jon came striding in like he owned the joint.

He walked right up to Darcy and planted one on her. I looked away in disgust. Sure I was a romantic at heart. I'd spent a good deal of time grooming myself today as I was meeting up with Twistypaws later on. But that didn't mean I liked seeing Jon pawing at my Darcy.

I could hear them talking all lovey dovey to each other. I'd had enough. I jumped down onto the counter between them trying to break it up. I purred and acted all cute and everything so that Darcy would take notice of me and ignore Jon.

Jon laughed at me and scratched my ears. "I guess we'll have to share Darcy," he said. "How does that sound to you?"

I meowed and pressed my head into Jon's hand trying to push him away from Darcy. I think I gave him the wrong idea though. Now he thinks that I'm okay with sharing Darcy.

He couldn't be more wrong. And I intend to show him!

**-End-**

# ACKNOWLEDGMENTS

Time flies over us but leaves it's shadow behind - Nathaniel Hawthorne

You can't turn back the clock. The clock will only turn forwards into the future - Tess Calomino

# BOOK 2 - MISTS OF THE PAST

# CHAPTER 1

*H*umming softly to herself Darcy Sweet carefully turned the pieces of chicken that were sizzling in the pan on her stove. She swept a bit of her dark hair back over her ear and smiled. The scent of the delicious herbs and spices they were coated in wafted up and she sniffed at the air appreciably.

Her eyes drifted towards the window. Looking out she could just barely see the neighboring house in the distance. It had been standing empty ever since her neighbor Anna Louis had been murdered just a month ago. Darcy had found her body. Then she endured the whole traumatic experience of bringing the murderer to justice.

Things like that happened in Darcy's life. She attracted trouble.

Darcy sighed. She supposed that the house would go on the market soon and be sold. The thought of it made her very sad. Of course, she hoped that her new neighbors would be nice and that she would like them. Life moved on. In this instance, she could hope it wasn't so, however.

She felt something nudging her leg and looked down to find Smudge, her black and white tomcat, rubbing up against her.

"Sorry Smudge old fellow," she spoke to the cat like he could understand her, "you can't have any of this chicken. It's for someone else." The cat gave her an offended look before turning and prancing away. Darcy smiled. He understood more than most people gave him credit for.

"Wow that smells really amazing." Darcy's boyfriend, Jon Tinker, entered the room and came over to her. He grabbed her around the waist and planted a kiss on her cheek. She leaned back against his chest as he rested his chin on the top of her head. "I didn't realize you were such a great cook back when I agreed to go out with you."

She wrapped her arms around his neck. "Well, I guess we haven't really known each other that long have we? And what do you mean, you agreed to date me? You were the one who asked me, Mister Police Detective."

He smiled at her with that special look he had just for her. All those events that had taken her good friend Anna from her and turned the town upside down last month had brought her and Jon together, as well. Jeff, her ex-husband, had been murdered also just days after Anna. It hadn't been a real great time for Darcy. But Jon had been there for her. Once she had gotten past the tough police exterior, anyway.

"No," Jon agreed with her. "I don't think I've had enough time with you. Definitely not. But we're going to make up for that now." She lost herself in his deep blue eyes and almost missed when he leaned over and tried to snag a piece of chicken.

Slapping his hand away she said, "Uh, uh. Not yet. You don't get to taste it until it's ready. Could you set the table please?" She smiled sweetly at him and he pretended to pout as he went to do what she'd asked. He knew where everything was in her house now, and flawlessly set out two plates, forks and knives and napkins and then glasses of water. When dinner was ready, she brought it to the table and they sat down to eat.

He took his first bite and made sure to let her see his eyes roll back with a little smile. She laughed at him, but appreciated the way he enjoyed the meal. The rice and apple side dish had been her great-aunt's recipe. After a few moments of silent eating, she brought up what had been weighing on her mind. "I was thinking about Anna as I was cooking the meal."

Jon looked at her for a long moment, chewing and swallowing his bite of food. The events of last month had been hard on her, and she knew it. She had lost a good friend and an ex-husband. Not to mention the small moment in time when she was almost killed by the murderer, who turned out to be a friend.

"There are no updates about Steve and Jess," Jon finally said to her. She knew he shouldn't even be telling her this much. It was a sign of how much he cared. "Their case is going to trial soon and after that we'll know more. Although it looks as though Jess may not have to go to trial thanks to her cooperating with us like she did."

Darcy started to twirl the delicate antique ring on her finger that had belonged to her great aunt Millie. Outside of the book-store that she operated in town, and this house that had been gifted to her by Millie, the ring was the greatest memento she had of a woman who had been so important in her life. Twirling the ring was a habit she had whenever she got stressed or anxious. And right now thinking about the events of the previous month was definitely making her anxious.

Steve Nelson, Misty Hollow's mayor at the time, and Jess O'Connor had been having an affair. Jess had worked at the bank, and the two of them had been skimming money from the council funds. Anna and Jeff, Darcy's friend and her ex-husband, had both worked out what was going on and Steve had killed them. When Darcy had stumbled onto evidence of what was going on, Steve had tried to silence her, too, and Jon had saved her. With Smudge's help, of course. They were both in jail now awaiting their fate.

Feeling Jon's eyes upon her frantic ring twirling, she abruptly stopped and jumped up out of her chair. "Sorry, I sort of zoned out there for a moment," Darcy said. She started to clear the table and kept her back to Jon as she wiped the tear from the corner of her eye. She dumped the dirty dishes in the sink, set the leftover chicken and rice into a container, and as she turned back to the table she found Jon standing there watching her. He had such a serious look on his face. When she tried to speak and couldn't find the words he pulled her into his arms and lowered his head to kiss her instead. It was a sweet, gentle kiss.

Pulling back he looked her in the eyes and said, "I love you Darcy."

She caught her breath at his words. Somehow it washed all the pain and bad memories away. "I love you too, Jon."

She'd known for a while now that she loved him. And in her heart, she had known that he loved her, too. He'd never said it before, though. Not before now.

He always knew just the right thing to say. Darcy was so glad that she'd found him.

$$\sim$$

THE NEXT MORNING Darcy was in such a great mood as she walked to work at the Sweet Read Bookstore. She had a definite spring in her step as she walked through the center of town. She waved happily to a couple of people she knew at the door to the book store, flipping the sign from 'CLOSED, THE END' to 'OPEN a good book today'.

Darcy went behind the counter to get things ready for the day. Sometime later the bell over the door jangled loudly and someone burst through the door. Darcy looked up to see her single employee Sue Fisher rushing in wearing a tight pair of jeans and a flattering red blouse, her blonde hair whirling around her shoulders.

"Sorry I'm late," she said by way of apology. "But I did bring coffee." She lifted a couple of cups up to eye level and Darcy smiled.

Darcy knew full well why Sue was late. The woman was only twenty, a college student, and Darcy was lucky to have her as an assistant while she was taking a break from her law degree for a year. Sue was one of the most level-headed women Darcy knew but she was still a young woman. She would have been having a good old gossip at the bakery when she picked up the coffees.

"So what's the news about town today, then?" Darcy was sure that Sue would have something to tell.

Sue handed Darcy one of the coffees and settled down on a stool behind the counter. It looked like she was settling in for a good long chat. Darcy took a sip of her coffee, a little smile playing around her lips.

"You will never guess it," Sue said to her excitedly, swinging her feet like a little child. "Helen is running for mayor."

Darcy didn't know what to say to that. Helen Nelson was the soon to be ex-wife of the former mayor of Misty Hollow, the same man who had murdered two people just to keep secret the affair he was having from Helen. She had been running things in the town since Steve had been arrested at the suggestion of the town council and the support of the voters, Darcy included. There was going to be a special election in a few weeks to decide on a new mayor. It would be wonderful if Helen was elected.

"Everyone thinks that Helen is going to win and become the new mayor. Wouldn't that be great?" Sue's eyes were wide and it was obvious she was eating the gossip up.

"They don't have this kind of drama in that fancy college town you used to go to?" Darcy asked her.

"Are you serious? The most we ever got there was professors hitting on us cute co-eds." She giggled as she said it. "Or stupid stuff like the captain of the football team stealing a police car. I much prefer this town. This place is interesting." She drew out the last word like it was a sweet piece of candy between her teeth.

"I don't know if murders qualify us to be interesting," Darcy tried to imitate the way Sue had said it but the word was more sour than sweet on her lips.

"Okay, yeah, I know what you mean, but apparently we're interesting enough to draw people here to live. According to Helen, a newlywed couple have moved into the old mill house." Helen hadn't just been the wife of the town's mayor. She owned and operated the Bean There Bakery and Café, the only bakery-slash-coffee house in town as well. The business had been at risk of closing before the scandal happened. But now, with all of the negative publicity, business was booming. Darcy was happy for her friend's good luck, but sad that it had come at such a price.

Sue continued, "Oh and Blake and Pete's cousin has moved to town as well." Sue looked coy for a moment. "Randy is thinking about moving here also." Randy was Sue's on again off again boyfriend. Darcy gathered that the relationship must be on again right now.

"What do you think about that then?" Darcy couldn't help ask the question.

Sue screwed her face up. "I'm not sure that it is such a good idea. We can't seem to settle into a steady relationship. We argue over the stupidest things. I'm just afraid that if he moves here it will be worse and we will break up for good."

Darcy considered that for a moment. "But wouldn't it be better to find out if the relationship is strong enough to withstand a closer proximity or not now instead of falling apart later when you are more invested in it?"

Sue shrugged. "Maybe. Right now I have work to do or my boss might get annoyed and give me the sack." Sue smiled and Darcy could tell that she was using humor to deflect Darcy away from the conversation so she let it go. She'd had enough turmoil in her own life the last few weeks to last a lifetime and didn't need to take on anybody else's.

Thankfully things seemed to be getting back to normal in

Misty Hollow. At least, a little bit. New people moving into town, Helen moving on with her life. Darcy herself hadn't had a single nightmare in the last two weeks. No visions or signs of impending doom. And the mists that gave the town its name had stayed away as well.

The mists always came in when that special kind of trouble that Darcy attracted to herself was about to happen. She shivered as she got back to work tidying up the shop. She was happy that there hadn't been any of that kind of trouble in a while.

LATER THAT DAY Darcy and Sue were busy unpacking a shipment of books that had just arrived. Business had begun to pick up again after a small slump which Darcy had assumed was due to the fact that most people read their books from an electronic device instead of the real paper product these days. Darcy had been afraid that she might have to close the bookstore and sell up. She was relieved that the crisis looked like it may have been averted, at least for the time being. New shipments were coming in every other week now.

Darcy was on autopilot, her thoughts on Jon. A singularly embarrassing but nice thought about his lips was interrupted by the bell over the door ringing as someone entered. Darcy looked up to see who it was. She felt a little thrill rush through her when she saw it was Jon. It was like her thoughts had conjured him up.

He smiled at her and she felt her heart skip harder as she smiled back at him. "Hi Sue," he called over as he walked in, keeping his eyes on Darcy. "Hello there, pretty woman," he said very quietly as he drew her to him and kissed her lips ever so softly.

She'd been right about those lips.

"Oh you two are so adorable," Sue said, watching them and grinning from ear to ear. "You're making me jealous. I think I'm going to take my break now." She grabbed her bag and with a last smirk in their direction she left the store.

Jon waited for the door to close and then swooped down and claimed Darcy's lips again with his mouth and his tongue and his full attention. He let her take a full breath half a minute later. When he held her at arm's length she looked up into his eyes and knew he was up to something. "You know what?" he said to her. "We've never been out to a restaurant. I want to take you out on a real date."

Darcy laughed and said, "I would love to go out on a real date with you." She lifted her head for a kiss but he pulled away from her sharply.

"Ouch! What was that?" He looked all around while rubbing the back of his head. There on the floor at his feet was a book. It had flown from its spot on a shelf a dozen feet away, through the air, to hit him.

"Millie, stop it!" Darcy tried to find her great aunt's ghost, but the woman wasn't in a mood to be seen today. The bookstore had been her great aunt Millie's back when she'd been alive. Now she haunted the place, always causing trouble and throwing things around the shop.

Jon laughed nervously, trying to act like what she had just done didn't bother him, but Darcy knew that he was uncomfortable. As much as he loved her he sometimes had a hard time with this part of her life. He couldn't completely accept that ghosts and communicating with those ghosts was real even though it had been her sixth sense that had helped solve the two murders just a month ago.

He went back to stroking her cheek and gently kissing her mouth, and finally it was time for him to get back to work. "I'll see you tomorrow night for our date. Pick you up around six?"

"I can't wait."

"So your first public date with Jon, hm? What are you going to wear?"

Darcy had met her sister Grace at the Bean There Bakery and Café for coffee that afternoon and had just finished telling her all about her upcoming date with Jon. They sat together now in a booth, sipping coffee. Grace's dark hair was cut shorter than Darcy's, in a professional style and tied back away from her face, and the blue pantsuit that she wore was pressed and perfect. Darcy felt underdressed in her khaki slacks and yellow top. Other than the minor differences, however, no one would ever doubt that the two of them were sisters.

Grace was a long-time officer on the Misty Hollow police department. Jon was her partner. They'd started together just before the troubles had hit the town a month ago, in fact. Darcy knew Grace and Jon had become close. She was hoping for a little insight.

"I don't know what to wear, tell you the truth." Darcy's face puckered into a frown. What did she have that was suitable for a dinner date? Going out for dinner wasn't something that she did on a regular basis. Or ever, for that matter. "Actually it might be fun to shop for a dress. It's been a long time. And shoes. Maybe some new eyeshadow, too. What do you think?" Grace smirked at her. "What?"

"Nothing. It's just nice to see this side of you."

"Side? What side?"

Grace rolled her eyes. "The normal, girl falling in love side. I like it. You should let it out more often."

Darcy grinned at her. "I haven't felt like this for a long time. I really like Jon."

Grace raised an eyebrow. "Just 'like'?"

Darcy felt her face flush. Darn it. She almost never blushed. She made sure to keep her eyes riveted to her coffee. "No, sis, it's more than that. I really think I love him. He said it to me, you know. Just yesterday. It was really sweet." She felt her face get hotter. "I'm not being silly, am I?"

Grace was quick to shake her head. "No, Darcy. You're not being silly. You're being a woman. Look, I know Jon pretty well now. I'd wave you off if I thought there was some reason for you not to go after him. This isn't me telling you not to do this. This is me teasing my little sister about her boyfriend."

She winked at Darcy and Darcy relaxed. Back when Anna and Jeff had been murdered, the whole investigation that Darcy had started into their deaths had gotten Grace's husband arrested. She had thought at the time that it would be the end to their friendship. They'd come through it, though. It was good to know she still had her sister to depend on.

"Can I fill that for you Darcy?" Darcy jumped a little and knocked her empty cup over, the white ceramic mug spinning on the tabletop before she could right it again. She had been in another world and hadn't heard Lily come up to them.

Lily Sutter had just started working at the bakery and was a young girl in her early twenties. Short blonde hair framed her delicate face and her pale blue eyes looked tired. "Thank you, Lily." Darcy held her cup out as the girl filled it for her. Darcy studied her as she turned to fill Grace's cup.

"Do you like working here Lily?" Darcy asked, a sudden curiosity about the girl making her ask.

"Oh yes, I like it very much," she answered. "It's so much better than the restaurant where I used to work in Edgeport. I was really worried when it closed. It's so hard to get a job these days, you know, and I thought that I might have to move to the city to find one. Helen has been a lifesaver for me." Edgeport was a slightly larger town, nearer to the coast, a few miles east of Misty Hollow. Darcy knew that Lily had lived in Misty Hollow all of her life, and had commuted to Edgeport each day for her job at the restaurant, but other than that she knew hardly anything about her.

She smiled at the girl. "You know I don't think you and I have ever had a chance to chat. How are things going for you?"

"Things are going fine, except I got into a big fight with my brother, Robbie, this morning. It's tough having him live with me."

Darcy didn't know that Lily had a brother. "Is he an older brother?"

"Yes, though you'd never know it. He couldn't get a job after he finished college so he decided to come back here to live with me for a while. Lucky me, right? Problem is now that our parents are gone and the family home was sold he didn't really have a home to come back to. So I couldn't just turn him out on the street."

"That was good of you to take him in." Darcy hadn't even realized Lily had a brother. "I hope your argument with him wasn't anything too bad."

"Nah, just typical sibling stuff," she said dismissively as she left and went back behind the counter to serve some other customers.

# CHAPTER 2

*D*arcy peered at herself in the bathroom mirror as she painstakingly applied the new eyeshadow and blush she'd purchased. She almost never wore makeup. It felt so strange to see her face like this. She was quietly humming a tune to steady her nerves. She had a few butterflies in her stomach which she thought was quite ridiculous. It wasn't as if she didn't know Jon. Not like she'd never gone on a date before.

Her cat Smudge came into the room and sat stoically watching her for a moment. Then he jumped up onto the vanity and tried to rub up against her. She gently pushed him away. "I can't have you getting your fur all over me."

She stared at the cat, willing him to understand. Smudge flicked his tail violently from side to side, annoyed at her. "Well, I'm sorry that I have a date tonight, but I do." Smudge mewled at her and jumped down from the vanity. He stalked out of the room and Darcy rolled her eyes.

Finally ready she went into her room to grab her purse and then headed downstairs to wait for Jon. When she was half way down she heard a knock at the door. He was early. Her breathing stalled and her heart kicked hard in her chest. She admitted to herself that she was more than a little nervous.

Opening the door to Jon she couldn't help but smile. He looked magnificent in his dark blue suit, a white shirt and a dark maroon tie. Her mouth watered a little at the sight of him. He looked gorgeous.

"Hello," he said softly as he leaned in to kiss her gently. He studied her for a moment. "You look great. Are you ready to go?"

She definitely was.

"THIS IS A NICE RESTAURANT," Darcy said as she looked all around. They had driven to the next town over, Meadowood, because Misty Hollow didn't have a restaurant of the kind that Jon had wanted to take her to, a sit-down restaurant with waiters and gentle orchestral music playing over the speakers.

The restaurant was dimly lit and very romantic with long, white table cloths and candles. While they waited for their food to arrive they sipped wine and talked about their childhoods. Jon was telling her about when he broke his leg while riding his bike.

"I was showing off for my friends. I felt like such an idiot when it happened but all my friends thought it was hilarious." Darcy laughed at his story and Jon pretended to be annoyed with her, frowning ridiculously which set off another bout of laughter from her. Darcy told him a couple of stories about when she and Grace were just kids. She chose a story that happened before she was such a disappointment to her mother.

Before their food arrived Darcy excused herself to visit the bathroom. As she was retouching her lipstick in the mirror she suddenly felt cold. A chill washed over her and sent shivers down her spine. It was growing dark in the bathroom.

Her sixth sense had her in its grip.

Suddenly she was catapulted into a vision. Like most of her

visions everything came to her in pieces. The vision was from the point of view of a man and she was in an unrecognizable apartment. She felt really sick, almost to the point of vomiting and her stomach was cramping with vicious pain.

There was a knock at the door of wherever her vision was occurring and another man entered the room. Darcy realized in shock that the other man was Jon. He looked younger. This wasn't happening now. It was in the past. When? Where? Then she felt another sharp pain. In the vision she, as the man, was on the floor and Jon was hovering over her. He reached out for her.

And then the vision snapped away like someone had changed the channel and she was back in the here and now.

She found herself on the bathroom floor. Yuck. She picked herself up and brushed off her clothes. What on earth was that all about? Where had it come from? And why was she having a vision of something in Jon's past?

Jon. She remembered that he was just outside waiting for her in the restaurant. She couldn't face him. She couldn't go back to that table and pretend she hadn't seen what she just saw. Worse, she couldn't just sit down and start asking him who the badly sick man from his younger years was. He still wasn't very accepting of her sixth sense. There was no way she could see him. Not right now.

She left the bathroom and fled the restaurant out of the back door.

AFTER THE CAB dropped Darcy home she ran inside and slammed the door behind her. She leaned up against the door panting, her heart racing. She took a few deep breaths to try and calm down. The vision in the restaurant's bathroom had really rattled her.

Smudge rubbed up against her leg as soon as the door closed and she bent to pat him. "I'm fine old fellow. Just a bit shaken up."

She headed upstairs, with her cat following her, and got changed out of her nice new dress and into her bathrobe. She was still jittery, still on edge.

She went into the bathroom to scrub at her makeup. Staring at her reflection in the mirror she was alarmed at how pale she looked. Her green eyes were almost luminous and her dark hair stood stark against the white of her skin. She looked deeply into her own eyes and asked herself for the hundredth time why she saw these things when no one else did. Was it hereditary? Something passed down from her mother or her father? No. Grace didn't have this issue. Darcy was the only one in her family blessed, or cursed, with it.

Loud knocking brought her out of her reverie. She knew it would be Jon. She grimaced and shook her head. "Oh for Pete's sake," she muttered. She should have just faced him at the restaurant.

She heard the door open and Jon called out, "Darcy? Darcy are you here?" She took a deep breath and went downstairs to find Jon hovering, very agitated.

"Oh, thank God," he said. She had expected him to yell at her or call her names or something. Instead she only heard concern in his voice. "I didn't know what had happened to you. What's wrong? Why did you leave the restaurant without telling me you were going?"

She knew she'd have to lie to him. At least for now. "While I was in the bathroom I started to feel really sick. I was feeling so nauseous that I didn't think, I just ran out and took a cab home."

She could tell that he didn't completely believe her. "All right. Well, I hope you feel better soon. I wish you would have just come and got me. I would have brought you home, you know." He tried to draw her into a hug but at the last moment Smudge jumped at him, growling. Jon quickly stepped back looking puzzled at the cat. Smudge had always gotten along well with him.

But he was loyal to Darcy.

"I guess he doesn't want you to catch whatever I've got. It's probably best not to get too close." Darcy figured it was as good an explanation as any. She felt her fingers fiddling with her aunt's ring, twirling it madly around and around, a mix of emotions burning a hole in the pit of her stomach. Jon's eyes drifted downwards and he frowned a little. He knew what it meant when she fiddled with the ring.

He didn't speak for the longest time. And then when he did, there was a distance in his voice that she could hear. "I'll call you in the morning to see how you are." He gave her one last intense look, and then left without another word.

After the door closed Darcy turned to Smudge and said, "Thank you. At least you and I understand each other." He blinked at her as if to say, of course we do.

She headed upstairs once again intending to go to bed. But after several minutes of tossing and turning she realized that she was too restless to go to sleep. She needed to figure out what her vision meant. She decided that she would go and find her sister, Grace. Like Grace had said, she understood a lot more about Jon than Darcy did. Maybe there were answers there. She threw back the covers and got out of bed.

DARCY RACED to Grace's house as quickly as she could. The good thing about living in Misty Hollow was that almost everything and everyone was within walking distance. Darcy didn't even own a car. Of course, that meant that when you wanted to be somewhere right now, you had to wait until your feet got you there.

When she finally made it to Grace's apartment, she banged on the front door until it was opened by a sleepy Aaron wearing light blue pajamas.

"Darcy. Is something wrong?" His voice was sluggish and disinterested as he rubbed his eyes. His brown hair was a tousled mess. She knew that he'd forgiven her for the whole thing about him being arrested when Jeff and Anna were murdered, but that didn't mean she was his favorite person.

Darcy shook herself and said, "Nothing's wrong. I'm fine. I know it's late and all, Aaron. I just really need to talk to Grace." Darcy spotted Grace shuffling towards them yawning widely. Darcy smirked a little when she saw the pajamas Grace was wearing. They were pink with little white lambs all over them. Cute.

"It's not that late, Darcy," Grace said to her with another yawn. "But we both need to be up early. What do you want?"

"I'm sorry for waking you up." Darcy felt really stupid now. How should she even start this discussion? "I really need to talk to you, Grace."

"Well come on in, then. I'm sure you're not going away until you get whatever it is out in the open." Grace knew something about Darcy's special abilities. Just not everything. She didn't want to know, for the most part.

Aaron gave Grace a sleepy little kiss. "This is clearly a sister's thing, so I'm going to go back to bed." Darcy said goodnight to him as he stumbled back down the hallway toward the bedroom.

Grace made some tea and she and Darcy sat at the kitchen table to drink it. "So are you going to tell me what this is about now?" Grace asked. "I'm betting this has to do with that sixth sense of yours?"

Anxiously twirling the ring around her finger Darcy took a deep breath and then explained her vision to Grace. "I really trust Jon. I do. But what I saw really shook me. I don't know what it all means."

Grace was silent for a moment. "Darcy, you need to remember that you suspected Jon of being a murderer before, based on some stupid visions, and you were wrong."

"Yeah, I know, Grace. I'm not saying he's done anything wrong. The vision just scared me, that's all. Is there something in Jon's past that I should know about? He and I are just starting out and it's going so well and...and..."

Grace sighed when Darcy fell silent. "Well. I can always ask him questions without him knowing what I'm doing. And maybe check with his superior at his old department. But it was just a stupid, well, vision. I wouldn't put much stock into it."

Darcy sighed with relief. "Thanks, Grace. I can't just ignore what I saw." She stifled a yawn as she rubbed a hand over her face. She sighed once again before she said, "Can I stay here tonight? I don't want to go back home."

Grace nodded. "Of course, you can. Take the guest room."

# CHAPTER 3

The next morning Darcy left Grace's house to go to work. She wore the same clothes she'd had on to go to Grace's the night before, but they would do. Grace and Aaron lived in a very nice upmarket apartment close to the center of town so it didn't take long for Darcy to get back to Main Street.

She had to physically restrain herself from going straight to the police station to talk to Grace, who had left for work early before Darcy was even awake. Darcy was glad she wasn't a police officer; the early hours wouldn't suit her. She reminded herself that Grace would come and find her as soon as she had news.

Before heading to the bookstore Darcy headed over at the Bean There Bakery and Café to get some coffee. She waved to Mrs Sparks as she passed the old woman working in her front garden, which was immaculate already. Darcy knew that she spent a lot of time tending it.

Lily was alone and was busy serving behind the counter when she entered the cafe. She looked a little flustered as she poured coffee for Darcy. She spilled a little over the brim of the cup.

"Sorry, Darcy. I'm just so busy what with Helen taking over the mayoral duties. She has less time for the café. I've had to take over the baking and the serving, too. I've even had to bring my brother in to help me." She ran a hand through her short blonde hair. "You don't want to hear all this. I love the baking part actually. I've been trying out new recipes. Here, take this muffin and try it. Let me know what you think of it." She shoved a muffin towards Darcy before darting off to serve someone else.

"Thanks," Darcy said quickly as she started to pour milk into her coffee.

Lily finished with the other customer and came back to stand at the counter in front of Darcy. She had a sly grin on her face. "Say, I saw Jon all dressed up and heading out towards your house last night. I've heard a lot of rumors about the two of you. Are you dating?"

The question took Darcy off guard and she nearly spilled her coffee. While she quickly shoved the top back onto the cup she mumbled some stupid answer about how you never know and then took her coffee cup and muffin and raced out of the shop.

~

DARCY FOUND herself staring out of the window yet again. She was at the bookstore and was supposed to be cataloguing some books she'd obtained from a second-hand store, but she wasn't being very productive. She kept watching and hoping to spot Grace coming with news.

"Hey, earth to Darcy." Darcy hadn't heard Sue come up behind her and jumped when she finally realized she was speaking to her. "You've been way distracted today. Get in too late last night? You expecting a visit from a hunky police officer or something?" Sue smiled slyly at Darcy with a wink.

As if on cue, through the window she saw Jon coming toward the store. She couldn't believe his timing. She turned quickly to Sue and said, "Jon and I had a big fight last night. I really don't want to see him right now can you cover for me?" Another lie.

She would have to decide what she was doing about Jon, and decide quickly, because she couldn't keep lying just to avoid him.

Sue nodded, though, and put a finger up over her lips while Darcy ran to hide behind the shelves in the back of the store. She only just made it before she heard the tinkling of the bell over the door as Jon entered.

"Hi, Sue," she heard Jon saying. "Is Darcy here?" Darcy couldn't work out his mood from the tone of his voice. Neutral, was the best she could decide on.

"Um...no, she's not here right now." Darcy could hear the nervousness in Sue's voice. Darcy knew she wasn't a very good liar. Jon was sure to hear the lie in her voice. She put her forehead down against the books and shook her head from side to side. What was she doing?

"Okay," Jon said a little too quickly. "When will she be back?"

"I really don't know, Jon." Darcy could just imagine Sue out there, twirling her finger into her hair. "She didn't say."

There was a moment's pause and Darcy heard that edge to Jon's voice he always got when he was suspicious. "Well, I thought she was sick, but she isn't at home. I guess she's around somewhere. Can you tell her I stopped by?"

Sue giggled nervously and said, "Sure thing."

He left the store and Darcy slowly came out of hiding. Sue practically pounced on her. "Come on Darcy give over. What's going on?" Sue wanted all of the details of their fight.

"It's nothing really. We just fought about silly little things last night. That's all. I'd really rather not talk about it. I'm going for a walk." She didn't wait for Sue's reply as she left the bookstore.

Darcy didn't get very far on her walk when she saw Grace walking quickly towards her. "I was just coming to find you," she said to Darcy.

"Do you have news?" Darcy was eager to hear what Grace had found out.

"Yes, I looked into some things." She looked around them and then continued, "But not here. Let's go and find a seat somewhere quiet."

"You want to talk at home?"

"No," Grace said with a shake of her head. "I don't want to wait that long."

They found a quiet spot inside the Gazebo in the town square. Grace wasted no time in getting to the point. "You remember that whole thing that you and Jeff told me about Jon back when we were investigating Anna's murder, right?"

Jeff, her late ex-husband, and Darcy had found an article about Jon being accused of murder back at his old precinct. It was all cleared up, but at the time it had seemed to indicate that Jon could perhaps be capable of murder. "Yes," Darcy said at last, after replaying some of those horrific events from just one month ago. "I remember. But he was cleared of those charges. The article said so."

"Well," Grace said with a twist to her mouth, "Maybe he was cleared or maybe that was just the story that they fed the newspapers. Cover ups do happen." She raised her eyebrows.

Darcy couldn't believe that Jon would be guilty of this but then again she didn't really know him that well either. She chewed on her bottom lip for a moment and then asked, "So who was the victim of the crime that Jon was investigated for?"

"He was investigated for the murder of a man called Kyle Young."

"Okay. I remember that the paper said Jon solved the crime himself and in the end it hadn't been a murder at all but a suicide."

"Which may be what happened. It also may not be. Not long after that he resigned from the police force there and came to work with us out here." She sat back on the bench and brushed her dark hair back.

"Look, Darcy, I'm not happy about this. This guy is my partner, and I trust him, and I think you two are good together. I hate that we're digging into his past this way but maybe...maybe there's good reason to. The details are sealed, which is strange. That raised my suspicions as it seems to indicate that there is more to it. I've got a contact in the State Police over near Pequot Lakes, where this all happened, and he says he can find out what really happened for me."

"Thanks Grace. I appreciate it." She sighed, still not sure what to make of it all. "I need to get home now. I'll talk to you later, okay?"

Grace nodded and Darcy walked away toward home. She had completely forgotten that she needed to go back to the bookstore. Right now she just wanted to be alone to think.

She had thought that this whole thing with Jon had been cleared up when Jeff and Anna's murderer had been caught. She thought she could trust Jon, that he was safe, that she could let herself fall in love with him.

Had she invited a murderer into her heart after all?

IT SEEMED as though she wasn't going to get space from Jon after all. As she got closer to home she could see him waiting for her on her front porch. Her steps slowed as she mentally prepared herself for a confrontation. He was sitting on the steps with his head in his hands and the sight of him gave her pause. She stopped a little way from the house to just study him.

Could he really be a killer? Hadn't they already been through this a month ago, settled it, moved past it? Yet, here they were all over again. She didn't really believe it but what about her vision?

Her visions were always right, even if she couldn't figure out exactly what they meant right off. It looked bad for him.

At the sound of her footsteps his head popped up and his eyes locked onto her immediately. He stood up slowly and waited for her to approach and when she was close enough he said in a demanding voice, "I want to know what's going on, Darcy. I looked for you here, I looked for you at the bookstore, everyone I talk to says they haven't seen you. What's going on? Are you avoiding me?"

Darcy decided that she couldn't avoid this anymore. She needed to know what had happened. More than that, she couldn't keep lying to him. "What really happened with Kyle Young?" Jon looked surprised by her question. She told him about the vision she had in the restaurant bathroom. She added the part about the dying man being Kyle, sure now that was who it had been.

"Darcy, we've been through this before." Jon started to pace. "You and this damned sixth sense. Why didn't you tell me about the vision last night? Why keep it from me?" He sounded very upset. "What? Do you think I actually killed someone? I can't believe that you don't trust me." He started to walk past her.

She grabbed his arm. "No, Jon. You don't understand. I never thought you really did it. I was just confused and anxious about the vision."

Jon shook her hand off and said, "Darcy you asked me all about this. I told you how all that happened, about how I was accused, and cleared, and I really thought this was done between us. I don't even know what I'm doing here." He stormed away from her heading back to town.

Darcy felt her temper rise and then quickly break apart. She'd accused him without proof. Again.

There was something her visions wanted to know, though, and Jon hadn't exactly tried to help her understand what.

# CHAPTER 4

*D*arcy was so upset over Jon's reaction that she couldn't sit still. She was pacing the length of her kitchen, backwards and forwards, until she could calm down somewhat. Only then could she admit that she was also really mad at herself. Why didn't she trust him? She loved him, didn't she? She should have talked to him right away about the vision she'd had instead of running away from him. She'd only made things worse now.

The case had been ruled a suicide, according to what Grace had found out, and she should have accepted that at face value. Or accepted what the old newspaper article had said about the whole thing. It was probably a very sensitive subject for Jon. It had been enough to drive him away from his old department.

She decided to stop being an idiot and go after him. Her mind made up, she left her house quickly. She needed to find him in a hurry if she was going to set this right.

She wasn't sure where he would have gone. She didn't find him on the path back into town so she went to the police station. The desk sergeant let her know he wasn't there. The next logical place to look was his apartment, which was located a little outside of the town center on the opposite side from where she lived. Before long she found herself climbing the creaking, wooden steps to his front door.

With butterflies rampaging around inside of her she lifted her hand and knocked on the door. Several agonizing moments passed where she was convinced he wasn't going to answer. She was about to knock again when she heard his voice through the door. "Go away Darcy, I don't want to see you right now."

"That's too bad Jon, because I'm not leaving. I messed up, and I need to let you know that, and I'll stay here all night if I need to." She stood up straight and propped her hands on her hips.

Jon sighed and then reluctantly opened the door. He walked away and she took that as an invitation to enter. Closing the door behind her she followed him into the entry hall and then into his living room. Not exactly sure how to start, she stood in front of him looking up into his face, her mouth opening and closing without any sound coming out. He just stood with his arms folded across his chest glaring at her.

She gulped a breath before finally speaking. Funny, now that she'd almost forced her way in here she didn't know what to say. "I'm so, so sorry. I messed up."

"You said that."

"Well, I mean it." She reached out for him and pulled him into her arms, hugging him close. He held himself stiffly at first but then she felt him relax into her and return the hug. She breathed a sigh of relief then. "I was just scared about what I saw and I panicked."

"I understand," Jon said into her hair. She could feel his warm breath on her head as he spoke. He dropped a soft kiss to her hair. "No, I actually don't. I'm not quite up to speed on your whole sixth sense thing. But I suppose I might have done the same thing if I'd had a vision like that." He pulled away slightly and wrapped his arm around her shoulders as he steered them towards the kitchen. He pulled a chair out for her and then went to one of the cabinets to take out two glasses and poured them each a small amount of whiskey from a bottle he had in the same cabinet.

They sat down at the table and Jon said, "All right. I'm ready to listen. Tell me more about the vision."

Planting her hands firmly in her lap so that she wasn't tempted to play with her ring, she went on to tell him what she had seen, not leaving out any of the details this time.

Jon took a big sip of his drink. He looked thoughtful. "Kyle was a really good friend of mine. He worked freelance as a private eye sometimes. There was this one murder case that I just couldn't figure out. The murderer had left a cryptic poem at the scene of the crime." He paused to take another sip of his drink. He put the glass down onto the table and started to roll it between his hands. Darcy could sense that telling this story was hard for him.

"I gave the poem to Kyle hoping he could figure something out. He always was one of the smartest men I know. A few days later he called me to tell me that he'd found something. The night that Kyle died I went over to his place to find out what he had learned." He paused again to take another generous sip of the whiskey. "When I got there Kyle was lying on the floor really sick, or something. He died within seconds of my arrival. I was in shock and I blamed myself for his death. Then, on top of all that, I was investigated because I was on the scene when he died. It was finally ruled a suicide but it took a while and in the meantime my career suffered. I had to leave town. I just couldn't stay after that."

Jon went quiet then and Darcy leaned over and kissed him. "That must have been so difficult for you." They sat in silence and Darcy moved her chair closer to lay her head on his shoulder.

Although Jon had explained the story something still felt off to Darcy. She'd told him everything. Was he holding back on her?

∾

DARCY WAS ALONE in the bookstore the next day, quietly sitting and reading one of her favorite books. There had been no customers today. Sue had the day off and Darcy quite enjoyed having the bookstore to herself. It gave her time to think.

As she was flipping a page in her story she saw Millie appear out of the corner of her eye. The woman always appeared in a long dark dress, a heavy broach around her neck, her translucent gray hair done up in that modest bun she had preferred to wear. Darcy turned to the ghost of her great aunt and smiled. "You're not going to throw a book at me, are you?"

Millie stared at her and then she eerily raised both hands. One hand was holding a letter, a sealed envelope. She could make out the name that it was addressed to. Detective Jon Tinker.

Jon.

Millie's other hand was closed. Darcy took a step towards her, wanting to see that letter more clearly, but as she tried Millie just disappeared.

Darcy didn't understand what was going on. Millie's messages were always cryptic, never clear or direct. And now she was giving her a message about Jon.

FEELING VERY SHAKEN up from seeing Millie, Darcy closed the bookstore and headed to the Bean There Bakery and Café for a cup of coffee to settle her nerves. She was hoping to have a chat with Helen. Talking to her friend always helped make her feel better. So when she saw that Lily was behind the counter she felt a little disappointed. It seemed that these days Helen was never around and Darcy missed her.

She moved up to the counter and gave Lily her order. Darcy knew Lily could tell how upset she was. Lily had to ask her twice how her day was going. Then when her coffee was ready, Darcy spilled it.

Darcy felt like an idiot. "I'm sorry, Lily. It's been a rough couple of days, I guess."

Lily nodded. "I used to have days like that too. I went to the doctor and got some anxiety pills that have really helped me. My brother, Robbie, he borrows them sometimes too, when he gets stressed." She winked at Darcy. "Don't spread that around though, okay?"

Darcy smiled at her and said, "Thanks. I mean, I won't. Isn't that dangerous, though?"

Lily shrugged. "He only uses what he needs." Then she was off to help another customer looking to order a cake for a birthday party.

Darcy appreciated the woman's attempt to help, but she knew that anxiety meds weren't what she needed. She had to confront her problems head on. She decided to go and talk to Jon about the letter. She'd kept silent about what she had seen the last time, and nearly put a permanent rift between herself and Jon. This time, she was going to try honesty.

*D*arcy hurried to the police station hoping to catch Jon there. The desk sergeant smiled at her and told her Jon was inside. She found him working at his desk. Before she had a chance to talk to him, though, Grace greeted her from her own desk. "Hi sis. What's up?"

Darcy smiled at her. "Hi Grace. I just wanted to talk to Jon."

Grace gave her a knowing look. Jon stood up without hesitation, though, and Darcy didn't have time to explain to her sister why she was suddenly all right with Jon again. He walked around to the front of the desk where Darcy was standing. "We'll just go for a walk and…"

"No need for that," Grace said. "I need to head on home anyway so I'll get out of your hair." Grace put the file away that she had been working on and grabbed her bag and coat. "I'll see you two later," she said with a smirk as she left the room.

Darcy shook her head at her sister and then turned back to Jon. Every other officer on duty at the moment was also out of the building, except for the desk sergeant up front who was separated from them by a wall. Now that they were more or less alone Darcy eyed Jon for a moment before she said, "Do you know anything about a letter? Something sent to you with your name on it? I think it might have something to do with my first vision."

Jon went pale when she said that. "How did you know?" he whispered. She told him about Millie's visit. He usually met her stories about Millie with scepticism but he didn't even blink an eye this time. He went back to his desk and pulled a letter out of the top drawer. Darcy drew in a sharp breath. It was the letter from the vision, with his name on it.

"I got this the morning after our date, after the vision you had in the bathroom. I hadn't told you yet, because...well, here." He handed it to her

"Shouldn't this be in an evidence bag?" She asked.

Jon nodded and said, "Yes you're right." Darcy realized then just how rattled he was by this.

She turned her attention back to the letter in her hand and carefully fished it out of the envelope. She held the letter by the edges as she read it.

It was a typed letter. A poem, actually, which read:

> *"Your time is up*
> *We've reached the end*
> *The wind is gone from your sails*
> *I've killed others*
> *Those who asked questions*
> *Those who told lies and tall tales*
> *I won't need weapons, not a gun or a knife*
> *If you try to find me, I'll end your life*
> *Stay away from me or you'll meet your fate*
> *With me there can be no clean slate*
> *Lo ti distruggero"*

"A YOUNG WOMAN called Emily Ayers was killed in my home town of Pequot Lakes," Jon said. "There were many poems found in her apartment but not in her hand writing. I was hell bent on finding her murderer and then when Kyle died, even more so. I never thought that Kyle killed himself, but everyone else did." He paused for a moment. "Right before Kyle died, he said two words. Misty Hollow. That was the reason that I asked to transfer to this police department."

Darcy fit that piece into the puzzle in her head. The murder Jon had been accused of had really been ruled a suicide. And from what Jon was saying, he hadn't actually believed it to be a suicide so he had left Pequot Lakes to come to Misty Hollow because he thought the real murderer might actually be here. He'd been following a lead.

"I was hoping I would find clues about the murderer," Jon said, confirming her train of thought, "but I haven't been able to." He speared his fingers through his hair. "I have been researching it and then I got this letter. I'm sure that the murderer lives in this town."

"You don't think they sent that to you from Pequot Lakes?"

Jon shook his head. "No. I'm sure that they're here. And I think I'm getting close. I think I've spooked someone."

"What about the last part of the poem, what does it mean?"

"It's Italian for I will destroy you. It was also on a bunch of poems in the first murder victim's apartment."

Darcy reached up to kiss him. She hoped to reassure him a little. She could see how rattled he was. "We will figure it out."

Here she was again, attracting trouble to herself. It just seemed as if she couldn't stay away from the dark mysteries.

A NIGHT'S sleep didn't make any of the problems popping up around Darcy seem any more distant. Walking into town from her home the next morning to meet Jon, she saw how the mist was starting to rise. That was never a good sign, but she'd gotten used to these mists rising whenever there was trouble in town. Trouble she always managed to find. She hoped that they could solve this crime quickly.

They, she had said. That made her smile a little. It wasn't just her alone in this situation. It was her and Jon. Together.

She started to walk briskly, in a hurry now to see Jon. She got to the police station in record time and found him engrossed in a report at his desk. She stopped just inside the doorway to look at him without him knowing and that familiar shiver that had nothing to do with her sixth sense rippled through her as she watched him. She felt her breath catch in her throat as he lifted his head and caught her with his eyes.

She moved quickly over to him, coming around his desk to lower her head and kiss him. It was a quick kiss, as she was aware of the few other people in the room who were more than a little interested in them. "Hello," she said, staring into his eyes, seeing the same emotions written in them that she was feeling herself.

"Hello," he whispered back. The feel of his warm breath on her skin caused her to shiver once again.

She pulled away and returned to the front of the desk to sit in the chair there. Crossing her legs and flipping her hair away from her face she felt so much better now that they being totally honest with each other. It felt good to be open with him again.

"I thought about the letter last night," she said to him quietly. "It has a stamp on the envelope and I think our first step should be to go to the post office with the letter and see what they can find out about it."

Jon looked at her seriously. "I thought about that too, but I'm not sure I want you investigating this with me. After all, the letter threatened me. People are dead because of this. You might be in danger also."

Darcy considered that for a moment and then said, "Are you going to give up?"

"No, of course I'm not. I need to find out who did this."

"Well, then I can't either. We're in this together." Darcy waited for him to say something as he looked at her. At last, he sighed and nodded his head. He leaned down and opened the top drawer of his desk to bring the letter and envelope out which were both now in an evidence bag each.

He got up and came around to where she was sitting and held out his hand to her. "Come on then. Let's go to the post office." She quickly took hold of his hand and jumped up to follow him out of the police station.

The post office was right across the square. It was nearly empty when they got there. A young man with stringy brown hair that he wore back in a ponytail was at the counter mailing a letter, wearing ripped blue jeans and a t-shirt with the name of some band Darcy had never heard of. She'd seen him around once or twice, and recognized him. It was Robbie Sutter, Lily's brother.

Darcy smiled and said hi to him. He turned with a half-hearted smile of his own, his eyes a piercing gray color. Robbie looked away when the postal worker, Blake Underwood, said, "There you go Robbie all taken care of." With a distracted wave of his hand, Robbie left.

When Robbie left Jon and Darcy moved up to the window counter to speak to Blake. Jon looked around the room with its post office boxes and mailing envelopes and such just to be sure they were still alone, and then took his letter out for Blake to see. "What can you tell us about this letter, Blake?"

Blake, a middle-aged man with a balding head of black hair, took the letter's envelope that was displayed in the evidence bag and turned it from one side to the other inspecting it closely. "It was hand delivered," he said looking from one to the other of them. Their blank looks must have been enough to encourage him to continue. "Even though there's a stamp there are no other markings. No cancellations, no routing city stamp."

"Which means what?" Jon asked him.

"Which means that it didn't come through the mail system."

Jon took the envelope back from Blake and he narrowed his eyes at them. "What's this all about?" They could tell that he was curious but they weren't going to tell him any more about it.

"It's a police matter, Blake," Jon said, hoping that would end it.

But Blake wouldn't be satisfied that easily. "Police matter? This is addressed to you, Jon."

"Blake, I hope I can count on your discretion in this." Jon waited for Blake to shrug his shoulders and walk away, then he and Darcy made their way out of the post office.

Walking slowly through town holding hands Darcy and Jon gave the impression to anyone looking that they were simply out for a leisurely stroll. They were actually talking about what they had learned, but Darcy sure didn't mind that they were using the walk as cover. His hand felt nice in hers.

"I can't help thinking that anyone could be the murderer," she said to Jon. "It's just like I felt a month ago, knowing one of the townsfolk had killed Anna and then Jeff. Now that we know the letter was hand delivered to you, it makes sense that you were right. The person probably lives right here in town."

Jon agreed but otherwise was quiet. Darcy hated seeing him like this. He was so stressed out. They needed to get more information and she realized that the best way to do that was to consult her sixth sense. She needed to do a communication with the other side.

She pulled on Jon's hand for him to stop. He looked at her with a puzzled expression as she said, "I have to go. Let's meet up at your house tonight, okay?" She gave him a swift kiss on the cheek and was off before he could say anything.

$\mathcal{D}$arcy raced to the bookstore to get what she needed for the communication. She gathered together some candles and incense, which were essential to a successful communication, and packed them into one of the store's plastic bags. Smudge jumped up onto the counter and she let out a little scream.

"Do you have to keep doing that to me?" She put a hand to her chest to try and calm her racing heart. Smudge just sat and looked at her like she was nuts. She laughed at him and ruffled his fur. "When did you leave the house, anyway? What would I do without you old boy?"

He gave her a little cat smile.

"Okay, tell me this, smart guy. Do I have everything I'm going to need?" She asked him. He meowed at her loudly. His tail was twitching madly as if to say "do you know what you're doing?"

"I have to do the communication Smudge, even though I don't want to. Try not to worry so much. I love Jon. If this helps him, then I have to try it." Darcy grabbed the bag off the counter and locked the door behind her. Smudge twined between her legs as she went.

She went back to her house for a few more items, and to wait until she knew Jon was off work. Then she went over to Jon's apartment with her bag of stuff. "Uh, what have you got there?" he asked as he let her in.

"Oh, just some bits and pieces I'll need." She looked at him for a moment trying to gauge how he would handle her saying what she had planned. "I want to do a communication with the other side to try to channel the spirit of Kyle. Hopefully he will give me more information."

He was shaking his head at her before she even had the words out of her mouth. "Jon, listen to me. I haven't chosen to do this lightly. Communications are a serious thing. When you open a door to the other side, it acts just like any door. Anything can come in, or go out. We have to do this, though. We need to know." She put a hand on his arm and squeezed. "You understand don't you?"

He looked at her intently for a moment and then nodded his head.

"Good. I need something from you. Do you have anything that belonged to Kyle? I didn't know him and it will be hard for me to call him without it."

Jon rubbed a hand over his face. "I don't know, let me think." He looked off into the distance for a few moments and then nodded his head. "Sure I do. Hold on a minute." He raced into his room and was back in seconds with a book in his hand. "I borrowed this book from Kyle years ago and forgot to give it back to him. I kind of held onto it, you know? After his death." He handed it to her and she put it inside her bag. It was a copy of The Bourne Supremacy.

Now for the next hard part, Darcy thought. "We should do this at my house. Millie and Smudge may be able to help." Jon looked a little wary when she said that but nodded his head in agreement anyway.

~

JON DROVE THEM. When they got to Darcy's house she wasted no time in getting things ready. She opened her bag and handed Jon nine white candles. "Would you set those up in a circle in the living room please? You'll see the marks from where I've put them before." While he did that she prepared the six incense sticks by putting them in her ceramic holder and lighting them. A heady Sandalwood fragrance soon filled the room.

She was pleased to see that Jon had lit the candles after arranging them in a circle like she had instructed him to. He hadn't spoken a word since they'd entered the house. She knew he was nervous about all this paranormal stuff. Darcy sat down in the middle of the circle and crossed her legs. "You should go and sit on the couch Jon. This could take a while."

She closed her eyes and focused on the book in her hands. The cover felt a little rough as she rubbed her fingers over it. Nearby her, within the circle of candles, mist coalesced in ethereal tendrils. She let it happen, let the bridge between this world and the next solidify until the mist became a spirit, became the form of a figure. A man, his face covered in shadow. He held his left hand up closed into a fist. He shook it with an eerie rattling sound.

"Are you Kyle?" Darcy asked. The shadowy form nodded its head. She'd invited the right spirit. "What happened to you?" The figure shook his hand once more, the rattling noise repeating, and then on feet not quite touching the floor he speedily glided towards Darcy. She threw up her hands to protect herself, knowing Kyle wasn't really there but also knowing that the dead could hurt the living unintentionally. When the ghost touched her, everything went black.

# CHAPTER 7

*I*n her vision, Jon leaned over her, reaching for her as she faded away…

Darcy wasn't sure where she was. She was lying on something soft, pillows piled behind her and the familiar feel of a thick comforter so she assumed that she was in bed. She didn't remember going to bed. Wait…what did she remember? Her mind was fuzzy and she was having difficulty focussing.

Her head was pounding and she wondered if she had a hangover. She didn't remember drinking the night before. She opened her eyes and then quickly slammed them shut again. The light was too bright and the room felt like it was spinning. Oh, her head.

"Thank God!" Jon's voice seemed to come from far away when he spoke. Jon. She remembered. Jon and she had been in her house, and they had been…doing something. She hoped it had been fun, at least, to justify the way she felt now. She felt a little better knowing he was with her, though. He pulled her in for a hug and she groaned. It was too much, too fast. The room was spinning madly. He let her lay back down on the mattress when she gently pushed him away.

She scrubbed a hand over her face and tried opening her eyes again. The light was still way too bright but better than before. "What happened?" she croaked out.

"Don't you remember?" Jon sounded concerned.

"No. I'm having a little trouble with that right now. Did we...you know?"

He smiled down at her. "Not this time, sweetheart. I brought you up to bed after you passed out."

"Passed out?" She scrubbed a hand over her face. She felt awful. What had happened to her? She looked around the room and saw the light on her bedside table still on, saw how dark it was outside. It must still be the same night. The same night when she and Jon had...

The communication. That's right. She had done a communication to talk to Jon's dead friend. And it had worked.

She started to feel really uneasy about something but just couldn't put her finger on it just yet. She looked back at Jon who was still staring at her with concern.

"I was talking to Kyle."

Jon sighed. "Yeah. You seemed to be talking to someone. Then you screamed and passed out. I rushed over to you but you wouldn't wake up. I picked you up and brought you up to bed." She glanced at him as he shoved his fingers through his hair and made it all stand on end. "I was really scared Darcy. I thought you were dying."

Darcy nodded. "Yeah, sometimes the communications can become pretty intense. I'm sorry. I should have explained it better. How long was I out for?"

"It was almost an hour." He was still looking at her with concern, like he expected her to keel over again at any moment.

"Thanks, Jon. You sure you want to get caught up with a girl like me?" She smiled as she said it, and she'd asked him the same question before, but she still worried he'd take his chance to run.

He took her hand in his as she sat up straight. "I've always been a for better or worse kind of guy. If you ever become too much for me, I'll let you know." He brought her hand up to his mouth and put a sweet kiss on it. "Don't worry. You're not getting rid of me this easily."

A warm sensation spread through her from the touch of his hand and his lips. Darcy soaked it in for a few moments, then got serious again and told him all about calling up Kyle. "Does the rattling sound mean anything to you?"

"No it doesn't." She could tell that he still didn't believe it all. He frowned and then looked at her. "Do you need anything? You look a little pale."

"I'm actually really thirsty, can you get me some water please?"

"Sure thing." He stood up but before he left the room he bent down and kissed her. "I'm just glad you're okay. It's all right if it didn't work." He gave her a long look before he left the room.

Smudge jumped up on the bed after he had left. They exchanged a silent glance. The cat had seen the whole thing. He knew it had worked just fine. So what had Kyle been trying to tell her?

JON STAYED with her through the rest of the night, curled up to her back, his clothes on, holding her because she was still rattled. His comforting heat lulled her to sleep before she knew it.

When she jerked awake the next morning, he was gone. But Grace was there. She had snuck into Darcy's bedroom quietly, and when she saw that Darcy was awake she held up her hand with a key on a ring dangling from her finger. "I hope you don't mind, I used the key you gave me. I didn't want to disturb you if you were asleep."

"That's fine." Darcy stretched and yawned. The room seemed a little emptier for Jon not being there. He must have left early to go to work.

"How are you?" Grace asked, frowning at her. "You don't look great."

"Thanks," Darcy grimaced at her sister and sat up. She felt incredibly hungry. Her headache from last night was mostly gone, with just a lingering touch at the back of her mind.

Grace grabbed the chair in the corner of the room and dragged it closer to the bed. She plopped down into it and ran her fingers through her dark hair. "I spoke to someone at Jon's old department, over in Pequot Lakes."

"What did you do that for? There was no need." Darcy stretched and wished she'd changed out of her clothes before going to bed. Oh well. She smiled at her sister. "I know the whole story anyway. He told me."

Grace's eyebrows shot up. "So he told you that he attacked someone?"

A cold shock spread through her at her sister's words. Darcy furrowed her brow and shook her head. "What do you mean?"

Grace gave her a long look. "Jon's file also had an attack charge on it but there were no details listed about it. I'm still trying to find out more information." She gave Darcy another look. "I do trust Jon, but be careful for me, will you sis?"

Grace stood up and returned the chair to the corner. She patted Darcy's leg through the blanket. "You always did follow your heart. Be careful it doesn't lead you down the wrong path, okay?"

Darcy said, "Yes, I agree. Thanks for coming Grace. Thanks for...looking into this."

After Grace had left, Darcy spent a long time thinking about what her sister had told her. Did this mean Jon was being dishonest with her again?

Maybe it was just a mistake. Was there anything to it at all? He was a police officer, for crying out loud, and sometimes cops were accused of using excessive force. Weren't they? She blew out a long breath and told herself she had to decide. Either she trusted Jon, or she didn't.

# CHAPTER 8

*D*arcy was feeling better the next day but had decided to stay home just in case. She didn't want to overdo it. The communication had taken more out of her than she realized. It had been so intense, this time. She never liked to perform those. It always seemed to sap away some of her inner strength. Some of her soul, to be more specific.

When Darcy had been just a girl, not even into her teens, she had delved heavily into the world of the occult. Spurred by visions she couldn't understand, visions that always came true in some way, she took out books from the local library and read everything they had to offer on the subject of the occult.

That's where she had first learned how to do a communication with the spirit world. She had been so proud of herself, up in her room, surrounded by a circle of candles, exhaling and inhaling and working up a connection to the other side that would bring forth a ghost for her to talk to.

After that night, she had taken all of the books back to the library and boxed up all of the candles and tried to deny the whole thing had ever happened.

Her sixth sense had other ideas for her.

She shuddered at the memory. This communication had felt different somehow, though, and had taken even more out of her than usual. She had called Sue early in the morning to say she was too sick to go into work and to ask the girl if she wouldn't mind taking care of things for her for another day. Sue had told her not to worry and that she had it all under control. Darcy didn't doubt it for a minute. She knew that she could always depend upon Sue.

She spent the morning taking it easy, just sitting on her couch in her living room, reading a book and drinking tea. She couldn't remember the last time she had done this. As relaxing as it was, she knew she wouldn't be able to put up with this inactivity for very long. Not only that, but thoughts of the problem of Jon kept bubbling to the surface, disturbing her calm. She was hoping her subconscious would come up with an idea of what to do about him, the letter, the threat, the vision, all while she read through chapter after chapter of a historical romance novel.

She was just getting to the good part in her book when there was a knock at the door. She was tempted to just ignore whoever it was but when they knocked a second time she knew that they weren't going to go away. "Oh for Pete's sake," she mumbled. Sighing, she put the book down. Checking out the window before opening the door, she was surprised to find Linda and Helen standing on the other side.

"Hello, you two. What a surprise." Darcy was genuinely happy to see them and stood back to let them enter. She noticed they had their arms full of plastic bags and paper sacks and a pot that Helen carried in both hands.

"We heard that you were a bit under the weather so we come bearing gifts," Linda said as she made her way into the house and straight into the kitchen.

"Are you alright dear," Helen said, looking at Darcy with a frown. "You look a bit pale. Never mind. Once you get some of my chicken soup into you, you'll feel better in no time." Helen indicated the huge pot of soup she held.

"And don't forget some of my tea," Linda called out from the other room. Darcy and Helen laughed as they followed her into the kitchen. Her two friends had been in Darcy's house a number of times. They knew to make themselves at home.

Linda was a tall woman, thin in that way that some women could pull off so easily, and always quick to smile. She worked at the library in town, one of Darcy's favorite spots, so they got to spend a lot of time together. Her red hair was curly on the ends and, as she was fond of pointing out, her natural color.

In contrast, Helen was a stocky older woman with graying dark hair. She wore a gray pantsuit with a crisp white blouse. Those weren't the clothes that Darcy was used to seeing her friend in. But since she'd began taking on the mayoral duties her husband used to perform, she'd stopped dressing like a bakery owner and started dressing like a businesswoman. Darcy had to smile. She thought her friend would make a fine mayor.

"Thank you very much for the gifts, I appreciate it." Darcy said as they sat around the kitchen table drinking tea and pushing spoons through steaming bowls of thick chicken soup. She was very touched by their thoughtful gesture. She also felt a little sad to remember how Anna, her neighbor, had been murdered just a few weeks before. Anna had always been stopping by to drop off food to Darcy or to just sit and visit. She missed her friend.

"How did you know I was sick anyway?" she asked. Knowing this town it wouldn't have taken long for it to get around that she wasn't at work. She almost never missed work.

"I saw Jon earlier," Helen said. "He told me. And Grace told Linda when she saw her at the bank earlier. So when Linda came into the bakery and we got to talking we decided to come and visit you together."

They sat and chatted over unimportant things for a while,

until Helen and Linda both said they had to get back to work. Darcy thanked them again and saw them out. Helen left the rest of the soup with her, and Linda left the crusty loaves of bread she'd brought. It was enough for two or three meals.

She actually felt much better after that little visit. Any trace of a headache was gone and she felt ready to dive right back into the mystery at hand. Darcy decided that she would ask Jon about the attack he'd been accused of. Hopefully he wouldn't be too mad at Grace for looking into it.

There had to be an end to the secrets between them, though, if their relationship was going to go anywhere.

"WOW, SOMETHING SMELLS GREAT." Jon sniffed the air as he entered Darcy's house. "What are you cooking?" He dropped a quick kiss to her cheek and then he headed for the kitchen with Darcy following him. She had to smile at the boyish way he was acting. Anyone watching him would think he hadn't eaten all day.

Darcy explained how Linda and Helen had stopped by earlier and dropped off some food, including the soup. Jon went over to the pot and lifted the lid to take a look. He sniffed appreciably again. Then he turned to her with a more serious expression. "How are you feeling today?"

Darcy nuzzled in close to him for a hug. "I'm feeling much better. Thanks for looking after me when I passed out. I just took it easy today. I'm back to my old self."

She went to the cupboard and took out two bowls. She served up the soup and cut pieces off the bread and they sat down to eat it. Jon was making all sorts of appreciative sounds and Darcy couldn't help but grin at him.

"What?" he said when he caught her looking at him.

"Nothing. I just like watching you." The soup wasn't the only thing that looked tasty, she thought.

Jon talked about his day while they ate and brought up the subject of the letter twice. Each time he paused like he was expecting her to say something. She kept quiet each time, though, knowing she had to bring up the subject of the assault with him, but wanting to wait until later. She wanted their evening to at least have one happy, normal moment before diving into whatever had happened in Jon's past again.

When they were done and had cleaned up the dishes they moved into the living room, each with a cup of Linda's special tea. Darcy was suddenly nervous at the thought of telling Jon what Grace had done, and what she had found out.

She cleared her throat as they sat down on the couch and she looked at Jon. "I have to tell you something."

He put down his cup on the coffee table and sat up straighter. "Okay," he said, a little defensively. "I'm listening."

She started twirling the ring on her finger frantically. It didn't help to comfort her at all. She said quickly, "I had Grace look into your file. I know about how you were charged for attacking someone, I don't want there to be any more secrets and I just want you to tell me about it." She cringed, ready for whatever his reaction might be.

To her surprise, he reached out a hand and laid it over hers where she was twisting her ring. "I understand why you looked into my file. It's all right. No more secrets."

She relaxed when she realized that he wasn't going to be mad and then waited for him to continue. "I attacked a man," he said. "A guy that I thought was responsible for Kyle's murder. After he died and after I found him there I, uh, went a little insane. I was so certain it wasn't a suicide, but no one believed me."

"Why did everyone think it was a suicide?"

"Kyle overdosed on anxiety pills. They were prescribed to him. He had to carry those things with him everywhere he went." Jon's eyes got wider. "You know, I didn't think of that. Maybe the thing that rattled in Kyle's hand in your vision was a pill bottle."

She couldn't hold back her surprise. "I thought you didn't believe in my sixth sense?"

He brought her hand up to his lips for a kiss. "What I believe doesn't matter. You believe it. And I believe in you."

Her heart melted. Not even her ex-husband, Jeff, had ever said those words to her. As she looked up into Jon's face, a realization of her own bubbled to the surface. "You know, Lily told me that she's on anxiety meds. That seems too much of a coincidence doesn't it? Do you think she had anything to do with it?" Darcy shook her head. There had been so many false accusations flying around town last month when Anna and Jeff were murdered. "She seems so nice but I've learned that people are often not what they seem. Oh, I just don't know."

Jon stood up. "Tell you what. I'll go and question Lily right now. Maybe being honest with her like we're being with each other will get some answers to all of these questions."

He started for the door and Darcy got up to follow him. He put a hand on her arm to stop her. "You stay here, this is police business. I'd feel better if you stayed here." He left as she was trying to formulate the words to argue with him. She stared at the closed door for several moments before throwing her head back against the couch. She couldn't say that she wasn't a little miffed about being left out of this, even if she did understand his reasoning.

She stayed at home for an hour, cleaning up, reading, pacing. Finally she couldn't stand it anymore. She had to find Jon and find out what was happening.

TEN MINUTES later Darcy arrived at the police station. She had practically run all the way into to town. Jon rolled his eyes at her when she came through the doorway.

"I knew you wouldn't be able to stay away for long," he

grinned at her. "You're starting to give our desk Sergeant fits, you know. You're in here more often than some of the people who actually work here."

She sat down at his desk with a little smile. It was true. Not only did trouble find her, but sometimes she actively sought it out. Finger combing her windblown hair, she said, "What happened?"

He shrugged. "Lily said she didn't know anything about any murder and refused to come in with me to talk. She got so agitated that she slapped me."

Darcy was shocked, but Jon put his hands up and motioned for her not to worry. "It didn't hurt. It did, however, make my job easy. I was able to bring her in for assaulting a police officer. I've been letting her cool down a bit before I question her."

"Are you going to charge her? Send her to court?"

"No. If I arrested everyone who got mad at me the jails would be full. It does give me an excuse to go and question her now."

Jon got up from his chair and moved towards the interrogation room. One of the interrogation rooms was fitted with a one-way mirror, and Darcy went to stand on this side of it as Jon went inside the room. She looked at Lily through the glass. Was this the murderer? How could they tell?

Some days, she wished her sixth sense could do more for her than muddle her life.

# CHAPTER 9

*D*arcy continued to watch through the one way glass as Jon questioned Lily.

"Have you ever lived anywhere else Lily?" Jon asked. "Do you know anything about Kyle Young?" Lily started to cry. "Do you enjoy poetry?" Jon kept throwing the questions at her, getting nothing but more crying for his efforts.

"I have no idea what you're talking about," Lily managed to say in between sobs. Darcy could see that Jon wasn't going to get anywhere. Not this way. Without waiting for permission she entered the room where Jon was interrogating Lily.

"What are you doing Darcy?" Jon asked. "You can't be in here." She ignored him and sat down next to Lily, taking hold of her hands. She had decided, watching all this, that she would try to use her sixth sense to get some answers. Darcy closed her eyes and concentrated. But nothing happened. She didn't feel anything. She let go of Lily's hands, stood up and left the room with Jon following her.

"What was that all about?" he demanded.

Darcy looked back into the room through the one way glass at the still crying Lily. "It seems like Lily is probably innocent.

239

You're not getting anything from her so I just wanted to try it my way."

He waited before asking, "And?"

She shrugged. "Nothing. I didn't sense anything at all."

Jon shook his head. "All right. But I want to hold her for a bit longer anyway…" He was interrupted by a commotion in the outer office. Darcy could hear a man yelling. They went to see what was going on and found Wilson Barton, the night shift officer, trying to calm down an irate guy in a gray hoodie and blue jeans.

It was Lily's brother Robbie. "You let Lily out right now!" He was demanding at the top of his voice. Jon went over to him and put a restraining hand on his shoulder but Robbie shook him off. "I want to see my sister right now! You have no right to hold her, she hasn't done anything wrong."

"Look, Robbie, is it?" Jon started to say. "You need to calm down. Your sister is being questioned and I know that you…" He was interrupted once again, this time by his cell phone ringing. He took it out and Darcy expected him to ignore it after looking at the caller display. Instead, he immediately thumbed the screen to connect the call. "Grace?"

Grace? Darcy stiffened as she heard her sister's name. While Officer Barton finally managed to escort the still upset Robbie out of the office, Jon finished his call and then turned to her.

"Darcy…I've got bad news. That was Aaron. Grace has been attacked."

~

JON TOOK them straight to Grace's apartment building. She was his partner, after all, and Lily wasn't going anywhere. Darcy was grateful for his company.

When they got there, Darcy pounded on the front door. "Darcy," Jon said, holding her fist in his hands, "it's all right. She said she was all right."

"It is not alright! Every time I get into these kinds of things, someone I care about gets hurt! Every time!"

Aaron opened the door at that moment and Darcy flew past him into the neat, orderly apartment. "Is she alright? Where is she?" Aaron pointed towards the bedroom and Darcy hurried down the hallway to get there. Jon stayed behind to talk to Aaron.

Grace was reclining on the bed with an ice pack on her forehead. Darcy was speared by alarm when she saw it. She dropped down into the chair next to the bed and immediately peppered her sister with questions.

"What happened sis? Who did this? Should we call the ambulance?"

"No, no I'm fine. Well, not really," her sister said with a wince. "I was coming into the house when someone hit me over the head with something hard. Right at my door. Can you believe it?"

"Did you see who it was?"

She went to shake her head but then stopped herself. "No. I didn't see who it was, I didn't even hear anything. Aaron found me lying in the entryway when he got home a little while ago. We figure I was lying there for about twenty minutes or so, give or take."

"Oh, Grace." Darcy was at a loss. "This is terrible."

"It gets worse," she said with a sober expression. "Apparently there was a typed note lying on my chest when Aaron found me." Grace handed the note to her in a plastic Ziploc bag.

*When you look into the past*
*You find nothing but strife*
*This warning will be my last*
*Stay out of a dead man's life*
*Lo ti distruggero*

Darcy's breath hissed in as she read the note, the same type of note and bad poetry that had been left previously for Jon. "I'm so sorry Grace." Darcy realized what had happened. When Grace went looking into Jon's files, she must have alerted Kyle's murderer. She was convinced now that Kyle had been murdered. If her spirit communication hadn't shown that to her, then this did. No one would go through this much trouble over a suicide.

"Don't worry about it Darcy, all right?" Grace took the note back and read it over again. "I'm a police officer. It's part of the job."

"I don't think getting mugged at the door to your apartment by a psychopath qualifies as part of your job, Grace."

"He didn't mug me. To mug me, he would have had to rob me after he hit me, and he didn't. So thank God for small favors."

Darcy tried to smile but she didn't find it very funny. "What about the ambulance?"

"I'm fine, sis. Really. But the doctor is coming over to check me out just in case anyway. Aaron already called. Don't worry."

Jon came in at that point and Darcy listened as Jon and Grace talked over the note and the particulars of the whole matter. Jon let on some of the secret information that he had already told Darcy about. He looked devastated that his old life had gotten both of them involved in this mess.

BACK AT THE POLICE STATION, Robbie was waiting for Jon outside. He approached them as they were just getting out of Jon's patrol car.

"You can't hold Lily she hasn't done anything wrong."

"Yes, I can." Jon said to him, holding up a hand as Robbie got a little too close. "I tried to explain to you earlier that she attacked me by slapping me across the face. I'm holding her on a pending assault charge. Robbie, go home. I'll be sure Lily lets you know what's going on."

But Robbie wasn't having any of it. He was shaking and his eyes were wide, his hands fisted at his sides. "You have to let her go."

Darcy moved in closer to Jon very carefully and laid a hand on his arm. "I have to talk to you Jon."

Jon didn't look away from Robbie as he nodded. "You try to calm down while I talk to Darcy okay Robbie?" He backed away from the other man carefully and he and Darcy went to the back of his car.

Darcy kept darting her eyes over to Robbie and then back to Jon. "You know Lily couldn't be the one who attacked Grace, right? She was here with you."

"I know that. The time frame matches up, from what Grace told us. That doesn't mean she didn't have an accomplice." He closed his eyes and took a breath and tried to calm his voice down. "I'm sorry. I just can't help but think that I got Grace hurt. I mean, how many other people are going to get hurt because my past is catching up to us? Are you safe around me, even?"

Darcy's eyes softened and she took his hand in hers. "It isn't your fault, okay? There's a crazy person out there and you aren't responsible for what they do. Not Kyle's murder, not my sister's attack, none of it. Okay?"

He nodded after a moment. "I know that. It's just...it followed me here." He looked deep into her eyes and she could see how tired he was. "It followed me."

# CHAPTER 10

"The town is buzzing with the gossip about Lily's arrest." At work in the bookstore the next day Sue was going on and on about everything that had happened. "Come on Darcy, tell me all of the details."

Oh for Pete's sake couldn't people in this town just mind their own business for once. "It was nothing really. Just a simple mistake." Darcy didn't want to talk about it, even with Sue. The woman kept twirling her blonde hair around a finger though, and asking the same questions. Thankfully Jon walked in just as Darcy was about to give in and tell Sue something just to get her to stop.

Darcy grabbed Jon by the arm and started to drag him outside again. She wanted to talk to him but without Sue around to overhear. "Do you have any leads?"

He shook his head and said, "That isn't why I came. Everything has been so crazy lately. I just want to spend some time with you." He paused for a moment and looked at her intently. "I need your key."

Darcy looked at him dumbly. "My key?"

He nodded. "I need to get into your house." She opened her mouth to ask why and he put a hand up to stop her. "It's a surprise." He smiled.

She shook her head. "I have a spare key in the potted plant on my front porch for emergencies. You can use that."

His eyebrows scrunched downwards. "That's not a very safe practice Darcy, even here in Misty Hollow. You should probably reconsider doing that, okay?"

Darcy pressed her lips together. She wasn't used to someone caring about her like Jon seemed to. She nodded. "Okay."

Jon visibly relaxed and then smiled at her. "Meet me at your house in an hour, okay?"

Darcy was surprised by the invitation. She wanted to keep working on this until it was solved, until they knew who was threatening Jon and who had attacked Grace. But, he looked so lost and needy that she couldn't tell him no. "Sure thing," she said with a smile.

He hugged her quickly. "Great, I'll see you then." He hurried away, and Darcy went back into the bookstore feeling happier than she had in a while.

"I see you and Jon are back on track," Sue said to her with a mischievous grin.

Darcy nodded her agreement. It felt good, even in the midst of everything else, to know this thing between her and Jon was so right.

DARCY WALKED home with a spring in her step. She had left Sue in charge of the shop again, joking that she'd have to turn the whole place over to Sue if this kept up. Curiosity burned at her. Jon had sounded so... Well, she wasn't sure exactly how to describe it. Mysterious, maybe? She was dying to find out.

She noticed that the fog was beginning to rise again but she chose to ignore it. She didn't want anything to spoil the lovely mood she was in right now.

As she climbed the steps onto her front porch, she could see through the front windows that Jon was already inside. She pushed the door open slowly and found that there were dozens of flowers everywhere in the hall. Vases full of roses and violets and other flowers. She stopped, mouth open, marvelling at the sight of it.

Jon came out of the living room with a huge grin plastered on his face. He handed her a glass of wine and leaned in to kiss her sweetly. "I love you Darcy."

"What is all of this for?" she asked him, laughing. Not that she was complaining. This was probably the most romantic thing any man had ever done for her. They moved into the living room and Darcy put her glass on the coffee table. She looked all around the room to find that Jon had dotted lit candles on tables and window ledges to give the room a warm glow.

Jon put his glass down next to hers and drew her into his arms. "To answer your question, I just wanted you to know that amongst all of this drama I know that I can depend upon you." Her breath caught in her throat and then his head was moving in closer to her again and he sealed his lips to hers. Tilting his head, he deepened the kiss. She was feeling dizzy when he leaned back a little and looked deeply into her eyes. "I am so glad to have you in my life, Darcy."

She smiled at him, her voice trembling. "I'm glad too."

He stepped away from her and moved over to the bookshelf and the stereo system there to put some music on. She sipped her wine and watched him through hooded eyes. He looked delicious. As he came back to her he held out a hand and she placed hers into it. He curled his fingers into her palm and his warmth seeped into her skin.

"You once told me that you love to dance. Would you dance with me now?"

Darcy had to catch her breath to answer. "Yes, I'd love to dance with you." He pulled her into his arms once again and held her close as they slow danced together for what felt like eternity.

# CHAPTER 11

The sun streamed through the sheer curtains and woke Darcy slowly the next morning. She stretched her legs and back languidly, her body liquid within the warm confines of her bed. Warmth radiated down one side of her where her naked body was sealed to Jon's. She laid her head on the wide expanse of Jon's chest and started idly drawing circles upon his warm skin with her fingers.

She felt him stir next to her as he woke up. "Good morning," she said in a husky voice.

She felt him run his hand over her hair, fingers sifting through the fine dark strands, as he yawned. "Good morning to you, too," he said. "Is it morning already?"

"Mm-hmm." She snuggled in closer. "I had no idea you were such a romantic. Thank you for last night."

Jon smiled and replaced his hand with his lips as he kissed her hair. "I'm surprised Smudge hasn't come and tried to attack me yet." Darcy giggled just as Jon's phone vibrated wildly on the bedside table.

"Nooo," Darcy groaned as Jon sighed and grabbed for the annoying little device.

Jon untangled himself from her and sat up, sounding surprised and excited as he spoke to whoever was on the other end of the phone. Darcy sat up with him, combing her hair back, eyes raking the line of his nude form. She had hoped that they could spend all day in bed together today, exploring each other...

When he hung up he just stared at the phone in his hand for a moment and then he turned to look at her. "I don't believe it. My old friends from college, Dale and Cindy, are in town. I haven't seen them for ages. We all used to be such really good friends."

"Uh," Darcy tried to be excited for him but she'd learned to hate coincidence. "Now? Are you sure this is a good time for a reunion?"

"I can't put my whole life on hold because of one psychopath. I won't let him tell me how to live my life."

Jon started to get up from the bed and then turned back to her, his hand falling in a very private spot. "They're going to meet me at my apartment. You want to come meet them with me?"

Darcy decided that meeting some of his friends would let her know more about his life. And, it might be just what he needed right now.

"I'd love to," she said, and then admired the view of his backside as he got out of bed.

Jon CALLED in to take a few hours off work. He got a hard time for it, considering Grace was already off herself, but ultimately it was all set and they were driving over to Jon's apartment. When they got there they found two people waiting outside who Darcy assumed would be Dale and Cindy.

Jon jumped from his car and ran up to greet them. "Guys! I can't believe you're here." Cindy, a short and athletic looking blonde hugged Jon first, in a way that seemed really familiar to Darcy. Then Dale shook Jon's hand. He was taller than Jon, stocky, and had a dark complexion with eyes to match. They both were wearing jeans and t-shirts, Cindy's just a size or two smaller than she needed, in Darcy's opinion.

"Guys I'd like you to meet Darcy," Jon said to them. They both greeted her warmly. Jon turned to her and said, "This is Dale and Cindy. We've been friends forever but they just got married recently. It took Dale years to coax her into it."

The other two laughed and Dale slapped Jon on the back. "Yeah, and you were supposed to be my best man, if you remember. How the hell have you been Jonno?"

They all headed inside Jon's apartment. Darcy listened as they talked about how they had all gone to college in Jon's home town of Pequot Lakes and how Dale had an aunt that lived in Misty Hollow. Darcy thought she knew everyone's family here in Misty Hollow. She still thought it was a strange coincidence that Jon's best friends from college not only had a connection to this place but were showing up now. But she reminded herself she wasn't going to let it disturb Jon's obvious happiness at seeing them. For the moment, she could set aside the buzzing in her sixth sense.

That didn't mean she wasn't going to be extra careful around them.

She pushed the thought out of her mind, reminding herself that not everything was murder cases and mysteries. She decided to let Jon and his friends catch up alone and told them she would see them later. She headed out the door and decided it was a good day to go to work after all.

SHE CHECKED in with Sue by pay phone, one of the few left in town that was located just outside of Jon's apartment complex. Sue assured her that, once again, she had everything under control and the new display of horror novels was coming along nicely. So before she went to work, Darcy paid a visit to her sister. Grace hadn't fully recovered from her hit on the head and was confined to bed rest. Darcy had rung her after the doctor had visited to find out how she was. It was a concussion, nothing worse, but Darcy still felt horrible that it had happened to her.

Darcy had phoned ahead, after talking to Sue, and been told by Grace to just come in. She used her spare key, and found her way down to the bedroom to sit in the chair by the bed again. "You look like you got run over by a chicken truck." Darcy joked with her sister.

Grace laughed, appreciating the levity instead of the grave concern everyone else had shown her. "I feel like I got beat up in a prize fight, is what I feel like."

Darcy hesitated. "I don't want to bother you with this if you're not feeling up to it, Grace."

"Oh, please. I'm so bored! Aaron won't let me do anything. He's been smothering me." She screwed up her face in disgust.

"He's just worried about you, sis. So am I."

"I'm fine. It's a bump on my head. You and Jon act like I can't take care of myself. Aaron, too. Just tell me what it was that you came here for."

"Okay," Darcy said, giving in to her. "I don't know where to go with any of this. Jon doesn't seem like he's interested in diving any deeper into it. I don't know if he's upset about getting you hurt or if he doesn't want to bring up bad memories or what. But I need to find out what's going on. Are you sure that you can't remember anything at all from the attack?"

Grace shook her head. "I've been trying to remember but I can't think of anything. Whoever it was that hit me did it just as I came in the door. I didn't have a chance to see or hear anything." She gave Darcy an encouraging look. "You'll think of something, you always do."

Darcy smiled back at her sister. "I hope you're right."

Darcy stopped by the Bean There Bakery and Café on her way
to work. She was glad to see Lily behind the counter serving a
customer. Darcy just hoped she wouldn't be too mad at her over
Jon bringing her in to be questioned. She made her way slowly to
the counter, not sure what sort of reception she was going to get.
Lily finished serving the customer ahead of her and turned frosty
eyes towards Darcy.

"What can I get you?" Lily asked, managing to make it sound
like an invitation to leave.

Darcy chose her words carefully. "I just wanted to apologize
to you for everything that happened. We were wrong. I was way
out of line, and I'm sorry."

Lily's eyes narrowed and turned even colder, if that was
possible. "Well that's just too little too late, isn't it? I'm not going
to accept your apology. What happened to me was unforgivable.
Thanks to you I've become the hot topic of gossip around town.
Everywhere I go I have people hassling me about what happened.
It's not pleasant. I'm a laughing stock." Tears moistened her eyes
and she tilted her head to the side. "So if you don't need anything
I am super busy and need to get on with my day. No? Good."

Lily walked away without giving Darcy time to say anything
more. She sighed. Well, so much for that. Just as she turned to
leave an angry Lily came rushing back and hissed, "I thought you
were my friend Darcy. Robbie is furious with both you and Jon,
too. I don't know if I can ever forgive either or you for what you
did to me."

"I'm so, so sorry Lily. I don't know what else I can say or do."
Feeling awful Darcy turned and left the shop. She was mad at
herself for doubting Lily and ruining a friendship. It was in the
name of solving a mystery, of finding whoever was threatening
Jon. Not to mention the person who had hurt her sister. That
might make it right, but it didn't make her feel any better.

THE REST of the day went by in a blur. Sue didn't say much, picking up on her dark thoughts. A few customers came and went, and she barely noticed what books they bought. That night when Darcy hopped into bed she couldn't help but think back to the night before with Jon. It had been a wonderfully romantic evening and she loved him more for the whole experience. Smudge jumped up onto the bed and curled up next to her. She wriggled around for a few moments, until she was comfortable.

Darcy soon drifted off to sleep and quickly found herself inside a dream.

She was sitting on the front porch with her great aunt Millie. Usually when Darcy saw Millie as a ghost her figure was vague and hardly defined. But in the dream Millie was just like Darcy remembered her when she had been alive. She was a young woman in the dream, the sun was shining brightly as she and Millie sat in rocking chairs drinking homemade lemonade.

The rocking of the chair should have been soothing for her but it wasn't. It was the rhythm of a beating heart, a tempo of something marching closer and closer. "I miss you so much Millie," Darcy said.

"I miss you too sweetheart." Millie smiled at her. Her cheeks were creased with laughlines. She looked happy. This was how Darcy remembered her from when she was just a young girl. It was how Darcy liked to remember her now.

"Millie," Darcy said to her, "can you help me with this mystery?"

In her dream, her aunt smiled at her and pulled out more pea pods from a bowl that suddenly appeared in her lap. She started shelling them without looking. "No child, I can't help you. I'm sorry. But you have more tricks up your sleeve than you think. You need to go back and to talk to Grace again. Grace is the key."

"What do you mean, Grace is the key? I don't understand." Darcy was confused. She saw herself take a pea pod that Millie handed to her. She ate it. It was sweet. She could feel the snap of it between her teeth.

Darcy sat bolt upright in bed gasping for air. She was disorientated. It was the middle of the night and dark in the room, where just a moment before she had been sitting in the bright sunlight with her aunt. She could still taste the sweet crunch of the pea pod in her mouth. She fumbled for the light switch and turned the light on. She squinted against the sudden harsh light as it filled the room.

Smudge meowed at her and she bent down to stroke her hand over his fur. "I'm fine, Smudge. I just had a strange dream. That's all."

Of course, she knew that wasn't true. She knew her special dreams from her normal ones. This had not been a normal dream.

She decided to go and see Grace in the morning.

"I knew it was you," Aaron said with a broad smile on his face as he opened the door to Darcy the next morning. "You're making a habit of banging on our door at an early hour."

"I'm sorry, Aaron. How is she?"

He didn't need to ask who she meant. "Grace just got up. You know the way down to the bedroom, right?"

"I do. Thanks." She gave him a quick hug. She had always liked Aaron, even when she'd accused him of having something to do with Anna's murder last month. He stood back to let her in and she went straight into Grace's room.

Grace was just sitting up as Darcy entered the room. Rubbing at her eyes and yawning she said, "What's wrong now, Darcy?"

Darcy went right to the same chair she'd used to visit with Grace yesterday. Sitting down she said, "I had a dream."

Grace rolled her eyes. "So what does that mean for me?"

"I, um, need to try something."

Grace was used to Darcy's strange habits. She might not understand them, or even want to, but she knew they always worked. "Sure, sis. I'll help any way I can."

"That's good, because I'm not really sure where to begin,"

Darcy said as she took Grace's hands between both of hers. "I'm going to try to figure out more about the night that you were attacked. Will you talk me through your night up to the last point you remember?"

"Darcy, we've done this already."

"I know," Darcy said with a patient smile. "Indulge me."

"Okay. Well. Let me see. I had gone grocery shopping and then I walked home." Darcy tried to visualize that. The images came to her slowly, her hands warm where she held Grace's. Grace continued, "I was reaching for my keys when I felt a sudden sharp pain and then the next thing I remember was waking up and Aaron was carrying me to the bedroom."

"Try to really picture those final moments," Darcy said. She closed her eyes. As Grace did as she asked, a clear image came to Darcy's mind. She no longer heard Grace's voice. She saw everything as it transpired in her sister's mind.

Grace walked up to her apartment door. She balanced a bag of groceries in one hand, and dug into her pants pocket for her keys with the other. Something hit her on the head and everything went black. No. Play that back. She was reaching for her keys and a thick, round piece of wood, like a cane, hit her at the base of her skull. Grace fell to the ground. She looked up at the attacker but his face was covered in shadow. His body was a blurred smudge in the memory. Blurry and undefined.

But there was something. A smell. A unique scent. It was almost like an herb. Rosemary, maybe?

Darcy snapped awake from her trance with a fantastic feeling inside. "I think that I was able to see a few things about what happened to you that you didn't remember," Darcy said to Grace. She explained how the attacker was definitely a man, and about the herb like scent.

"I'm glad to help," said Grace a little skeptically as she squeezed Darcy's hands.

"I'll keep you updated." Darcy rose and stretched. "I need to go and tell all of this to Jon."

DARCY STOPPED by Jon's apartment hoping maybe to catch him home if he had taken some more time off to visit with his old friends. He wasn't there, as it turned out, but Dale and Cindy were. They welcomed her in.

"Hi," she said to them. "Um. I thought maybe Jon would be here."

"We came over to have breakfast with him," Dale told her. "But he had to get to work. He told us we could hang out here for the day."

Darcy made small talk with them for a while. She was getting a strange vibe from Dale. She might have been tempted to chalk it up to a little latent jealousy on her part as they had known Jon so much longer than she had, only she knew to trust her feelings. Even when they turned out to be wrong. As soon as it was polite to leave she said goodbye and headed over to the police station. Darcy found Jon busy at work behind his computer.

"Oh hi, Darcy. You're out and about early today." Jon got up to kiss her. She leaned into him, encouraging his affection.

He sat back down in his chair and she took the one in front of his desk. "Yeah. I needed to see Grace. I, uh, swung by your apartment to see you. Dale and Cindy told me you were here."

"Oh yeah? You three have a nice visit?"

It seemed important to him that she did, so she told him yes, keeping her feelings about Dale to herself for now.

"I hated to leave them there at my apartment," Jon went on, "but I got a call this morning from the Lieutenant at my old police department. He's sending over the files from the first murder case by special courier. They should arrive any second."

"That's great. Speaking of that, I learned something important about the man who attacked Grace. I was able to read Grace's memories this morning."

"You...did what now?"

She laughed at the expression on his face. "Just listen." She told him how she had walked through the event with Grace, experienced it with her, and had seen a man and how that man had a specific scent like the herb Rosemary.

Jon looked a little dumbfounded. "I don't understand how you're able to do this."

Darcy shook her head. "If I ever figure it out, I'll let you know."

"Okay, so let's say what you saw is correct." He waited for her to nod his head, then continued. "Do you have any ideas about who it could be?"

"Just one. But you won't like it." Jon raised his eyebrows. No stopping now. She took a deep breath and then just blurted it out. "Dale gives me a weird feeling."

Jon shook his head vigorously. "Come on, Darcy. You're wrong. Dale's a nice guy. I've known him and Cindy since college. I would have picked up on something like that."

"Look, I don't know them like you do. I know that. And I don't mean to upset you, Jon, really. But don't you think it's strange that he has family here in Misty Hollow? Strange that right at the time you start getting hand delivered letters from a psychopath, Dale and Cindy show up?"

"No, I don't. They're friends, Darcy. And Dale grew up here. There's nothing strange about it." Jon stiffened his back and Darcy knew that she wouldn't change his mind. "I need to stay here and wait for those files to arrive. Why don't I see you later?"

Darcy knew when she was being dismissed. She didn't want to push him further. She said goodbye, and he said goodbye, and she left knowing that she would have to take things into her own hands.

DARCY HEADED BACK to Jon's apartment. As she walked she noticed that the mists around the town had now gotten thicker. Bad things were happening. The town always knew. So did her sixth sense. She passed several of the town folk as they went about starting their day. Helen was entering the mayoral offices, Blake was opening up the post office, Aaron was going into his accounting office and Robbie and Lily were opening the bakery. She saw Sue opening up the bookstore. She stopped to ask her to watch the store for her and was surprised when Sue told her she had it taken care of before she even asked.

"I guess I've been doing that a lot lately, haven't I?" she asked Sue.

Sue winked at her and then went inside the store to turn the 'CLOSED, THE END' sign to 'OPEN a good book today'.

She knocked on Jon's door when she got there. Dale was standing on the other side when it opened. "Hey there," he said. "We didn't expect to see you again so soon. Uh, come in, I guess?" He stood back to let her enter.

Darcy could see Cindy in the little kitchenette off the living room and there was a lovely aroma of frying bacon and eggs in the air. "Hi," Cindy called out to her. "Want to join us for breakfast?"

Darcy's mouth began to water and her stomach rumbled reminding her that she hadn't yet eaten this morning. "That would be lovely. Thank you."

"That's great. It will give us a chance to get to know each other," said Cindy as she brought the food to the table to serve.

Darcy sat down at the small round kitchen table. "I'd like that. Dale, I was surprised to know you had family here."

"Sure do," he said. "I've always liked it here. I'm glad to be back. So, tell us, Darcy. Have you and Jon been together very long?"

"Oh, yes. Tell us about how you and Jon met?" Cindy added. "Back in college we thought he'd never find a decent girl."

"Tell me about it," Dale said. "You remember that one girl he dated? The one from your sorority, Cindy? Crazy girl?"

"You mean Karla? Wow. Wack job," she said in a sing-song voice. Darcy did her best not to make a face. These two were starting to grate on her nerves. She didn't want to know about Jon's past love life and she didn't want to talk about her and Jon either. She wanted answers to all of the questions this mystery had brought up. Dale had dodged her so far. She'd have to pin them down.

"Truthfully, I'd rather talk about you two." Darcy looked at Cindy and then Dale who both looked a little put out that she'd changed the subject. Maybe she was being rude but that was too bad. Finding out who the mysterious poet was had to come first.

Stuffing food into her mouth Darcy watched Dale and Cindy closely. "So tell me guys. What did you study in college? Was it English, maybe?"

Not the best way to start an interrogation, she thought to herself. But it wasn't like she could just come out and ask if either of them liked poetry or spoke Italian. She couldn't just dive in to ask if they had known Jon's friend Kyle, either. She had to be smart and subtle.

Before she could get any answers from them at all, though, the door slammed open and Jon stumbled into the apartment. He was holding a piece of cloth to the side of his head, and Darcy could see dried blood on his shirt.

She jumped up from her chair, spilling her plate across the floor. "What happened?!"

Darcy ran to him in a panic. Jon held her into a hug. She could tell he was hurting. "I was attacked," he told her. "Just like Grace. I got hit from behind as soon as I left the police station."

"Why would you come here?" Darcy fussed. "You got hit on the head, you wonderful idiot. Why wouldn't you go to the hospital?"

"Darcy, it's not that bad," he told her, reminding her of how Grace had reacted under the same circumstances. "It hurts, sure, but the bleeding has stopped. No reason to go to the hospital. What I need to do is start getting serious about finding this guy."

Darcy held onto Jon's arm like she was worried he would fall to pieces in front of her if she didn't. Dale and Cindy hovered nearby, obviously upset that their friend had been hurt. Not caring if they heard or not, Darcy asked Jon, "Did you see anything? Do you know who did this to you?"

"No, I didn't see anything," he answered. Then he inclined his head pointedly at Dale and Cindy. "But I know who didn't do it. Anyway, whoever it was snuck up behind me on the street. Broad daylight, everything. They hit me from behind. I never even saw it coming."

"Did they want anything? Take anything? Leave something with you?"

Dale cleared his throat. "You mean like one of those poems

you told us about, Jon?" Darcy turned to him in surprise. "Yes, Darcy. Cindy and I knew what you were getting at with your stupid questions. I'm not concerned about that right now. I just want to know that Jon is okay."

When she turned back to Jon, he had an "I told you so" expression on his face. "No, they didn't take anything from me or leave anything. They just hit me and ran. One of the other officers found me out there and helped me get up and back into the station. I filled out a report and came back here. Figured I'd find you here, Darcy."

Darcy twisted the antique ring on her finger for a moment, then took Jon's hands in between hers. "Can I try the same thing with you that I did with Grace?"

He smiled at her. "I was hoping you would, actually." He set aside the cloth and gave her his hands.

She felt a bit uncomfortable doing this in front of Dale and Cindy. They wouldn't know what she was doing. They'd probably think she was crazy, and maybe Jon too. But she had to do it. She pushed her discomfort aside, and took Jon's hands in hers.

Acutely aware of the audience watching her and still holding his hands she instructed him, "Take me through what happened." He did as she asked, relating the whole thing just as he remembered it. As he spoke, his words came to life and Jon's apartment faded away. Their hands warmed up and a tingling sensation crept up her back. Darcy saw everything through Jon's eyes. He left the police station, in a rush to get somewhere, and then as he stepped out the door and turned left, pain blossomed in the back of his head and he collapsed.

She had him tell it again, and then a third time, and the images got stronger as she did. The figure was still in the shadows behind him, but this time she caught the same smell she had with Grace's attacker. It smelt delicious, liked baked bread and herbs.

The world rushed back in on her and she was back in Jon's apartment again.

"I recognized the scent this time, Jon! It's from the bakery. I remember talking to Lily about the new recipes she was trying. It was Lily all along!"

"Well, she must have had help," Jon said as he stood up. "She was locked up when your sister got attacked, remember?"

"Okay, so she had help, but I'm telling you I know that smell."

Dale and Cindy exchanged a glance. "What smell, exactly?" Cindy asked them.

Jon gave them a weak smile. "I'll explain it to you later. Right now Darcy and I have to go find someone."

He stood up, slowly, with a twinge that he tried to hide from Darcy. "Come on. We have to go and get Lily. This time, we won't let her go until we know what's going on."

Darcy thought that sounded like a great plan.

DARCY AND JON went straight to the bakery. As they entered they could see Lily behind the counter serving a customer. They waited until she was finished before moving up to the counter. When Lily saw them she said, "What are you doing here? I don't really want to see you two, I've had enough of you."

"Well that's just too bad," Jon said as he walked behind the counter while pulling out a pair of handcuffs. "I'm arresting you for assault. I need you to come down to the station with me." He stopped in front of her with a wicked smile. "Unless you want to try hitting me again?"

Lily started to cry. "I don't know why you're doing this to me." She let Jon put the handcuffs on without a fight, and Jon led her out of the shop and into the street where a crowd was gathering already.

Darcy cringed when she saw Helen rushing down the sidewalk to find out what was going on at her shop. "I'm sorry, Helen," Darcy said to her. "I'll explain it later, I promise."

Helen gaped at her. "This is exactly what you did with me last time, Darcy. Can't you keep out of things?"

Darcy didn't know what to say to that. She just knew she had to find out who was doing all this. She turned away, her eyes low. The fog was rolling in thick around them. The troubles were definitely not over.

When they reached the police station Jon led Lily straight into the interrogation room. Darcy watched from the other side of the one way glass as Lily cried and Jon settled himself across from her.

"What do you know about Kyle Young?" Jon asked Lily.

Lily was still sobbing and took a few moments to get herself under control. Jon waited. "I told you before. I have never heard of Kyle Young. And I'm done. I don't know why I am here and I refuse to say anything else without a lawyer present."

Jon sighed and stood up. Taking Lily by her elbow he escorted her to a cell. The look she shot Darcy on the way by could have melted lead.

"So now what?" Darcy asked him when he got back. She had hoped that Lily would confess to the murders, to Kyle's and then also to the one Jon had Kyle looking into when he'd been killed.

Jon shrugged. "We wait for her lawyer to get here I guess. I should have just started with asking about the assaults on me and Grace." They went out to the front office of the police station and sat down at Jon's desk to go over what they knew.

It didn't take long for Lily's brother Robbie to burst into the police station. They could hear him out front arguing with the secretary, demanding to be let in.

Jon rolled his eyes. "This, I didn't really need."

He went out to the front area, being buzzed through with a grateful expression by the little old woman who acted as the department's secretary. Darcy followed. When Robbie saw them, he stepped toward them, stabbing his finger in the air at Jon. His eyes and his hair were both wild. "I want to see my sister. Now!"

"Robbie, we don't let people we're holding have visitors." Jon tried to crowd the man back to the door. "I'm sorry. She's asked for an attorney. When he gets here, maybe you can talk to her then. Now, I'm going to ask you to leave. Got it?"

"No. You arrested my sister, Jon," Robbie grated through clenched teeth. "My sister! You let her go now or I'll bury you!"

Jon's eyes narrowed and Darcy took a step back. "Now you listen to me," Jon said, pointing a finger of his own. "You leave, now, or I'll let you join your sister in the cells. You think that's going to help her any?"

Robbie clenched and unclenched his fists. Then he turned on his heels without a word and walked out.

Darcy looked up at Jon. "Wow. I don't think I've ever seen you that upset."

"Yeah, well, he was getting under my skin. Bury me? Seriously? Who talks like that." He stopped with his hand reaching for the door to go back into the station. He turned to Darcy. In that moment, she got it too.

"The person who writes the poems. That's who."

Jon nodded. "Exactly."

Darcy couldn't believe she hadn't seen it before. "Robbie's been helping Lily at the bakery. He would have picked up the same smell on him of herbs and baking."

"Let's go back and have a talk with Lily about this," Jon suggested, nodding to the secretary to open the door again.

"Don't we have to wait for her attorney?" Darcy asked him.

"Only if she's a suspect. Right now, she's just a witness for all I know."

As they went back into the building, they heard a loud noise that sounded like a crash come from the cells. Jon and Darcy and the two other officers working at their desks rushed into the cell area. In the cell on the left, behind the floor-to-ceiling bars, they found Lily on the cement floor shaking, having some sort of fit.

"Damn it. One of you guys go get the keys," Jon said to one of the two uniformed officers. The man ran off. Darcy put her hands to her mouth. The cell was brightly lit by the overhead lights and the sunlight slanting through the barred window at the back of the cell. "We need to get her to the hospital immediately. This doesn't look good."

"What could have happened?" Darcy asked.

The officer arrived back with the keys and when the door slid open to the side with a rattling clank, Jon rushed in. He felt for her pulse, checked for her breathing. "I don't know what happened to her. She looks like she's having some kind of seizure or something." He knelt there with a puzzled look on his face. Then he picked up one of Lily's hands.

"Look at this," he said to them, showing the backside of Lily's left hand. "There's some kind of red welt here. Like a bee sting."

Darcy couldn't understand what was happening. She knew one thing. If she and Jon hadn't brought Lily into the police station, she probably would still be fine.

She knew something else, too. They had to find Robbie. Fast.

## CHAPTER 14

*D*arcy sat in one of the uncomfortable plastic chairs while Jon paced the hospital waiting room waiting for news on Lily. Meadowood's hospital was the closest and it had still taken them fifteen harrowing minutes at top speed in a patrol car to get there.

Jon took out his cell phone and tried again to contact Robbie. Every time he called, it went to voicemail. It was nearly an hour later when a doctor approached them.

"Detective," the man said. He was an older man, balding, heavyset, with thick glasses. "Thanks for waiting. Miss Sutter received a toxic mixture injected directly to her bloodstream through that site you found on the back of her hand. The labwork finally came back on her blood. It appears to be a combination of a common prescription anti-anxiety medication and a couple of toxins. The injection caused the reaction, the uh, seizure that you saw."

Jon nodded along like he understood all that. All Darcy got out of it was that Lily had been poisoned.

"Will she be all right?" Jon asked the Doctor.

"I believe so. It's going to take some time, though. We've put her into a medically induced coma while we detoxify her system. We'll know more in a few hours."

"I understand, Doctor." Jon looked like he might understand it, but he didn't like it. "Look, I don't have any jurisdiction here in Meadowood, but I've called and asked the local police to post two officers outside her room for her own protection. They should be here shortly. I'm going to leave you my cell number. If anything comes up or if her condition changes, I'd appreciate a call."

The doctor took Jon's card, then dipped his head to them before going back through the swinging doors under the sign marked "Emergency."

"Now what?" Darcy asked Jon.

"I don't know. We need more proof. I'm going to get a search warrant so that we can look for evidence at Lily's place." He pulled his cell phone from his pocket again to make the call. "Then I'm going to try Robbie again."

AFTER JON GOT the search warrant approved over the phone he and Darcy drove back to Misty Hollow and went to Lily's place. The fog was thick and heavy now. Even though it was still the middle of the day, Jon had to turn on the headlights of his patrol car. Darcy shivered, knowing that it wasn't a good sign.

Lily's apartment was in one of several apartment buildings just down a side street from the center of town. Jon didn't hesitate at all about bringing Darcy with him. She was his partner in this now, with Grace down and out. He still touched the side of his own head tentatively from time to time, but wouldn't admit it still hurt.

When they entered Lily's apartment, Darcy couldn't get over how messy it was. There were clothes everywhere, scraps of paper, baking sheets piled high in the kitchen, clothing thrown around the floors, both Lily's and what she guessed were Robbie's clothes as well. The place looked like a bomb had hit it.

Jon set about looking for evidence. Lily's room was one of two bedrooms opposite the bathroom down the hallway, just as messy as the rest of the place. It took some time to go through everything in the mess. There was little of interest. A note on Lily's bedside turned out to be a to do list written in loopy cursive. A laptop next to the note was password protected and Jon told her they'd have to collect it for forensic analysis.

The bedroom next to Lily's was obviously a man's. "Robbie's," Darcy pointed out to Jon. "She said her brother was staying with her." It stank of old socks and bad body spray. It turned up empty as well.

Back in the living room, they located a row of books on a shelf. "Hey Jon, look at this. There are heaps of poetry books here."

"Any of it in Italian?" Jon asked with a snort. "Nevermind. It ties in. I was just hoping to find more, you know?"

"Then let's keep looking," Darcy offered, squeezing his arm in compassion. This must be so hard on him, to know this trouble that he thought had been behind him had come knocking on his door again.

They went back to looking through the apartment. After a few minutes Jon found a red sweatshirt with a college logo on it hanging on the backside of the bathroom door. He held it up for Darcy to see. "This is where I went to school."

"Why would it be here?" Darcy wondered.

"It's a man's sweatshirt. So, it's Robbie's. Do you know anything about where he went to school?"

Darcy shook her head. "Lily never talked about it with me."

"Well, if Robbie lived in Pequot Lakes, he could have known Emily, the original victim in the case, and maybe even Kyle. I don't know why Robbie would have done it though, but it could definitely fit."

"Well," Darcy said as she thought it through. "Let me ask you this. How do you think Lily got attacked in her cell?"

"Simple," he said, and it didn't surprise her at all that he'd already figured this out. "Someone injected her with a needle through that cell window. I've been telling the Chief ever since I got here that we need to close that off. She must have put her hand up on the windowsill and then whoever came along attacked her."

"But why would she look out the window. Who could have coaxed her to it?"

Light came on in Jon's eyes. "Robbie. He was there at the station, and I wouldn't let him in. The little punk must have gone around behind the station where he knew we wouldn't be watching, called his sister to the window to talk to her, and then jabbed her with a needle."

"We need to find Robbie fast, before he tries to cover his tracks and hurt someone else," Darcy said.

∼

DARCY AND JON weren't sure where to look for Robbie so they just started walking the streets. They tried to act casually, like they were just out for a leisurely stroll. They asked anyone that they saw if any of them had seen Robbie. No one had.

Darcy saw Aaron walking down the sidewalk toward them. He smiled and waved as he saw them. "Hi Darcy. What's the news on Lily?"

"We don't know yet," Darcy answered truthfully. "You wouldn't happen to have seen Robbie anywhere around, would you?"

Aaron nodded and pointed down the main street. Darcy could tell from the expression on his face that he knew something was up. "I just saw him head into the bakery a few minutes ago. What's going on, Darcy?"

"Sorry Aaron, can't stop to talk," Jon stalled Aaron off. "Thanks for the info."

The two of them raced off down the street back towards the bakery. Darcy reached the front door just a little before Jon and he grabbed her hand as she was about to open it.

Jon opened his mouth to speak but she knew what he was about to say and cut him off. "No, I will not stay outside while you go in."

"This could get dangerous, Darcy. I want you to call the office and get more guys out here. I'm the cop. Let me do my job."

"I don't care. I'm not letting you go in there alone. Too many people have been hurt already, including you. Let's just catch him, okay?"

Jon smiled at her and squeezed her hand. "Okay, but stay behind me and do as I say." She saluted him cheekily and she could see he was trying to suppress a grin.

All the same, he made that call to the police station before he turned to quietly open the door.

They stepped into the dimly lit bakery not knowing what to expect. It was dim inside as the lights hadn't been turned on. They moved through the open eatery area stealthily. Darcy nearly jumped out of her skin when she heard a loud bang come from the kitchen. It sounded like someone knocked a pan to the floor. From under his left arm, concealed under his suitcoat, Jon pulled his semi-automatic handgun. He raised a finger to his lips at Darcy, indicating he needed her to be quiet. She nodded an emphatic yes that she understood.

As they got closer to the kitchen Darcy could hear a muffled voice. The kitchen was divided from the front part of the business by a swinging door with a rectangular window in it. Both she and Jon squeezed in close and looked through. Robbie was in there, bent over the central counter where food was prepared, scribbling a note.

Jon looked at Darcy, his eyes serious. He mouthed the words:

*Three, two, one*. Then he burst through the door, Darcy tight on his heels, yelling for Robbie to put his hands up. Robbie bolted in a panic for the back door. Jon chased after him.

Darcy looked at the note on the table that Robbie had been writing out. She knew she had to follow after Jon, but she took a quick glance before picking it up to bring with her.

> *You should have stayed away*
> *Now you and your girlfriend will pay*
> *Lo ti distruggero*

A COLD VICE tightened her heart as she ran out after Jon.

As Darcy went out the back door she could see Robbie sprinting down the alleyway and it looked like he was going to get away from Jon.

Just as Robbie made the mouth of the alley and looked back with a smirking grin on his face, a black and white dash tangled up between his legs and Robbie tripped, falling hard to the ground on his hands and knees. His fall gave Jon the time he needed to pounce on him and lock his arms behind his back. He took out his handcuffs from their case on his belt and had Robbie's hands secured in only a few seconds.

As Jon pulled Robbie to his feet, Darcy felt something rub up against her legs and looked down to find Smudge at her feet. He meowed, a self-satisfied cat smile on his face. She bent down and scratched between his ears. Smudge purred as he leaned into her attentions. "Good job, Smudge," she told him.

After all, it wasn't every day her cat caught the bad guy.

# CHAPTER 15

*B*ack at the police station, Darcy, Jon, and Grace were sitting around Jon's desk while he filled Grace in on what had happened. Grace had heard the call for backup come in across the police scanner, and she just knew her sister would be at the heart of it all. Turned out, she was right.

"Robbie gave a full confession for both murders after we brought him in," Jon was explaining. Darcy knew how relieved he was, even if he was trying not to show it. He'd been proven right after all this time. His friend Kyle hadn't overdosed. It had been a homicide after all, meant to cover up the first murder of Emily Ayers.

He smiled over at Darcy before continuing as if he could hear her thoughts. "Robbie had been dating Emily in college and when she broke up with him he got so mad that he ended up killing her in his rage."

Darcy wondered at the matter-of-fact way he could say that. For a police officer, this must all seem routine. For her, it was a tragic thing that a woman should lose her life because she didn't want to be with a man anymore and he couldn't deal with it.

"So," Grace said, trying to understand the story Jon had laid out for once already, "Robbie found out that your friend Kyle was investigating him for Emily's murder, so he decided to put an end to Kyle's investigation."

"Exactly," Jon said. "He wanted to throw off suspicion so he thought of a way to get rid of Kyle by making his death look like a suicide. He'd been using his sister's anti-anxiety meds already anyway, so it was a small thing for him to break up some of the pills into a powder. He said he went over to Kyle's place under the pretence of confessing. That was what Kyle meant when he said he had something to show me. He thought he'd have the whole thing wrapped up for me. Instead, Robbie put the powdered medication into a drink and Kyle overdosed on the stuff without even knowing what was happening."

Anger had seeped into his voice. His friend had lost his life trying to do him a favor. That was a lot to bear.

"So why did he try to kill Lily?" Grace asked.

"He was afraid of what she might say," Jon answered. "He figured his sister wasn't stupid, and she'd put together that he had access to her medications as soon as I asked her. Not to mention it would only be a matter of time before Emily Ayers' name rang a bell with her. Her brother's girlfriend. Lily would have figured it out."

"She might not have said anything," Darcy pointed out. "She was in no hurry to cooperate with us."

Jon shook his head. "Robbie couldn't take that chance. So, he ground up more of the medication into a solution of water and household cleaners, and put it into a syringe. He only wanted to see Lily so badly because he needed to get the shot to her." He grimaced. "Our back window allowed him to do it anyway. The Chief is already hiring someone to block those windows up."

"And," Darcy chipped in the final piece, "when he knew we were getting close to figuring out it was him, he attacked you, Grace, and left us a note trying to scare us off."

"Right," Jon agreed. "And when that didn't work, he got desperate enough to attack me, thinking he could either kill me or incapacitate me, and sidetrack the whole investigation that way. He let his emotions get the better of him on that one, though. Broad daylight, in front of a police station." He snorted. "As soon as he hit me he saw half a dozen people out on the streets. He got scared and took off, waiting for another chance that never came."

There was a moment of silence, all three of them reflecting on the insanity that had unfolded in their sleepy little town. Then Grace stood up, stretching, rubbing at the back of her neck subconsciously. "Well, I for one am very happy you two figured it out. I'm glad to hear Lily came out of the coma, too. That's a bit of good news."

"Yes," Darcy said, her voice quiet and thoughtful. "I don't know if she'll ever forgive us, though."

"You guys saved her life, sis," Grace said. "That's something to be proud of. Anyway, I'm going to go…do some stuff. I'll be back in a half hour or so."

She winked as she said it, and Darcy's cheeks reddened to think her sister was intentionally giving her and Jon some alone time.

After she'd left, Jon got up to put the file away in the cabinet. When he came back to the desk Darcy stood and wrapped her arms around him, hugging him to her tightly. She laid her head on his chest and sighed. "I'm so glad this is all over with. Do you think we'll ever be just a normal couple?"

"Well, I don't have any more secrets in my past. So there's that. But normal?" He thought it over for a moment and then shook his head. "No. You're too special to be normal. But that's okay. I don't care what happens as long as I get to be with you. I do think that we need a holiday though." He grinned at her before lowering his head to hers. Their lips met in a kiss that warmed her blood and turned her thoughts…hot.

She was happy he was hers, too.

**-The End-**

# BOOK 3 - FROM THE ASHES

# CHAPTER 1

*D*arcy Sweet lifted her face into the cooling breeze that was blowing into the car through the open window. Her long dark hair was flying all over the place but she didn't care. She closed her eyes and just enjoyed the feeling of it.

She was tired all the way into her bones. It was a good kind of tired. After spending a wonderful long weekend in a cabin in the mountains with her boyfriend, Jon Tinker, she was ready to get back to their regular lives again. They had hiked through the forest and hills every day before collapsing exhausted into each other arms each night.

Not too exhausted to make the weekend…very memorable.

The weather had been perfect all weekend but it had been starting to turn cold and there had been a hint of snow in the air just before they had left. Summer couldn't last forever, she mused while she idly hummed along with the radio. It had been good to get away. They'd certainly earned it after the last few months, where murder seemed to follow them like a stealthy shadow.

She let her eyes slide shut, and with a sigh, relaxed her body further back into the passenger seat. It had been a long time since she had been that physically active, but it had been fun. It turned out Jon was a bit of a nature lover, very knowledgeable about the native flora and fauna, and he'd shown her a lot of things she'd never known, even living in a rural town like Misty Hollow for a big part of her life.

After a time she opened her eyes to check on their progress. They slid shut again on their own when she realized they weren't anywhere near to home yet. It was almost too much effort to keep them open. The road they were travelling was practically deserted this late in the evening. Between the quiet all around her and the drone of the tires on the roadway, she could feel herself drifting toward sleep. She decided not to fight it if it came. She felt safe with Jon driving. She felt safe with him in everything.

She sighed when she felt Jon's hand settle on her knee. Lazily, she opened her eyes to look over at him.

"About another hour, Sweet Baby," he said quietly to her.

She smiled at him. "Sweet Baby" was his new nickname for her. It had been something that he came up with this weekend, a long story that led to his calling her that during a very, very passionate moment. It made her smile and blush to remember it.

She was disappointed that their weekend had to end so soon. There would be others, she knew, but they would have to work them into their schedule of work and private life. She sighed, wishing there could be more time for just the two of them.

As if sensing her mood, he squeezed her leg and said, "We'll go away together again very soon."

His hand felt good on her leg. Maybe when they got home, she'd be awake enough to let him put his hands on her some more. She could feel her cheeks heating at the thought. He definitely brought out a side of her that few men had ever been able to. She liked that about him.

She drifted off to sleep with thoughts of Jon creating vivid dreams to occupy her mind as he drove them home.

As Darcy was unpacking her suitcase the next morning her black and white cat, Smudge, jumped up onto the bed and planted himself right in the middle of the clothes she was trying to pile neatly on the bed. He sat and glared at her, his green eyes flashing.

"Don't give me that look, Smudge. It's not like I left you completely alone to fend for yourself. Grace was here every day to feed you and I know she spent time with you, whether you want to admit it or not, so you can just stop pouting."

She knew he was upset with her for leaving him for the weekend, not to mention kicking him out of bed last night while she and Jon...said goodbye. Smudge had definitely been a little jealous that she was spending so much time with Jon these days. For a long time now, it had just been her and Smudge in this big old house her aunt had left her. He had been her best friend in the world, the only one that really understood her. He would just need some time to get used to there being someone else in her life.

Darcy pulled the clothes out from underneath him when he refused to budge. He rolled over with a surprised mewl and with one last dirty look jumped off the bed. He ran out of the room with his tail held high.

Darcy shook her head and grinned as she threw the last of her dirty clothes in the laundry basket. She heard Jon turn off the shower just as she was leaving the bedroom to head downstairs to make breakfast. She considered peeking in on him, but gave him his privacy instead. For now.

Downstairs she got the box of powdered pancake mix out along with the quart of milk. She mixed everything together and poured it out into the pan and then waited for it to bubble. She was happily whistling a little tune as she flipped the pancakes when Jon finally came down into the kitchen. It was still before eight o'clock, but it was a Monday and both of them had work to get to today.

He came up behind her as she was cooking and wrapped his arms around her from behind. He dropped a kiss on the slope of her shoulder as she leaned into him. "Good morning beautiful," Jon's voice trembled along her neck.

"Good morning to you too," she said. "Careful, you'll make me burn these." She didn't try to move him away though as she took up the last pancake and stacked it onto the plate. Turning in his arms, she kissed him quickly.

They sat down at her small dining room table with cups of coffee and plates of pancakes. Pouring syrup on hers in random patterns, Darcy sighed loudly.

He looked at her with those bright blue eyes and raised his eyebrows in a question. "So, did you think about my question?"

Yes. She certainly had. He was so darn cute with an errant lock of his dark hair flopping down over his forehead and she couldn't squelch the urge to reach across the table to push it back into place.

He grinned at her as he captured her hand. "Don't try to distract me," he said to her. "What do you think about us moving in together?"

Darcy shrugged and said, "I'm not avoiding the question. Believe me, I thought about it a lot this weekend. I'm just not sure how it would work with our two schedules and you having to do your police detective things and, I mean, what would everyone think?"

"That I'm a lucky guy?" She thought he was trying to lighten the mood but it fell flat. He looked at her intently and she couldn't work out what he was thinking. After a long moment he sighed and said, "That sounds a bit like an excuse to me." His eyes bored into her while he waited for her to respond.

She took a deep breath and said, "Okay, you're right. I'm just not sure about it. Don't get me wrong I like the idea of living with you but I'm also a bit apprehensive about such a big commitment." She screwed her face up as she tried to get her point across without offending him. "You know I was married and that relationship didn't turn out so great. I guess I just want to be sure this time. We haven't really known each other that long."

She could see he was considering her words. His eyes softened as he quietly said, "Feels like I've known you forever…" Darcy's heart stuttered at his words but before she could say anything he continued, "But okay, I admit the idea was spur of the moment. Things are going really well with us though, don't you think?" He said as he finished off the last of his pancakes.

"Of course I do. We're…we're good together." She couldn't quite meet his eyes. After she had divorced her ex-husband, there had been nights that she wondered if she'd ever find a man to share her life with again. Or ever want to, considering how she and Jeff had parted company. With Jon, though, it was like everything worked. They'd had their problems, to be sure, in a big way. They'd worked through it all, though, and they knew everything about each other's lives. It was as solid a foundation for a lasting relationship as she was ever likely to find.

"Okay, so then what's worrying you?" he pressed. "We've been through murder together. Literally."

"I know, and now everything is settling back to normal life and I love that about us, Jon, I really do." She stood up and took both their plates to the sink, bending down to kiss his ear as she passed him and whisper, "Just give me a little more time with it, okay?"

She hoped that would be enough for him. True, the little town of Misty Hollow had become a nightmare for weeks on end. That was all past them now, and even the trouble that always seemed to follow Darcy around had let her be for a while now.

Somewhere in the back of her head, though, that little voice kept nagging at her: "Yeah, but for how long?" Trouble seemed to find her even if she wasn't looking for it.

～

Darcy unlocked the front door to the Sweet Read bookstore and swung it open as she went inside. She flipped the sign over from "CLOSED, THE END" to "OPEN a good book today" and then dumped her purse and tote bag on the desk small office near the back of the store. She had closed the store for the long weekend while she was away and even though it had only been four days it felt like forever. There was so much to do to get the place back to how she wanted it. She grabbed a duster and walked all around, cleaning and making sure everything was in order.

It was very peaceful inside the store at this time of morning and she soaked it up. There had been too much upheaval in the last few months and she was glad it was finally back to normal, or as normal as it could be for her. She reminded herself that Jon coming into her life had been part of that upheaval. So it hadn't been all bad.

A little while later Darcy was busy rearranging a display shelf of books, bringing out ones that dealt with Halloween and Christmas, when her one and only employee Sue Fisher arrived at work.

The young girl gave Darcy a quick hug. "How was your weekend? Did you and Jon get up to anything exciting?" Sue took off her Fall jacket, smoothing out the wrinkles in her blue top, her blonde head bobbing up and down. Sue was a college student on a break from her studies for a year while she decided whether she wanted to continue with her law degree or not. Darcy was glad that Sue had decided to spend the time working in the bookstore, which she seemed to love doing. Sue had proven invaluable as an employee on more than one occasion. She was a whirlwind of energy and could often brighten up the darkest day.

"We had a great weekend," Darcy answered her now. When Sue smiled in that coy way she sometimes did, Darcy swatted at her shoulder. "Not like that. Well. Mostly not like that. Actually, I have something to show you."

Darcy went to the desk in the office and grabbed her bag as Sue followed her in. She carefully removed a couple of old looking books with dark, worn leather covers and placed them gently onto the desk. Their pages were a faded and mellow off-white, and other than the wear on the corners and around the spine, they looked to be in quite good condition.

Darcy enjoyed books for their own sake. In a world where the printed word was being rapidly replaced by mass-produced e-books, finding treasures like these here was getting harder and harder to do. "I visited a rare book store while we went out for lunch on Saturday and found these." She indicated the books lying on the desk. "I've been searching for something like these for quite a while now."

Sue was looking at the books with interest. "What are they?" She picked one of the books up carefully, like she was handling fine china, reading the faded gold lettering along the spine, then opening the cover to the title page.

"Histories," Darcy said with a smile. "They are histories of the old towns in this area and Misty Hollow is mentioned in them a few times. I haven't had time to read them yet, but I hope to soon."

"Oh yeah?" Sue asked her, that coy look in her eyes again. "What kept you from reading them? Hm?"

"Sue," Darcy emphasized her friend's name, laughing as she did.

"What? I like to live vicariously through other people." She humphed and carefully placed the book back down on the desk. "Randy and I broke up. Again."

"Oh, Sue." Darcy didn't know what else to say. She knew that Sue and her on-again off-again boyfriend were never going to work out their troubles, but it wasn't her place to say so. "Want to go over to Maxy's after work and talk about it?"

Sue thought about it. Maxy's had recently opened and was the only bar in Misty Hollow, a nice place with low lighting over tables that served red wine more often than it served domestic beer. Finally she shook her head, though. "No, that's all right. I was just going to have an early night. Some other time though okay?"

Darcy nodded. The bell over the door jangled as it opened announcing the arrival of a customer. Sue took the opportunity to end their conversation about Randy as she went to see what Beatrice Miller, one of a group of elderly women living in the town's assisted living complex, might want to buy today. Beatrice waved at Darcy. She was one of her book club members and a good friend. Sue was already lost in conversation about what book Beatrice might like to try today.

Darcy shook her head and made herself realize that Sue's life was her own and that Sue needed to make her own decisions about her love life. She shrugged and turned to pick the books up to put them back in her bag.

The one closest to the edge of the table shifted suddenly like it had been shoved and started to fall to the floor.

Darcy lunged to catch the fragile book, managing to save it in midair before it hit the floor. She let out a quick relieved breath. Just then she caught a ghostly whisper of a playful laughter echoing through the store. "Millie," she said under her breath. Aunt Millie had left her the bookstore, too. She just hadn't gotten around to leaving the place after she'd died.

Darcy tsked at the woman's shadow, knowing that her aunt had always loved to play pranks. She put the bag with the two books in them on the floor where there was no place for them to go. Unless Millie decided to pick them up and move them somewhere else.

"Good to see you, too, Aunt Millie," Darcy whispered as she went to help Sue.

# CHAPTER 2

*L*unch time came around very quickly. Darcy had plans to go and get something to eat with her friend, Linda. She found Linda walking down the street toward the book store and waved in greeting. Linda was a tall woman, graceful, and always quick to smile. Her red hair bounced in tight curls as she came toward Darcy in a flowing pink dress.

Linda wasn't alone. "Hi Darcy," she said. "Hey, welcome back from your vacation. Um. I hope you don't mind, but I was wondering if we could talk over lunch? This is Sarah Fender." Linda held a hand out towards the girl as she introduced her.

"Hello Sarah," Darcy said. The girl gave her a quick, shy nod. She had the smooth, flawless skin of the young. Darcy was a little envious of her beautiful shiny dark hair and deep blue eyes. Her clothes were very simple and plain. She was probably all of eighteen or nineteen, and very nervous about something if the constant twisting of her hands around themselves was any indication.

"Sarah is nineteen," Linda explained, meaning Darcy had been right. "She lives with her dad, Louis. You know him don't you

Darcy? He owns the Hometown Real Estate Company here in town."

Darcy did know Louis. By sight, anyway, but she'd never had any real reason to have anything to do with him. She nodded. "So, is everything all right? This was just a lunch date, right?"

Linda sighed. "Well, Sarah and her dad are really good friends of mine. I wouldn't usually do this, you need to understand, but for them..." Linda chewed on her lip, maybe trying to decide upon the right words. "We have a favor to ask you," she said at last.

"Okay," Darcy said slowly, not sure what they wanted. The other two women were looking at her intently and Darcy got the impression this favor, whatever it was, was very important.

Linda looked relieved. "Well, Sarah's mother, Angelica, died in a house fire when she was a toddler. You might not remember, because it was years ago but her family lived in that big manor house just outside of town on O'Leary Lane. The fire completely destroyed the house and it took poor Angelica with it."

"No, I remember that," Darcy said. "I don't remember much about it specifically but people talked about that fire for years after." She caught the look on Sarah's face and gave her an apologetic glance. "I'm not sure what you could need from me though?"

Linda put a hand out to rest on Darcy's arm. "Everyone in town knows that you're special, Darcy. You, well, know things. Things about people that are gone." Darcy raised her eyebrows but didn't say anything. Linda flushed a little and then quickly added, "Sarah and I have been talking and there's something that's bothered her for years. Something she saw that day and she can't let it go. She's haunted by it."

Haunted. Darcy looked at Sarah. She could see it now, in the girl's eyes. There was something to a person's eyes who had seen more than they should have. When they had seen something they couldn't explain. Ghosts, or spooks, or worse. It was a darkness that defied any light to touch it. Sarah had that in her eyes.

The world around everyone was supposed to be normal. Plain, simple, normal. There was more to it, though. The other side. The place where the spirits of the departed went. Sometimes, those spirits stayed here with the living. Not everyone could see them. Darcy could. Darcy had gotten used to it and even been able to use her talent to help others from time to time. More often than not it landed her in deep, deep trouble, but that didn't stop her from trying. She knew what it was like to see ghosts like Aunt Millie who refused to move on.

She knew what it was like to see the things that were worse, too.

Darcy tried to do the math in her head. The fire had been about fifteen years ago, just before Darcy had come to live with Aunt Millie permanently, so Sarah would have been about four. What could she have seen? What could a little girl being saved from a devastating house fire have seen to put those shadows in her eyes?

"Darcy?" Linda was saying. "Sarah really needs the kind of help that you can give. Like I say, I wouldn't usually ask this because I know how you don't like to talk about these things, but it's her mother. I knew Angelica, too. She didn't deserve what happened to her. She was a good, loving mother."

Tears slowly leaked out of the sides of Sarah's eyes. Darcy had already decided to help, but seeing those wet trails on the girl's cheeks cemented her decision for her.

"Do you think you could find out anything about that night for her?" Linda asked.

Hinting awkwardly around the subject Linda didn't actually come out and ask Darcy if she would communicate with Angelica's ghost but Darcy knew that was what Linda wanted her to do.

Darcy smiled at Sarah. "Of course. Any friend of Linda's is a friend of mine."

Sarah visibly relaxed and even managed a smile. Darcy was glad she had agreed to help. She just wasn't sure if Sarah would be ready for what came next.

"I'll need something that belonged to your mother," Darcy told her.

# CHAPTER 3

*D*arcy dropped the pen onto the desk and stretched. She had been slaving over the bookstore's accounts for most of the afternoon in between serving customers. They had done more business than usual today, and she was glad of that fact. There had been a steady stream of customers in and out all afternoon. Losing a lot of her customers to ebooks meant the book stores revenues had steadily declined over the past few years. This place had been Aunt Millie's dream and then Darcy's own dream as well. If she didn't find some way to bring in more cash flow, however, it might end up being just a memory.

That cold fact sat heavy on her heart but she tried to rationalize that it was just the way of all business. Further back in the store, three books fell off shelves in quick succession, *thump, thump, thump.* Darcy smiled. Aunt Millie didn't like the idea of losing the shop either.

She looked at her watch and was surprised to see it was almost closing time. The bell over the door jangled once more, and when Darcy looked up to see who it was she saw Sarah approaching the counter.

Cashing out a purchase for a customer, Sue's face brightened. "Hi Sarah. Wow, I haven't seen you for ages!"

Sarah smiled back. Darcy guessed it figured that the two of them would know each other, being so close in age. The two of them exchanged chit chat about their lives for a few minutes.

"I actually came to see Darcy," Sarah said after a minute or two. She rocked on her feet uncertainly.

Sue looked a little confused but took the hint. "It's good to see you again, Sarah. We should get together and do something some time."

Sarah seemed to be more at ease around Sue. "The last time we got together to do something," she said, "we ended up with that boy, what was his name?"

Sue rolled her eyes. "Kevin. Yeah, I remember."

"Do you remember almost getting arrested?"

Darcy raised her eyebrows at that. She would have never thought Sue was capable of doing anything to get arrested at all.

Sue slid a quick look at Darcy and then away again. "Well, we'll find something that doesn't involve church steeples, is all. I'll talk to you later, okay?"

"Okay." Sarah watched Sue walk away into the stacks of books and then turned to Darcy. "Thank you so much for doing this Darcy, I really appreciate it. I really know so little about by mother, and what happened that day. I have never been able to really get closure. Anything you can tell me would be such a relief."

Darcy nodded, reminding herself to ask Sue about churches and getting arrested later. "Can you tell me what you saw? What do you remember?"

Sarah scrunched her face up. "It was a long time ago. And it was dark. Except for the flames, I mean. But I remember seeing two figures at a window while the house burned. Why would there be two?"

Just like that, the good mood Sarah had put herself in while talking to Sue evaporated and the shadows were back heavy and dark in her eyes.

"I'm so sorry about you losing your mother," Darcy offered. "I'll try to help in any way I can."

Sarah nodded at her. "Linda mentioned you could...learn things that no one else could."

Darcy nodded her head. "It's a lot to accept, I know. I don't talk about it much so you'll just have to trust me, okay?"

The girl nodded at Darcy and then held out her hand. In it was a slim gold chain with little charms hanging off it. "This bracelet belonged to my mother. Will this work?"

"This will be perfect." Darcy took the piece of jewelery from Sarah's hand and held it up. The charms dangled and swung. A cat, a heart, a book. Happy things from a happy life.

"Great." Sarah looked at her watch. "I have to go but please, let me know if you, um, find out anything."

"Sure. I'll call you later tonight, probably. Or tomorrow depending on how things go." Sarah squeezed Darcy's hands in hers, and then turned quickly and left the store.

Darcy would try and communicate with Angelica as soon as she got home. Jon was working late, and it would be the perfect time. Hopefully she would be successful in contacting Angelica and then she would be able to give Sarah the information and closure she was seeking.

WHEN DARCY ARRIVED HOME LATER she locked the door behind her as she didn't need anyone accidentally walking in and disturbing her.

Smudge greeted her as she carefully placed her bag with the treasured books in it on the table in the entryway. He was winding his way around her legs rubbing up against her. "Oh really?" she asked. "Forgiven me just like that, have you?"

Smudge meowed and purred, as if to say, "Aw, how could I possibly stay mad at you?"

He stuck to Darcy's side as she prepared for communicating with Angelica. She placed six incense sticks in her ceramic holder and lit them. Soon a heady Sandalwood fragrance filled the room

She gathered up nine white candles and placed them in a circle on her living room floor with a little dish under each to catch any wax that might drip down. She lit the candles in order, creating the energy of the circle, and then stepped into it, to the very center.

She sat down crossed legged on the floor as Smudge paced the circumference of the magic hub she had created.

She held the bracelet that Sarah had given her in her hand and called out for Angelica.

Nothing happened.

Darcy tried again, concentrating some of her own force and will into the calling. She searched out through the circle of energy she had created. She searched in dark places where no one answered her.

After several failed attempts at connecting with Angelica she looked down at Smudge confused. She couldn't feel any presence of Angelica. Nothing at all. This had never happened to her before. Even if she hadn't been able to get any information she had always been able to get a sense of the person.

There was only one explanation.

"Smudge," she said, "I don't think that Angelica is dead."

# CHAPTER 4

    *E*arly the next morning Darcy was lying awake in her bed and was absently running the bracelet through her fingers. Jon had stopped by for something quick to eat the night before, talking endlessly about some case he was working on. The small town of Misty Hollow had become less and less of a small town, and there was always work for him to do. He had tried to turn the conversation to the subject of them a few times before giving up when she hadn't been very talkative. After a kiss that had turned into two or three more, he had left to go home saying he had an early morning.

She hadn't been able to sleep much herself, and now here it was the start of a new day. The failure of last night's communication still tangled in her mind with the same answer coming up over and over. She hadn't been able to reach Angelica's spirit, because Angelica wasn't dead. Which made no sense because Sarah was so sure her mother was dead. So was Linda. So was the whole town, for that matter.

Darcy decided not to tell Sarah or Linda yet, not that she would even know what to say to them. Frustrated with the situation she got up and started her morning. After a quick shower in nice hot water she dressed in a pair of faded jeans and a bright yellow T-shirt. With her comfortable sneakers on her feet she was ready to face the day.

When she finished dressing she put the bracelet in her pocket. Even though it was still early she decided to head into town. She wanted to talk to Jon about Angelica. Maybe he could shed some light on this mystery.

Darcy arrived at the police station before eight o'clock. She said hello to Sergeant Fitzwallis, the front desk sergeant. He was an older man with thinning gray hair but with a face that was hard as stone. "Jon's inside," he told her, hooking a thumb at the wall behind him as if she didn't already know where the Officer's desks were in the building.

She thanked him and he buzzed her through the main door. Four or five other Officers were already at their desks, busily working. Jon saw her from across the room, waving her over with a genuine smile on his face.

"What are you doing here?" he asked, grabbing her hand and pulling her into him for a quick kiss on her cheek. "I'm sorry, I can't do breakfast I've got a ton of work laid out for me today."

"No, that's fine," she said as she sat down in the chair opposite his at the desk. He looked really fine this morning in a crisp white shirt and a strong blue tie that brought out the color of his eyes. "I actually came to talk to you about something."

"Oh?" he said in a distracted way, reading through a piece of paper he held up off the desk. "What's up?"

Darcy gave him the quick version of how Linda and her friend Sarah had asked her for help in contacting Sarah's mother, the whole story about the fire, and then her failed communication last night. "I'm sorry, I know you're still a little uneasy with me talking about my, um, abilities."

He shrugged. "I'm in love with you. All of you." Still, he lowered his voice to a whisper. "That means accepting the part of you that deals with ghosts and feelings from beyond, too."

She smiled at his characterization of her abilities. She loved this man so much. Her sister, Grace, knew what she could do too, at least a part of it, and there were others like Linda who knew a little, too. But no one had ever made her feel like it was all right to be who she was, ghosts and all, until Jon.

"So, what?" Jon asked her. "You think Sarah's mother is still alive? Is that it?"

Darcy nodded.

"Is it possible that this Angelica just didn't want to speak to you?" Jon asked her. "I mean, ghosts don't have to pick up the phone when you call, do they?"

Darcy thought about it, her forehead scrunching up. "I don't know, I guess. I've never had trouble contacting the other side before."

"Maybe the bracelet wasn't Angelica's."

Darcy stared at him. She hadn't even considered that. She'd have to make sure with Sarah that the bracelet was, indeed, her mother's.

Jon tilted his head back and forth before finally nodding. "I'll look into it for you. Even though I'm swamped today."

He scratched at his neck and she knew what he was fishing for. "How about I make it worth your while."

His eyes lit up. "Tonight?"

"Tonight," she promised, feeling her cheeks blush. What was it about him that made her do that? She stood up, and hugged him tightly, knowing he had to keep up his tough guy persona here at the office.

"Love you, Sweet Baby" he said to her.

"Love you, too," she answered.

LUNCH TIME ROLLED AROUND VERY QUICKLY for Darcy. She knew she had to call Sarah and tell her something, but she had been avoiding it all morning, working hard at rearranging shelves in the bookstore that didn't really need to be rearranged. When the clock on the wall struck noon with a muted note, she sighed and left the store to get lunch. A new deli had opened in town just last week, and she decided to try it.

There were a few people in the La Di Da Deli when she walked in. Her friend Helen, now the town's new mayor, owned the Bean There Bakery and Café on the other side of town, which specialized in delectable pastries and cakes. The new place seemed to sell more sandwiches and that type of thing, which opened up the food choices for the townsfolk. In a town as small as Misty Hollow it didn't make sense to have two businesses offering the same type of fare.

Darcy ordered a chicken salad sandwich. The owner of the place, Clara Barstow, served her. Wearing a white apron over a blue dress, and with her light brown hair done up in a bun, she reminded Darcy of someone's kindly old aunt. Darcy guessed that Clara was around fifty, maybe. Her smile made her look younger.

As the weather was turning a little cold outside Darcy decided to eat her sandwich inside even though there were pretty round tables set up on the sidewalk outside the deli. As she sat eating, her sister Grace walked by the big glass window and saw her. They waved to each other and Grace came inside.

"How was your trip, sis?" Grace asked as she sat down at the table with Darcy. She was in her work clothes, a dark blue pantsuit with matching jacket. She'd been letting her dark hair grow out and it now hung down past the collar of her crisp white blouse. "How did you like staying in a cabin?"

"The trip was amazing and we loved the cabin. We went hiking every day and we had such a great time together." Darcy set her sandwich down. "I took a ton of photos. You want to see?"

"Maybe later." Darcy could tell her sister had something she needed to say. "I was going to come over tonight and talk to you.

I wanted to call yesterday, actually, but Jon and I are working on a case that sucks up most of our attention."

"Yeah, he told me. What's up?"

"Well I hope you got plenty of relaxation on your trip..." Grace sighed and continued, "Because I have some stressful news."

Darcy's breath caught in her throat and she could feel her heart begin to beat faster. "What is it?" she asked with panic in her voice. She had gotten used to horrible things happening in this town and assumed the worst. Darcy began to fiddle with the antique ring she always wore as she always did when she got anxious or upset.

Grace sighed out a breath. "Our mother is coming to town. She'll be here tonight."

That was bad news but not nearly as bad as Darcy had been imagining. She laughed with relief. "Is that it?"

"Isn't that enough?" Grace answered with the corner of her mouth twisting up.

She and Grace had never had a great relationship with their upper class mother, Eileen. Darcy in particular was just too different for their mom to understand or relate to. Her mother had always been embarrassed by her. But still on the scale of bad things that could happen, their mother visiting was not the worst.

"Why didn't I know about this?" Darcy asked. "I didn't get a call or anything from her."

"She called me Sunday. I didn't want to call you while you and Jon were on vacation and ruin your time away. Apparently she just decided on the spur of the moment to come up. Or, so she said." Grace was chewing her thumbnail. Their mother was not known for being spontaneous and Grace was clearly nervous about this visit.

Darcy put a hand over her sister's hand to calm her. "Remember she likes you better than she likes me. Me, she just thinks I'm weird. And there's something else that might keep her attention settled on me," she added with a grimace.

"Huh? What do you mean?"

Darcy looked up at the ceiling, tilting her head to one side. "Jon asked to move in with me."

"Darcy!" Grace broke out in a wide smile. "That's great. A little gross, considering he's my partner, but still it's great. Uh, it is great, isn't it?"

"Um...Yes, I guess it is." Grace gave her a puzzled look. "I mean, sure. I'm just not sure if I'm ready for it, you know?"

Grace pushed Darcy's sandwich to one side and leaned in to her. "Sis, it's been a long time since Jeff and you lived together. I get being nervous. But Jon is a great guy. And the two of you are great together. I've seen it. Don't let old ghosts get in the way."

Darcy had to smile at the way her sister put that. "Old ghosts." Her life was about old ghosts, it seemed, both the real kind and the ones she carried in her mind. "I understand what you're saying, Grace. Still...I just need to think about it."

"You want me to tell him to slow down for you?"

"No, don't do that," Darcy was mortified at the idea of her sister getting involved in her private life. "Jon and I will work it out. Really."

Grace tapped her finger on the table in a mischievous way. "I'll bet he's incredible in bed, isn't he? All those quiet, strong types are. That's why I married Aaron."

"Grace!" Darcy's face was heating up and she hoped no one was close enough to hear. "You're not wrong," she admitted.

The two sisters shared a laugh at the expense of their men and the moment helped ease the worry about why their mother would be coming back to Misty Hollow now. Still, Darcy had to wonder.

DARCY WAS BACK at work in the bookstore that afternoon with Sue. The younger woman was happily chattering away about Misty Hollow's annual harvest festival that was due to begin Monday of next week. She and Sarah had made plans to go together.

Sarah. Darcy had almost forgotten. She had to make that phonecall yet, but she still wasn't sure what to say.

Sue's description of the festival distracted her. A lot of the townsfolk would be competing in different recipe categories for all sorts of prizes, including the coveted harvest festival trophy. The trophy was a huge three foot solid silver replica of Misty Hollow's two hundred year old gazebo in the town square. It was a huge honor to win the trophy. The winner got to keep it for a whole year until the next harvest festival winner claimed it.

"Oh," Sue went on, "and all the food! I can't wait to taste Henrietta's jams again. She only brings them out for the festival. They are to die for."

Darcy appreciated Sue's flair for the dramatic. Henrietta was an older woman who lived quite a way outside of town. She was something of a local figure, making these amazing jams that she only sold once a year at the harvest festival.

Darcy knew she couldn't put off explaining what she had found to Sarah or Linda any longer. Of course, she wanted to have something to tell them, rather than the nothing that she had right at this moment. She left Sue in charge of the bookstore and went back over to the police station. She figured Jon would have found out something by now. She hoped.

There was a different desk sergeant when she came in this time. She could never remember this guy's name but he smiled and waved and buzzed her through just the same. Obviously, she was getting to be something of a regular around here.

Jon was at his desk, and when he saw her coming he didn't smile or get up to greet her. She missed half a step, a frown on her face. "Something's wrong, isn't it?"

That brought a short laugh from him. "This is our life we're talking about. Something's always wrong somewhere."

She knew he was trying to be funny, but it didn't strike her that way. Trouble always followed her. Everyone in town thought of her that way. She didn't want Jon to think of her like that, too.

"I spent all day looking over the files about the fire in Sarah's parent's house," he said to her, obviously missing her reaction to his little joke. "I even called up some of the police officers who worked the case back then." He looked at her intently as he said, "There was never any body recovered from the fire."

"What does that mean?" Darcy asked, confused.

"It means," he said, "that you were right. She could still be alive."

# CHAPTER 5

*J*on opened an old and worn manilla folder lying on his desk. "This is the actual case folder I got out of the archives. The fire was ruled as accidental. Wiring, is what it says. That would make sense. Those old houses usually have bad wiring. Sarah's father, Louis, grabbed Sarah when he smelled smoke and ran with his four-year-old daughter out of the house."

"Where was Angelica?" Darcy asked.

"Louis' statement says he didn't know. He'd been taking a nap upstairs. His daughter's room was next door. When he got downstairs, the fire was already spreading and the only thing he could do was get him and Sarah out." He turned a page. "The fire department arrived ten minutes after the first call went out. By then, it was already too late."

"And no body was found," Darcy stated.

"Nope. Louis went on to say that he tried to get back into the house but he couldn't and he was afraid that his daughter would try to run in after him if he stayed inside too long. Poor guy."

Darcy had to agree. Only…maybe not. "Why did Angelica get listed as dead if there were no remains found?"

Jon looked at the file in front of him again. "There was one police officer who said he saw Angelica through a window, trapped in the house while it was burning, but he couldn't get a second look because the fire was too strong. The daughter, Sarah, said she had seen her mommy inside the flames, too. The report assumes her remains were burned up. And since she was never heard from again, it was a safe assumption."

Darcy thought about it. Angelica, in the window of the burning house. Kind of like what Sarah said she saw. Only Sarah had seen two shapes, or at least her four-year-old mind had seen two. Hm.

"Well," Darcy said, "we should try to contact the police officer then to find out what he saw."

"Now you're thinking like a police officer. Only, I tried to do that already. His name was Grant Peterson, and he died a few years ago. Old age, I think. He was seventy-three."

Darcy smiled at him warily. "Well, we can still contact him. We just have to do it my way."

～

SOMETIME LATER DARCY headed back to the bookstore. She needed to get things ready for the book club meeting that was being held later that evening. The Sweet Read book club held meetings at Darcy's bookstore twice a month. She'd been doing the club now for a few years, and they'd gained a number of members. There were now thirteen of them who came on a regular basis. There had been five new members who had joined in the last month just after the tragic deaths of Anna and Jeff.

Setting things up gave her time to think about things. A number of the book club members were older residents of the town, women and men both, and she decided that the book club meeting was a great opportunity to grill some of them about Angelica and the fire.

Darcy sent Sue, also a member of the book club, to the Bean There Bakery and Café, after the bookstore closed, on a coffee and pastry run. Just before six o'clock the members started drifting in. Cora Morton and Evelyn Casey were the first to arrive like they always did. They were a couple of matronly women, always dressed primly with their gray hair pulled up into matching buns and they were also two of the biggest gossips in Misty Hollow.

Beatrice and a few others came in not long after. It looked like it was going to be a good turnout tonight. Even better, Darcy thought.

Darcy greeted them as Sue arrived back from her run to the bakery. They all helped gather up the chairs from the reading nooks in the store. People gathered napkins with pastries and cups of coffee and settled in. Conversation was a low buzz punctuated by laughter.

Dawn Wagner arrived just then. "Oh Darcy, Helen asked me to apologize that she can't be here today. She's doing some Mayoral thing or other." Dawn's eyes were wide behind her thick glasses as she spied the pastries on the table. She quickly moved over to grab a choice éclair and a cup of coffee.

The last four members, Isaac Gibbs, Tommie Sullivan, Rosie Weaver and Preston Morgan arrived together.

Darcy wasn't sure how to broach the subject of Angelica and the manor fire so she let the others talk about the book they had all been reading for the last couple of weeks. "Silver Twilight," by a relatively new author. A lively discussion ensued and Darcy sat back quietly plotting how she could bring around to where she needed it to go.

It was Cora Morton who gave her the perfect opening. Cora had been telling them how her son was a fireman in Stonehill, a large city about fifty miles away from Misty Hollow, just like the main love interest in the book. She was bragging about it, actually, and the conversation got bogged down around that point.

Darcy took her chance and started asking all sorts of questions about her son's job and Cora ate up the attention. Casually, Darcy asked, "Has your son ever worked at the fire department here in Misty Hollow?"

"Oh, yes," Cora said, delighted. "He started his career as a volunteer fireman here in Misty Hollow. Went to the city not long after, though. They pay the firefighters there, you know." Cora was nodding her head and puffing up in pride.

"Was he here when the Fender's house burned down? You know, their old manor house?"

"Oh sure. He talked about it for weeks. It was one of his first call outs and he was so excited about it. Sure was a tragedy though, that beautiful young woman cut down in the prime of her life." Several of the others agreed with her. Some wandered off to refill their coffees but most were paying rapt attention now.

"You knew Angelica Fender, Cora?" Darcy asked.

"Yes I did. Not very well, mind you, but enough to say hello in passing. I think we spoke a few times at the grocery store. She was always baking something, that one."

"That was big news around here, back then," Beatrice put in, earning a glare from Cora. "I remember the funeral. Buried her out in the cemetery on Applegate Road. Nice service."

"Buried her coffin, you mean," Cora argued, trying to gain control of the conversation back. "Remember? They didn't have a body to bury. No wonder, either, the way that place burned down."

Darcy's heart skipped a beat. So everyone remembered there had been a funeral without a body. No one had wondered, back then, about the reasons for the empty coffin. Now, Darcy had every reason to wonder.

# CHAPTER 6

"I can't believe that no one in town even wondered a little bit about whether Angelica died in that fire or not." Darcy was sitting at Jon's kitchen table after the book club meeting ended. She was looking over the reports that Jon had found and drinking hot cocoa.

He was splitting his attention between her and his case file from work. Whatever this other case was he was working was taking up a lot of his time. She didn't mind. He was hers, even when he had to pay attention to his cop stuff.

"Did you talk to Sarah's father?" Darcy asked him suddenly. "I keep wondering what Louis thinks. Does he believe his wife is dead, too?"

"I didn't even go near him," he said absently, making a note in his own file. "This was supposed to be a quiet look into the facts, remember? What are you going to tell Sarah and Linda?"

"I'm not sure." Darcy hadn't gotten around to calling Sarah like she'd promised. She felt bad doing that but she still didn't have any answers. "I want to wait and contact Grant's spirit before I tell them anything. I absolutely don't want to give them false hope. On the other hand I don't want to lie to them, either."

Darcy had convinced Jon to let her contact Grant later that night at the police station. Darcy didn't have anything that had belonged to Grant, so being in a place where he had worked was the best she could do. They were going to wait until late, another few hours, so that there was no chance of being disturbed.

The ringing of the phone in Jon's apartment made her startle. He smiled at her reaction and she stuck her tongue out at him as he got up to answer it. "Hello. Yup. She's here, hold on." He handed her the receiver without any explanation and then went back to his file.

"I've been trying to get you at home all evening," her sister Grace said to her. "When are you going to move into the twenty-first century and buy a cell phone?"

Darcy rolled her eyes. "Oh I don't know, probably the twelfth of never." She absolutely loathed the things. She'd had one for all of two days once. Turned out ghosts could make phone calls. She'd smashed it to pieces and never looked back. "Why? What's wrong?"

"Our mother arrived two hours ago." Darcy could hear the tension in Grace's voice. Her and Aaron's apartment was small enough, and with their mom staying there, tensions were sure to flare.

Darcy had thought about offering her house to stay in, but the arrangements had already been made, and she wasn't all that hot to throw the idea out, anyway. "How many times has she asked you about making grandkids for her?" she asked her sister.

"Too many. She's asking about you, too. Get your butt over here and take some of the heat off us."

"I'm busy tonight Grace, but I will come over tomorrow morning first thing."

"Oh no, uh-uh. You need to come over right now. Mother is insisting."

Darcy sighed. So much to do, and now this. There was no putting it off. When Eileen Sweet demanded, Eileen Sweet expected people to jump. "Fine. Tell mom I'll be right over." She hung up and handed the phone back to Jon.

He gave her a curious look. "Bad news?"

"I have to go and see my mother."

Looking up from his file, he raised an eyebrow at her. "You know, I had to hear about your mom visiting from Grace."

"So did I." Darcy got up and gathered her things together.

"Should I go with you?" Jon asked.

Oh, how she wanted to take him with her. He would be a perfect shield when her mother got too pushy. She sighed and shook her head, though, deciding to take it easy on him. "No. Thank you, but it's fine. I'll go over by myself for right now."

"Are you sure? I could always ask her what she thinks of me moving in with her daughter."

Darcy was shocked. "Don't you dare!" She playfully pushed him by his shoulders and it turned into him catching her around her waist and pulling him down into his lap. She sat there, nestled against him and slapping his chest. "You listen to me, Jon Tinker. You are not to mention to my overly stuffy mother anything about you wanting to move into my house, or about you sleeping in her daughter's bed, or—"

"Or about what we did in the cabin all weekend?" he teased.

"Definitely not that!" She didn't know whether to hit him again or laugh so she did both. "You promise me right now or you won't get any more of what we did in the cabin. Ever."

He laughed with her. "Okay, okay, I promise. But only if you promise to sit down with me and have a real conversation about me moving in with you."

Darcy realized she'd trapped herself. Somehow, though, she didn't mind. "I promise," she told him, leaning up to kiss him tenderly on his lips.

~

ON THE WALK over to Grace and Aaron's apartment Darcy tried
to get her head in the right spot for a visit with her mother. She
tried to be happy about her mother being here, tried to muster
some enthusiasm. It was her mom, after all. She fiddled with the
antique ring on her finger like she always did when she got
anxious or nervous about something. It was her Aunt Millie's
ring. All she could think about as she spun it on her finger was
how Millie had been more of a mother to her than her real
mother.

She had lived with her aunt for years, growing more and
more distant from her mother. It wasn't anybody's fault really.
Her mom just wasn't ready to accept Darcy for who she was.
Millie had been. She'd accepted Darcy without question.

When she reached Grace's front door she took a deep breath
and then raised her hand to knock. Before her hand even made
contact with the door it swung open wide with Grace standing
on the other side. Her sister grabbed her by the wrist and pulled
her inside.

"What took you so long?" Grace hissed under her breath. She
dragged Darcy to the kitchen where Eileen sat, drinking a cup of
tea, sitting like the queen of her domain.

Her mother had always been a very proper woman. She
looked older than the last time Darcy had seen her, with a few
more lines on her face and with her professionally styled short
hair completely silver now. She was wearing one of her trade-
mark fashionable outfits. Tonight it was a navy skirt and light
blue silk blouse, with a red silk scarf tied around her neck. Darcy
always felt like such a scruff standing next to her. The jeans and
t-shirt she was wearing today didn't help her feel any different.

Eileen looked her youngest daughter up and down slowly,
and then stood up and awkwardly embraced Darcy. Darcy was
surprised by the hug. Her mother had never been a particularly
affectionate woman. "It's been much too long Darcy," she said,
that same haughty ring to her voice.

"Uh, you too, Mom." Darcy couldn't keep the question out of her words. This was more attention than her mother had given her in the last sixth months combined.

They all sat down at the kitchen table. Aaron was staring blankly at the floor and Darcy guessed that he had already been harangued by Eileen to the point where he didn't want to say anything at all.

"Well I can only stay for a minute. I have something I need to do tonight," Darcy said with a smile, trying to keep the conversation going. They chatted a little about the weather, the upcoming harvest festival and other mundane things. No matter what they said, though, Darcy got the impression that something was about to be brought up that she wouldn't like. It would be time to make her escape any minute.

Suddenly Eileen speared her with a sharp look. "When am I going to meet this man you've hooked up with?"

Darcy stiffened. "His name is Jon, Mother."

Eileen ignored Darcy's reaction. "What's he like? Not that I would know, since you've never introduced us." She was irritated by her mother's accusation.

"Mom, we've only been dating a couple of months or so." Darcy was annoyed to see the relief on Grace's face that their mother was targeting her now. "He actually asked to come over tonight but I told him it was just family."

Aaron rolled his eyes. Thankfully Eileen didn't notice.

"I tell you what," Darcy said to her mom, standing up from the table, "I'll see you tomorrow. Maybe we can have lunch together. Me, you and Jon. Okay?" She said goodnight to Grace and Aaron and walked out of the apartment, proud of herself for not rising to her mother's bait. It might have been the first time in her life.

y the time she got back to Jon's and he drove them to the police station it was almost midnight. They used Jon's keys to get in the back door. The police force staffed only one or two officers each night, and right now both patrols were out on the streets somewhere. Jon showed Darcy the plain metal desk that Grant used to sit at, explaining the Chief had pointed it out to him when Jon had asked. It was just like all the others in the room, and it was someone else's now, of course, but it should still hold a connection to Grant.

Darcy sat down cross legged right on top of the table. She levelled a look at Jon and said, "Don't you dare make any jokes. This is necessary."

"Of course it is," he said drily. "How else would you do this but sitting your rear end on the desk?"

"You can leave if you want to. I know this sort of thing makes you uncomfortable."

"Your rear end does not make me uncomfortable."

She smiled at him. "Silly boy. You know what I mean."

He shook his head. "I can handle it." He moved back to lean

against one of the other desks and crossed his arms over his chest, watching her.

Darcy nodded and then closed her eyes. There was no room to use the candles here, plus it would take too long to go and get them from home. She breathed deeply and tried to tap into the gray fog in the recesses of her mind that was her channel to the other side. She didn't know how other people with her sort of gift did this. This was just how she did it. How she had taught herself to use her sixth sense.

In the mists of her mind's eye, a figure appeared. She was surprised that she could feel Grant's presence so quickly. A tall man, dark and shadowy, wearing a police officer's uniform and waiting for her to say something.

"Are you Grant Peterson?"

The figure never spoke. It never moved. Yet it answered her.

*Yes.*

"Grant, we need your help. The fire at the Fender home. What happened the night of the fire at their manor house? Did you see Angelica in the building?"

*Yes.*

Chills ran up Darcy's spine. The connection was very, very strong. Whatever Grant knew, he desperately wanted to help her. "Grant, this is important. Angelica's daughter, Sarah, is troubled. She thinks there's more to the fire and her mother's death. Did you see Angelica die?"

*No.*

Okay, Darcy thought to herself. That was less than helpful. "What did you see?"

*Tried to save her, tried to help her.*

"What did you see?"

*She was there in the house standing waiting for me, standing there. She waited for me until I saw her, waited for me then ran back into the flames, ran back in.*

"She went back into the flames? Into the fire?"

*Yes.*

"Is it possible she got out another way?"

Grant's spirit swirled and shifted. He didn't know.

"Thank you, Grant. I'm sorry for disturbing you."

*Not done, more to tell.*

"More?" Darcy got excited and had to force herself to stay calm to keep the connection alive. "What is it?"

*Someone else in the flames, saw them, think I saw them, another person standing in the flames.*

"Someone else? Who?"

*Look for the man who was there in the flames, I think.*

"You think you saw someone else?"

*Yes.*

Jon's voice interrupted her. "Someone else? Who?"

Darcy's eyes snapped open and the mists cleared away and Grant was gone. She reached for him, felt for him, but he'd said all he wanted to say. He was gone.

"Jon," she said in frustration. "You can't talk to me when I'm doing that. The connection with these spirits can be very fragile."

His face fell. "I'm sorry, Darcy. I didn't think."

"No, it's okay. I should have told you. I think Grant was done anyway." Darcy filled him in on what Grant had told her. "I'm not sure what it means. It doesn't prove she's alive or dead, really. And the idea that someone else might have been in the house with her? What do you make of that?"

He shook his head. "Since when should it be easy?"

She couldn't argue with that.

# CHAPTER 8

The butterflies were fluttering wildly in Darcy's stomach as she brewed tea and arranged some cookies on a plate. She took the plate to the table, barely missing stepping on Smudge once again. He'd been under her feet all afternoon. "Cat, you need to stay out of my way."

Earlier in the day she had called Linda and asked her and Sarah to come over. She was really worried about telling them what she had found out. This was always the problem with a request like this. She never knew what she was going to find out and when people started digging into the past the answers weren't always ones that people liked.

When there was a knock on the door just fifteen minutes later her heart skipped a beat. She opened the door and made herself smile at Sarah and Linda. "Hi guys, come on in. I have tea ready in the kitchen."

Linda looked at her oddly as they sat down at the table and Darcy poured them each a cup of tea. Sarah watched her every move, her hands wringing themselves again, her face anxious. "What have you found out Darcy?" she asked finally.

Darcy had already decided to be completely honest with her.

She just wished they could have taken their time a bit more. "I don't know how to put this, Sarah. Um. It might even be a little disturbing for you. Are you sure you want to know?"

Sarah was nodding before Darcy could even finish the question. "Yes. I'm sure."

So Darcy took a deep breath, and came out with it. "I wasn't able to contact your mother's spirit. That's unusual for me. So I had Jon do some research. Um. There is a chance your mom is still alive."

Sarah gasped and dropped her cup as her hands flew to her mouth. The cup fell to the floor and broke in two. She blinked repeatedly and otherwise sat there motionless. Linda sat frozen with her cup halfway to her mouth, which was hanging open in surprise.

Darcy was prepared for a thousand questions and she knew the answer to each one would only lead to more. How could she explain what she'd just said? Linda, of course, knew about her abilities and was quite used to Darcy just knowing things. Which was all well and good, but that wouldn't help her explain it to Sarah.

Unless she just spilled it all and let Sarah decide for herself.

"I spoke to Grant Peterson," she explained slowly. "He was a police officer who was there the night of the fire."

Sarah put her hands back into her lap. "Was? He was a police officer? What is he now?"

"Dead," Darcy answered her. "He's dead."

Darcy looked over at Linda for support. Her friend just shrugged and put her tea cup down.

Sarah cleared her throat and shook her head. "That's insane."

That was the response Darcy had been expecting. She didn't let that bother her. Too much. "I have an ability to, um, well... speak with the dead. It's a sixth sense. You're going to have to trust me on this, Sarah."

The girl laughed. "Just trust you. Okay."

Linda reached over and put her one of her hands over Sarah's trembling ones. "Sarah. You can trust Darcy. I've known her for a number of years and what she's telling you about what she can do, strange as it seems, is true. Let's hear her out."

Darcy was able to relax some knowing that Linda was there to support her. She waited for Sarah to nod, her eyes still focused on the table, before she went on. "Grant saw your mother that night in the fire. But he saw her run into the fire, not away from it."

"I don't understand," Sarah said.

"Well, I'm not sure I do either to tell you the truth."

"Did he… Dear God this is insane." Sarah took a deep breath and then finished her question. "Did the dead man say anything else?"

"Well, yes. He said he thought that he saw another person in the house with your mom. A man."

Now Sarah's head snapped up. "Just like I saw?"

Darcy wished she could just tell her yes and make her feel better. That wasn't how it worked, though. "I don't know. You saw two people in the fire. Grant said he saw your mom, and then saw a man, but he wasn't even sure about that. Could it have been your dad?"

"No." Sarah shook her head, rubbing at the corner of her eyes where tears had collected. "Dad couldn't get back in. He tried, but I was so scared and he had to stay out with me…"

"It's not your fault, honey," Linda said to Sarah. "You were just a little girl."

Darcy chewed on that bit of information. Louis hadn't been able to get back in to his wife. Not without leaving his little girl behind and afraid. What an agonizing choice that must have been. But if the man Grant thought he had seen in the fire wasn't Louis, then who would it have been?

～

THE NEXT MORNING Darcy woke up feeling more tired than when she had gone to sleep. Her mind would not stop thinking about the whole situation with Sarah. Having come up with no answers at all, it kept asking the same questions over and over deep into the night.

When Darcy walked to work through the town center she stopped in her tracks to take in the sight before her. She was stunned by how transformed the area was. Everyone had been very busy the last week setting up their stands for the festival and putting up decorations of colored leaves and stacks of haybales. The stands were set up on every available space and each one was decorated beautifully with colorful banners so that the area looked like a sea of blues, greens, yellows and reds.

Darcy saw Henrietta buzzing about her stand where she would be selling jams at the festival, now just a couple of days away. Darcy went over and said, "Hi Henrietta."

"Oh, hello there Darcy, how are you doing? Looking forward to the festival are you?"

Darcy smiled at the woman and said she was. Henrietta was a bit of an enigma. She acted like an old woman, with her cane and head of very frizzy, white hair. Her face and voice seemed so much younger, though. Darcy had seen her several times before and never been able to guess her age.

"You going to come and buy some of my blackberry jam this year?" Henrietta asked her.

"If I can get here in time. Last year I missed out, you know."

"Don't worry, Darcy. You're one of my favorite people. I'll keep some under the table for you."

"Thank you so much, Henrietta. I really need to go, though, or I'll be late for work." With a little wave Darcy moved on along the path towards the bookstore.

Her thoughts quickly went back to Sarah and her mother. Henrietta had lived in town for a long time, Darcy thought. She lived away from most everyone, too, so she might have a different take on things. Darcy made a mental note to catch back up with her and ask if she knew anything about the whole mystery.

Then she remembered she'd promised to meet her mother for lunch. She might have to put off investigating anything until after that.

DARCY WORKED her way through the morning with Sue talking about the festival and Sarah and even a little bit about Randy, her ex-boyfriend. When the bell over the door jingled she turned to see her mother walking in. Oh no, was it lunchtime already? Jon. She hadn't even called him yet to tell him they were supposed to meet with her mom!

Her mother was impeccably dressed once again in another fashionable skirt and silk blouse, this time a lovely pale yellow color. Eileen leaned in to give Darcy the same kind of quick hug she had the night before and then stepped back looking around the store. Darcy couldn't tell what she was thinking from her carefully neutral expression, but she was sure it wasn't good.

It wasn't like her mother to be so quiet but Darcy let her be. Sue wisely found other things to do that somehow always kept her on the opposite side of the store from them.

"You know," Eileen said at last, "it looks just like I remember. You really haven't changed it much. I could even expect to see Millie walk through that door any moment like she used to, exclaiming that some tragedy was about to happen." Eileen scrunched up her face. "She was a little strange, your Aunt Millie." She looked thoughtful. Darcy took offence at her dig at Millie. She'd been a wonderful woman and Darcy missed her terribly.

"This store has always had a strange atmosphere to it. Can

you feel it?" Eileen shivered a little, rubbing her hands up and down her arms.

"I think it has a great atmosphere," Darcy said stiffly, more than a little offended.

Eileen pierced her with her stare. "Yes you would, wouldn't you?"

Darcy knew exactly what Eileen meant by that. She was referring to Darcy's sixth sense. Her mother had never been able to come to terms with it. Darcy could sense the conversation heading into old, familiar territory so she decided to put aside her hurt feelings and change the subject.

"Actually, mom, the store isn't exactly the same. I changed the name and I've modernized it a bit. We've even added several new sections." She moved over to where her mother was standing and pointed them out.

"Oh yes, you have." Eileen wandered over to one of the shelves and ran a finger along the spines of the books. She slid one of the books out of its place in the row. Eileen ran her fingers lovingly over the cover with an odd look on her face.

She turned to Darcy holding the book up for her to see with a small smile on her face. It was a copy of "Pride and Prejudice."

"Did you know," she asked, "that I named you Darcy because of this book. I was going through a phase where I used to read this over and over. I think I was a little in love with Mister Darcy. When you were born I just knew I had to name you after him." She studied the book for a few moments more before putting it back in its place. "Silly thing to do wasn't it?"

Darcy wasn't sure if she was supposed to answer. Her mother never talked about her personal life like this. It was sweet, in a way, and along with the hugs and the attempts to be nice her mother was starting to worry her.

She turned to Darcy and with no warning asked, "When am I going to meet this Jon person of yours?"

The rapid change of subject threw Darcy for a moment. She

shrugged. "Actually, I was supposed to invite him to lunch with us but I haven't had the chance to call him." It was a little lie, but it was easier than saying she'd just forgotten.

"Oh really Darcy dear, that's not an answer. I think you should have us all over to your house to dinner tomorrow night so that I can get to know this new man in your life. Let's hope he's an improvement on Jeff."

Darcy didn't know how to respond to that. Her ex-husband, Jeff, had been murdered a few months ago. Was Jon an improvement over Jeff? Without a doubt. But Jeff and she had started to reconnect just before his death and she had been incredibly sad that he had been killed.

"Mom, how about we just go for lunch today? I'll call Jon and maybe he can meet us."

Eileen gave her another sharp look. "Nonsense. I didn't come all this way out here to the backside of the civilized world to not meet him. I'll see you at your place for dinner tomorrow night. I'll make sure Grace and Aaron are there on time. The Lord knows that was never your sister's strong suit."

She made her way to the door. Turning before she left, she gave Darcy another long look, and then she was gone.

"Wow," Sue said from the other side of a book stack where she'd apparently been hiding for a while now. "I've heard you talk about your mom. Your stories didn't do her justice."

Darcy sagged against the counter feeling thoroughly frazzled. She wasn't sure how she was going to get through an entire dinner with her mother. The one bright spot was that at least Jon would be there with her.

## CHAPTER 9

*L*ater that day when lunch time rolled around Darcy found that she wasn't very hungry. So she decided to skip lunch and take a walk out to the cemetery on Applegate Road.

In general, she tried to avoid the cemetery. Ghosts and spirits anchored themselves to the living world at whatever place they felt most tied to. That's why houses became haunted by those who used to live there, and why those same ghosts never moved on to haunt deluxe apartments in Beverly Hills. They liked the familiarity of what they knew.

Sometimes, the deceased ended up tied to their gravesite. It was a lonely existence for them, as far as Darcy had been able to determine, and it made many of them irrationally angry. That was a lot of emotion in one place for someone as sensitive to the other world as Darcy was.

It took her nearly a half an hour to walk out past the school and the town hall to lonely stretch of road where the town's cemetery was. It had stood in this same place for more than a century, predating the incorporation of the town, even. There was one corner of the place that had headstones from the early

1800s and another where there was only flat stones on the ground with names on them that might have been even older.

Darcy was very glad she was coming here in the daytime.

The rusted wrought iron fence around the three acre plot of ground had an archway that faced the street with Misty Hollow Cemetery written in metal letters across the top. Leaves skittered across the ground in a sudden wind. The grass was kept mowed and the trees inside the cemetery were ringed with red mulch. It was a nice, peaceful place.

The headstones on this end were newer, some with dates that were only a year or two old. Aunt Millie's grave was in here, too, next to her husband Frank's. Darcy decided to visit it later. Right now she had to search for Angelica's.

Up and down two rows Darcy searched, her eyes darting everywhere, catching fleeting movements of gray figures that she knew were the spirits that resided here. They kept their distance today, and she was grateful for it.

In the third row back from the front, Darcy found a short, squat black stone with the Fender's names. Angelica on the left, with her date of birth and death, and Louis on the right with just his date of birth and a blank for when he passed on, too. Darcy liked these kind of stones. They spoke of the dedication people had to each other in life.

Kneeling down at the site, she felt her hand along Angelica's name. She closed her eyes and reached out with her sixth sense and tried to feel anything of the woman who was supposed to be buried here. Again, there was only that dark emptiness. Nothing. Not only was Angelica's body not here, her spirit wasn't, either.

More proof that she might be alive.

Darcy opened her eyes to find several faces staring back at her.

She jumped back with a little squeak and nearly tripped over another gravestone before she got ahold of herself. The misty, blurred figures of two men and a woman stood there, faces indistinct, clothing matching eras of a different time, shifting in and out of focus. They drifted closer to her again and she held up a hand as if to push them back.

"I don't have time for you today," she whispered. "I can maybe come back some other time, all right? We'll talk then?"

They stared at her silently. She felt stupid, trying to order them around. They weren't even really here, in the strictest sense. Anyone else looking where Darcy was wouldn't have seen anything. Finally, one at a time, they started to fade away until only the woman was left. She was a young, young girl, maybe all of twelve in real life, with wide eyes and a cute face.

As the girl started to drift apart and disappear as well, Darcy suddenly had a thought. "Wait. Do you...do you know an Angelica Fender?"

The girl seemed to laugh at her, then shook her head, and with that she melted away.

Darcy sighed out a deep breath. Well, it had been worth a shot.

A hand settled on her elbow and made her jump again. Turning, she saw Sarah standing there, an embarrassed look on her face. "I'm sorry," she said to Darcy, "I didn't mean to startle you."

"No, no you didn't. I mean, you did, but it wasn't..." She inhaled deeply and tried to settle herself. "It's fine. I just wasn't expecting to see you. You know, here."

"I come here every few days to visit with my mother." Sarah looked down at the gravesite. "Seems kind of foolish now, if she isn't even dead."

"I don't know that for sure," Darcy said quickly.

"But you're pretty confident, right?"

Darcy twisted the antique silver ring on her finger. She couldn't lie to Sarah. "Yes. I'm pretty confident."

Sarah nodded, her blue eyes sad. "I don't know what to feel about that. If mom's alive, why did she leave me? If she really died in that fire, then why do I feel that there's so much more to what happened?"

"I don't have answers for you, Sarah. I'll keep looking until I find some though. I can promise you that much." She felt a little better when the girl worked up a smile. "Hey, I tell you what. My Aunt Millie's gravestone is in this same cemetery. Want to come with me while I pay my respects?"

Together, the two women walked down and over a couple of rows to where Aunt Millie's white marble stone stood. Next to it was Uncle Frank's, a man that Darcy had hardly known as a little girl before he passed away. On both of the stones, at the top, Millie had paid to have pictures of her and her husband colored into the glaze on the stone. They had been transferred over to the stone from real photos of them both, and they looked remarkably life-like. Millie's gray hair was done up in a bun, her eyes sparkled, and she was smiling.

Darcy knelt and said a little prayer, something she did infrequently but with conviction each time she did. When she stood up again Sarah was staring at Millie's headstone.

"Is that your aunt?" she asked Darcy. There was a strange look on her face.

"Yes, that's Millie. She was my great aunt, actually, but that's such a mouthful... What is it?"

Sarah was still staring at the gravestone. Without answering, she reached into the back pocket of her jeans and took out a slim woman's wallet. Zipping it open she removed a photo and handed it to Darcy.

"That's a picture of my mother," she explained. "I keep this with me to remember her by. Look at the woman in the photo with her."

Angelica had been a young woman in the photo. Long blonde hair swept over one shoulder, and she was smiling at the camera. Standing next to her was a much older woman, her brown hair already mostly gray. Darcy was shocked to see the face of her great aunt Millie staring back at her.

"Why do you think your aunt would be in a photo with my mom?" Sarah asked. "Were they related? Are you and I related?"

Darcy shook her head. "I don't think so. I knew my mom's family pretty well." Still, there was something familiar about Sarah's mother. Something about the eyes, she thought. "Maybe Millie and Angelica were friends?"

Sarah took the photo back and carefully put it away. "Maybe. I mean they both lived here in town. It is a big coincidence though, don't you think?"

"Yes," Darcy said quietly. "Quite the coincidence, isn't it?"

In the back of her mind, though, she had to wonder. Had this mystery just gotten more mysterious?

In the corners of the graveyard, fog started to lift from the ground.

# CHAPTER 10

*L*ater that night Darcy went over to Jon's. The mists that had given the town its name began to crowd in along her feet. They always came in when something was wrong, Darcy had found. She was shaken by what Sarah had shown her in the cemetery. She needed to talk to someone about it.

When Jon opened the door to let her into his apartment she didn't say anything, she just slipped into his arms and hugged him tight, pressing her face into his chest. She breathed him in and it calmed her. He let her stand there like that for several moments before he broke the silence.

"What's wrong?" Jon said as he ran a soothing hand over her hair.

She sighed that the moment of peaceful comfort was over, and gently pushed past him to let the door close. "Can we sit down? I need to talk to you about this thing with Sarah and her mom. And I really need a drink. Do you have any of that wine left?"

Jon raised an eyebrow at that but went to the cabinet to take out the bottle of dry red wine they had started a few days ago.

Two glasses in his one hand, bottle in the other, he met her at his couch in the living room.

"Thanks," she said as he poured her some in the long-stemmed glass. He took a sip of his drink and then leaned back next to her, loosening the top two buttons of the dress shirt he still had on from work.

He was patient with her, letting her sip and ruminate and take her time before she brought up what was bothering her. "I went to the graveyard today. To look at Angelica's grave."

"That sounds...well actually that sounds dreary." He picked her feet up off the floor and put them across his lap. Putting his drink down on the coffee table, he took her shoes off one at a time.

When he started rubbing the soles of her feet she thought she might swoon.

"Oh, yes, that feels good." She sipped her wine and let the warmth and pressure he was applying relax her body.

"So what happened? Did you see Angelica's ghost?"

She looked at him, wondering how he possibly put up with her and all her eccentricities. He was wonderful, she decided. That must be the answer. "No, I didn't see her ghost." She left out the part about seeing three others. Jon was wonderful, no doubt, but she didn't want to push her luck. "What I did see was a picture of Angelica."

"Oh? How did you see that?"

Darcy went on to explain to him about Sarah arriving at the cemetery, about seeing Millie's grave and about the photo Sarah showed her.

"I told her it was just a coincidence, but now I don't know. Why would Millie be in the photo with Angelica? What was the connection there? Is it possible that Sarah and I are related?"

"I don't know," Jon answered with a shrug and a very pleasant motion of his thumbs under her right big toe. "I guess you could ask your mom. I mean, she's in town."

"Yeah. That reminds me." She gave him her other foot to do the same heavenly things to as she dropped her news. "We have a date to have dinner with my family tomorrow night."

Jon's eyebrows rose. "In the middle of all this? Are you sure now is a good time?"

"No. With my mother, I'm never sure. How about you? Aren't you still busy with that case?"

He shook his head and ran his finger up her foot, making her twitch and giggle. "Grace and I finished it today. Bernard Munson was stealing scrap from around town for resale. So my night is free. I meant the stuff with Sarah and her mom."

"I know what you meant," she said, sinking lower on the couch to brush her foot around his chest. "I figure I can spare a few hours for my family. How about you?"

He smiled at her. Then he caught her foot and brought it up to kiss her toes. "I would do anything for you."

Yup. He was wonderful.

DARCY WENT to work from Jon's apartment the next morning, leaving him snoring in bed as she snuck out before seven o'clock. She wanted to get to the bookstore early so that she could talk to Millie uninterrupted. It had occurred to her last night that she could just go to the source with her questions. She might not be able to find Angelica to ask, but she had Millie.

She locked the door behind her and then stood in the middle of the store. "Millie?" she called out. It took only a few seconds for the vague shape of her great aunt to materialize, sitting in one of the reading chairs. She smiled at Darcy as if she was encouraging her favorite niece.

"Hi Millie. Can you help me with something?"

Her aunt nodded, moving her hands in a rhythmic motion that looked like she was knitting. Darcy remembered how she

used to talk with her great aunt for hours at a time about everything under the sun while the woman would sit and work her
knitting needles. The memory made her smile.

"You know Sarah? The woman I've been trying to help? Are
we related to her at all?"

Millie shook her head no. She tapped a finger to her nose, and
Darcy got the feeling that there was more to tell. Talking with
spirits was beyond frustrating sometimes. Some wouldn't stop
talking. Some never spoke at all. Millie was the second kind.

"Do you know anything about Angelica being alive?" Darcy
tried. Millie shook her head again, her face shifting from surprise
to sadness and a host of emotions inbetween.

"There's something going on here and I need to know what it
is." Darcy took a few more steps toward Millie. She wished she
could just reach out and hold her aunt again. She twisted the ring
on her finger. Millie looked down at the motion and smiled.
Darcy could tell she was pleased.

"Can you help me with any more information?" Darcy asked.
She watched as Millie's ghost rose and floated to the back of the
store, where the office was. At the desk, Millie reached up to the
shelf on the wall and with a wave of her hand spilled everything
on it to the floor.

Her aunt turned to her with a smile and a wave, and then she
somehow turned sideways and disappeared.

"Thanks. That was a lot of help," Darcy said sarcastically,
bending to clean up the mess. The shelf had been where she put
her personal books, ones she had read and planned to read again,
plus some knick knacks that were too solid to be hurt by the fall.
As she picked everything up and put it back in place she found
something she'd forgotten about.

Millie's journal. The little book with its black leather cover
had been sitting up there for a couple of years now. Darcy had
skimmed through it a couple of times after her aunt's death, but
it had been too painful for her to read properly back then. She

had shelved it up there with the intention of reading it later. She hadn't thought about it in forever. Inside it were her aunt's observations of the town and its people and her own private thoughts. If Millie had anything at all to share with Darcy about Angelica, it would be in here.

"Thank you Millie," Darcy said out loud, hoping her aunt could hear her.

IN HER OWN VERY neat handwriting, Millie had filled every page in the book. Darcy enjoyed reading her aunt's almost poetic observations of the quaint little town she had lived in for most of her life, but that wasn't relevant to the issue at hand.

By lunch time Darcy had finished the book. Realising how hungry she was, she closed the shop up and hung out the back in an hour sign. Sue had taken the day off. Darcy hoped she was spending it with Sarah. The girl could definitely use a friend right now.

Darcy went to the La Di Da Deli. Clara waved to Darcy as she came in, the lunch crowd keeping her busy. When Darcy made it to the front of the line she ordered two sandwiches, one for herself and one for Jon.

They chatted as Clara made the sandwiches. The subject of the harvest festival inevitably came up. "I'm really excited for the festival this year," Clara said as she cut the sandwiches in half and wrapped them in wax paper.

Darcy inhaled the smells of fresh meats and cheeses with a smile. "Why didn't you open up this deli years ago? Come to think of it why did you live out of town for so long? You could have been making a fortune with this place all along."

Clara tensed up visibly as she tried to put the wrapped sandwiches into brown paper bags. "I couldn't have lived in town before now," was all she said as she put the sandwiches in a bag.

Darcy took the food and decided to drop the subject. Clara obviously had her reasons and just as obviously didn't want to talk about them. For now, Darcy had enough problems of her own to deal with. She paid for the sandwiches and with a last smile at Clara left the deli. She headed for the police station to talk to Jon about what she had learned in Millie's journal.

THE DESK SERGEANT buzzed Darcy through to the office. As she entered she could see Jon working at his desk. She stood just inside the doorway and took a moment to take him in. He looked so serious as he worked on the paperwork in front of him. When he finally looked up, his smile lit the corners of his beautiful eyes.

She walked over to his desk as he stood up to kiss her on her cheek. "I brought sandwiches," she said as she held the bag up.

"Fantastic. I'm starving."

They sat at his desk and opened the sandwiches. Inbetween bites Darcy told Jon about finding Millie's journal, overlooking how it had been Millie who showed it to her.

"It actually clears up a lot of our questions. We're not related, first of all, but Millie was a close friend of Angelica. She was almost like a daughter to Millie, from what I can gather. Sarah wouldn't remember it now, all these years later, but Millie and her mother were practically inseparable." She took another bite of her sandwich and chewed it thoughtfully. Jon finished up his sandwich and scrunched the paper up to toss it in the bin.

"Okay," he said. "That's not really helping us figure out what happened to Angelica, though. Was there anything else of interest in your aunt's journal?"

"There sure was." Her face split into a huge smile. "Millie had abilities like mine. She was able to communicate with the other side. In the journal, Millie said that our power has been passed through the generations and that our family is the oldest one in

Misty Hollow." Darcy had been so excited by this information. It helped to explain why she had such a strong connection with Millie even after her death.

"Really?" Jon asked her. "She never mentioned it to you?"

"No, she didn't, but she always took me under her guidance. She taught me it was all right to be who I am, to experience the things I do. My mother made me feel like a criminal, practically. Millie made me feel like family." She finished a last corner of her sandwich and then tossed her wrapper after Jon's. "Who knows? Maybe if she'd lived a little longer she would have told me about her abilities, too."

The journal said that apparently Misty Hollow had always been a hotbed for strange occurrences and Millie had been kept just as busy as Darcy was. "The last page of the journal speaks about Millie trying to help Angelica."

Jon sat up straighter. "Help her? Help her how?"

"It doesn't say," Darcy said, her disappointment obvious. "Millie knew the reasons and she didn't see fit to write them down."

With a sigh Jon stood up and offered her his hand. "So the search continues. Look, I'll dig around into what was going on in the town back then. Maybe there's an answer in there some-where." Darcy took his hand and stood up. He kissed her quickly. "Thanks for the sandwich."

"No problem." She looked at the clock that hung on the wall over the door. "I should get back to work."

Jon grabbed her hand, though, and pulled her back towards him. "Not yet. You surprised me with lunch. Now I have a surprise for you. It's out back. Come on." He tugged on her hand and dragged her out the back of the police station.

At the door he stopped and said to her, "Close your eyes."

"Do I have to?" He nodded and with a grin she let her eyes slide shut. She heard the squeak of the door as he opened it and then he guided her through. She felt the cool air caress her face as he positioned her just so.

"Okay, you can look now."

She slowly opened her eyes and there in front of her was a shiny new red and white Titan Pathfinder Mountain Bike. She was stunned.

"Wow. That's…" She was speechless. "Jon, what's this for?"

"It's for you. You've mentioned a few times that you should get a bicycle instead of walking everywhere. I saw this yesterday in the window of the bike store over in Meadowood. I couldn't resist. I could just imagine you riding it. Think of it as an early birthday present."

Darcy couldn't believe it. Yes, she'd mentioned getting a bicycle. Several times. She never thought that Jon would go out and do this for her, though. "Jon, I don't know what to say."

"Say you love it," he suggested. "Say I'm the best boyfriend in the world and you have no Earthly idea what you would do without me."

She couldn't stop grinning at him. "I love you. I love it. You are the best boyfriend in the world and I have no Earthly idea what I would do without you."

"There." He winked at her. "That wasn't so hard, was it?"

She slid into his arms. "It's getting easier by the day."

"Think how much better your life would be if we were together all the time, under one roof."

"Subtle," she said sarcastically.

"Subtlety was never my strong suit. I still think you should think about it."

"I am," she admitted, snuggling into him.

THAT AFTERNOON DARCY left work early to go home and start the dinner for the get together her mother had insisted on. She wasn't the greatest cook by any means and she spent an hour just nervously flipping through recipes. When she had it narrowed down to what she would be able to cook with what she had on hand, she set water to boil and collected ingredients from cupboards.

Smudge jumped up onto the counter and planted himself in the middle of the recipe book she was looking at. He stared straight at her with that way he had. "Smudge you're making me even more nervous. Shoo." He refused to budge, and she sighed loudly and gave up trying.

The phone rang right then. "Saved by the bell eh Smudge?" She raced to pick it up. It was Jon.

"Jon, so help me, if you're backing out of this dinner I may have to disown you," she said, only half joking.

"No, no, I'm not backing out. I'll be there for sure but I just found out something and wanted you to know right away." He paused and she nearly reached through the phone to make him say whatever it was quicker. "Sarah's dad, Louis, broke his arm and a leg a few days before the fire."

Darcy's eyebrows shot up. That was interesting. "Was it an accident?"

"He reported it as one, but the doctor made a notation in the paperwork for our department that it appeared to be caused by blunt force trauma."

"Uh, Jon I don't speak cop talk. What does that mean?"

He laughed at her and translated. "It means he was hit by an object like a pipe or a baseball bat. It's just the doctor's opinion, though. No one ever followed up on it and Louis never changed his story that I can see."

"It must be connected." Darcy sniffed the air. The dinner! "Oh my gosh I've got to go. See you later." She hung up before Jon could say anything else and raced back into the kitchen.

# CHAPTER 11

*W*anting to look her best Darcy dressed carefully in a sleek black dress, one of the few she owned. She had always been a jeans and t-shirt kind of girl. Tonight she wanted to impress, though. Her mother was always full of comments about the way Darcy dressed. She was hoping this way, at least, that would be one less thing for Eileen to gripe about.

She had managed to finish cooking the seasoned chicken breasts and pasta without any major disasters. The table was set, the salad started. She was even surprising herself.

The doorbell rang at exactly six-thirty. Darcy opened the door to find Grace, Aaron and Eileen on the other side. She put on her best smile and soon everyone was seated at the kitchen table while Darcy flitted about doing last minute things like putting the rolls in the oven. Without asking, her mom sat down at the head of the table. Sitting ramrod straight she folded her hands in her lap.

As her mother was checking her watch for the third time and raising her eyebrows, Jon came walking through the door with the cheesecake she had asked him to pick up from the La Di Da deli. Darcy swept over to him and took the desert out of his hands. "Thank goodness you're here," she whispered.

Jon kissed her modestly on her cheek and whispered back. "I'm always here for you. We should talk about Angelica later." Then, after introductions were made, he sat down across from Grace and Aaron. Eileen began to chat with him about the town, the upcoming harvest festival and his police work. Darcy was relieved that her mom was being so civil with him. It made a pleasant change.

Darcy served up the dinner which was surprisingly good. She got compliments from everyone, including her mother.

As the night progressed and things seemed to be going great Darcy relaxed a little. Eileen had been very well behaved and hadn't said anything inappropriate all night.

She should have known it was too good to last. Darcy was serving slices of the cheesecake when Eileen asked Jon right out of the blue, "So Jon, when are you going to propose to my daughter?"

The room went completely silent and Darcy felt the heat rushing into her face as her cheeks turned bright red.

"When the moment is right," Jon said without missing a beat, as if he'd been expecting the question. "We've actually been talking about our next step, haven't we Darcy?"

She sat down a little heavily with her own plate of cheesecake and stared at him dumbly. Somehow she couldn't help but think that her mom would know that he'd been asking to move in with her and, worse, that she had been seriously considering it. All she could do was nod and hope the truth didn't show in her eyes. She felt like a school girl caught making out in her room.

Eileen beamed, though, happy at the news. "Excellent! Don't wait too long, Jon. Life goes on without you if you do."

Grace and Darcy exchanged another glance. Their mother was definitely acting differently, Darcy decided. Something was up.

The evening wound down not long after that, with hugs all around and a handshake between Aaron and Jon. Even her mom gave Darcy another of those awkward hugs.

When the others had left and it was just Darcy and Jon, she turned to him and stomped a foot, even if she couldn't keep the smile off her face. "I can't believe you said that!"

"Said what?" he asked innocently, collecting dishes and bringing them to the sink.

"That bit about us discussing the next step in our relationship."

He came back to her, the table half cleared, the sink full of dishes, and pulled her into his arms, softly kissing her neck and sending an electric thrill up her skin. "Well, aren't we discussing that?"

She melted. "Maybe we should discuss it more. Upstairs."

The night had been nearly perfect. She had Jon to thank for it, and maybe even her mother a little bit. As Jon led her up the stairs, she wondered again why her mom was really in town.

THE NEXT DAY was Saturday and as much as Darcy wanted to sleep in next to Jon's warm body, she had too much to do. She showered quickly before Jon even got up and went downstairs to call Linda. She asked her to bring Sarah and meet her at the bookstore. No one would disturb them there on the weekend, and they could talk privately about what she had discovered so far.

She got to the store long before Linda and Sarah and used the time to reread parts of Millie's journal. Millie had written a detailed passage about recreating moments from people's lives and delving further into their pasts. Darcy wondered if that technique would work for her.

The bell over the door jingled as Linda entered the store, followed by Sarah.

"Darcy, what did you find out?" Sarah asked immediately. She looked like she'd slept in the red sweater and dark blue jeans she had on.

Darcy led them over to one of the reading nooks and when they were all settled in chairs, she started with the last thing they had found out. "A few days before the fire, your father broke an arm and a leg."

Sarah scrunched her face up. "Yes. He still walks with a limp. He always said it happened when he fell off a ladder. Why?"

"It may not have been accidental. Do you know of any reason why someone would want to hurt your family?"

"I have no idea. My father just owns a very small real estate business. There's nothing much there that could have gotten him into trouble."

"Could we maybe ask him?" Darcy suggested. "I wanted to talk to him, but I didn't want to do it without asking you first. Does he even know you've been asking about your mother?"

Sarah leaned back in her chair, her hands in her lap. "Dad doesn't like to talk about my mother. Every time I bring her up, he changes the subject. Maybe you'll have better luck. You can come and meet him tonight, if you want. He had to go into work for a little bit today."

"Good," Darcy said, glad that Sarah was okay with it. She really didn't know where else to turn.

"What about Millie?" Linda asked her. "Sarah told me about the photo. I knew those two were friends, but it never occurred to me to mention it."

Darcy was surprised that Linda had known about that all this time when she herself was only just finding out. "Um. Well, it turns out that Millie and Sarah's mom were good friends, like you say. I'm sure that's all there was to it."

She left the other part out, about Millie wanting to help

Angelica out. No sense in mentioning it until she understood it better.

〜

THAT EVENING Darcy rode her new bike over to visit Sarah and Louis at their home. Sarah answered the door to Darcy's knock and brought her into the living room with a nervous smile. Entering the room Darcy felt like she had been transported into another era. Dark, antique wooden furniture was tastefully arranged against oak paneling on the walls. A mantel clock ticked softly above an empty and clean fire place. It was like the picture of a perfect home in a Norman Rockwell painting.

Louis sat in one of the chairs, a newspaper open on his lap. He was a middle aged man with dark hair that was graying at the temples and thick round glasses perched on his nose. He had a kindly face and after all of the introductions had taken place he smiled at Darcy before asking her if she would like some tea.

"That would be lovely, thank you Mister Fender."

"Oh, please call me Louis. Mister Fender is my very elderly father." He grinned at her and then left the room to make the tea. Sarah offered Darcy a seat and they sat on the wingback couch facing the chair Louis had been in, a low and wide coffee table between them. They chatted about mundane things until Louis returned a few minutes later with a tray laden with tea and cookies.

They chatted about the upcoming harvest festival while they sipped their tea. Darcy was itching to ask Louis the questions they had but she wanted Sarah to direct the conversation. This was her father, after all. Eventually Sarah cleared her throat and put her teacup down on the table.

"Dad, we wanted to ask you about…" Sarah looked at Darcy for encouragement and then continued. "About Mom and the fire at your house."

Louis just looked at her and then put his cup down next to hers. He sat back in his chair and folded his arms across his chest defensively.

"We've talked about this before," he said shortly.

"I'm trying to help Sarah learn more about her mother," Darcy told him, hoping to ease his concern.

"I know who you are, Darcy. Everyone in town does. I know how you like to go poking into places you aren't invited. Why would you want to dig into such a horrible time? That fire was the worst thing that happened to me and you need to stay out of it." He punctuated his warning with a shake of his finger.

Darcy didn't let his angry tone scare her. "I'm sorry you feel that way, Louis. Don't you think Sarah has a right to know about her mother?"

He actually jumped up out of his chair at that point, scaring both women. His voice began to raise in volume as he spoke. "If Sarah has questions about her mother, I'll be the one to answer them."

Darcy wondered at his extreme reaction. It seemed totally out of place.

"Dad," Sarah said quietly, "I have asked these questions. You won't talk to me."

He softened his tone a little as he turned to her, crossing his arms once again. "Some things are better left alone, Sarah. Your mother's death is one of them."

"Is my mother alive?"

That simple little question stopped him cold, his eyes popping, his mouth open with no sound coming out. With shaking hands he pushed his fingers through his hair. "Why would you ask that?"

"Dad we aren't trying to upset you. Just, please answer me.

Darcy thinks that my mother might still be alive."

"Oh. Darcy thinks. I see. Well, Darcy needs to leave our family alone and not poke into things that are none of her business."

"I asked her to do this," Sarah started to explain.

"I don't care!" Louis shouted. "I said leave it alone!"

Sarah got up in a hurry from the couch and rushed out of the room. Darcy stared at Louis, not sure what to do. "I think maybe I should leave. I didn't mean to upset you Louis. Please...tell Sarah I'll talk to her later."

As she headed for the door Louis grabbed her arm and swung her around to face him. His fingers dug into her when she tried to pull away from him.

"I can't let you leave until you promise to drop this," he said desperately. "You have to stop digging. You have to promise me you will stop."

Darcy tried to keep herself calm. "Why? Why, Louis? What are you afraid I'll find?"

He dropped her arm, realization of what he was doing written on his face, and then stepped away from her. "Nothing. There's nothing to find, and you need to keep it that way. Now, please. Get out."

Darcy found her way to the door and left as quickly as she could, more convinced than ever that in spite of what Louis said, there was a lot more going on here than anyone knew.

The next morning Darcy cycled into town. She was thrilled that Jon had done this for her. There was a certain freedom in feeling the breeze in her hair as she rode and of being able to go wherever she wanted more quickly than just walking.

She was there before she knew it and took mental note to not leave home so early any more. She wouldn't need the thirty minutes to walk to work anymore.

She jumped off the bike at the beginning of Main Street. Her plan was to walk around town for a while, maybe clear her head and figure out another direction to come at this mystery from. She saw tendrils of mist in the shadows, being burned off by the rising sun, and did her best to ignore them.

In the town square everyone was working hard to finish setting up for the harvest festival. She walked her bicycle around, looking at everyone's booths, at the decorations, at the people rushing back and forth. Darcy saw Henrietta walking and waved to her. The elderly lady waved back and then steadied herself with her cane. Again, Darcy tried to guess the woman's age. Old, was the best she could come up with, chuckling to herself.

When she passed by Helen's stand she stopped to say hi. "Hello, Helen. Almost ready for the festival?"

Helen propped a hand on her hip and wiped her brow with her other hand. Her old button-up shirt and jeans were dusty and there were dark grass stains on the knees. "Getting there Darcy, getting there. Oh my you have a bicycle. How wonderful. When did you get that?"

"Friday," Darcy answered with a smile. "It was an early birthday present from Jon."

A middle aged woman came up behind Helen, waiting to be noticed. "Oh," Helen said finally. "Darcy, this is Elizabeth Archer my new baker. She's a damn fine one too. She's been a lifesaver for me, with all of my work as mayor now."

Darcy held out her hand for Elizabeth to shake and noticed that the woman had several scars on the left side of her face. Long, auburn hair hid most of them, but they looked a lot like burn scars to Darcy.

Darcy's mind jumped to conclusions. Here she was, trying to decipher a mystery of a burning house and a missing woman, and a new woman shows up in town at the same time, with burn marks on her skin. The face looked different, but people could change their appearance, especially if plastic surgery had been needed to remodel burned skin. And hair color was easily dyed.

Could it be?

"Where are you from Elizabeth?" Darcy asked, trying to rein in her suspicions and act natural.

"Around." Was all she said. She stared at Darcy with hard eyes and then turned on her heel and walked away.

"I'm sorry about that, Darcy," Helen said. "Elizabeth is a very private woman. She hasn't even really opened up to me. But she can bake like nobody's business. Here. Try one of Elizabeth's muffins. It's a new recipe."

Sliding her eyes away from Elizabeth she took the proffered

muffin lying on a brown paper napkin. "Thanks Helen. Lily isn't working for you anymore?"

"Oh, no. After all that business with her brother, and him trying to kill her, she had a bit of a breakdown. Poor girl. She's having a 'holiday' for an unspecified period of time."

Helen put air quotes around the holiday part and Darcy knew that the poor girl was probably under a psychiatrist's care somewhere. She couldn't blame her after what had happened.

Darcy took a bite of the muffin. It was wonderful. "Oh my gosh this is delicious."

"I told you they were good." Helen grinned at her.

Darcy chatted a little longer as she finished the muffin. Then she said her goodbyes and hopped back on her bike. The town was beautiful this early in the morning, adorned with the colored leaves of Fall. The mists that lingered were the only thing that dampened the scenery but she could ignore them.

Mostly.

IN HER BOOKSTORE, the door locked and the closed sign out, Darcy flipped through the books she had purchased about the town's history on her weekend with Jon. It was all interesting stuff. As she leafed the pages one at a time she was surprised to see a section labelled with Louis Fender's family name. She read that a few decades ago Louis' ancestors had owned practically the entire town and several of the surrounding towns. For a time, nearly everything around for miles in every direction was Misty Hollow.

That explained Louis having a job as a real estate agent. She wondered how much property he still owned from what his family had passed down generation to generation.

There was a knock at the door. Darcy looked up in confusion. No one would think the store was open. Not on a Sunday.

Through the glass front of the doors she saw Sarah standing there, a light gray hoodie closed tightly against the slightly chill breeze. Darcy closed the book before going to let her in. This was another piece of the puzzle that didn't quite fit and she wasn't ready to throw something else at Sarah.

Sarah came in looking sheepish. "Hi Darcy. Look I'm really sorry for the way my father behaved last night. I'm not sure what got into him."

"Don't worry about it, Sarah. Obviously we hit a sore spot with him. It could be nothing more than he misses your mom." Even as she said it, though, it didn't sound right to Darcy.

Sarah nodded, her eyes focused away from Darcy. "That's not why I'm here, though. I thought of something last night. It might mean nothing, or something, I don't know, but our house has been broken into several times over the past few years." She took a moment to shrug. "They never take anything, though. At least not that my dad has told me. The way he acted last night, I got to thinking maybe he's hiding more from me than just what my mom was like. Maybe there was something taken that he isn't telling me about? He reported it to the police each time," she added, with an expectant glance at Darcy.

"Okay, I'll ask Jon about it," she said. "He can pull up the police reports."

## CHAPTER 13

As soon as Darcy got home she went right to her phone and called Jon. He was off work today because of the weekend but he said he'd had some things to take care of, slyly pointing out that he wouldn't have to take care of his own place if he lived where she did. She had kissed his cheek and called him cute and now here they were, with her calling him for help.

"Hey Sweet Baby," he said to her, using his little pet name for her. "What's up?"

She told him all about Sarah's house getting broken into several times and that Louis had supposedly reported it each time.

"Hm," he said, and she could hear him snacking on something. "Well, I only looked into the things that were happening in town around the time of the fire, not since, so I'll check. First thing in the morning. Anything else?"

"No." She sighed. "I wish there was. Oh. I was looking in those books I bought on our trip, you know, the history books? Turns out most of the area all around here once belonged to Louis Fender's family. Including all of Misty Hollow."

"Wow. They must have been rich. I wonder what happened to all that money?"

"Who knows. I've never had that kind of money to worry about."

He laughed at her little joke but then cleared his throat. "By the way, I ran into Eileen today." Darcy tensed when she heard her mother's name. "She was acting strange, sneaking around town. It was like she didn't want to be seen. She was startled when I said hello to her."

"That might just be mom being mom." Darcy thought about it though. She'd already decided her mother was acting odder than usual. She wasn't going to burden Jon with that, though. She hoped it would just work itself out in time. Her mom couldn't stay in Misty Hollow forever.

She almost kicked herself for even thinking it. She loved her mom, but large doses of her were hard to take.

"So, want to catch dinner tonight?" Jon asked her.

She caught herself twirling her hair with a finger. "You could pick something up and come over here."

"I could do that, couldn't I?"

"Pizza," she told him. "With anchovies."

"Yuck. Only if I can have mushrooms on my half."

"Yuck to that, too." They laughed. "I love you, Jon."

"I love you, too."

Smudge jumped on her shoulders as she said it, meowing into the phone.

"Aw," Jon said. "Smudge loves me, too?"

Darcy looked at her cat. He lowered his eyelids and jumped away gently, landing softly on his feet and walking off with his tail in the air. "Uh, sure he does. What's not to love?" she told Jon. They said goodbye again and she hung up.

Smudge looked at her from around the doorway to the kitchen. "Well, you'll just have to get used to him, Smudge." She hung the phone's handset back into its cradle. "This one is here to stay."

THE NEXT MORNING she untangled herself from Jon and left him snoring in bed. Putting a note on the table, she reminded him to look into the break in reports from Louis Fender, and said she loved him. Biting her lip, she hastily added a little heart, feeling like a schoolgirl again with her first crush.

On her way biking into work Darcy stopped at the Bean There Bakery and Café to get a coffee. There were other places in town to get coffee, but this was Helen's business and Darcy liked to help her friends out.

The café was packed this morning and Darcy said 'Hello' to many of them as she walked up to the counter. Leo Hanway was in a particularly dour mood today and only grunted at her. She rolled her eyes as she turned away from him. He wasn't a very likeable man.

Elizabeth was working behind the counter, busily serving the breakfast crowd. The woman's auburn hair was pulled back into a tight tail exposing more fully the pale red splotches of the burn marks on her cheek. Darcy tried to examine them without staring.

When it was her turn she made sure to order one of the muffins that Helen had let her try along with her coffee. "You're really busy this morning," she commented to Elizabeth. The woman nodded without really answering.

"Hey, do you mind if I ask where you're from?" Darcy asked her.

Elizabeth shrugged. "I don't mind. It doesn't mean I have to answer." She handed Darcy the coffee and muffin. "If you really have to know, I'm from a little town about two hours north of here."

Darcy waited for her to say the name of the town. When she didn't, Darcy just smiled and turned to leave.

"Do you always ask this many questions?" Elizabeth said to her before she could step out of line.

"Not always," Darcy said. "Do you always avoid answering them?"

There was just a ghost of a smile on Elizabeth's face before she turned to the man behind Darcy to take his order. Darcy left the store, wondering about Elizabeth and her secrets and if she might really be the missing Angelica. She would have to tread lightly with the woman if she didn't want to spook her. Maybe she should ask Jon to look into Elizabeth Archer's past.

She would need to catch up with Jon later this morning and see if he'd managed to look up the police reports on the break ins at Louis' house. She could talk to him then about Elizabeth.

She felt bad sometimes, putting so much on Jon. It seemed like any time she got into these situations, she took up a lot of his time helping her find answers or peek into people's pasts. Well. He never complained about it. And she knew she couldn't do it without him. They were a good team.

Balancing the paper bag with her muffin and the cup of coffee in one hand, she walked her bike back down the street to the bookstore to open it for the day.

Sue came in not long after, chipper as ever. "Hi, Darcy. Did you have a good weekend?"

"It was...productive," Darcy decided to tell her.

They went through the first couple of hours in the store cataloguing the store and discussing possible new purchases. The mystery and horror sections were selling pretty well now, with the Halloween season just around the corner. The first customer didn't walk through the doors until almost ten o'clock, a mother and her three young children who Darcy knew pretty well. They were looking for kids books, new ones that they hadn't read yet.

"I tell you what," Darcy said to her, looking at the clock on the wall. "How about I have Sue help you with that. I have a short errand to run. There's a great new book we took in about a basketball tree. I think you'll like that one."

With a nod to Sue, she slipped into her light fall jacket and went to get on her bike. She figured she'd given Jon enough time to check on those police reports.

~

"I CAN COMPLETELY VERIFY that there is no record of any robberies at Louis' house."

Darcy was confused to hear that. She was sitting at Jon's desk at the police station, drumming her fingers on her knee. "That means Louis lied to his daughter about that. Why would he lie about reporting those break ins? And who breaks into a house without taking anything?"

"Are you asking me or just thinking out loud," he asked with a little smile.

"Well I was just thinking out loud but since you're offering your vast police experience, you tell me."

He sat up a little straighter in his chair. "In my experience, if there really were break ins to the home, and you're sure there were because Sarah told you there was, then it's one of two things. Either the person who did the breaking in is known to the homeowner, or there was something stolen the homeowner doesn't want anyone to know about."

"Like what?" Darcy asked.

"Like drugs, usually, or money that the person wasn't supposed to have in the first place. Things like that."

"Hmm. Well. Louis struck me as strange, and really nervous with me asking questions, but he didn't seem like the kind of guy to be involved in drugs. And even though his family used to be wealthy land barons he only runs a small real estate business now. I doubt he had any secret money that he was hiding.

Plus, Sarah said there were several break ins. Why keep breaking in?"

Jon nodded to everything she said, encouraging her that she was on the right track. "I think," he said when she finished, "that leaves the idea that Louis knew whoever was breaking in."

Darcy turned that over in her mind. Someone Louis knew. Like maybe Angelica?

"I did find something else out," he said to her, drawing her attention back to him.

"You're holding out on me?" she teased. "What do I have to do, bribe you?"

"Bribing a police officer is illegal. I do accept kisses in lieu of cash, though."

She rolled her eyes but gladly leaned across his desk and kissed his soft, warm lips.

"There," he said as he sat back in his chair. "Paid in full. I figured if Louis was trying to make false claims on his home-owners insurance something might show up in his financials so I went over and checked with Mark at the bank."

"Wait, don't you need a subpoena for that?" Darcy asked.

"Usually we need a warrant to search records. But this is such a small town and everyone knows me, so I can usually ask nicely and get at least a little information. Mark says there's nothing odd in Louis' accounts, just the income from his business and a few other small deposits here and there."

"Well, that's not unusual," Darcy said, waiting for something more.

"True, that's not strange at all. But the fact that his daughter, Sarah, is getting a check for a large sum of money every three months is. A different amount every time."

Darcy's curiosity was piqued. Why wouldn't Sarah have mentioned that to her? She didn't know the answer to that, but she was definitely going to find Sarah and ask.

It turned out she didn't have to look for Sarah very hard. Biking down the street back to the bookstore, Darcy saw her walking up the sidewalk.

Braking to a stop in front of Sarah, Darcy smiled. "Hi, Sarah. Hey, I was just going to go look for you."

"Really? Did you find something out?" the girl asked hopefully.

"Why didn't you mention that you were getting checks for money every three months?"

Sarah blinked at the direct question. "Because I didn't think it had anything to do with, well, anything. I won a scholarship when I was in grade school. Something for gifted children I think. I've gotten it all my life. Why would that be important?"

Darcy felt foolish now. Of course it would be something that simple. "I'm sorry, Sarah. I guess I'm just at a loss to find answers to all your questions. So you're still getting money from this scholarship? You're out of school now, right?"

"Well, yeah, but I'm not going to look a gift horse in the mouth, you know?" She smiled at Darcy and pulled an envelope out of her back jeans pocket. "Actually I'm going to deposit the check now. See?"

She pulled it out and handed it to Darcy. The check looked just like any other check. In Darcy's hands, though, the paper felt…prickly. Like there was something wrong with it. She knew when to trust her sixth sense. She studied the check closer, reading Sarah's name, the amount—seven hundred and twenty dollars—and the company that issued it. There was no return address.

"What's the Accountable Student Foundation?" Darcy asked.

"I don't know. The group that gave the scholarship, I guess."

Darcy saw the letters in the name of the company shift on the check. Like they were twisting somehow while they stayed still. Then the first letter of each word in the company name lit up, gold against the black ink.

Her eyebrows shot up.

"Sarah, what was your mom's middle name?"

"Uh, Sybil. Why?"

Darcy knew what her sixth sense had been trying to tell her. Angelica Sybil Fender.

Accountable Student Foundation.

ASF.

She had to check out her hunch, though. Even if her sixth sense was almost never wrong, she still needed proof.

"Sarah, before you go to the bank would you mind coming with me to visit Jon at the police station?"

On their way back to see Jon, Darcy explained to Sarah everything that he had told Darcy about the break-ins to Louis and Sarah's house. The girl was surprised and a little sad to learn her father had lied about that. She had to wonder what else her father had been lying about. Sarah just wished there were more answers to give her.

Jon was at his desk still. He looked up as she approached and smiled. "Wow, twice in one day. What do I owe this to?" The smile slipped a bit when he saw that Sarah was with her.

"Jon," Darcy said, "I know I keep taking up your time but this is important. Can you look up the Accountable Student Fund for me?"

"Of course. It'll cost you though." He arched an eyebrow and she knew what his price would be.

"Okay, okay," she agreed in mock frustration. "But later. At home."

She caught Sarah's look. The woman knew exactly what Jon was charging her.

He turned to his computer and did a number of searches, both public ones and official ones that she wouldn't have been able to access. Darcy watched him work over his shoulder and saw the results of each so she wasn't surprised when he shook his head and said, "There's nothing by that name." He looked up at her. "What is it?"

Sarah held up her check. "It's the name of a company that has been sending me checks from a scholarship I won as a little girl. How can it not exist if it's sending me money?"

Jon and Darcy exchanged a glance, and he nodded. Turning to Sarah, she said, "I think the money is coming from your mother."

## CHAPTER 15

*J*on's eyebrows dipped as he said, "What are you talking about? Where would she get all that money from?"

"The Fender family used to be very rich," Darcy theorized. "They made a lot of money off selling land around and in Misty Hollow. They owned tons of the buildings in town."

"Sure, Darcy," Sarah said to her, running a hand through her dark hair. "But my dad isn't rich. He just has his real estate business. The money that I get from this scholarship has made the difference between paying bills or not, sometimes."

"Maybe he didn't lose the money," Darcy said to her, "maybe Angelica has it."

Sarah thought about that in silence. "I don't get it. You mean to say, my dad gave all his money to mom so she could go live some secret life but now, rather than have any contact with me, she's sending us money under a false name so that we don't go broke?"

She was angry and Darcy couldn't blame her. For now, everything pointed to exactly that. As hard as her own mother had been on her when Darcy was growing up, she couldn't imagine what it would be like to have a mother who had completely abandoned her.

"There's something else," she said to Sarah. "I think that your mother is alive, and here in Misty Hollow."

Jon's expression was only slightly less shocked than Sarah's. Darcy hadn't planned on telling Sarah this part yet until she had more information, but in light of the checks and everything else, it seemed like now was a good time to test out this part of her theory.

"Would you mind coming with me to meet someone?" Darcy asked. Sarah bit her bottom lip and wrung her hands together roughly, but nodded and stood up, ready to see where Darcy was going to take her.

THE MORNING RUSH had subsided in the Bean There Bakery and Café. Elizabeth was cleaning down tables. Darcy could see another employee, a man she didn't know, busy in the back through the swinging doors with the round windows in them. Elizabeth looked up at her, then with a roll of her eyes went back to work.

Sarah pointed to Elizabeth when her back was turned. Darcy whispered, "Yes. Does she seem familiar?"

Swallowing, shuffling her feet, Sarah shrugged helplessly. "I don't know."

Darcy figured it would be hard for Sarah to know. She had been a young girl when she last saw her mother, and the only other thing she had was photographs. "Maybe you could be sure with a closer look," she offered. Then, raising her voice, she said, "Elizabeth, could you come here for just a minute?"

The woman turned, her auburn hair falling back for a moment to expose the burn scars, and then stood with her hand on her hip. "If you aren't here to order anything, I don't have time." She looked straight at Sarah, with no recognition and no change in her expression. "So, unless you want something...?"

It was Sarah who shook her head and told Elizabeth no. Then she took hold of Darcy's elbow and pulled her back outside.

On the sidewalk, Sarah leaned back against the wall of the bakery and closed her eyes. Darcy wasn't sure what to say. "You don't think that was your mother?"

"No," Sarah said immediately. "I saw her face. It's not her."

"But the burn marks," Darcy said. "Could she have had plastic surgery or something?"

"It's not her." Sarah was insistent. "My mother could have changed her whole face over and I would know. It's the eyes. I've studied her photos so many times, wondering what kind of woman she was like that I would know." Tears came to her eyes as she tried to blink them away. "I would always know by her eyes."

Darcy felt horrible for Sarah. They were no closer to finding out what had really happened to her mother. If anything, it felt like they had taken a giant step backward.

AFTER SARAH HAD GOTTEN AHOLD of herself enough to walk back to her car, Darcy returned to the bookstore. The festival was due to begin that night and everything was looking great in the town square. There was a sea of color as far as the eye could see and everything looked so festive. It made Darcy feel warm inside to know that something happy was taking place in spite of everything else.

Darcy and Jon were supposed to meet up with Eileen, Grace and Aaron around five o'clock, after she closed up the store, and walk around the stalls with them. There was always so much to do at the harvest festival. She didn't like that the festival would take so much time away from her investigation into Angelica's whereabouts, but one more evening couldn't matter, she figured.

All day she tried to think of some way to move this investigation along. She was convinced that Angelica was still alive. She was almost positive the money that was being sent to Sarah was coming from her mother. The questions that remained troubled her, though. Where was Sarah's mother? Why was she staying away? What had caused the fire at their manor house?

She tried to talk to Millie all day, when Sue wasn't looking. She caught a glimpse of her aunt, once, smiling and nodding like she was trying to encourage Darcy. Thanks, she thought to herself sarcastically. That's a big help.

Sue had been antsy since after lunch and Darcy finally took pity on her and let her go early to get ready for the festival. "Thanks, Darcy," she said. "Randy agreed to meet me and Sarah for the festival and maybe he and I will have a chance to talk about…you know. Me and him."

Sue's face colored as she smiled a wry smile. Darcy wished her good luck, remembering being young and in love herself. That was how she and her husband Jeff had ended up together, after all. She hoped Sue had better luck with Randy.

Around four o'clock Darcy decided to close the bookstore up for the day. No one was coming in anyway with all the doings in the square. She called Jon and he said he was free to meet her early, too. It was nice to know that Jon was going to be with her and her family tonight. Her mother was going to be with them, and she might need his calm support.

Leaving her bicycle locked inside the bookstore when Jon picked her up, they met up with the others outside of Grace and Aaron's house. Eileen was very polite to Jon and Darcy began to wonder if her mother was honestly making an effort to be nicer to her daughters.

They walked through the town, weaving in and out of all the crowds of people that were milling around, admiring all of the stands and booths that had been put together for the festival. There were colored lights strung between the buildings and all around the gazebo and trees in the town square. Darcy thought it looked a little like Christmas.

"This is wonderful," her mother said. "I had forgotten how pretty this town could be."

Darcy smiled. "I'm glad you're enjoying yourself, Mom."

"Well, I wasn't sure I would when I first came."

Grace rolled her eyes. Darcy caught her eyes and they shared a look. Yup. That was the Eileen they both remembered.

As the sun inched its way down toward the horizon in a clear sky, the mists collected at the edges of the square and around the buildings. Darcy knew what that meant. For the moment, she let trouble take care of itself. Maybe if she did that, it would iron itself out for a change.

Things were going great as they sampled some of the food placed out by the different vendors and bought a few little things here and there. Darcy said hello to several people she knew, including Linda who was with her mother and sister, as did Grace and Jon and Aaron. Eileen smiled at a few. She'd been away from town for a long time but was still recognized by several people, which surprised Darcy.

At one point during the evening, after the sun had gone down far enough to be only a bright line along the horizon and for the streetlights to come on overhead, Darcy saw Sarah walking with Sue. There was a young guy with them too, tall and pale and graceful in that way that some men could carry off so well. This must be Randy, Darcy thought. She smiled. No wonder Sue was working so hard to keep a relationship with him.

Sarah and Sue were laughing at some joke when Darcy and the others came up to them. "Hello you two," Darcy said to them. "Great festival isn't it?"

They both agreed. Sue pulled the guy with them forward by his wrist. "Darcy, this is Randy." She said it with a smile, and

Darcy couldn't help but notice that he returned it when he looked at her.

"Good to meet you Randy. I've heard a lot about you." Darcy shook his hand and then she and Sue began talking about the festival and the town and just general small talk. Sarah joined in, and it was good to see her relaxed after the way the past week had gone for her.

Randy told them he had to go help a friend for an hour or so but promised Sue he'd be back. They kissed each other lightly on the lips before he left. Darcy could see both of them were holding back because of the audience they had. Sue told him to hurry back.

The group went back to their conversation, Grace and Jon telling the story of their latest arrest of Bernard Munson for stealing scrap metal. When they were finished, Darcy asked Sue, "have you gotten any of Henrietta's jam yet?"

"No, I was just heading there now. I hope there's some left!"

"Wow, the way you've been talking about it all week I figured it would have been the first place you went." Darcy saw the look of confusion on Jon's face. "I don't know if you would have met Henrietta yet, Jon, but her jam is famous in town. We should go get some, too. She promised to save a jar for me."

"Hey, no fair!" Sue laughed.

Eileen cleared her throat. "Actually, Darcy, I'm pretty tired. Perhaps Grace and Aaron could take me back to their place now?"

Grace kept her face carefully neutral but Darcy could tell she didn't think much of that idea. Her husband, Aaron, saw it too. "I tell you what, Eileen, how about I take you back?" he said. "Why don't we let the sisters have some time together?"

The look of absolute gratitude on Grace's face showed the love those two had for each other. Darcy had always been impressed at how strong their marriage was. Her mom looked at her daughters, at Grace and Darcy, and smiled a genuine smile.

"Very well, Aaron. Thank you." She hugged Grace first and then Darcy, a bit less awkwardly then the last time. When Grace hugged Aaron, she whispered something in his ear that Darcy couldn't make out. Whatever it was brought a smile to his face.

As they started to walk away, Jon kissed Darcy lightly on the cheek and said quietly, "I think I'll help Aaron out. That okay?"

She hugged him tightly. "I knew I loved you for a reason."

"Hey, Aaron, wait up," Jon called out to him. "How about some company?"

"Well, I guess it's just us girls," Darcy said with a smile. "Let's go get some of that jam.

Henrietta was serving a few people at her stand, the once tall stacks of jam jars dwindling rapidly. Sue bounced on her feet when they were almost there. "Come on, Sarah. You haven't tasted anything until you've tried her apple-blackberry jam."

The four of them waited in the short line until it was their turn. Henrietta greeted Grace and Darcy with a warm smile. Her eyes twinkled in the glow from the strung lights around her booth and she wiped her hands on her white apron. "I was wondering when I would see you two. Oh, and you too, Sue. You never miss a chance to buy from me, do you?"

"Sure don't," Sue agreed. "I'm hoping you have some of my favorite left."

"Right here," Henrietta said as she picked up a small glass jar with a bright white and green label. "I have some nice raspberry this year, too. Turned out good."

Darcy and Grace looked over the kinds she had to offer and picked a couple of jars each. Sarah hung back a little, idly watching the rest of the festival. Henrietta made change for Darcy and then thanked her as she turned to ask the next people in line what they were interested in.

"You want anything, honey?" she said to Sarah.

Sarah turned back from watching a juggler with bowling pins. "No, thank you. I'm—"

She stopped, and stared. Darcy scrunched her eyebrows down as she saw the way Henrietta's expression changed from surprise to carefully neutral.

Sarah's hands shook as she put them up to her mouth. She stepped closer, ignoring everyone's stares. Darcy couldn't believe it when she finally understood.

"Mom?" Sarah asked Henrietta, hope making her voice tremble.

# CHAPTER 16

"Sarah, you can't be sure?" Darcy hadn't meant it to come out as a question but with so many dead ends resulting in nothing up to this point she was sure this would be another one.

Sarah put her hands down on the edge of the booth's counter. Henrietta swallowed but didn't look away. "It's you. It's you," Sarah kept repeating.

"Uh, Darcy, what's going on?" Grace asked her.

Darcy shook her head. "Henrietta. You know what she's asking, right?"

"I...I..." the woman stuttered, swallowed again. "I can't..."

"Darcy, it's her," Sarah insisted. "Look at her eyes."

Darcy did. At first she didn't see it, but then she called up an image of the photo Sarah had shown her of her mother. The eyes. The eyes were the same.

When she'd brought Sarah to see Elizabeth in the deli, so sure that she'd found Angelica, Sarah had said she would always know her mother by the eyes. That her mother could have had plastic surgery, even, and she would still know her by the eyes. Sarah had been right. Henrietta's eyes were the same ones from that photo.

It suddenly made sense to Darcy why she had never been able to put an age to Henrietta. Plastic surgery. She had paid to have her face altered to look older even though she wasn't. Apparently had the shape of her nose and cheekbones changed as well. But there was no denying it.

Henrietta, the kindly old woman who lived just outside of town and came in just once a year to sell her jams, was Angelica Fender. Sarah's mother had been here the whole time.

"All right," Grace said, annoyed. "Somebody needs to talk to me. What in the world is going on?"

"Grace I need you to arrest Henrietta," Darcy told her sister. "She's Sarah's mother."

"Darcy!" Sarah objected. "You can't have her arrested!"

"She faked her own death, Sarah. And ask yourself this. Where did the money come from that she's sending you? Why did your father get his arm and leg broken before the fire happened? We've solved one part of the mystery. There's a lot more to find out. Your mom has a lot of explaining to do."

"But Darcy…"

"No, honey," Henrietta—Angelica—said. Her voice was suddenly that of a much younger woman and Darcy began to realize just how complete her disguise had been. "Your friend is right. I have a lot of explaining to do. I don't want to run anymore. I don't want to hide from you anymore."

Angelica slowly untied the apron from behind her and let it drop to her feet. Tears were heavy on her cheeks. "I'm your mother. I'm so sorry, Sarah."

Grace took out a cell phone to call one of the officers on duty to come down to where they were. "You're going to explain this to me, right Darcy?"

Darcy went over to Sarah and put an arm around her

shoulder as Sue held her hand. "Once we're down at the police station, Angelica can explain it to all of us."

~

GRACE SETTLED them in one of the police station's interview rooms. Her, Darcy, Sarah, and Angelica. Randy had returned just as they were walking Angelica out through a gawking crowd of people. Sue realized how personal and embarrassing this was for her friend. She quietly wished Sarah good luck and left with Randy, promising to catch up with her tomorrow.

Grace had called Jon and filled him in as best she could, passing the phone to Darcy as she read Angelica her Miranda Rights before beginning what promised to be a very complicated interview.

"It's really her, Jon. I can't believe it." Darcy stepped away from the table a little bit and kept her voice low. "I can't talk now. Can you make it back?"

"Sure. I'll be there in ten minutes."

Hanging up she passed the phone back to Grace. "Henr— Angelica here," Grace corrected herself, "just waived her rights and says she wants to speak with us," she explained.

Angelica's cheeks were still wet. Her tears had washed away a layer of makeup that she had been using to make her skin appear paler. She had left behind her cane at her booth in the square, apparently not needing the device that Darcy had never seen her without. It was no wonder no one in town, even those who had known her before the fire, had recognized her now. Between the cosmetic surgery and the incredible act she had been putting on, Angelica had literally become a whole new person.

"I don't want to keep these secrets anymore," she choked out now, carefully keeping her eyes away from Sarah. "I've lied for too long."

"Mom..." Sarah hesitated when she called Angelica that, like the word was strange to her or hurt to say. "Just tell me why, please? You've let me and dad think you were dead all these years. Why?"

A sad smile crossed Angelica's lips. "There are too many questions in there to know where to begin."

"How about you start at the beginning," Grace said, her notebook out and a pen ready in her hand. Darcy knew the camera in the corner would be recording everything, too, but her sister had always been this thorough.

"The beginning?" Angelica repeated. "The beginning of the story was wonderful. When I first married Louis, he had just inherited the business and the family fortune. We were so in love in those days. Everything was perfect. We tried for a few years for a baby. I wanted a family so badly. Then I got pregnant with you, Sarah. I was so happy."

Darcy watched Sarah's face. She was lost in her mother's story, the untold story of her life that not even her father had told her.

"Louis was rich back then," Angelica continued. "I can't say that I married him for the money but it certainly didn't hurt."

Darcy nodded. "His family inherited money from the land sales they made."

Angelica looked surprised. "That's right, actually. When this area was first settled back in the 1700s, it was Louis' ancestors who got the land grant. They kept the area in the family until his great-great-grandfather started selling off pieces at a time. The money from it had amounted to a small fortune."

She took a sip of water from the glass in front of her. Grace scratched some notes down and waited for Angelica to continue. "Then something happened that I really hadn't planned on. Louis and I fell out of love. Oh, it was just small things at first and I figured, hey, everyone goes through this. We'll get out of it. Only, we didn't."

Sarah made a small strangling sound and shifted in her seat.

Angelica looked at her then with sympathy. "Oh, honey. I really didn't want you to hear about all of this. Ever. I was young, and stupid, and there's no real way to explain it other than to say it happened."

"What happened?" Grace asked, pen hovering over paper.

Angelica's eyes took on a faraway look. "I fell in love. Again. His name was Milton Strader. He swept me off my feet and made me feel like I was sixteen again. We fell so hard and so fast that we…well, we decided to do something stupid."

"No. Oh, no," Sarah whispered.

"Did Louis know about the affair?" Grace asked her.

Angelica hesitated, and then she nodded. "Yes. He found us one day, a few weeks before the fire at the manor house. He was so mad. I'd never seen him that mad. He rushed Milton and kept punching him and Milton did the only thing he could." She took a deep breath, the memory obviously painful. "He defended himself. He hit Louis with a baseball bat. Ended up fracturing poor Louis' arm."

There was silence as everyone in the room soaked that in. Then Grace prompted, "Then what happened, Angelica?"

"Well. Louis ran. He just ran to his car and drove away. He was so mad or so in pain or something that he drove the car into a ditch and broke his leg, too. He was so embarrassed by the whole thing and by what I had done that he just told everyone his injuries all came from the accident. It was just easier. I never told anyone the truth."

Sarah had been wringing her hands over and over. Now she clenched her jaw together as her face reddened.

"I knew," Angelica said slowly, "that I couldn't stay with Louis after that. But I couldn't leave him, either. He wouldn't give me a divorce. What's more, without him I had no money. No way to support myself. Milton was the love of my life but he had nothing, either. So together we devised that stupid idea."

"You stole from Louis," Darcy guessed. "Then you planned out a way to disappear."

"I didn't steal everything he had. Just what I figured was mine. Just half."

"It was marital property," Grace pointed out in a matter-of-fact tone. "You didn't steal it. It was as much yours as his."

She looked at Grace like a ton of bricks had just fallen on her. "I...didn't know that. I swear, I didn't. I thought I would be kicked out into the cold with nothing."

"My great aunt Millie was a friend of yours back then," Darcy said. Grace raised an eyebrow to that but didn't interrupt her sister. "I found her journal a little while ago. The last thing she ever wrote in it was that she wanted to help you fix a mistake you had made. I take it she knew about you taking the money? About you wanting to leave?"

Angelica nodded enthusiastically. "Good old Millie. She tried to talk me out of it. She said I should stick it out for your sake, Sarah. I should have listened. I should have listened. I was young, though, and in love, and I thought I knew best." She glanced at her daughter and then quickly looked away again. "Not that any of that is a good excuse."

"No," Sarah said in a clipped voice. "It's not."

"Tell us about the manor fire, Angelica," Grace said to get the interview back on track again.

"I set it, of course." She said it so matter-of-factly that Darcy wasn't sure she'd heard it correctly at first. She looked at each of the women in turn, reading their shocked expressions correctly. "It was the only way I saw out of the situation. I was going to disappear with Milton. It was a Monday evening, I remember, and I had the whole house to myself. I picked up Milton, we went there together, and I packed only the things that meant the most to me. While I did that, Milton messed with the electrical box and then stuffed it full of old rags. A few sparks later, the place was on fire."

"But I was in there!" Sarah shouted, standing up from the table, her hands fisted at her sides as she yelled out her frustrations. "Dad was in there! You nearly killed us both!"

Tears started in Angelica's eyes again. "I'm sorry. Oh, honey I'm so sorry. You weren't supposed to be home. When I left, Louis said he was going to take you to his mother's for the night to visit. I couldn't have known he didn't go. We were sleeping in separate bedrooms at that point and you were in his room. For all I know he heard me in the house and just didn't say anything because we were fighting all the time. If I had known, oh Sarah if I'd only known, I never would have put you in danger."

"Really?" her daughter quipped. "You didn't have any trouble abandoning me."

Angelica wiped at her tears, smearing makeup as she did. "That's where you're wrong. I never stopped thinking about you. I never stopped regretting leaving you. I walked away from your father, not you. I just didn't see how I could take you with me. With the money I had stolen," she glanced at Grace as she said that, "Milton and I set up new lives. New identities, new names. I even had some plastic surgery done. But I kept coming back. I couldn't help it. I kept coming back to the house to check up on you."

The break-ins, Darcy realized. The break-ins had been Angelica coming back to check on her daughter. That was why there was never anything reported stolen. If Angelca had taken a photograph or two from Louis' house, he would never report it. She probably could have robbed him blind, and he wouldn't have reported it, for that matter. He just told Sarah that he had to keep her from knowing. Which meant...

"Louis knew you were still alive, didn't he?" Darcy asked. Grace smiled quickly at her sister, pleased with that bit of deductive reasoning.

Sarah held her breath until her mother answered. "I think so. Well. I know so, even if I can't prove it. He saw me in the window of the manor house the night of the fire. I made sure of it. It was supposed to be part of the act so everyone would think that I perished in the flames."

She looked again at her daughter, who turned away in disgust. "I'm sorry, Sarah. I'm so, so sorry."

Sarah tried to answer but her voice was too choked up. Shaking her head, she rushed from the room.

*J*on arrived at the station a few minutes later. The interview was over and Grace was already typing up the reports. Darcy sat with Jon to fill him in.

"When I first saw the photograph that Sarah showed me of her mom I thought there was something familiar about her. Something about her eyes. It turns out I was remembering what Henrietta's eyes looked like."

"You mean Angelica, right?" Jon clarified.

"Right. I know, it's hard to believe. She paid for facial reconstruction, dyed her hair white, walked with a cane. She did everything she could to keep people from recognizing her, all so she could be in town once a year to catch a glimpse of her daughter."

"Hard to hate her when she did all that, I guess."

"Well. Sarah isn't about to forgive her anytime soon. She's been here in town with her daughter for years, keeping away from everyone. Sarah never went up to Henrietta's stand before so there was no way she could have known her mom was right there. That's a lot of hurt to get past. She thought her mother was dead all these years."

"Don't forget," Jon said. "Her father's been lying to her all this time, too. So now she has reason to hate them both. She's going to need a good friend to help her through this."

He looked at her in that way he had and Darcy knew what he meant. "I plan on checking up on her tomorrow. And Sue and Linda said they'd do the same. Between the three of us, she'll always have someone to talk to."

His hand found hers across his desk. "You're a good person, Darcy Sweet. Very few people I know would put this much effort into helping someone out that they hardly knew."

Darcy shrugged, a little embarrassed by his compliment. "So is Angelica in a lot of trouble?"

"Yes. She may have thought she had reasons for what she did, but she still broke the law and put a lot of people in danger, including her own daughter. That boyfriend of hers, too, that Milton guy."

"Right. Too bad he died."

Angelica had further explained that after being together with Milton for nearly eight years, he had died of an undiagnosed heart condition. That had left her all alone and it was right around that time when she started showing up in town as Henrietta, kindly old woman. She had missed her family so much but that was the only way she could think of to see them again. That, and breaking into Louis' house.

It had been Milton that Sarah saw the night of the fire in the window with her mother. Just four years old, she couldn't describe him or even explain fully what she had seen. It had been Milton who the ghost of Officer Grant Peterson had told her about seeing as he tried to save Angelica from the fire, not realizing that she didn't need saving.

All of it fit together nicely, now that they had Angelica's confession. She had even shed a little more light on the checks that Sarah had gotten all of her life. That was money from a trust fund account Angelica had set up for her daughter with part of the money she had taken with her when she'd disappeared. It matured at different rates based on the stock market, and that was why the amount was always different. It really had eaten at her, leaving her daughter behind. So she gave what she could to make sure her daughter would never want for anything.

Angelica just hadn't realized her daughter only really wanted one thing. She had only wanted her mother back.

"Now that she has her mom in her life again," Jon said, coming around the desk to Darcy, "maybe the two of them can find some way to reconcile."

She stood up with him and folded herself into his arms. "Maybe. I hope so, anyway."

"Let me talk to Grace for a minute and then I'll drive you home," he told her. "No sense both of us being up until dawn."

Darcy looked at him, waiting.

"What?" he finally asked her.

"I'm waiting for you to say something about how it would be easier if you moved in with me and then you wouldn't have to go home to your lonely apartment when you get done."

He laughed and took her hand in his. "I could still do it if you want me to. Seriously, though, I think I've said enough on that subject for now. You know what feels right for you. I'll go along with whatever you decide. As long as I have you."

Darcy leaned her head against his shoulder. She loved this man so much. "You'll always have me, Jon."

He pulled her into a deep kiss, and didn't let her go until the room spun around her. "I love you, Sweet Baby."

"I love you, too."

## CHAPTER 18

*L*ater that week Darcy was at Grace and Aaron's saying goodbye to their mother. Darcy knew there was something her mother was still not telling her. She was determined to find out what was going on before she left.

"Okay Mom, what gives?" Darcy crossed her arms and held her mother's gaze. "All visit long you've been acting strange."

"She's right, Mom," Grace said in agreement. "We know something is up. Might as well tell us. You can't hide it from a couple of ace detectives like me and Darcy."

"Mmm…" Eileen looked thoughtfully at Darcy and then at Grace. Finally she sighed loudly and threw her hands in the air. "Okay. You're right. There is something going on. I just didn't know how to tell you girls."

"You're not sick are you?" Grace asked. "I remember you had that scare at your last checkup."

Eileen shook her head. "No, no, it's nothing like that. It's a good thing, actually." She paused and looked intently at the two of them again with a wide smile. "I'm getting married again."

"Married!" Darcy and Grace exclaimed together.

Eileen laughed then. "Yes, married. You make it sound like it

375

would never happen for me again. You have your wonderful Aaron, Grace. Darcy, your Jon seems like a wonderful man. Is there some reason that I shouldn't be happy, too?"

"We didn't mean it that way, Mom," Darcy said to her while Grace asked who the person was and if it was anyone they knew and when could they meet him and so on until Eileen finally held a hand up to ask her to wait.

"He is a perfectly nice man. His name is James Bollinger. You've never met him. He's a retired businessman. What else do you want to know?"

"Everything," Darcy told her. "You wait until you're leaving to drop this on us?"

They laughed together, and Darcy couldn't remember the last time they had been this happy to be together. Eileen went on to tell them all about how they had met on a cruise last year. Darcy and Grace asked her questions until they had no more questions to ask. Then all too soon, it was time to say goodbye.

Darcy noticed that the hugs between them weren't so awkward this time.

A FEW DAYS later Darcy was in her kitchen washing dishes, Smudge winding his way between her legs, when a car horn blasted out front of her house. Confused, she looked up at the clock. It was just after six thirty. Who would be visiting now, and why would they beep the horn instead of coming to the door?

She went outside to find Jon, sitting in his car, smiling at her. He honked the horn once more and then got out of the car, running over to her to pick her up and swing her around until she squealed.

"I have a surprise for you," he said when he put her back down. "How about we go back to the cabin this weekend to celebrate?"

"Celebrate? Celebrate what?"

"Us. You. Me. Everything. You reunited a mother and a daughter. Us solving a case no one even knew was there to be solved. Your mother's getting married. Pick one."

Darcy laughed. "That sounds amazing. When are we leaving?"

"Friday. I took the day off, we can leave in the morning and get a head start on the weekend."

Her heart leaping in her chest, she took him by the hand and pulled him toward the house. "Why don't we go upstairs and get a head start on the weekend right now."

He didn't argue. Smudge saw them as they walked through the kitchen, his eyes narrowed. He sneezed once, shaking his head, and Darcy got the message.

If Smudge had to share her with someone, he was glad it was someone who loved Darcy as much as Jon did.

**-The End-**

# BOOK 4 – THE GHOST OF CHRISTMAS

First published in Australia by South Coast Publishing, December 2013.

# CHAPTER 1

*D*arcy Sweet shivered as the cool air in the room penetrated the thick blankets that covered her bed. She snuggled up closer to her cop boyfriend, Jon Tinker, snoring softly beside her. She was wide awake watching the shadows flitting across her bedroom wall as the moonlight played between clouds. Jon mumbled in his sleep as he threw his arm around her pulling her even closer to him. Darcy grinned. She loved the feel of his body against hers.

She couldn't blame him, it was freezing in her room. She wriggled her feet and could feel Smudge, her black and white cat, lying at the bottom of the bed. After a few months of her and Jon being together, the big tomcat was starting to like Jon more. Enough to be in the same room as him anyway.

She sighed, not sure what was causing her sleeplessness. Perhaps it was the fact that Jon had brought up the subject of them living together again. Not just spending their nights together, but actually living together. He'd been quiet about it for several weeks but he had slipped it into the conversation once again last night at dinner. Darcy wasn't sure why she couldn't just say yes. They spent most of their free time together these days anyway. It seemed the logical thing to do. But still she couldn't give him that commitment.

Outside her window, the clouds gathered. The moon all but disappeared and there was a different feel to the air. Instinctively, she knew what it meant.

She reached over and shook Jon. He stirred and mumbled something that sounded like, "Leave me alone." She couldn't be sure. She shook him again, more forcefully.

He snapped awake and sat up quickly, looking all around. "What? What is it?" he demanded in a sleepy voice.

She smirked and dragged him back down with her, wrapping her arms around him. Jon rubbed a hand over his face and checked the time. He groaned and turned to look at her. "What is it?"

She realized she must have alarmed him. Who could blame him, she thought, after the last few months full of murder and mystery. "Everything is fine." She put a hand on his arm. "In fact, something wonderful is about to happen. We have to get out of bed right now though, or we'll miss it." She jumped up and dragged on her winter coat and boots. "Come on, get all bundled up so we can go."

Jon hadn't moved. He sat there shaking his head and staring at her like she was mad. "Go? Go where? It's the middle of the night for goodness sake."

Darcy just smiled at him. "Come on. You'll like it, I promise."

He shook his head again but reluctantly got out of bed. "Why do I need to bundle up, exactly?" He shivered, his naked chest exposed to the air in the room. "It's chilly enough in here as it is."

"We're just going to the front yard. Now come on." She raced out of the room ahead of him, her pajamas thin comfort against the cold air until she pulled on her heavy red winter jacket.

A few minutes later they were standing in her front yard. "Yup, I was right," Jon mumbled behind her as he rubbed his hands together. "Colder out here. You're a goofball. You know that, right?"

Darcy just smiled at him. Jon grumbled but didn't turn to go back in. That was true love right there, she said to herself.

"So what are we...?" Jon trailed off when the first flakes of snow fell to the ground.

Darcy was grinning like a fool. "Oh, I love this time of year don't you?" Winter was her favorite season. She was so happy that it was snowing. Only a few more days until Christmas and the whole town of Misty Hollow had been talking about how it was going to be a green Christmas this year. Now there was a chance there would be thick, fluffy layers of snow after all.

"Yeah, well it is kind of pretty I guess," Jon said with a little frown. "But it's still damn cold. Can we please go back inside to the nice warm bed?"

Darcy's smile widened even more. She leaned up to kiss him. "Thank you," she whispered. This was going to be the best Christmas ever now that she had him.

~

DARCY TOOK a sip of her coffee as she slid a sideways glance at Jon. He was thoughtfully chewing his toast and she could almost hear the wheels in his brain working.

She slowly placed her cup down on the table in front of her and took in a breath, knowing something was wrong but not understanding what. She was about to ask him when he suddenly sat forward and looked directly at her. "How did you know it was going to snow last night? Did it have anything to do with...you know?" He wiggled his fingers in front of his face as he said it and she knew he was referring to her psychic abilities.

Darcy laughed and shook her head. "No, silly. There's no paranormal weather vane. Well. Not that I know of. I could just feel it in the air."

Jon looked relieved as he sat back in his chair. Darcy's smile turned into a frown. All the time they had spent together, all the things he had seen her do, and still he was uncomfortable with her abilities. It made her a little sad.

"Do you wish that I didn't have them?" she asked suddenly. She realized it wasn't all that suddenly. The question had been nagging her at the edge of her mind for a while, she just hadn't had the nerve to ask. She held her breath waiting for his answer.

"Well...honestly, yes, I do." He couldn't quite look her in the eyes anymore. Darcy felt hurt by his admission, even though she had kind of been expecting it. He had never actually come out and admitted it before though. He had always covered it up with a quick comment on how he loved every part of her or whatever.

She let the matter drop. Was he having doubts about their relationship? If he was, did she really want to know?

They finished up their breakfast in silence. Darcy sensed that something had shifted a little between them and it made her very uncomfortable. She quickly packed her dishes into the sink to do later and ran upstairs to finish getting ready for work.

When she came back downstairs Jon was waiting in the entryway for her. He gave her a long look but didn't say anything.

As he opened the door for them to leave Darcy paused before going through. "Um…" Jon eyed her warily. She sighed and said, "I just wanted to remind you that the Christmas Pageant is coming up and I volunteered us both to help with the costumes and the sets."

He looked at her for a moment like he had been expecting her to say something else. Then he shrugged and said, "Sure."

THE FIVE MINUTE drive into town had been a silent one and Darcy was very tense by the time Jon parked in front of the police station. She quickly leaned over and kissed him on the cheek before jumping out of the car. If he had anything more to say, she didn't want to hear it.

She was already on the sidewalk and on her way to her bookstore when Jon yelled out behind her, "I'll see you for dinner later, okay?"

She stopped walking and turned to face him. Relief washed through her. What had she been worried about? She and Jon were perfect together. She smiled and waved to him and turned away again with a heavy weight lifted off her heart.

As Darcy walked slowly through the town she marvelled at how beautiful everything looked. There were holiday lights strung from all of the buildings and a dusting of snow had clung to the ground. It certainly was beginning to feel like Christmas. She loved this time of year. This would be the first Christmas she would get to spend together with Jon, which made it even more special.

Should she be worried about them, she wondered? She had thought he was becoming more accepting of her abilities. It sure had seemed that way when she had used her abilities to solve the mysteries that they had become involved in while getting to know each other these last few months. She had thought that he was even beginning to appreciate how her connection to the other side could help. She shrugged. Obviously she was reading too much into it. Jon loved her. Otherwise, he wouldn't keep nagging to move in with her, right?

She flushed a little at the thought of him living under her roof. Waking up with him every morning, laying down with him each night, knowing that every part of her life was shared with someone else. She hadn't done that since her late ex-husband, Jeff. Maybe it was time to let it happen again.

As Darcy walked further into the center of town she could see that a large stage was being constructed for the Christmas Pageant in the town square. It was very near to the Bean There

Bakery and Café, which belonged to her friend Helen Nelson, who also happened to be the Mayor of their little town.

The Christmas Pageant was a really big deal in Misty Hollow each year. It featured the church choir singing carols, a huge nativity scene, and Santa handing out gifts to the children. There was a lot that went into making it all happen.

Darcy decided that she could do with another cup of coffee and as she headed for the café she passed by Mrs. Sparks hanging a wreath on her front door. Darcy had the sudden thought that she had no clue what the older woman's first name was. Mrs. Sparks had lived in Misty Hollow for years, in one of the few original old century period houses in the center of town. She was kind of in a hurry to get her coffee and then open up the bookstore or she would have stopped and chatted, maybe asked her name and how she had come to live here. Another time, maybe.

Darcy entered the Bean There Bakery and Café and was happy to see Helen working behind the counter. It was rare to see her in the shop these days. Being the town's mayor took up so much of her time.

"How are things, Helen?" Darcy ordered her coffee at the same time and accepted the warm cup from Helen's hands.

Helen ran a hand through her graying hair. "Great Darcy, just great."

"And the pageant?"

"Oh the pageant is going great, except for Mister Baskin." Helen pulled a face as she said his name. Roland Baskin was notorious as the town's resident grump. He had always hated the Christmas pageant with a passion, claiming it was too loud and there was too much hubbub. He'd earned the nickname of the Grinch among the kids in town. "He is already protesting about the pageant," Helen said.

"It wouldn't be Christmas if he didn't," Darcy said with a smile as she picked up her coffee and headed for the bookstore.

AFTER THE WORK day was done, passing quietly with few customers in the store, Darcy headed to the police station to catch up with Jon. The desk sergeant waved her through, buzzing the door open that separated the lobby from the officer's desks, and she found Jon on the phone. When he hung up he looked distracted. When he noticed her he startled and tried to cover it with a quick hello.

She stopped. He seemed so distant. The good feeling she had gotten back about their relationship started to slip away again. She spun the antique silver ring on her right hand ring finger. It was a nervous habit she had whenever she was stressed or anxious. The ring had belonged to her great-aunt Millie when she had been alive, along with the house that Darcy lived in and the bookstore. Darcy had inherited all three. The ring meant a lot to her. In times of stress she sought its comfort.

Jon finally smiled and she thought maybe she had only imagined the way he had looked at her. She stepped closer to his desk, and as she did he stood up. "I have to go and help out the guys in Meadowood tonight. Um. Raincheck on dinner?"

Darcy felt her mood deflate again. These ups and downs were getting exhausting. "Oh, okay. Is everything alright?"

Meadowood was the next town over from Misty Hollow and was quite a bit bigger. The crime rate had increased over there in the last few weeks as Christmas got closer. It wasn't unusual for that township to ask for help from the surrounding departments, including Misty Hollow, but still Darcy couldn't help but feel like Jon was making up excuses.

Rifling through the papers on his desk he said, "No, baby. Everything's fine. They had a tip that a larger burglary is going to take place tonight. They're asking for help. That's all."

Darcy hoped that he wasn't using that as an excuse to avoid

her. Even as the thought flashed through her mind she felt foolish for it. "No I understand. Just be safe. Okay?"

"Of course. Thanks for being understanding." He leaned into hug her, holding her tightly. She reached up for a kiss but he was already walking past her for the door.

"I'll see you later, all right Darcy?"

The door closed behind him with a very final-sounding click. Sometimes she wished that her abilities extended to sensing what living people were feeling and thinking. Sometimes it was so much easier to communicate with ghosts than it was with real people.

Realizing she was starting to draw the stares of the other officers in the room she quietly slipped out the door and headed home.

DARCY STOOD BACK with hands on hips to admire the Christmas tree she was decorating in the living room of her home. She looked it up and down and this way and that. It looked pretty good but it needed something else. She riffled through her decoration box looking for the perfect ornament when her hand landed on a delicate silver angel. She hung the ornament on one of the top branches and stepped back again to admire her handiwork. Perfect.

Darcy laughed when Smudge jumped up and swiped some of the candy canes lower down on the tree. He had been trying to knock them all off as soon as she put them on. It had become a sort of a game. "Stop it Smudge. I have it looking perfect. Don't ruin it."

He gave her a glare with his wide green kitty cat eyes and then skulked away. They had worked out a language between them over the years. She didn't know if he actually understood what she said or what she meant, but either way, Smudge had been her closest friend for a long time.

As Darcy straightened the tree once again she shivered with a sudden flash of cold. Rubbing her hands up and down the goose bumps on her arms she looked all around for the source of the cold. A draft, maybe? Had she left a window open?

Darcy went around the room, and then the rest of the downstairs checking the windows one by one but they were all shut and locked. It wasn't that.

She breathed out. Her breath plumed.

Still shivering she wandered back to the living room and stood with hands on her hips. Listening carefully, she heard noise where there was just silence a moment ago. Outside something whirled and paced, like a gale force wind. Her front door started banging with the force of it and she jumped.

It almost sounded as if someone was knocking. Strange.

She went to the front door. It thumped rhythmically against its thick wooden frame, thump, thump, thump. Curious, she reached out to open it, startled when it blew inwards with force enough to knock her off her feet before she'd even touched the handle. Stunned, her vision sparking with stars, she looked up into the face of the night.

The ghost of an older man stood there. Graying dark hair, wide face, clothes that were wrinkled and unkempt. He reached his arms toward her and she felt the waves of frigid cold coming off from him.

"Who are you?" Darcy asked as she pushed herself to her feet again. Ghosts in her life were nothing new. She had spoken to any number of them. Usually, however, they didn't make house calls.

The ghost raised his arms up above his head and as he did so Darcy was pushed back by a harsh gust of wind. She felt fear ripple in her belly. She had never met a ghost where this happened before.

*"My name is Roger,"* she heard the spirit speak, a watery voice that touched the furthest corners of her mind. *"Many years ago on Christmas Eve I was murdered."*

Ghosts were rarely this direct. The ones who were able to speak to the living usually had to do so in riddles or snatches of remembered conversations. Roger here seemed to have no trouble communicating. Darcy centered herself and prepared to do what her gift allowed her to do.

Communicate with the dead.

"Why are you here?" Darcy asked. She shivered again. "And why did you bring all this cold?"

*"I am too angry to rest!"* The ghost shimmered with his rage. *"I need peace!"*

"Roger," Darcy said as she searched for some way to calm the spirit down, "you have the option to leave. Go on to the next place."

*"No!"* he shouted, his face distorting before snapping back to the visage of what he must have looked like in life. *"I was murdered! I want justice!"*

Before Darcy's eyes, he seemed to shrink down, become smaller even as his voice became quieter. *"I can't rest until I know who killed me."*

There it was. This was what most restless spirits wanted. Darcy sighed. Here we go again. "If you want," she offered, "I can help you with that."

Roger smiled at her. The wind died down, the cold receded, and then the ghost simply faded away.

Smudge wound his way around her ankles. "Big help you were," she muttered. "You could have at least hissed at him or something."

The tom cat meowed loudly. Darcy laughed and picked him up, scratching his ears until he purred.

Well, she thought to herself. What do I do now?

*D*arcy straightened the last piece of tinsel on the Christmas tree that had been mussed by the ghost's cold breeze. She had to smile as Smudge crawled under the couch for a moment only to re-emerge with an ornament in his mouth. He trotted over to her and dropped it at her feet.

"Good boy. Are there anymore lying around anywhere? Our friend Roger certainly made a mess didn't he? Who do you suppose he was?"

Darcy carefully picked up the last pieces of the broken colored ball ornaments that were lying on the floor and threw them into the trash. The ghost had really done a number on her Christmas tree. Several of her favorite decorations hadn't survived the violent wind that had accompanied him.

She picked up some magazines from the floor and straightened them into a neat pile before dropping them down onto the coffee table. Smudge waddled over to her and dropped another ornament at her feet once again. She bent to pick it up and placed it back on the tree.

Darcy propped her hands to her hips and did a slow rotation

around the room. It looked like everything was back in order. While she had been tidying up she had been going over the mystery of Roger's visit in her mind. She couldn't shake the feeling that he was familiar to her. Somehow, she thought that she may have seen a picture of him at one time.

If he came knocking on the door, she reasoned, maybe he had been a friend of her Aunt Millie. Maybe the picture was in her great-aunt's journal.

A cold gust ruffled her hair.

The journal was at the bookstore. She grabbed her coat and shrugged into it, looking around the empty house as she did. She wished Jon were here. Just to have someone to talk to. Of course, he was already freaked out by her abilities and Roger the ghost hadn't exactly been gentle about his request for help. Maybe it was better that Jon wasn't here.

Darcy stopped suddenly, one arm in and one arm out of her coat. She hadn't meant that to sound the way it did. She couldn't take the thought back, though. It was there now.

She shoved her feet into her boots and headed out of the house.

THE TOWN CENTER looked practically deserted when Darcy cycled into it. Her bicycle was newly fitted with all terrain tires and thankfully the snow was only a dusting. She didn't know what she would do once it got deeper.

Outside the bookstore she leaned the bike up against the wall and quickly unlocked the door to rush inside. Twinkling white Christmas lights lit the corners of the room and the stacks of books, strung around the bare ceiling beams and pull away hooks on the walls. The tinsel taped to the end of each row of books glittered in the muted light and the cut out paper snowflakes swayed softly on their strings in the gentle breeze coming through the open door.

She closed the door softly and went into her small office near the back of the store. There, on a shelf above her desk, she slid the journal out from between a copy of Pride and Prejudice and a first edition of Palmer's Journal, then she sat down to read through the leather bound book her aunt had kept such careful notes in.

In the light of her desk lamp she slowly flipped her way through the book, carefully studying the photos that were pasted into several of the pages. She had read through her aunt's journal any number of times, and knew entire passages by heart. Was there a photo in here that could help her?

A dozen or more pages in, Darcy saw it. A picture with a bunch of people, all of them labelled, looking like a committee for one of Misty Hollow's many festivals. She traced her finger over the man who had visited her, standing near the back of the group in the faded photograph. His name was scrawled under the picture. Roger August. He looked exactly the same, wide face etched with fine lines around his eyes, thick dark hair turning gray. A scowl set into his mouth. There was no other information on the page to give her any idea who he was or how her great-aunt knew him.

She had the next step, though. Now that Darcy had Roger's full name she would go and ask Jon for help in looking him up. She decided to do that tomorrow. Jon was gone for the evening, after all, and he had said he wouldn't be coming over.

She tried not to let that thought bother her. They weren't spending every night together. One night didn't matter, in the bigger picture.

The picture in front of her hadn't been much help. There was a lot more about the story to learn. She slid the journal back onto the shelf and stood up to leave. She was almost to the front door when she heard the journal fall to the floor back in the office.

"Oh for Pete's sake," she said as she went back to pick it up. "Millie. Stop it. I have to get home. I'll be back tomorrow, I promise."

Her aunt still haunted the bookstore. For some spirits, like Roger, hanging around the mortal coil was a sign that something was unresolved from their lives. For Millie, it just meant she was somewhere she loved to be. This bookstore had been her life, so to speak, and the memories that Darcy had of being here with her would always be some of her most cherished. Millie loved to play little pranks now by throwing books or knocking things over in the store. Darcy just didn't have time for it tonight.

The journal had fallen back open to Roger's photo. Darcy looked at it again, deciding she hadn't missed anything, and putting it back on the shelf once more.

As she turned to walk away, the book fell again. She growled between her teeth. Turning back, she saw the book was on a different page this time. A page showing a picture of one of Misty Hollow's many previous Christmas celebrations. A group of children were on stage, singing carols. One girl stood in front of the rest of the group, doing a solo by the looks of it. The photo was dated, thirty five years ago.

Was Millie trying to tell her something?

THE NEXT MORNING Darcy cycled into town early to see Jon before he went to work. She had on her heavy winter coat. Last night's encounter with Roger made everything seem colder somehow.

There weren't many people out and about this early in the day. Darcy had gotten up before dawn and headed out before seven. Jon's shift would start in an hour or so, depending on how late he had been out last night in Meadowood. Maybe he'd decide to stay home.

She went to the Bean There Bakery and Café to get some breakfast for the two of them first. She was delighted to see that Helen was working behind the counter again.

There weren't many people in the café this early in the day. Leo Hanway, who always came into the café for breakfast every day, was sitting in his usual place and was reading his morning paper. "Hello Mister Hanway, how are you?" Darcy said with a smile as she walked past him towards the counter.

He nodded hello to her but didn't speak as he turned a page of his paper and shook it out, holding it up in front of his face rather rudely. Darcy had always thought he was a bit of a strange man and not very likeable. He kept mostly to himself and could be a bit curt at times. He was just one of the dozens of unusual characters who lived in Misty Hollow. The place seemed to have more than its fair share.

Darcy sighed as she turned towards the counter. "Hi Helen," she said. Helen had come up to the counter when she was talking to Leo.

"Hi Darcy what can I get for you?" Darcy ordered two coffees and two muffins. "Thanks," she said as Helen set the order down in front of her.

"Going to Jon's for breakfast?" Helen asked with a smirk. Darcy just grinned as she left the shop without answering.

At Jon's front door Darcy knocked a couple of times before he opened it yawning loudly. "Hey you," he said, sleepily looking at her with his eyelids low. He was still in his pajama bottoms and an old t-shirt.

She laughed and said, "What sort of greeting is that?"

He rubbed a hand over his face and with a grin said, "Sorry. I'm really tired this morning." He yawned again. His eyes lit up when he saw that she had coffee and muffins from the bakery. "Oh thank goodness, coffee."

She grinned back at him as he stepped aside to let her enter. Taking one of the styrofoam coffee cups from her he took a big sip. "Oh my God, that is so good." He flopped down into one of the chairs and put the cup down onto the coffee table in front of him. He reached up like a little kid when she held up the blueberry muffin. She made him pay for it with a kiss first.

"So how did the stakeout go last night?" She asked, sitting down next to him.

He swallowed his mouthful before answering. "Fantastic. Got the little, um, thieves," he said, covering up the term he obviously wanted to use instead. "We arrested them, finally, but they didn't show up until three in the morning. That's why I'm so tired." He took another sip of his coffee. "But this coffee is making me feel much more human. Thanks."

"My pleasure," she said as a warm glow spread through her. Any awkwardness from yesterday was gone. He was Jon again and they could sit together in comfortable silence. His eyes slid shut again for just a moment before they snapped open. She felt guilty for waking him up. "I can leave if you want to go back to bed."

"No, baby. Thanks, but no. It's fine. I have to get ready for work anyway." He shoved the rest of the muffin into his mouth and Darcy took another bite of her own. They chewed in silence for a few moments.

"So, tell me more about your stakeout," Darcy asked him, wanting to work up to asking him about Roger.

He shrugged. "We arrested four men. Boys, really. The oldest was just twenty-one. It was pretty routine, but it was nice to do it the old fashioned way for a change."

Darcy frowned, confused. "What do you mean?"

Jon gave her a long look through tired eyes and then said, "Lately I've been arresting people based on weird visions that my girlfriend has had."

Darcy sat back, trying not to be offended. He must not have meant it the way it sounded, she thought. She knew that Jon wasn't completely comfortable with her psychic abilities but what he had just said…it sounded like he resented them. Now she didn't want to tell him about her vision of Roger the ghost or ask his help.

Darcy could feel the tears coming. There was no reason to cry. She knew that. She just couldn't make it stop. Standing up she kissed him goodbye and quickly left without saying another word.

THE WHOLE REST of the day Darcy was out of sorts. Even Sue Fisher, her always bubbly assistant, couldn't bring her out of the unhappy mood she was in. Darcy had thought things were going so well with Jon, but this thing over her abilities was becoming a giant rift between them.

She closed up at the end of the day with a sigh of relief. The bookstore was usually soothing to her but today it had been a grind. She headed over to the police station.

In the back of the police department, after being buzzed in, she found her sister Grace. She was older than Darcy, and her dark hair was a little shorter, but the resemblance between the sisters couldn't be denied. She looked up now from her computer screen, a little smile erasing some of the lines around her eyes when she saw Darcy.

"Hey sis. What are you doing here? Jon's gone home." Grace waved at the chair on the other side of her desk and Darcy flopped into it. "What's up?"

Darcy explained everything about how she'd had a vision of a man named Roger August, who had been murdered. "I kind of need your help, Grace. Can you find out anything, do you think?"

Grace studied her for a moment. "Why aren't you working on it with Jon?"

Darcy bit her lip and looked away. She didn't want to try explaining to her sister the feeling she had that something might be wrong between her and Jon. She could be wrong, after all. He had been happy to see her this morning. If it weren't for those constant comments about her abilities… "I've loaded him down with a lot lately," she decided to say. "Could you do it for me this time? You know I wouldn't ask if it wasn't important."

Grace looked at her intently for a moment and then shook her head. "Uh-huh, no, that's not it. There's something else." Darcy sighed. Trust her sister's eagle eye. She took a deep breath and then explained what had happened between her and Jon that morning.

Grace chewed on the inside of her lip. "Well, I do understand where Jon is coming from…"

"Oh for Pete's sake, not you too," Darcy said with an edge to her voice.

Grace held up a hand and said, "Your visions and whatnot can be a little hard to accept, Darcy. Even for me, someone who has known you all of your life. Doesn't mean I don't love you, sis. You know that Jon loves you too, right?"

Darcy calmed down a little and nodded. "Oh, sure. I know. I just, um, don't want to put too much on him." The excuse sounded weaker every time she said it.

Grace shrugged and turned back to her computer. In a few minutes she had looked up Roger August and found out that he had died some twenty years ago. "He was killed in his house on Christmas Eve," Grace said as she read the report out loud to Darcy. "These are files that were copied over after we got our computer system, from the old paper files, so they aren't exactly complete. It says he was shot in the back, no leads, no one ever arrested. That's about it."

"That's it? Nothing else?"

Grace shook her head. "Guess you'll have to rely on your abilities to get you anything else on this one."

Darcy pressed her lips together. Her abilities. Right.

For the first time in her adult life, she came very close to wishing her abilities would leave her alone.

"Twenty years ago?" Darcy repeated what Grace had said. "That means that the killer could still be alive."

Suddenly solving this mystery had become much more dangerous.

# CHAPTER 3

*E*arly the next morning, after a very sleepless night of tossing and turning, Darcy pulled out all of the old photo albums she had stuffed in the back of her closet. Some had belonged to her great-aunt and they'd passed to her with the house.

Jon hadn't come over last night either. She tried not to put too much thought into that.

As she sat cross-legged on the floor of her bedroom, she wondered if Roger August would be in any of the pictures. Worn pages flipped between her fingers, old photographs held in place with plastic corners at their edges. She started with the old albums of her aunt's figuring that there was a greater chance of finding something useful in those. Thankfully her aunt had taken the time to leave notations under them with names of people, dates, places and so on.

She didn't find a single photo of Roger in any of them. What a waste of time. At least it had kept her mind off Jon for a while. She wasn't sure what to do about him, or if she should do anything, or if she should just let it alone. If she said anything, would it make it worse? Was there anything even to make worse?

Exasperated, she threw herself back on the rug with a little groan. Smudge came over to see what was wrong, nuzzling her cheek with his nose until she started rubbing his ears and neck. His purring was loud, and comforting.

Darcy figured she could at least solve Roger's problem. She could find out who killed him, and give his spirit some rest. Thinking on how to do that she decided she could talk to other townsfolk, particularly the people who had lived in the town for more than twenty years. There was a good chance that somebody would remember him, especially if he had been involved in town affairs like that photo in her aunt's journal suggested.

At least it was a place to start.

AFTER WORK THAT DAY, Darcy took a stroll through town, taking in the sight of all the pageant preparations that were going on. Several of the town's residents were there, helping in one way or another or just watching, and she used it as an opportunity to casually ask about Roger August.

She looked all around at the work that was being done. There were a lot of people working on the stage development, including her friends Helen, Sue and Linda. Her brother-in-law, Aaron was also working there and he lifted his hand to wave at her. She smiled and waved back at him. Clara from the La Di Da Deli was busy hammering nails into the framework and Leo Hanway was looking at some papers that looked like they may have been plans for the stage structure.

One after another, Darcy talked to the older residents of the town. There were several people she asked who either said they had never known the man or who only remembered that he had died, and nothing more. She was beginning to wonder if Roger had made any impact on the town at all. How could he have lived here and no one remember him?

Leo Hanway, for instance, looked bored with her questions. He didn't seem to be helping with the work either and explained to Darcy that he was only there because the others needed to borrow his tools. He was more than happy to talk about how he had worked in construction before being forced to retire because of his cancer. He went on and on about being a foreman and how he'd even built some of the houses that were still standing here in Misty Hollow, but had no interest in discussing anyone named Roger August.

Helen Nelson, taking a break from her duties as mayor to pitch in with the preparations, told Darcy that she knew a little about Roger August. "He used to be friends with Wally Marlow when he was mayor all those years ago." Helen stopped what she was doing and brushed her hands on the front of her puffy white coat. "He had a daughter. I just can't remember her name. I know she had a different last name than his." Helen shrugged and apologized for having to go off to help someone else.

"Thanks Helen, you've been a help." Darcy smiled at her and was about to leave and go back to the bookstore when Helen put a hand on her arm to stop her.

"You should keep an eye out for Roland Baskin. He's going around with that petition of his to stop the pageant. Thankfully, no one is signing it. Still he might know something about Roger."

Darcy nodded. She wasn't looking forward to talking to that old grump. Maybe someone else would know something.

HER INTERVIEWS HAD TURNED up hardly anything on Roger. Hard to believe a man could live his whole life in this town and not have anyone remember him. Later that night when Darcy was back home she gave Grace a call.

"Hi sis," Darcy said when Grace answered.

"I'm real busy right now, Darcy. I can't really talk."

"Okay, I know. I'm sorry. I found out Roger had a daughter, though. Can you find out for me who she is?"

"Yeah alright, but I can't do it until tomorrow. What was her name?"

"I don't know."

Grace blew out a breath over the phone. "You don't ask for much, do you?"

"Thanks sis," Darcy said. Grace had to go so they said their goodbyes.

She hung up the phone thoughtfully. She realized that she would have to tell Jon the truth. She couldn't keep hiding it from him and using her sister, his partner at work, this way. Reluctantly she pulled on her coat and boots and started off for Jon's apartment.

AS JON SWUNG the door open to Darcy's knock the smile on his face was wide and genuine. She thought he looked happy to see her and was glad about that but she could only raise a small smile in return.

She didn't know how to start. She felt tense and unsure of herself, so much so that she started to pace around his living room.

Jon stood with his arms folded, watching her. "What's wrong?" he said with no trace of the smile on his face now.

She stopped pacing and made herself look at him. "I have something to tell you. It's nothing really. It's silly actually." She tried to smile but it slipped. His face looked like it was carved out of stone. Taking a deep breath, she tried to rush through what she needed to say.

"Look I don't know why I kept this from you. I had a visitation from a spirit of a man named Roger August and he needs my help because he was murdered here in town years ago and, well, you know how I'm the only one who can help in situations like that. I asked Grace to look into it and she's going to let me know what she finds out."

She thought she would feel better after saying it out loud but she found the lump in her throat was still there. Jon didn't look any happier when she had finished speaking, either. Fidgeting with her ring, Darcy tried to explain herself. "I guess I kept it from you because of what you said about my abilities making you upset. You know? You've never said anything like that to me before and I didn't want it to get in the way of you and me."

Jon just stood silently with his arms folded. He didn't say a word. Darcy felt him putting a wall up, like he had raised some invisible defense between them. She sighed. This hadn't helped at all.

"Please tell the truth about how you feel about my abilities," she asked softly, terrified of what his answer was going to be.

"Okay," he said, "I'll tell you. They make me uncomfortable and I wish that you wouldn't use them. It seems to me you're just asking for trouble and we don't need any more of that." Darcy bit her lip, but he had more still to say. "I'm also really mad that you kept this latest vision or whatever it was from me."

Darcy didn't think that was entirely fair. "You can't have it both ways, Jon. Either I should have told you or I shouldn't have. Which one is it?" Her feelings were in a knot, and she felt like she'd been punched in her gut. Anger like hot bile stirred in her.

"I just want you to be honest with me Darcy, that's all. When you have one of these visions you should tell me about it instead of keeping it a secret." He stabbed the air with a finger.

Darcy could feel tears stinging the corners of her eyes. This was getting out of control. They were both mad, about the same thing, and she knew she should just admit it to him and try to fix it. She just didn't know how to get past it. "I should tell you? Every time? What, even if it upsets you like you are now?"

They stood there, both of them staring, neither of them

willing to give an inch. Finally, when she couldn't hold the tears back anymore and they started to fall, she turned away. "I have to go," she said as she moved towards the door.

"Darcy, wait," he said when her hand was on the door. "I don't want this to affect you and me."

"You just think I can put away my abilities like taking off a shirt?" she accused him. "You just want me, without the abilities, is that it?"

When he didn't have an answer for her she walked out and closed the door behind her.

# CHAPTER 4

*D*arcy stomped the length of her living room and then back again. She knew that she was overreacting, but she was just so upset with Jon for not accepting her for who she was. She had hidden her abilities from Jeff, her late ex-husband, whenever she could, and it had been part of the strain that finally led to their divorce. She didn't want to have to do that same thing with Jon. A small part of her knew that he was just concerned for her, and she couldn't really blame him, considering how her abilities had gotten her into danger in the past.

Those same abilities had brought murderers to justice, though. Without her, the mysteries this town had fallen into in the past few months would have gone unsolved. She knew that. It scared her a little, too, if she was being honest. Just like it scared Jon.

But right now she was just too upset to think about being honest or fair. The hurt was pulsing though her fast and heavy.

Smudge came rushing up to her, meowing loudly and jumping into her arms. Her faithful cat pushed against her chin with his head, meowing again. He knew when she was upset. At least someone in her life was always there for her. Picking him up gently, she headed upstairs for a nice warm shower. Maybe that would help to calm her down.

She went through the bathroom on her way to the bedroom, turning the shower on to make sure it would be nice and hot when she got in. Smudge jumped down out of her hands and hit out at the cascading shower. He loved playing in water but quickly tired of the game today and raced from the room. She smiled at his antics.

Testing the temperature, she started to slip out of her clothes when she heard a thump in the bedroom. Running in, she saw that Smudge had knocked over one of the photo albums she had been looking through that morning. Now he was pawing at the pages, sniffing at one page in particular.

"Smudge, stop that!" she said, shooing him away with a hand. "Come on, now. You can't even read!"

But she could. On the page Smudge had been sniffing at was a picture of a little girl. A little girl in a Christmas dress of white and reds. The name underneath read Katrina Settler.

It was the same girl from her Aunt Millie's journal. She studied the photo to be sure, but yes, there it was. The same girl.

In her world, things never happened by coincidence.

WHEN DARCY WOKE up the next morning she felt a bit calmer. She got up slowly and started to get ready for her day, thoughts of Katrina Settler and how she tied in with Roger August running through her mind. She felt confident that she knew who the girl was. She just had to have it confirmed.

Jon took up a lot of her thoughts that morning, too. As she went about her usual morning routine she was deep in thought about the events of the day before.

She thought about her psychic abilities and how they impacted on her life, and now Jon's life. He had been unfair to her. She thought about his comments and how hurt she had been by them, but then a new thought occurred to her.

Would she give her abilities up if she could? It would certainly make her life safer and easier. She wasn't sure that she would ever do that, though, even if she could. Communicating with spirits from the other side was so much a part of her now that she just wouldn't be who she was without them. And she liked who she was. She didn't want to change. Not for anyone. Not even Jon.

Just before she was ready to leave the house she gathered up the costumes for the pageant that she had finished putting together as promised and folded them into a large duffle bag that she slung crossways over her shoulder. She handled them with care as some of them were very old and had been used in the pageant for many years. She had just needed to patch them up a bit as they had been showing some wear and tear. A couple of them had needed altering a little to make them fit better. She put Santa's hat in last on top of the rest and zipped up the bag, then headed downstairs ready to leave for work.

THINGS WERE a little slow at the bookstore today and Darcy kept herself busy by rearranging some of the shelves. Sue had the day off so Darcy was by herself and was finding the store just a little too quiet for her liking. To make matters worse there had only been two customers the whole time the store had been open today. It was the age of electronic books. The store was actually seeing less and less income, and she knew there might come a day when she would have to consider selling it.

The bell jingled into her thoughts as someone entered the bookstore. On her knees at the end of the mystery section, Darcy looked up to see who it was.

"What are you doing down there?" Grace asked as she came closer. "Are you okay?"

Darcy smiled at her sister. "I'm fine. I've been doing some rearranging." She stood up and swiped at the legs of her jeans to clean off the floor dust. She and Sue would definitely need to spend some time in the near future cleaning the place up.

Grace folded her arms and stood with one hip cocked. "I talked to Jon this morning. He was in a grumpy mood. The kind a guy gets into when he argues with his girlfriend." She arched an eyebrow and let the statement hang in the air.

Darcy sighed. Her sister was sharp. There wasn't much that she missed. "Jon and I had a big fight," she said. "He said things, I said things. It's all over my…you know. My abilities."

Grace didn't look surprised. In fact, she smiled. "Well. It's about time something went wrong with you two."

Darcy was horrified. She gaped at her sister. "What do you mean?"

Grace patted her sister's arm. "I didn't mean anything bad by it. I just meant that you and Jon have been getting along so well that it almost isn't natural. You had to get into a fight sooner or later."

Darcy relaxed a little and smiled wryly at Grace. "Thanks, that makes me feel so much better. So you think our problem was that we were too perfect?"

"Something like that."

Darcy let the smile slip a little. "You know how I told you ages ago that he wants us to move in together?"

Grace nodded. "I haven't heard you mention it lately."

"He went quiet on the subject for a while. He was supposed to be giving me time to think about it. But the other night he slipped it into the conversation again."

Grace's eyebrows shot up. "Really? I take you said no."

Darcy winced. "Yes. I just kept putting him off and putting him off, and now it looks like I made the right decision because can you imagine what this would be like if we lived under the same roof?"

"It would be just like every other relationship out there, sis. Couples fight. It's part of life. This won't be the last one you and Jon have either. You're not giving up on him after one fight are you?"

Darcy searched for the words to explain it. She really thought her sister would have understood her better. "I don't know. If he can't accept that part of me what future do we have? It's who I am, Grace."

Grace shook her head. "I'm sure you'll work it out. Just don't give up. Okay?" Grace smiled at Darcy and then pulled a piece of paper out of her pocket. "About Roger August's daughter. I have a name for you."

"Is it Katrina Settler?" Darcy asked.

Grace blew out the breath she had been about to speak with. "You already knew? Then why did you...oh. Right. You know, I can understand why Jon would say your abilities are annoying."

The look on Darcy's face must have made Grace realize what she had said. "I didn't mean it that way, sis. I was just kidding."

Darcy tried to play it off. "That's fine Grace. I understand. So what did you find out?"

"Well," Grace said, "she lives on the outskirts of town. Roger never married and Katrina was born out of wedlock. She was an only child and was raised by her mother, Agnes Settler, who was a single parent. Roger had visitation rights to see his daughter." Grace consulted the paper again. "Katrina is married to one Joseph Samson but I can't find anything on him at all. That's about it." Grace handed Darcy the piece of paper.

"Thanks for doing that Grace, I appreciate it."

"No problem. I have to get going, though. I'll catch up with you later. Just take it easy on Jon, all right? Everything will work out. You'll see."

Darcy hoped that she was right about that. She was having a hard time imagining her life without Jon in it.

~

DARCY BREATHED a sigh of relief as she flipped the 'OPEN a good book today' sign to 'CLOSED, THE END.' She was so glad that it was the end of the day. She hefted the dufflebag up onto her shoulder and started walking her bike across to the town square to drop off the costumes to Helen.

She dropped her bike gently down onto the snowy grass and walked towards Helen. As she got closer she could see that the other woman looked very distraught. When Helen looked up and spotted her she put her hands up into the air and she said, "Thank God! Darcy come here, quick. Something has gone horribly wrong with the pageant."

Darcy tensed. "Helen, what is it?"

"Harry and Madge have both come down with some horrible sickness." Darcy relaxed a little. "They were going to play Santa and Mrs. Claus. What will we do now?"

Darcy realized what that would mean for the pageant. Santa had to be in the pageant or it would be ruined for the children.

"You and Jon will have to do it," Helen said suddenly. "You're the only two volunteers left that aren't in the show."

Darcy could think of nothing she wanted less. She was still mad at Jon and she could only imagine that he was still mad at her, too. What would it be like to stand on the stage together as such a famous married couple as Santa and his wife? She couldn't see any way to get out of it, though, and the pageant meant so much to her and everyone else in town, so she begrudgingly agreed.

Helen hugged her. "Oh, thank you. One less thing to worry about. Are those the costumes? Oh, Darcy you're a life saver! What would I do without you and Jon?"

Helen smiled at her and Darcy could only smile back, wondering what Jon would say about all this. She said goodbye to Helen and started to walk towards the police station to tell Jon the news.

She hesitated, knowing that anything she said to him now would probably only make things worse or spark another argument. One of them needed to apologize first before anything could be healed between them. It would probably be her. Jon was stubborn, in his own way. She wanted to do it, too, because she wanted them to be back to the way they were. Just not right now.

Sighing, she picked up her bike and started to ride in the direction of home.

# CHAPTER 5

*O*nce again Darcy found herself wide awake when she should have been sleeping. Only this time she knew what the problem was. She wished that she had gone to Jon's apartment after work and apologized. Her anger at him was gone and she missed him badly. She just hoped that she hadn't ruined things with him.

She wondered why she was putting all of the blame on herself. He had started the argument, after all. Maybe she should hold her ground and wait for him to apologize to her first.

She rolled over onto her side and looked out of the window. It looked much as it had the other night with the heavy cover of dark clouds in the sky. Her window was open just a crack and a trickle of a breeze was coming through. She could sense the possibility of snow once again and it was kind of comforting. She smiled.

Quickly sitting up and jumping out of bed she raced downstairs to put on her coat and boots. If she couldn't sleep she might as well go outside and watch the snowflakes fall for a little while. The fresh air might do her some good.

As she pulled open the front door the cold air stung her face and took her breath away for a moment. She raced down the porch steps and stood in the front yard. She lifted her face to the sky just as the first snowflakes began to fall. She took a deep breath and let the frigid air burn her lungs. It was magical. The only thing missing was Jon.

"Can I join you?" She startled a little as his quiet voice came from behind her. She thought that she had imagined it for a moment.

Darcy turned to find him standing behind her. Then Jon suddenly moved and closed the space between them. He pulled her into his arms and kissed her deeply.

"I'm sorry." They both said at the same time when they pulled apart for air. They laughed together.

"I love you Darcy, and I accept all of you. I've been an idiot but you understand, don't you? I'm just so worried about all of the danger that your abilities seem to attract to you. That's why I said that I wished that you didn't have them. I don't want you to get hurt."

"I understand," she said to him, so grateful to hear those words that she could barely stand to breathe. "As long as you can understand that these abilities are a part of who I am and I can't change that."

He wrapped his arm around her shoulders and she melted against him. They stayed like that for a long time just watching as the snowflakes fell.

DARCY EXPERTLY FLIPPED the pancake she was cooking and then shrieked as Jon grabbed her around the waist from behind. He pulled her in close to his body, her back to his front, and kissed her neck. Darcy giggled and nearly knocked the frying pan to the floor. Still, that didn't stop her from bending her neck further to allow him easier access to kiss her more.

"I'm starved," he whispered in a sultry way, making her shiver as she thought of things other than food. "How long until we eat."

Darcy grinned at him over her shoulder. "Not long." She was so happy that things between them seemed to be back to normal. Or even better than normal.

They sat in silence for a few minutes as they dug into their pancakes. Darcy remembered her conversation with Helen. Quickly chewing and swallowing her mouthful of food she said, "Oh by the way they need us to play Santa and Mrs. Claus in the Christmas Pageant."

Jon almost choked on the mouthful of pancake he was eating. "We're what now?"

She grinned at him and said, "You heard me."

He rolled his eyes at her. "Okay, I'll do it for you but I don't want this to become a yearly thing. I'm too young to be Santa Claus."

Darcy grinned at him before she jumped up and ran into the living room where she picked up the Santa suit she had been mending. She raced back into the kitchen with it and handed it to him. He ran his hands over it. The suit was soft and worn and probably had been used for generations.

Jon held the suit out in front of him and frowned. "Whoa, I am going to need to eat a boatload more of those pancakes if I'm going to have a belly like Santa to fit into this."

Darcy laughed as she took the hint and went to make another batch.

AFTER BREAKFAST JON drove them into town in his police car with Darcy's bike stowed in the trunk. On the short trip he asked her about Roger August and the vision she had. She told him all that she knew so far. It seemed like now that they had made up he was ready to help her solve this. Her heart felt light.

"I need to talk to Roger's daughter, but I don't know where she lives exactly," Darcy said as they pulled into a parking space outside of the police station.

"Okay I can find out her address for you. Let's get inside where it's warm." He rubbed his hands together as he blew his hot breath onto them. Darcy grinned and followed him into the police station.

As they settled down at Jon's desk, he turned his computer on while Darcy waved to a few of the other officers still at their desk. They were getting used to her being in the building with Jon by now. Moments later Jon had Katrina's address. He wrote it down on a post-it note and handed it to Darcy. She read it to herself. It wasn't that far away from the center of town here.

"Do you want me to come with you when you visit her?" Jon asked her.

"No thanks, I can handle it on my own." She smiled at him. He looked at her skeptically, more of that overly protective nature that kept him harping on her abilities. She had to insist, though. Katrina might be more open to talking about what had happened to her father if Darcy was alone. A police officer, even Jon, might be intimidating for her. She reached out to hold his hand in hers. "I'll be fine, Jon. I promise."

"Made up so soon?" Darcy jumped when she heard her sister's voice behind her. She turned to find her sister standing there with arms folded across her chest, smiling smugly at the two of them.

Darcy glared at her before turning back to Jon. "Ignore my sister," she said as she stood up and moved around to his side of the desk to kiss him goodbye. "I'll see you later."

DARCY WAS STANDING behind the counter of the Sweet Read Bookstore when Sue entered in a rush, cold air flowing in behind her. Her blonde hair had escaped from her knitted cap and she pushed the strands back as she plucked the hat off along with her mittens. She smiled mischievously at Darcy.

"I have some gossip for you about Mister Baskin, our resident grump," she said. She was obviously eager to spill whatever it was. Darcy rolled her eyes. Misty Hollow was always rife with some sort of gossip. "Have you heard about this petition he's spreading around to stop the pageant? He's already gotten a few signatures on it. Now he's going to take it to Helen. Can you believe it?"

"He can't possibly have enough to keep Christmas from coming." Darcy giggled as she said it, imagining that scene from the Grinch where the green-furred meanie was staring down at Whoville and scheming to take their Christmas away. "Let's just hope no one else signs it."

Sue nodded and blew hot air onto her hands to warm them. "On another note I have something good to share." She reached into her bag and pulled out a present wrapped in brightly colored Christmas paper. She shyly handed it to Darcy. "Merry Christmas boss."

Darcy smiled as she took the gift from her. She placed it on the counter in front of her and said, "Thanks, Sue. I have something for you, too." She bent down and picked up a gift bag from under the counter and handed it to Sue.

The younger girl's face beamed. "Thanks so much."

They both ripped into their gifts. Darcy peeled back the paper from hers to find a copy of 'Forgotten Bookmarks: A Bookseller's Collection of Odd Things Lost Between the Pages'. Her eyes grew wide. "Oh Sue, thank you so much. This is incredible." Darcy was very touched by her friend's thoughtfulness. She had wanted to find a copy of this book for a long while now. Now here it was, in her hands.

"Oh wow, thanks Darcy," Sue said as she held up a huge, warm looking scarf, all fuzzy and red. Then she realized what she had and could not sit still. Bouncing up onto her feet she danced in a little circle. "Darcy! Oh, wow, Darcy! This is a Nordstrom solid woven cashmere scarf! Oh my God! You are the best! I love it!" Sue wrapped it around her neck and moved over to the mirror on the side wall of the bookstore. She modelled for herself, smiling widely.

"I take it you like it?" Darcy asked jokingly.

"This is so warm! I'm going to wear it all the time. Thank you!"

The two women shared a quick hug before Sue got to work behind the counter, still wearing the scarf. Darcy smiled, thinking to herself how this was one of the reasons why she loved the holidays so much. The good feeling of giving a friend a gift that you knew they would enjoy. It reminded her of how thankful she was to have good friends in her life.

Jon's present was carefully hidden away in her house. She hoped he liked it as much.

DARCY LEFT work right after lunch, leaving the store in Sue's capable hands. She wanted to visit with Katrina Samson. She headed out of town on her bike, knowing she could have called for a taxi or borrowed someone's car, but she had wanted to enjoy the feeling of the fresh air on her face. She didn't really mind the cold. Not when it was wrapped up in the feeling of the holidays like this.

Jon's directions said that Katrina's house was by Bottleneck Lake and would be fairly easy to find. She hoped that he was right. She rode on towards the lake along the deserted road. There used to be five or six houses built up around the lake back in the nineteen-fifties, from what she understood, but the ones that still stood were abandoned now. Except, apparently, for Katrina Samson's house.

An uneasy feeling started to settle in her stomach as the house came into view. It was surrounded by tall trees and it was in desperate need of repair. A couple of the shutters out front were hanging off to an angle, and she could see where the shingles were starting to rot in several spots. There were curtains drawn over every window. Darcy couldn't tell if anyone was home or not.

As she pulled up to the front of the house she could feel her cheeks and hands stinging from the cold. She chastised herself for not wearing gloves so her hands were at least protected. She imagined that her face must be glowing red by now from the brisk cold air. She hopped off her bike and wheeled it up to the porch steps. It occurred to Darcy then that perhaps she should have let Jon come with her after all. She had no idea what Katrina would be like or what the whole story was.

Then her mind took a horrifying twist. What if Katrina had killed her father? Darcy was halfway up the steps and almost onto the porch when she thought of that scary notion. She had faced a few murderers thanks to her special gifts, and she wasn't looking forward to meeting another. Especially in an out of the way and secluded place like this. She decided that she was going to leave and come back later with Jon. Yes. That sounded right.

She turned around to go back down the steps when she heard someone open the front door. She froze in place.

"Who's there?" The woman's voice sounded quiet and sweet. Not able to hide, Darcy turned back to the middle aged woman peering through the screen door at her. The woman's blonde hair was done up in a bun and she was wiping her hands on an apron worn over a simple flower-print dress. She certainly didn't look very dangerous. Darcy climbed back up the steps and gathered her courage.

"Hello, Mrs. Samson. My name is Darcy Sweet. I own the Sweet Read bookstore in town." The woman nodded, her face curious, so Darcy continued. "I know this will sound strange, and

I know we've never met, but I was hoping that I could speak to you about your father."

The woman's face puckered into a frown. "My father? Goodness, why on Earth would you want to talk to me about my father?"

Darcy smiled, thinking reassuring thoughts, hoping to persuade Katrina that she wasn't some crazy person come knocking on the door. "I've heard about your father's murder. I was hoping that maybe you could answer some questions for me."

Katrina's expression never relaxed, but she did nod and open the door for Darcy. "I don't mind, I suppose. Please come in."

She held the door open for Darcy. It was dark inside the house with very few lights on. Katrina shut the door behind them and shuffled ahead of Darcy into the kitchen. "I was just finishing up some baking before I tried to take a nap. My husband is away this week and I've been sleeping none too well without him."

"I'm sorry. I won't keep you long, I promise." Darcy took a seat at the little kitchen table when Katrina waved a hand at one of the chairs for her.

"It's no bother, Darcy. I will say this is odd, though. No one has asked about dad's death for years. Can I get you something to drink to warm you up? You must be frozen coming all the way out here on a bicycle. I have coffee or tea, or I could maybe rustle up some cocoa, if I've got any."

"Some tea would be great, thank you." Darcy rubbed her hands together, just getting the circulation back in them now.

Katrina shuffled around the kitchen in worn slippers that looked too big for her feet, grabbing cups from a cupboard over the sink and taking tea bags out of a metal canister. Putting the kettle on the stove to boil, she sat down with Darcy and folded her hands on the table. Frowning she said, "Now why did you come out here and bring all this ancient history up?"

Darcy felt sorry for the woman. "I didn't mean to intrude on your grief."

To Darcy's surprise, Katrina waved her hand as if she were swatting away the thought. "Don't worry over that. I came to terms with dad's death a long time ago. No suspects, no arrests."

"But your father's case is still open, isn't it?"

Katrina smiled sadly. "For the police, maybe. Not for me. I know exactly what killed my father," she said, pausing for that to sink in for Darcy. "Everyone thinks that it was a gunshot, but the real culprit is the Santa suit."

Darcy thought that she must have misheard. "I'm sorry. What?"

"My father played Santa in the Christmas pageant and that's the reason he died. The suit is haunted."

# CHAPTER 6

*D*arcy was sure she looked as shocked as she felt. Katrina thought that the Santa suit was haunted. Darcy's first reaction was to say that wasn't possible. But she lived in a world where specters showed up on her doorstep and children in graveyards followed her every step.

Haunted clothing? It wasn't the strangest thing she'd ever heard of or seen.

The kettle whistled and Katrina got up to pour water over the bags. "Can you explain that to me?" Darcy asked her.

"I can, but you wouldn't be the first one to just write me off as insane." She said it with a smile, but Darcy could hear the hurt behind those words. She herself knew what it was like to have to keep secrets from people because no one would ever believe you, and to be ridiculed even when you knew you were right.

Maybe she and Katrina had more in common than she realized.

Putting the cups of tea down on the table, Katrina looked thoughtfully into the distance. "My dad was very involved with the town. He always helped out with the festivals and pageants. Everyone in town liked him. So you see, no one had a reason to kill him. The night he died was the night after the Christmas pageant. It was the first year that he'd played Santa." Katrina paused to take a breath. "When I saw him that night in the suit he looked really nervous, almost sick. I had never seen him look that way before. The very next day he was killed."

Katrina focused back on Darcy and took a sip of her tea. "So you see, I know what killed my dad. That suit is haunted. By what, I don't know. But whatever it is killed my dad. As sure as you and I are sitting here, that's what got him killed."

That night Darcy lay awake in bed once again. Her visit with Katrina was running through her mind on a continuous loop. Could the suit be haunted? Could a ghost be responsible for Roger's death? Why? Why would a spirit do something so drastic? There were documented cases of poltergeists destroying property, even hurting people. As far as she knew, however, there had never been a ghost that actually killed someone.

That didn't put it beyond the realm of possibility. Especially if the ghost haunting the Santa suit—if there was one—had a grudge against Roger August. There were too many questions and absolutely no answers. She needed to speak to Roger once again.

Communicating with the other side was meant to be done in specific steps. She didn't like to use them because of the drain on her physical and mental energy, but in situations where she had no other choice, they were her measure of last resort.

Smudge followed her around the house as she got together the thick white candles, sticks of incense in a ceramic holder and the old bed sheet that she used when she performed the ritual here in the house. Setting the sheet out in the living room, she put the candles around the edges in an exact pattern and lit each one in order. After lighting the incense sticks she sat in the middle of the circle of candles, cross-legged, and cleared her mind.

Nearby her, within the circle of candles, mist formed in slithering tendrils. She let it happen, let the bridge between this world and the next solidify as she poured her own self into that connection, reaching out for Roger August.

She waited. Nothing happened.

"Roger?" she asked. "Are you there?" No one answered her. She couldn't get any feel for him at all, which was very unusual. The last time that had happened, it had meant the supposedly dead person she was trying to contact was still alive. She didn't get the feeling that was the case here, though. There was something else going on. It was like something was blocking her. Keeping her from communicating with Roger's spirit.

Standing up, stretching, she checked the clock and only then realized that three hours had passed. When she put herself into that state time had no meaning. She could have sat there for a day or more without realizing it, and in truth she had done that once. It was dangerous, to sit there for that long. There was a real risk that her body could die from inattention even as her spirit continued to search for a connection.

A wave of dizziness swept over her and she caught herself against a nearby wall. Smudge looked up at her, his head cocked. "I'm all right, boy. Just need some water." She collected the candles, snuffing them out in proper order, and then put them away again for next time.

It was when she was heading to the sink for a glass of water that the thought hit her. What if the Santa suit that Katrina had told her about was the same one she had now, the same one that the pageant had used for years now?

She raced back into the living room and picked up the suit. Tentatively she held it out at arm's length and inspected it closely. It looked old, but there was really no way of knowing for sure if it was the same suit or not.

She closed her eyes and tried to feel for any strange, haunted powers that the suit might be holding. A snap against her fingers startled her into dropping it to the floor. She flexed her hand, feeling foolish. Just a static electric shock. That's all.

Still, she went and got the candles back out, and formed the circle around the suit with the candles lit. Lighting the candles wasn't really the smartest thing to do but she didn't feel like she had any other choice right now. The circle would contain any spirit for the night. Smudge looked up at her and blinked.

"I know," she said. "It's foolish and dangerous. But I'm not sleeping in the same house with a possessed Santa suit without some precautions."

Darcy and her cat stared at each other and then she laughed out loud. This was ridiculous. Feeling silly, she took herself back up to bed.

But, even though it was dangerous, she didn't blow out the candles. Just in case.

THE NEXT MORNING Darcy was at work when Jon stopped by. Nothing had happened overnight, and the suit was right where she had left it when she woke up. She'd stuffed it back into the pack with her Mrs. Claus suit, and tried to put her energy into thinking up a good way to solve this mystery. A way that didn't involve theories about possessed clothing.

Jon smiled at her. He looked excited. In his hands he was carrying a large, thin book.

"What's that?" Darcy asked.

"Well," he said, obviously proud of himself. "Your boyfriend has been combing through boxes of old files and photos in the basement of the police station. Now, he did this because he loves you, and because he's sorry he ever made you doubt that. Now. Guess what I found?"

He was so excited he was about to burst and Darcy found herself excited too without even knowing what he was talking about. "So tell me already," she laughed.

"Your loving boyfriend, who expects to be rewarded for staying up most of the night going through album after album, found, among hundreds of photographs, a single photograph of your dead man." Jon dropped the book down onto the counter with a flourish and opened it up to a page marked with a scrap of paper. "In this photo album there were pictures for the old Chief's retirement party years ago. And here," he pointed to one of the pictures, "is a picture of Roger."

Darcy looked at it, understanding Jon's excitement now. "You really are the best boyfriend in the world."

"Yes," he agreed. "I am."

Darcy kissed him on his cheek, but whispered a promise to thank him more later. In the photo stood a very stern looking Roger, and next to him was a female police officer. The photo was labelled, Roger's name, and then Rose Abbington. Darcy pointed to the woman. "Who is this?"

"I don't know. A friend of Roger's, maybe. I'll ask around when I get to the station today. Somebody may remember."

"That would be great, Jon. This is one more step closer to finding out who Roger was. If we could find this Rose, and talk to her, she might be able to help."

Not to mention that Darcy would be able to stop putting protective circles around costumes.

DARCY FLIPPED the store's sign to 'CLOSED, THE END' and pulled the front door of the bookstore shut behind her as she left. She hopped on her bike just as Helen began calling for her from the town square. Darcy headed over to her with a smile.

Helen smiled back at her and said, "I just wanted to thank you again for taking over for Santa and Mrs. Claus this year. We need a hundred more volunteers like you and Jon."

"You're too kind, Helen." Darcy debated with herself, but then asked the question anyway. "Say, that suit for Santa looks very old. Do you know how long it's been used in the pageant?"

"Well I'm not really sure," Helen said, thoughtfully pursing her lips. "I know it's been used for years. Might even be the original suit the town used back when the pageant first began thirty five years ago."

A chill ran down Darcy's spine that had nothing to do with the weather. If the suit had been around that long, then it was the exact same one that Roger had used the day before he was killed. She realized Helen was looking at her oddly as she stood there silent, so she started up a conversation about something else entirely, and then a few minutes later said her goodbyes and headed for home.

As she rode her bike out of town, she couldn't help but notice the way the mists were rising in the shadows. It was an eerie thing to see in the cold. Sunlight sparkled on the coalescing vapors as they hung low to the ground. The town had been named after this very phenomenon, this mist that was always present here no matter the time of year. Of course, Darcy knew that they came out strongest when something bad was going to happen. Or when danger was coming.

When she made it home, brooding about Santa suits and dead men and how she always managed to get herself caught in the middle of these mysteries, she was a little alarmed to find the door unlocked.

Carefully she let herself in, the smell of cinnamon and apples filling her nose. Jon's humming reached her from the kitchen. She relaxed. What a wonderful surprise. He must have used the spare key that she kept in the pot plant on the porch to let himself in. She fully expected to get another lecture from Jon some time about it. She had kind of promised him not to keep it in the pot any more. Oh well, couldn't be helped now.

"Wow. What is that wonderful smell," she said as she took her coat and hat off.

She stopped to admire Jon's jeans straining tightly over his perfect butt as he was bending over at the oven, looking at whatever was cooking. He stood up with a smile and moved over to pull her into his arms for a kiss. "I'm cooking an apple pie. It's something my grandmother always did around the holidays and it helps me feel closer to her." He hugged Darcy to his body tightly. "I've missed you these last few days. Let's not fight anymore."

Darcy tensed and he felt it. Pulling back he gave her an intense look. "What's wrong?" She could feel him tensing up also. Was it always going to be like this between them?

"I have something to share with you, but you're probably not going to like it. Again."

He dropped his arms away from her and her heart stopped beating for just a moment, until she realized he wasn't walking away from her. Instead, he took her hand and led her to the couch in the living room. "Tell me what it is," he said to her.

She took a deep breath and explained about what happened with Katrina and what she said about the Santa suit. She had expected Jon to play it off with a joke. Or, maybe she had been hoping he would.

"Do you think it's haunted?" he asked instead.

"No, I don't think it's haunted," she said, a little exasperated. "I'm not even sure that's possible."

"But you said you put one of those candle rings around it."

She knew her cheeks reddened. "Yes. I did. It was silly."

"All right. Then I'm sure it's fine," Jon said. "Besides, who's ever heard of a haunted Santa suit?"

*D*arcy knew it was very early before she even opened her eyes. The sun wasn't even up yet. It was the weekend again and she should be sleeping in. She sighed as she thought about all of the work she needed to get done today in time for the pageant that night.

She lay there for a while listening to Jon's rhythmic breathing. After several minutes she knew that she was too wide awake to try and go back to sleep so she slipped quietly out of bed, dressed and headed down to the kitchen for breakfast. Soon, she had eggs scrambling and bacon frying.

Looking still half asleep Jon shuffled into the kitchen in time for her to scoop eggs onto a plate. "Good morning," she said to him. He yawned in return, smiling like a little boy.

As they sat down to eat breakfast Darcy reminded him about the pageant that night.

"I'm ready," he assured her. "Although I will have to check and make sure there aren't any ghosts inside the Santa suit before I put it on."

Darcy laughed. She felt relaxed that Jon could joke around about it.

They finished up breakfast and Darcy packed the dishes into the sink while Jon got showered and dressed. He came back out clean and looking good enough that she couldn't take her eyes off him for a long moment.

When he winked at her she cleared her throat and then said, "You need to meet me in the town square around six o'clock this evening to get into costume."

"Yes ma'am," he said cheekily with that grin still firmly planted on his face.

JON DROVE THEM INTO TOWN. She didn't even bother bringing her bicycle this time because she and Jon were meeting up again for the pageant that evening. In the town square, everyone was hustling about doing last minute preparations. After kissing Jon goodbye so he could stop into the station and ask around about Rose Abbington, Darcy went to the bookstore so she could put the box of costumes somewhere safe. Then she went over to the Bean There Bakery and Café to get a large coffee. She'd need it to get through the day.

When she entered the café she saw Helen sitting at one of the tables frantically flipping through a notebook and scribbling things down. She looked pretty frazzled. Darcy sat down across from her. "Is everything all right?" she asked Helen.

Helen looked up at Darcy with wild eyes. She ran a hand through her graying hair and said, "Oh I'm just stressed about this damn pageant. This is my first year doing it as mayor and I just want everything to go perfectly."

"Oh, Helen you'll be fine. You're one of the most put together women I know." She saw that bring a little smile to her friend's face. "So I take it that Mister Baskin's petition didn't get anywhere?"

"Oh at least one thing went right and worked out for the town. He didn't get enough signatures. I'm still surprised at all the signatures he did get, though." Helen rubbed her eyes. "I'm so tired already and the day has barely begun."

Darcy smiled at her. "I've got the rest of the costumes over at the bookstore. When you're ready, let me know and you can do your final review of them." Darcy stood up and placed a comforting hand on Helen's arm. "Everything is going to go perfectly."

"Thank you Darcy, I'm not sure what I would do without you."

AS SOON AS Darcy entered the bookstore a chilling, violent wind picked up. It viscously swirled around the store knocking books to the floor, knocking knick knacks over and sending her paper snowflakes flying like they were the real thing.

"Oh for the love of God," she muttered. Why did this particular ghost have to be accompanied by such a powerful wind every time he wanted to make contact?

Darcy watched as Roger's spirit materialized out of nowhere. *"I cannot find peace until I know."*

"I need more time," Darcy said, a little grumpily. What did this ghost expect? She was only human.

Roger ominously held up two fingers and then abruptly disappeared. She didn't even have time to ask him why she hadn't been able to communicate with him the other night.

"Hey!" she shouted after his disappearing image. "What did that mean? Was that a threat?" There was no answer, not from beyond the grave.

Two fingers. Did that mean two days? It would be Christmas in two days and Darcy hoped that she would have solved the mystery by then. Of course, it could have meant two hours or two minutes or two lumps of sugar in his coffee, for all she knew. If ghosts wanted faster results, they could try using a language that the living could understand.

She picked up the fallen books and placed them back on the shelves. Shaking her head she gathered up the costumes and headed over to the town square.

DARCY HELPED Jon into the Santa suit jacket and rearranged the padding for the Santa belly. As he pulled the hat and fluffy white beard on she stepped back to look at him. "You make a pretty convincing Santa," she said with a wide smile.

He frowned at her as he adjusted the beard. "This thing is itching me already. Exactly how long do I have to wear it for?" She knew he was only pretending to be annoyed as his eyes were twinkling almost as brightly as the little colored lights strung all around the stage area.

"Not long, now don't be such a grouch." She nudged him in the ribs and he couldn't suppress his smile any longer.

The pageant was due to start in about thirty minutes and there was a lot of activity going on behind the stage.

Everything looked beautiful with the trees on stage decorated so lovely and all of the sparkly lights hung about the place everywhere. It looked magical.

The town square was filling up with townsfolk eager to watch the pageant. Darcy was sure that it was going to be a hit. Helen would be so happy, she thought, after all the work she'd put into it. As if on cue, Helen appeared on stage beside her, trying to be everywhere at once.

"Let's see you in your Missus Claus outfit then," Jon said jokingly. Darcy quickly donned the outfit which magically turned her into a plump older woman in a red dress with green trim. She pulled on the wig of white hair and then settled the round wire-rimmed glasses on her nose.

"We make quite the couple," Darcy said to him, her voice pitched higher. Jon laughed and kissed her. Darcy blinked through the glasses and decided to do without them. They were pinching her nose and giving her a headache. They actually looked like they might have been someone's prescription glasses instead of costume fakes. She left them behind on her duffle bag.

They moved closer to the stage area to listen to the carolers singing a jaunty rendition of Jingle Bells followed by a more sedate Silent Night. Darcy laughed at Jon's attempt to hug her from behind, their fake padding making it difficult.

The carolers sang several more Christmas songs and the audience joined in. Each person had a lit candle and Darcy thought that it looked magical to see the little flames swaying in time with the music. She was feeling very mellow and happy and was looking forward to this first Christmas, her first together with Jon.

When the carolers had finished singing it was time for the school children to perform the nativity play. They did a great job and almost moved Darcy to tears. At the end of the play the carolers returned and everyone sang Away in a Manger. As the song was ending Helen came up to them and told them to get into place. They were going on straight after the song was finished. They were to sit in a fake sled together and then the children would come up on the stage to sit on Jon's lap and tell him what they wanted for Christmas.

Darcy smiled up at Jon, turning to say something to him, just as some motion above them caught her eye.

She pulled Jon forward and between his weight and the awkward phony girth of their costumes they ended up toppling over onto the stage in front of the carolers and the entire town.

Behind them, the metal truss that had been holding up the

stage curtain came crashing down onto the stage. Everyone went silent.

"Dear God," Jon breathed. "That could have killed me."

Darcy let him help her up, eyeing the Santa suit he was wearing.

# CHAPTER 8

The show must go on.

The fake sleigh was moved down to the front of the stage so Mister and Mrs. Claus could sit in it and let the children tell him what they wanted for Christmas. Helen had been a wreck as the stage collapsed around them, but Darcy and several of the others pointed out that no one was hurt and there was no reason to disappoint the children. This was the solution they had come up with.

Kids sat on Jon's lap and gladly pretended he was the real thing. He did his best to be cheery and not at all upset that he had nearly just been killed. Several of the parents whispered questions asking if he was okay. He would spout "ho ho ho, of course!" and they would smile and move on.

Darcy knew better. They weren't okay. This mystery had almost just cost Jon his life. That damned suit might not be haunted, but there sure was something more than either of them knew going on here.

WHEN THE PAGEANT HAD ENDED, Darcy and Jon hurried to her bookstore and stripped out of their costumes there. Neither of them wanted to go backstage to do it, not after the stage setup had tried to kill him. Jon threw the Santa suit on the floor and looked at it like he expected it to bite him.

"No way. No way did a suit just try to kill me." He ran his hands over his head repeatedly as he paced. Darcy picked the suit up, her hands shaking. Jon snatched it away and tossed it down again. "Don't touch that thing! What should we do with it? Burn it? Is there an exorcism for clothes?"

Darcy tried not to find that funny. Nothing about this was humorous. "I don't think we should get ahead of ourselves," she said. "I'm still not willing to say this thing is haunted."

"I say we burn it. I'll buy the town a new one."

The idea was tempting. Still, if there was a spirit in it, bad things might happen if they tried to destroy the suit without first destroying or dispersing the entity within.

"Look, Jon, I'll store it for now." He gaped at her. "I'll put it in a protective ring. I have some sacred earth in the back. If I lace it with sugar then anything that's inside the ring will be stuck there until I break the circle."

After a moment, he shifted his stance and crossed his arms. "Obviously, there's a lot more to your abilities than I realized."

"There is. I'll tell you all about it." She hesitated. "If you still want to hear it?"

He sighed, but came to her and folded her into his arms. "I do. I promise. Just, not right now, okay?"

She knew that was the best she was going to get. She just hoped it wouldn't be the way it always was between them.

AFTER PUTTING the Santa suit into a paper bag from behind the sales counter in the store and placing the protective ring around it, she and Jon went to Darcy's house where Jon made cocoa for the two of them. He dropped a couple of marshmallows into each cup and Darcy giggled. "Aren't we a little old for marshmallows?"

"I nearly got killed today. You nearly got killed with me. I don't care how old I am, I want marshmallows."

She took a sip and the extra sweetness from the gooey marshmallows made it that much nicer. She licked her lips and let the warmth from the drink make her feel better. "Okay, you're right, it is delicious. Thanks."

They headed into the living room and got comfortable on the couch next to each other. They were quiet for a few minutes while they sipped at their drinks.

"So what should we do next?" Jon asked.

Darcy frowned. "I know you'll be against it but I need to do a communication with the other side."

"A communication?" Jon said.

"Um, yes. I tried it once already but there was no contact. I think I need to push it more. There was a block to the communication that I don't understand. I need to get by that block. That's the only way we will know if something is wrong with the Santa suit or if something else is really going on here."

Jon was quiet for a moment until he said, "I understand. You should do whatever it takes to solve this. Just like you always should. I shouldn't stand in the way of that."

His understanding made Darcy feel all warm and happy. She smiled at him and said, "Remember how I told you before about how Millie wrote about her abilities, that they were the same as mine?" He nodded. "Well, I remember reading in the journal something about a way to meditate before a communication to enhance the connection. I'm going to go and get the journal, it's back at the bookstore. The Santa suit, too."

His face twisted when she said it. "Do we have to?"

"I know you don't want to be anywhere near it. Neither do I, but I think we'll need it."

"Fine. But I'm going with you," Jon said. "It will be quicker if I drive and I don't really want you wandering around on your own this late at night with that crazy violent ghost out there somewhere."

Darcy felt a warm feeling spread through her at his concern. It was nice to know his love was there for her.

As soon as they arrived at the bookstore Darcy went to get the journal. As she reached for it the book flew across the room at Jon. With lightning fast reflexes he reached up and caught it before it could smack the side of his head.

"Millie!" Darcy yelled at her aunt. She wasn't sure if Millie was just making trouble, playing pranks like she always did, or if she was trying to tell them something. "Are you trying to warn me about something, Millie?"

The book wrenched out of Jon's hands and flew back across the room towards her, falling softly into her hands. "Thanks. That was very informative." She rolled her eyes and opened the journal to the page she needed. Refreshing her memory, she nodded firmly. "Yes. This, and the suit. You want to grab that?"

"No. I will, because I love you, but I don't want to."

She smiled at him. "Just be sure to break the circle with your toe first."

He eyed her skeptically, but she watched him as he did exactly as she had instructed. In the meantime, she got the candles out that she kept in the shop. Never know where you might need to use them, she always figured.

With the journal firmly in her hands and Jon carrying the paper sack with the suit in it, they left the bookstore and went back to the pageant stage. Darcy wasn't too keen on being around here this late at night, especially after what had happened earlier.

"Why here?" Jon asked her. He checked his watch, finding out exactly what Darcy had already known. It was after midnight. Everyone had gone home. Everyone, that was, except for them.

"This is where the event happened. If there is any connection between our world and a ghost living in this Santa suit, it will be strongest here."

"Do you ever keep track of the number of times during the day you say things like that with a straight face?"

She shrugged, taking the package with the suit from him. "It's who I am. I've gotten used to it."

He watched her silently. She desperately wanted to ask him what was going through his mind, but this wasn't the time or place.

The area was completely deserted as Darcy had known it would be. Yellow barrier tape surrounded the stage until the town's work crew could come out tomorrow and remove the broken staging. By mutual consent, they set up right in front of the stage.

Darcy set the candles, lit them, and set the Santa suit on the ground in front of her. She realized that she was very tense and tried to relax and breathe deeply. If she was honest with herself she could admit that she was a little apprehensive about doing this particular communication. Roger had scared her during the couple of times she had communicated with him previously.

This time, when she sat cross-legged, it was to study her aunt's journal for a minute or so until she was sure she had the basics of the technique down.

"Thank you, Millie," she whispered. She looked at Jon and said, "I need total silence to do this, okay?" He nodded but didn't speak. She could see he was tense and she guessed he was worried about her doing this. She wouldn't be doing it if it wasn't very necessary. Then she began.

The flames from the candles spread a soft, flickering light where there was only darkness otherwise. In her mind, she recited the words from her aunt's journal.

*"To be better protected from, and better connected to, the other side, you must have a very firm grip on your own life. You must be certain your life is in order, before you can attempt to order around the stronger spirits that you may encounter."*

Which made sense. She thought about her life now. She and Jon had been fighting, and headed down a road to breaking up. They were back together now, stronger in many ways than they had been. He was accepting of her. She had that in her life, and she could build on that foundation to become stronger.

She was stronger.

She took hold of the Santa suit and called out for Roger August. For a few moments nothing happened, just like before. Something was blocking her. It was Roger himself, she realized. His spirit was trying to keep her from seeing what she needed to see. With a force of will, she pushed that barrier aside, and made the connection. She was inside Roger's memory.

She saw him, Roger, in the Santa suit waiting behind a stage and she realized that this must be that long ago pageant. The one twenty years ago just before he died. The image faded in and out between scenes of him talking to kids and then walking off stage when the pageant was done and then suddenly Darcy heard a grunt of pain. She saw Roger limping away from the stage. He was injured, somehow, but still alive. The viewpoint shifted and she saw one last thing before the images vanished. A man, standing in shadows behind Roger. There was no way to see his face. Yet, somehow he looked familiar.

Darcy tried to push harder, to see more, but she felt the force against her multiplying. She was snapped forcefully back to reality, Jon holding her arms as her head lolled to the side.

"Darcy, are you okay?" Jon asked. His voice was tight with worry.

"Yes, I think so," she said. The night was dark around them. The candles were knocked over, their wicks trailing wisps of smoke. The Santa suit was on the ground a good distance from them in a heap as though it had been thrown aside.

Jon pulled her into him and hugged her tight. "I couldn't wake you," he said as he pulled back to look at her. "The wind was so strong." He hugged her to him once again.

"Wind?" She remembered something then, something of a cold arctic blast that pushed her around while she was trying to hold onto the connection of the communication. Roger August. Or was it something else?

Darcy's mind was still on the image that she had seen. And then it came to her. She realized who the man was. She pulled back out of Jon's arms a little so she could see him. "I think that Mister Baskin killed Roger."

# CHAPTER 9

"When you weren't responding to me, back there in the town square, there was an icy wind blasting around us." Jon's eyebrows were drawn down in a frown of worry. They were sitting in Darcy's kitchen, huddled around cups of hot chocolate. Darcy just couldn't seem to get warm. "Why was this one so violent?"

"One of the entities involved in this is trying to keep me from seeing into things. They're exerting a force working against me."

"One of the entities?" he asked, his eyebrows shooting up.

"Right. At first, I thought it was Roger himself. Now, we have to consider the possibility that the suit really is haunted in some way by something. So that's why I say, one of the entities."

"Could it be something else entirely?" Jon asked her.

Darcy appreciated the way he was making an effort to understand this part of her. With a smile she couldn't quite suppress she leaned across the table to kiss his cheek. "I'll know more when we talk to Roland Baskin."

"You're sure it was him you saw in the vision?"

"Very sure." Darcy shuddered as she remembered. "I saw a younger version of Mister Baskin in the background, standing behind Roger August just as Roger got hurt somehow. It must have been him."

Jon nodded. "We should go and talk to him in the morning. Right now I think we both need sleep."

"I wish that you could take my visions as evidence and arrest him or at least bring him in for questioning," Darcy said, putting a hand over a yawn she hadn't felt coming until he mentioned sleep.

"You've done your part," Jon said to her. "Now it's time for old fashioned police work to do the rest."

"POLICE STATION FIRST," Jon told her. "I'm all for confronting Baskin, but I want to look up a few things first."

As they drove into town the next morning, Darcy noticed the fog being burned away by the bright winter sun. Most of the snow still clung to the ground, and the mists were quickly receding back into the white ground cover. She didn't think Jon had seen them.

He let her out in front of the bakery and then told her he'd meet her over at the station. "Make mine black," he told her, holding her hand briefly before letting her go. She knew he'd never admit it, but he was still shook up over last night.

When Darcy entered the café she could see that Elizabeth Archer, Helen's assistant, was working behind the counter. Helen was nowhere to be seen. "Helen not working today?" Darcy asked Elizabeth.

"No. What can I get you?" Darcy had always found the middle aged woman to be rather abrupt. With those scars on her face that she kept hidden behind her long auburn hair, Darcy didn't doubt that she'd had a rough life. Even after Elizabeth had been in town now for several months, Darcy knew little about her.

With the coffees in hand Darcy made her way back to the

police station. She'd remembered to bring one for the desk sergeant and he smiled at her in appreciation as he waved her through to the offices where Jon worked. Sergeant Fitzwallis was an older man that Darcy had gotten to know pretty well after so many trips here to visit with Jon and Grace. "Come back when you can bring me a sandwich, too, you hear?"

Darcy laughed and promised she'd bring him some of Jon's apple pie next time she came through. He acted surprised that Jon would be able to cook anything past boiling water.

That was Jon, she thought. In his own way he had as many layers to his life as she did to her own.

As she came through the door she could see Jon tapping away at his computer, looking thoughtfully at whatever he was reading. He looked up and smiled at her when she set his coffee down in front of him.

"Have you found anything yet?" Darcy asked him.

"Noise complaints. Baskin has literally filed hundreds of noise complaints. All around Christmas, most of them related to the pageant." He shrugged. "Other than that, there's nothing on him. Either in our database or anywhere online that I can think to look."

Darcy thought about that. "Well maybe he just wasn't caught for anything before."

Jon made a noncommittal face, then took a big slurp of his coffee. "Won't know until we ask, I guess. Ready to go and have a chat with him?"

JON KNOCKED on the front door of the small, well-kept cottage. It had been a short walk to Baskin's house, here on a quiet street just off the main town center.

Baskin answered with a grumpy expression, shoulders hunched, eyes narrowed. "What do the two of you want?"

Jon kept his voice calm and even managed a smile. "We would like to speak to you about the Christmas pageant."

He looked from Jon to Darcy and back to Jon again. He made no attempt to invite them in. "What do you want to know?"

"Why don't you like the Christmas pageant, Mister Baskin?" Darcy asked him. If he wasn't going to let them in, they needed to get to the heart of their questions quickly.

Baskin scowled at her. "It's too noisy, that's why. I'm old and I just want a peaceful life but every time there is something to celebrate Misty Hollow makes the biggest racket. And that stupid Christmas pageant is the worst." He waved his hands animatedly, his voice growing angry. "I thought I could get enough signatures to stop the damned thing, but I should have known better. This town never listens to reason. I've been trying to stop that stupid pageant for years but it never works. You should know," he said to Jon, "you nearly died in it yesterday, didn't ya?"

"Now how did you know that, Mister Baskin?" Jon asked him with deceptive politeness. "I figured a man like you who was so dead set against the pageant wouldn't have been there at all."

Baskin scratched at his balding head. "I wasn't there. I was out of town, just like every year. Can't stand to be here. It's just all around town this morning, is all."

"Oh? And where exactly were you when you were out of town?"

Baskin sighed loudly. "I was in Meadowood with my daughter, if you need to know. What's this all about?"

"Do you have any proof of that?" Jon pressed.

Baskin glared at Jon. "What is this, an interrogation?" Baskin snapped. "I do have proof actually." He pulled his wallet out of the back pocket of his trousers and showed them a receipt from a dinner with his daughter. "There. If you need to know so badly, there it is. I always pay."

Jon and Darcy looked at the receipt carefully. It was time stamped for a half hour after the pageant began. Assuming the credit card number on the receipt matched Baskin's then this gave him an alibi. They thanked him for his time and left him grumbling in his doorway.

In the car on the way back into town Jon said, "So much for that. Wouldn't we have seen him around the stage, anyway? Someone would have. You can't cause that kind of trouble without someone seeing it."

"You're probably right," Darcy agreed. "Now what?"

"We need to talk to everyone else who was behind the stage last night to see if they know anything or saw anyone acting suspiciously. I will get a couple of officers to do that. Right now I am going back to the station and do some more digging into Rose Abbington. The female police officer in that photograph. I was working on that angle when this thing with the suit and the pageant came up."

He pulled into the parking lot in front of the police station and shut the engine off. "I don't know, Darcy. Maybe this Roger guy, er, ghost is barking up the wrong tree. Maybe there's a simple explanation and his spirit is just refusing to believe it?"

How did she explain this to him, she wondered. "It doesn't actually work that way," she said at last. "The spirits of the dead are aware of certain information that they can't necessarily pass on to us. If Roger says he needs me to find out who murdered him, you can bet that it wasn't an accident or a simple mugging or something like that."

He looked at her skeptically, but didn't say anything. Instead he leaned across and kissed her. It was the best answer she could have hoped for.

"Okay. I have a couple of things to do so I'll see you later?" she said. He nodded and she jumped out of the car to head over to the bookstore. She knew what she needed to do now. Although it was dangerous she didn't feel like she had another option. She needed to try and communicate with Roger again. Otherwise they were at a dead end.

But before she could go home and do that she had a special book club Christmas meeting to attend to. Life went on even if the dead needed her attention. The mystery of the Santa suit would have to wait for a couple of hours.

THE BOOK CLUB group were in high spirits as they took turns reading passages from Charles Dickens' 'A Christmas Carol.' Darcy thought that the book was fitting with what she had been going through with her own Christmas ghost, plus it suited everyone's holiday mood so well. She could just imagine Roland Baskin as Scrooge, humbugging his way through life. What had happened in his life, she wondered, to make him hate Christmas so much.

She was anxious to get home and begin her preparations to summon Roger August's ghost again. All through the book meeting she fidgeted and tried to apply herself to the reading of the book. Afterward, everyone stayed to try some of the delectable treats that Cora Morton and Evelyn Casey had brought in.

Preston Morgan had brought in a huge batch of his special recipe eggnog and Darcy was sure that the group would be tipsy before they started filing out. Maybe she should just have one of the group lock up for her, when they left. She wished that Sue had been able to attend this meeting but she'd had a family gathering to get to so it was left to Darcy to handle it alone today. Which was fair enough, as Sue had worked most of the day covering for Darcy while she had been out with Jon investigating the mystery.

She stayed longer than she wanted to, checking her watch when no one was looking. She had to admit everything was tasty, though. Maybe just one more fruitcake cookie.

She was about to make her escape when she realized that the

group before her presented an opportunity she shouldn't pass up. At least half of the book club members had lived in Misty Hollow for more than twenty years so she figured that any of them could have known Roger. Maybe they would have information about his murder. She just needed to find the perfect opening in the conversation to bring it up casually.

In the end it was easier to do than she had thought it would be. Tommie Sullivan, who was on about his fifth glass of spiked eggnog by then, started to reminisce about Christmases past. Something in The Christmas Carol story had set him off and he started rambling about lost friends. Darcy was surprised to hear him say Roger's name.

"You knew Roger August?" she asked Tommie.

He looked at her with slightly unfocussed eyes and hiccupped behind the sleeve of his blue knitted sweater. "He was my best friend at school and the friendship lasted after we finished school. It wasn't right how he was cut down like that. And they never did find the culprit who did it."

Several of the group were listening now, and Tommie began eating up the attention. "He was shot in the back in his own home on Christmas Eve. Twenty years back now. A Christmas never goes past without me thinking about him. It was such a waste. He was such a good person at heart. Grump of a man toward the end of his life, though. Give old Scrooge a run for his money."

"Or Roland Baskin," Cora said, and the whole group laughed with her.

"He was still my friend though," Tommie lamented. "Wasn't right what happened to him."

Darcy asked Tommie for more details and got several stories about stuff they had done in school. None of that helped her, though, and no one else seemed to know him at all. As the group split up for the night and said their goodbyes, Darcy came back to the realization that she would have to call on Roger's spirit again.

~

DARCY WENT BACK to her house quickly. No sense wasting time on this. Sitting cross legged in the living room, the candles arranged, the Santa suit that would allow her to forge a connection to Roger in her lap. Then she took some time to think about her family and Jon, grounding herself in the good things in her life. She had a lot of blessings to be thankful for, and she called upon them all now.

She reached out, putting her energy into the calling, merging with the mists that acted as a conduit between life and death. She felt the resistance, the same force as before acting against her, but she was able to slide through it easier now, and when she was past it she was transported into a new vision.

She was at the police station here in town, but it was years ago, old style furniture and a square metal clock on the wall like she'd seen in movies set twenty or thirty years ago. In the vision she moved, walking through the station, gliding around a corner inside the building until she saw Roger kissing a woman. In the vision she stopped, the scene before her coming into crisp focus. She could clearly make out Roger's features, and those of the police woman, Rose Abbington.

They turned to look at Darcy, shock on Rose's face, anger on Roger's. She went to take a step toward them—

Darcy was thrown out of the vision in a cold blast of air. She looked all around the room and found that once again her home was a mess with objects scattered all over. One of the candles had toppled over with its flames till burning, hot wax dripping onto the hardwood floor. She quickly dove for it and righted it before it could cause a fire. Maybe she should invest in some bases for the candles if this was going to keep happening.

Then she remembered the vision. Roger and Rose were lovers. She needed to tell Jon. Now.

# CHAPTER 10

*D*arcy rode her bike hard through the crunching snow and was out of breath by the time she reached the police station. It was after noon now, but she knew Jon would have waited for her here. She was surprised to find Grace there as well.

"I need to find Jon," Darcy said to her sister, still trying to catch her breath from the ride.

"Well. Glad you two are still made up," Grace said with a smile. "He's in the back room, sis. He's pouring through old boxes of case files. I'm guessing he's doing that on a Sunday for you?"

"Yes. That's true love, isn't it?" They laughed at her little joke, then Darcy raced into the back to find Jon sitting at an old wooden table with cardboard boxes piled in front of him. He looked up when she entered and smiled at her.

She smiled back at him and said, "How's it going? Have you found anything yet?"

"Well, Rose wasn't romantically involved with Roger. She had a fiancé. She took time off after Roger died, though, which as far as I can tell was unusual for her. They must have been close friends." Darcy opened her mouth again to tell him what she had seen in her vision just as he flipped a page. "Oh, it says here that she never married. At least while she worked here. I wonder what happened with the fiancé."

The pieces of the puzzle began to click together in Darcy's mind. "Who was her fiancé?" she asked.

Jon frowned and shrugged. "Beats me. That wasn't something the personnel files listed."

Darcy bit her lip and hoped Jon would take what she had to say with the same trust he had shown her the past few days. "I uh…I communicated with Roger again. Now, before you say anything, we both know it was important and I had to do it and I'm sorry I didn't tell you ahead of time but we're both working so hard to figure this out and we had to know." She was frantically twisting the antique silver ring around and around her finger as she spoke.

She stopped when he took her hands in his and held them still. "I get it," he said softly. "I damn sure am not happy about it, Darcy, but I get it. We'll talk about it later. Just tell me what you found out."

Darcy swallowed, knowing he wouldn't be satisfied until they had talked more. She promised herself to have a long talk with him as soon as all of this was figured out. For now, she had to tell him what she knew. "I saw Roger and Rose kissing and then being caught by someone. Right here in the station all of those years ago. I think whoever caught them was the one who killed Roger."

"So who would know who Rose was engaged to?" she asked.

He smiled, standing up and stretching his back out. "The police officer's best investigative tool of the twenty-first century, that's who."

"What do you mean?" she asked.

"Why, the internet, of course," he explained. "Come with me."

A few minutes later a website for public records gave them the information they needed. Rose Abbington had been engaged to a man, and they had gone so far as to obtain a marriage license.

They read the name together. Darcy gasped.

Rose had been engaged to Leo Hanway.

DARCY HAD last seen Leo Hanway as he was loaning his tools to the volunteers building the stage for the pageant. In Darcy's mind, it all made sense. The "accident" that had nearly killed Jon and her could easily have been staged by someone like Leo Hanway who had a background in construction. Now that she knew Leo had been engaged to Rose Abbington and had seen her and Roger together, that added up to motive.

"I understand why Hanway would kill Roger," Jon said to her. "But why would he want to attack me? That I just don't get." They were on their way to Leo Hanway's house right now to talk to him about the murder of Roger August twenty years ago.

Darcy had thought about that very question too. "He was in the town square when I began asking questions about Roger. He actually told me he didn't know Roger August. So, obviously he lied, but he must have thought we were getting close to uncovering the truth. Attacking you was probably his way of making sure no one ever found out what he did."

"You mean, attacking us," Jon pointed out. "He had to know you'd be right there with me."

Darcy had thought of that, too. Maybe she had been the intended target all along.

It didn't take long for them to reach Leo Hanway's house over on Miller Drive. When they knocked on the door Leo Hanway answered, opening it just a crack. He peered out at them through the small opening. "Jon. Darcy. What is it?"

Jon leaned closer to Leo's face in the doorway. "We want to

ask you some questions about the night of the Christmas pageant." He didn't specify which one.

No sooner had he said that than Leo slammed the door closed. They could hear him running back into the house. Jon turned to her with a look that clearly said "here we go again."

Thrusting his shoulder against the door once, and then again, Jon forced it inward and they took off after Leo. At the back door to his house they caught him, pulling him back inside by the scruff of his neck and both arms even as he thought he was free and clear.

"Ow! Stop it!" Leo screamed and squirmed as Jon held one of his arms behind his back, twisting painfully. "I didn't mean to hurt anyone!"

"Sounds like an admission to me," Jon said. "Leo Hanway, you are under arrest for assaulting a police officer and an innocent bystander, who also happens to be my girlfriend."

Leo slumped against Jon's grip, knowing he was beaten. Darcy waited for him to look her in the eye, then said, "We have some questions about the murder of Roger August, too."

At the police station Darcy and Grace were waiting in the main office. Jon was in the interrogation room with Leo Hanway.

"So now maybe Roger can rest in peace," Darcy said. She had been filling Grace in on the whole story, including the 'haunted' Santa suit.

"What a way to spend Christmas Eve," Grace said.

Jon came into the office and stood next to the desk where they were sitting. He ran a hand through his hair, leaving it mussed and out of place. "Is everything all right?" Darcy asked.

"As fine as it can be, I suppose," was Jon's answer. "He confessed. He discovered that Rose and Roger were having an affair and was so upset that he decided to kill Roger. His first attempt was the night of the Christmas pageant. He dropped a sandbag from the stage on him but it only injured his leg. When that didn't work he snuck into Roger's house on Christmas Eve and shot him in the back. Roger never saw it coming." Jon sat down on the other chair across from Darcy. "He also confessed to attacking me and you, Darcy. He got scared when he thought that we were getting too close to solving the case and panicked."

"He confessed to all that?" Grace said with surprise.

"Yeah, solving this case was easy in the end. He didn't even try to pretend it wasn't him. He told me he doesn't have a lot of time left. Cancer, apparently. Rose Abbington died a few years ago and he's got no reason to keep it inside anymore, I guess. He's very sick and was grateful just to get this off his chest. People are like that, sometimes. He did seem honestly sorry about attacking us, if that means anything."

"So, no haunted Santa suit, then?" Grace asked with a smirk.

"No," Darcy agreed. "No haunted Santa suit."

IT WAS LATE when they reached Darcy's house and they headed straight upstairs to the bedroom. They collapsed onto the bed both too exhausted to even bother with changing out of their clothes.

"So," Jon said, his voice thick with coming sleep, "explain something to me. Why were you having such a hard time contacting Roger's ghost? What was standing in your way?"

Darcy rolled into him more. "Like I said, I think someone didn't want us to know the answer. Someone, a spirit, was trying to block my efforts and that made communicating with Roger more difficult."

"What? Who?"

"The person who loved Roger but had secrets of her own to keep. I figured it out when you told me Leo had said Rose

Abbington had died. That was a piece of the puzzle we didn't have. Rose was having an affair with Roger. She wouldn't want that to come out. At the same time, she might have still felt something for Leo, too, and not wanted him to get in trouble."

"Wow," Jon said to her. "I guess true love extends even beyond the grave."

With her head on his chest, she sighed. "Of course it does."

Darcy was about to close her eyes when something caught her eye in the corner of the room. She tugged on Jon's arm. "What?" he mumbled.

"Roger has returned," she said as she pointed at the ghost shimmering in the corner. Something was different about him. His ghost seemed calmer and more peaceful. His scowl was replaced by a beaming smile and there was a glow to him that hadn't been there before. The cold that he had always brought with him wasn't there this time, either.

Darcy started to explain what was happening to Jon but he put a hand on her arm to stop her. "I can see him," he whispered. There was wonder in his voice.

*"Thank you so much for what you did for me. Now I can rest in peace,"* Roger said. That was all. When his ghost vanished the clock struck midnight.

Darcy turned to Jon and said, "Merry Christmas."

He was still staring at the place where Roger had been standing. He slowly turned to look at Darcy. "How did I see him?"

"Welcome to my world," she said, snuggling down under the covers with him.

DARCY SLOWLY OPENED her eyes as excitement filled her from head to toe. It was Christmas. She jumped out of bed and smiled when Jon complained in his sleep. Smudge lifted his head to glare at her for being up so early and taking away part of his warmth. It seemed that she was the only one interested in starting the day.

She rushed over to the window and looked out to find that it had snowed through the night. A sigh escaped her lips at the sight of the wonderland outside of her window. Thick snow covered everything and the tree branches were hanging low under the weight of it. The morning shone clear and bright. The mists were gone again. For now.

This day was going to be the best Christmas ever, she just knew it. She spent a few moments thinking about the night before when Jon had seen Roger's ghost. That had been a true gift. He would never doubt what she could see now. Not after seeing Roger for himself. She truly felt that their troubles were behind them at last.

She took a quick shower and headed back into the bedroom to dress. She found Jon awake and looking out of the window. "It snowed overnight," he said, happy and a little drowsy still. His hair was sticking up at all angles and he looked adorable. Smudge was nowhere to be seen now and Darcy figured he was probably in the kitchen already waiting for his breakfast.

Jon came over to her and pulled her into his arms. "Merry Christmas Darcy," he said as he lowered his head to kiss her lips.

"Jon," she laughed, "I'm naked!"

"Oh, how scandalous," he teased.

He was so nice and warm and she snuggled in closer to him. They stood like that for a few minutes and then she said, "Come on we need to get ready. Grace and Aaron will be here soon."

"Spoil sport." Jon grinned at her and then sobered. "About last night…"

"Roger's ghost. I know." She shook her head as she picked out her clothes. "I don't know what to tell you, Jon. It was real, I can tell you that. And, I can tell you I'm very happy that it happened. Let's just call it a Christmas miracle and leave it at that, okay? At least for now."

Jon nodded. "I can do that. I could help you get dressed, too, if you want?"

She laughed as he made a grab for her. "Go get showered," she squealed, happy to be with the man she loved on this magical Christmas day.

∾

THE FIRE FLICKERED and danced in the fireplace as Darcy, Jon, Grace and her husband Aaron all sat around Darcy's decorated Christmas tree. There was a lot of laughter and joking going on as they exchanged gifts.

"Wow, thank you so much for this book Darcy, I've been looking forward to this one." Aaron smiled at her as he flipped through the pages of the latest spy novel. Grace was trying on her new boots from Aaron and was walking backwards and forwards in front of him pretending she was in a fashion parade.

Jon handed Darcy a brightly wrapped gift and said, "I hope you like this."

She ripped the wrapping away and sucked in a breath when she found a rare copy of one of her favorite books, Mansfield Park. "Oh my, Jon..." She looked at him watching her. "This is so...I have no words to describe how much this means to me. Thank you." She leaned into him and kissed him. "I love you," she said in a low voice that only he could hear.

His face broke into a beautiful smile as she handed him his gift. "Merry Christmas Jon." She'd been dying to give this to him.

He ripped the paper off the small box and slowly flipped the lid off. He stared at the contents for a moment and then looked up at her shaking his head. "Is this what I think it is?"

"What do you think it is?" She said teasingly. By now Grace and Aaron had stopped their fooling around and were watching with interest.

Jon took the end of the ribbon that was inside of the box and pulled it out slowly to reveal a brand new shiny key hanging from the end. He laid the key in the palm of his hand, almost reverently, and stared at it.

"Is this…?" he tried to ask. "Are you…?"

Darcy was amused at his surprise. "Yes, Jon. I'm asking you to move in with me."

She squeaked when he hauled her into his arms.

"I love you so much Darcy." And then they were kissing each other passionately and the world disappeared.

Until Grace said, "About time."

A loud crashing noise had them pulling apart in alarm. Darcy turned to find that her Christmas tree was sprawled across the floor with decorations spewed everywhere. And there sitting on top of the upturned tree was Smudge looking very pleased with himself.

The four of them looked at each other before breaking out into laughter. Smudge may have accepted Jon being part of Darcy's life, but he wasn't above reminding them that he was the center of attention.

Darcy picked him up from the tree and held him in a tight hug. "Merry Christmas to you, too, Smudge."

**-The End-**

# BOOK 5 – THE STOLEN VALENTINE

# CHAPTER 1

*D*arcy Sweet folded another piece of tape against the back of the big red heart she had cut out of construction paper and decorated with scrapbooking lace. She positioned it just right on the end of one of the metal bookracks in her store, the Sweet Read Bookstore. It was the final touch among all the other Valentine's Day hearts, cupids and roses. When it was in place she stood back to admire her work.

"I think it needs more streamers," Sue teased her. Sue Fisher, Darcy's young and enthusiastic assistant, tapped a finger against her lips. "Yes. And maybe some more roses. There has to be some left in Misty Hollow somewhere."

"Very funny," Darcy told her, sticking her tongue out. She did a slow circle in the middle of the store, checking out the decorations that hung from the ceiling or were propped up on the tables in the reading corner or just stuck on the walls and windows. "I think it looks good. Have you ever seen a better looking Valentine's Day display?"

Sue raised her dark blonde eyebrows. "Nope. It's the best I've ever seen," she said, her tone flat.

Darcy wondered what was eating at Sue. Come to think of it

the girl had been a bit distracted all morning. "Um, Sue? What's up?"

At first she thought Sue wasn't going to answer her. She kept her head down over the magazine she'd been leafing through half-heartedly all morning. Darcy was just about to let it go when Sue suddenly dropped her hands to her lap and smiled in a sheepish kind of way.

"I've met someone new," she said.

"Well, that's good isn't it?" Darcy asked. Sue had finally broken up with her on again, off again boyfriend Randy just before Christmas. Darcy had never really cared for the guy anyway. Sue had never seemed happy with him. Now with a new guy, and at Valentine's Day no less, maybe Sue could be happy again.

Sue's smile got bigger. "Oh yes Darcy, he's the most wonderful guy. It's only been a few weeks and already I just can't stop thinking about him. He could be, you know, the one," she said, her fingers making air quotes to show how serious she was. "His name is Zachary Kendell. I met him at college. Same courses. Same taste in music. He even likes mustard on his hamburgers. Can you believe it?"

Darcy couldn't help but smile back at her. "Yes. I can believe it. It's the season of love after all."

"Oh, well, now, I wouldn't use the big L word just yet," Sue said, but even as the words were coming out her cheeks were coloring red. "Anyway, with winter break and all, he promised to come visit me here. Maybe you'll get a chance to meet him."

Darcy could see Sue really had strong feelings for this Zach. Not that it surprised her. Darcy had fallen for her boyfriend, Jon Tinker, within days of meeting him. They'd taken the big step now of moving in together. She'd never been happier than she was waking up next to him each and every morning.

"So, yeah," Sue continued. "Things are going really well with us. I'm just kind of worried, you know?"

"Worried? About what?"

Sue grimaced and then sighed. "I'm worried about Valentine's Day." As Darcy scrunched her face up in confusion, Sue quickly explained, "I'm worried that it's going to put too much pressure on him. You know how guys are. I don't want Zach trying to go over the top or stressing that I won't be happy with whatever he does. I don't want him to think I expect some big gesture."

Darcy thought about it. "Can I give you some advice?"

Sue practically beamed at her. "Oh Darcy, I've been waiting all morning to ask you! You're the perfect person to give me advice. You and Jon are like the most loving couple I know. Tell me. What are the two of you doing for Valentine's Day?"

Darcy bit her lip and kind of rolled her eyes as she sat down in the chair next to Sue's. "I have no idea. I keep trying to get hints from Jon but he won't tell me anything."

"Or maybe he doesn't have anything yet," Sue said.

Darcy giggled. "He better have something or I'll make him sleep on the couch for a month!" The two girls laughed together. "No, really. I don't care what he does. I just want it to be from the heart. Anything he does that he really means will be fine for me."

"Is that your big advice?" Sue asked, a little disappointed.

"Yup, that's it. That's what you need to do with your new guy. Find something to give him from the heart, and let him know that's all you want from him in return. Expensive doesn't make something special. Love does."

She felt foolish, talking like this about her and Jon and love and all. She chalked it up to Valentine's Day being next week. Love was in the air. It was in her thoughts, too. Turning the antique ring around her finger like she did when she was nervous or distracted, she realized that Sue was still staring at her. She shrugged her shoulders. "I just wish I knew what I could get Jon."

"You should take Jon to the dance in the square on Valentine's Day," Sue suggested with a smile. "You know. A man, a woman, music, dancing. And...whatever." She winked at Darcy when she said it.

Darcy knew Jon was something special in her life. They had gone through a lot together, what with his being a police officer and her special gift. It had taken a little while but he accepted who she was now, all of her, and she loved him all the more for it.

Of course, there were the mysteries and murders that had swirled through their quiet little town over the last year or so, too. Hard to forget those.

To Sue, she said, "Dancing? That sounds like fun. Jon is not such a great dancer when you put him on the spot, but at home, every once in a while he'll take me by my hand when we're alone and the radio is playing some silly song, and we'll just dance around the kitchen forever."

"See? That's what I'm talking about. That's the kind of romance I want to find with someone. Guys are just jerks, that's what I think."

Darcy looked at her out of the corner of her eye. "What about Zach? Is your new guy a jerk?"

Sue's face melted into a dreamy smile. "No. No, he's not."

Darcy got up and went to fiddle with straightening the books in their stacks. "Well, I already volunteered to help plan and decorate the town square for the dance. I'll ask Jon if he wants to take me there for Valentine's Day."

"Shouldn't he ask you?" Sue suggested.

"Sure. But here's my other bit of advice. Don't wait for the guy to ask you to do things, if there's something you really want to do. We aren't kids anymore, and love takes two people."

Sue nodded, looking for all the world like she was taking notes in her head from everything Darcy was saying.

Pulling back her long dark hair from her shoulders, Darcy looked around the empty store. Business had dropped off during the last two weeks, but it was sure to pick up for Valentine's Day. Either people were buying books for loved ones or people buying books about how to meet people. Or even the older ladies coming in to buy romance novels, who like to live vicariously through the dashing deeds of fictional men and women living in perfect worlds.

Darcy's life had been anything but perfect, but she wouldn't trade it for anything. She wouldn't give up her friends here in Misty Hollow or her incredible boyfriend Jon or even being the owner of her Great Aunt Millie's bookstore.

Just as she was thinking that, all of the streamers hanging from the ceiling fluttered to the floor in a messy heap.

Darcy shook her head, hearing faint musical laughter that seemed to come from all around her. Departed, but not forgotten, Great Aunt Millie could be a real handful when she wanted to. Sometimes, she wished she could be the owner of a store that wasn't haunted by the former owner. "Oh for Pete's sake, settle down, Millie," she whispered.

The laughing faded away. Sue sighed heavily and pushed her magazine aside. "I'll get more tape," she said.

# CHAPTER 2

*D*arcy turned the sign on the door from "OPEN a good book today" to "CLOSED, THE END" and pulled the door tightly shut behind her. She'd had a few sales today and tomorrow a shipment of books was due in for their Valentine's Day display, and even Great Aunt Millie had settled down after her one act of mischief. All in all, it had been a good day.

As she was locking up, she thought about how she would soon be able to ride her bike to work once again. Small patches of snow still spotted the streets and lawns around her from the freak storm they'd had just three days ago, but the weather looked like it was starting to fine up a bit. February and March were traditionally mild months in Misty Hollow. No reason to think this year would be any different.

It was still really cold right now, though, and as she headed over to the Bean There Bakery and Café on foot she huddled deep into her warm winter coat, the white one with the fake fur ruff around the hood. Jon had given it to her as a belated Christmas gift. Or, so he said. Sometimes she thought he just liked to spend money on her. Not that she minded. As long as he didn't go overboard. She was just a simple country girl, after all.

She laughed at her joke, knowing full well there was nothing simple about her life. "Darcy Sweet," she thought to herself, "you are a complicated woman with a full life. Just accept it."

She pushed the door to the café open and could see her friend Helen Nelson working behind the counter. Helen was the owner of the café but she had also become the mayor of Misty Hollow after the previous mayor, her husband, had been arrested. That had been when Darcy and Jon had first met. What a way to start a relationship.

The place was almost empty at this time of the day, closing time, when most everyone in town was either headed home or going to work in the next town over for a night shift.

"Hi Helen," Darcy called out as she approached the counter. The warmth in the place was penetrating through her coat and into her body. She shrugged off her coat and laid it over the back of a chair. She'd always liked the cozy, comfortable place Helen had created here. Everyone in town came through here at least once a week. Helen was as much of a mainstay in the town as the persistent mists that gave their town its name.

"Oh, why hello Darcy," Helen greeted her with a warm smile. "Would you like a coffee?" She had been busy rolling dough for some sweet confection, but when she saw Darcy she set that aside and wiped her floured hands off on a cloth and then tidied her graying hair.

"A coffee sounds wonderful, Helen," Darcy told her as she stood at the low glass counter. "It's very chilly out. Mind if I stay here for a while and chat?"

"You know you're always welcome in my store. Take a seat. Anywhere will do. I'll bring you that coffee. And maybe a blueberry muffin?"

Darcy said yes to the muffin—she would have been a fool not to say yes to Helen's baking—and then sat down at a nearby table and sighed. The day hadn't been any longer than most, but it sure felt like it had. Rubbing a hand over her face she tried to stifle a yawn just as Helen set a cup of fragrant coffee in front of her along with a huge muffin on a little plate. Darcy smiled at her friend as Helen sat down across from her.

"You look really tired, Darcy," Helen said to her, holding a ceramic coffee cup of her own between her hands. It was one of those oversized ones, glossed in a riot of colors. Helen didn't bring them out much because people kept walking off with them. "Now, you aren't working too hard, I hope?"

"Look who's talking," Darcy said back to her with a teasing smile. "I'm not the one working two jobs."

"Bah. Running a town like this doesn't take a whole lot of time when you've got good people working for you. And the bakery is just fun. Oh, did I tell you I'm going to hire another worker?"

Darcy started to say something about the last few workers Helen had hired, but thought better of it. No sense dragging up bad memories. "Someone from in town?" she asked instead.

"Um, no. No. I met him on that trip I took a few weeks back. The cooking convention? He really enjoys cooking."

Helen realized she was rambling and stopped herself by taking a sip of her coffee. Darcy noticed the way the older woman's eyes grew distant. She suspected that there was more to Helen wanting to hire this man than just his being a good cook. Good for her, Darcy thought to herself. She and her husband had divorced already, and Darcy knew Helen had been lonely. Apparently not any more.

"Oh, by the way, Helen. That reminds me. I'm not going to be able to work the dance on Valentine's night. I'll still help you guys decorate for it, of course, but I really want to go with Jon to the dance itself. I hope that's okay?"

Helen laughed. "That's totally fine, I understand."

They chatted for a while about mundane things while they drank their coffee. Darcy left a little later and headed over to the police station to see Jon.

# CHAPTER 3

*A*s Darcy entered the police station she dropped a brown paper bag onto the counter in front of Sergeant Fitzwallis, one of the front desk sergeants of the Misty Hollow police department. Darcy had gotten to know most of the men and women who worked here on a first name basis. That was what happened when you were dating a police officer.

The gray-haired man's eyes looked eagerly at the bag. "What's this, then?"

Darcy smiled at him. "Oh it's just a little gift from me to you, Sean. You work too hard."

"Muffins, is it?" He opened the bag and inhaled deeply. "Ah, I'd recognize the smell of Helen's baking anywhere. Thanks, Darcy. You know you don't have to bribe me, right?"

"I'd never dream of bribing a police officer. That's illegal."

They shared a little laugh as Sergeant Fitzwallis buzzed the connecting door open between the station's lobby and the inner areas where the officers did their work. "You bring anything for Jon, did you?"

"Just me," she answered him.

Darcy found Jon and her sister Grace both at their separate

desks bent over case files, busily scribbling notes or turning papers. Grace lifted her head as she heard Darcy come in. She was dressed in a button-up white shirt and her short dark hair was perfectly in place, as usual. She smiled at Darcy, but in a distracted way.

"Hi sis," Grace said. "What's up?"

"Nothing. I just came to see Jon for a few minutes before I head home." He stood up as she got closer, her ruggedly handsome dark haired man, and their kiss was gentle and loving. She caught her sister's carefully schooled expression. Grace was happy for them. For the longest time, Darcy had been sour on the whole prospect of love, after her husband had divorced her and become a jerk.

She caught herself. Best not to talk that way about the dead. Not even Jeff. Not when the dead had a habit of talking back to her.

"I thought you'd be on your way home by now," Jon said to her as he touched her forehead quickly with his and then sat down again. His slacks and dark blue dress shirt were wrinkled, his tie loosened at his neck. His blue eyes lit up, though, as he looked at her. "We weren't supposed to go anywhere tonight, were we?"

"No, no," she told him. Sometimes he got so caught up in his work that he forgot dinners or other small things he'd promised to take care of, like how he was constantly forgetting to pick up milk. "I wouldn't mind a ride home, though. It's cold out there!"

Grace laughed from her desk as she closed one folder and opened another. "You only live just outside of town, Darcy. You always used to walk without complaint before you met Jon."

"Well. I guess I'm getting soft. Or maybe I just want to spend time with him."

"Ah, young love," Grace said in a teasing voice. Darcy stuck her tongue out at her.

Grace pretended not to notice, but Darcy could tell. "Jon was just telling me all about his plans for Valentine's Day," Grace said to her, an eyebrow arched.

Darcy sat down in the chair in front of Jon's desk. "Ooh. Tell me."

He shook his head, though, with a glare at Grace for spilling that out. "I have some plans. It's supposed to be a surprise, though."

"Well, I do like surprises. Hey, I was going to suggest we go to the Valentine's Day dance in town here. You up for that?"

He paused, and she could see him thinking about it. "That should fit in with my plans. You know I can't dance to save my life, though."

"That's okay. You've got your surprise to fall back on, don't you?"

He put a finger up against his lips, silently telling her that she'd have to wait to find out.

Darcy felt warmer inside knowing he was planning something as a surprise. She wished she had thought of something for him by now. For all her talk to Sue about getting something from the heart for the one you loved, she knew it wasn't always that easy.

Darcy turned the question back around on Grace. "What are you and Aaron doing?"

Grace rolled her eyes. "I'm not sure. I haven't been feeling that great lately. I've just got no energy to do anything."

"You work too many hours," Jon said to her.

"Look who's talking," she shot back.

"Wait, sis," Darcy said to her. "If you aren't feeling well then you should go see Doctor Sandal."

Grace waved her off. "I've already got an appointment for tomorrow morning. I swear, Darcy, between you and Aaron I can't step sideways without somebody worrying I'm going to break a nail or something."

Darcy would never tell her tough cop sister this, but she did worry about Grace. Especially after she'd been attacked right here in town and almost ended up in the hospital. She knew it was Grace's job, and police work was dangerous, but that didn't mean she wouldn't worry.

The phone at Jon's desk rang at that moment and Darcy's hopes for a ride home sank. "Misty Hollow Police Department, Detective Tinker speaking. Yes. No, I can do that now." He smiled apologetically at Darcy. She nodded and leaned over the desk to kiss the top of his head. Oh well.

Thankfully, Grace took pity on her. "I'll drive you home, sis. Come on." She stood up, grabbing her jacket from the back of the chair. "You and me can catch up on the way. Then I think I might go home. Get some of that rest I've obviously been missing out on."

Darcy noticed how pale her sister's face looked. She hoped whatever was going on with Grace it wasn't serious.

# CHAPTER 4

*D*arcy drained the pasta and stirred in the sauce. She dumped the salad that she'd just made into a bowl and then the pasta went into another serving bowl with the creamy white sauce. It was a little after seven o'clock now. Later than she liked to eat dinner to be sure, but Jon's shift was only just now getting over. He'd be home soon and she wanted to have dinner waiting for him. She wasn't always able to do it for him.

He did this for her every once in a while, too, only Jon wasn't the greatest cook, outside of a few recipes he knew like his grandmother's apple pie. When he made dinner it usually consisted of take-out pizza or fried chicken.

She had been working on autopilot as she tried to think up the perfect Valentine's gift for Jon. He had one already planned for her. Why had she waited so long to start thinking about this?

She brought the plates and silverware over to arrange on the table and then sat down to think some more. She'd already thought of getting him some of her favorite books, but as much as she loved the man, reading just wasn't one of his hobbies. Jon didn't have a lot of time for reading. They watched movies, usually, when they were home together. She'd have to think of something else.

Dinner plates set and food on the table, she blew an errant strand of hair out of her face and looked at the white plastic clock up on the wall. Hmm. Where was he?

A knock on the front door surprised her. She looked over to her black and white cat, Smudge, laying peacefully in the middle of the kitchen floor. Smudge would have jumped up and hissed or ran away if he sensed anything wrong. The only person she was expecting, though, was Jon.

"Jon?" she asked out loud as she went to open the door. "Why are you knocking?"

She opened it to find her sister Grace standing there. "Uh, hi sis," she said. "What's up? I was expecting Jon."

"Jon got stuck working late. There was a break in to someone's house and he needed to go to the scene. He won't be too late. I told him I'd let you know since I, uh, wanted to come over anyway. Can I come in? It's freezing out here."

Darcy noticed the odd expression on Grace's face almost immediately. At first she attributed it to how her sister had said she'd been feeling tired, but it was more than that. Grace had changed out of her work clothes into jeans and a black sweater under her puffy white winter coat. For all of that, Darcy could see how tense her sister was.

She stepped back for Grace to move into the house. They went into the kitchen, Darcy waiting for her sister to explain what was going on. Shaking her head, Grace went to the table, sat down, and looked up at Darcy.

"I'm pregnant," she said.

Darcy blinked at her. "Wait. What?"

Grace laughed. "I know. I can't believe it either."

"But...how do you...when did you...Grace!" Darcy couldn't make herself finish a thought. Laughing, she went over to her sister and hugged her fiercely. "This is wonderful! Wait, I thought you weren't going to the doctor's until tomorrow?"

Grace smile was a little hesitant. "Well, I wasn't feeling good like I told you and after I got home Aaron pointed out to me that I hadn't had my...you know, yet. So I put two and two together and went to the store for a pregnancy test."

Darcy couldn't help herself from teasing a little as she brought a chair over closer to Grace and sat with her. "Way to go, detective."

Grace rolled her eyes. "Whatever. I've been busy. Me and Aaron both. There's just so much...and now a baby...oh, man!"

Darcy laughed with her sister and they hugged again. She was very happy for Grace. She and Aaron had talked before about starting a family, Darcy knew, but like Grace had said something always seemed to get in the way. Grace's job as a police detective, mostly. "Are you and Aaron okay with this?"

"Well, we have to be, don't we? But, yeah. We're good with it. You should have seen him when I told him, Darcy. He was more excited than I was. I've never been so happy. I still want to go to the doctor tomorrow to confirm it and have everything checked out, but this is for real."

Jon came home not long after that. Darcy had convinced Grace to stay for dinner and talk longer, and he stopped still as he walked into the kitchen to find the two of them staring at him with big smiles on their faces.

"What?" he asked.

Darcy and Grace both spilled the news at once, and after a moment to let the information sink in, Jon hugged Grace and congratulated her.

"Well," he grumbled, "I guess I really better have something good to give Darcy for Valentine's Day, if this is what you're giving Aaron!"

# CHAPTER 5

*D*arcy woke the next morning with Jon's arms wrapped around her. She snuggled into his warmth for a while, just enjoying the feel of him. When she checked the clock on their bedside table it was five minutes before the alarm was due to go off. She decided to let Jon rest and slipped out from under the covers to tiptoe out of the bedroom and to the shower.

Smudge trailed along behind her and jumped up onto the bathroom sink to curl his tail around his feet and blink at Darcy.

She shivered a little as she slipped out of her pajamas and turned the water on steaming hot. Then she reached over and scratched Smudge's chin. He leaned into her and started purring.

"What do you think, Smudge? Am I ready to be an aunty?" Remembering Grace's news from last night she smiled. Smudge smiled at her, his expression almost human. Darcy could hear his thoughts, almost, telling her that she'd be a great aunt. After all, she always kept his food dish full and his water fresh, didn't she?

Looking at her reflection in the mirror, at her heart-shaped face and her green eyes still a little red with sleep, she ran a hand down the flat of her stomach. Maybe there'd be a baby in her future someday, too. It had been what she always wanted with

Jeff, until it became obvious that she and her now deceased husband weren't going to be able to stay together. Now with Jon, she wanted to try again. When they were ready.

She could hear the alarm going off in the bedroom and quickly stepped into the shower, drawing the curtain closed behind her. She let the water slough down her shoulders, then lathered her poof and got to washing up. She knew she'd have to be ready when Jon left if she wanted to ride into town with him.

Hmm, she thought to herself with a wicked smile. Maybe it would be quicker if he joined her...

JON LET her out at the intersection where he had to turn right to get to the station and she had to turn left to get to the bookstore. He offered to drive her all the way but she told him it was okay and she could walk. She was glad she had when she saw Grace walking into the Bean There Bakery and Café. She hurried over in the direction of the café to catch up with her sister.

She found Grace just giving her order at the head of the short line of customers. Elizabeth Archer was working the counter today, her auburn hair pulled back into a net to reveal the scars on the left side of her face. Elizabeth was still short tempered whenever anyone talked to her, but she'd been in town long enough now to be comfortable with letting those scars show. It hadn't always been that way.

Darcy waved to her sister as Grace took her purchase from Elizabeth in a small brown paper bag and turned to leave. They went over to one of the small tables near the front windows instead, and leaned in close to whisper.

"Aren't you supposed to be at the doctor's?" Darcy asked.

Grace laughed, genuinely more happy than Darcy had seen her in a while. "Stop pushing me, sis. My appointment isn't until ten. I've got time."

Darcy kept her voice down, fully aware how much some people in town liked to gossip. She didn't know how many people Grace had told her secret to or if she even wanted anyone else to know about it yet. "So, this puts a whole new spin on Valentine's Day, doesn't it?"

"I'll say. Aaron immediately started making all these plans to go out and celebrate and I had to rein him in and tell him just to keep it quiet for now. At least until the doctor tells me everything is okay."

"Well, now you know why you've felt so tired."

"Yup. Hey, how about you and Jon coming over for dinner tonight? The four of us can at least celebrate for now, and then Aaron can take me out to dinner on Valentine's Day or whatever it is he's going to plan."

"What a great idea, sis. Want us to bring anything?"

"How about something to drink? Just nothing alcoholic."

"Of course. I know how this works." She checked her watch and found she was late to help Sue open the bookstore. She promised Grace again that she and Jon would be over tonight, and hurried back out into the cold.

As DARCY BUSIED herself with dusting the shelves and books in the store she let her mind drift again towards what Valentine's gift she could get for Jon. She was still completely stumped.

Some of the books in the store had sat in place for months. She'd have to clear out her stock soon, maybe even put out a discount display to try and clear some of these out. She pursed her lips. Not long ago, Jon had suggested to her that she start selling electronic reading devices, maybe even offer a selection of electronic books to borrow like libraries did. It wasn't a bad idea, but she'd resisted the suggestion. She wanted to keep the store going just the way her great aunt had done. Books were special to her. She had to wonder sometimes, though, if the rest of the world still felt the same way. Maybe Jon was on to something.

Thinking of her Great Aunt gave her an idea. She decided to have a look through her Great Aunt Millie's journals. They had helped her with so much in the past whenever she'd been stuck. Maybe she would get some inspiration from them now.

Stepping into the back office, she took down the old leather-bound books and sat down to peruse them. She slowly flipped through the pages of old photographs and precise, flowing penmanship. She smiled at the way she could hear faint echoes of Millie's voice as she read. It was all interesting, but there wasn't anything that was jumping out at her yet. Nothing to suggest what a young woman in love could do for her boyfriend on Valentine's Day.

The bell over the door jingled as someone entered. Sighing, closing the journal she'd been reading through, she stepped out of the office to find her friend Helen walking towards her with a smile. Her graying hair was done up just so and she wore a smart blue pantsuit today, obviously attending to her mayoral duties instead of the bakery.

"Hi Darcy," Helen greeted her, pulling off purple knitted gloves. "Are you busy? I was hoping that we could have a chat about the Valentine's night dance."

"Sure Helen." Darcy took Helen's coat and hung it on the rack behind the checkout counter. "I'm not busy right now at all. Sue's off running an errand for me so it's just us. What's up?"

"Well, it's hard to have a dance without a band," Helen told her as they sat down at one of the reading tables. "The one we had lined up quit at the last minute. Something about the lead singer having medical issues. I offered to pay them to just do instrumentals, but they insist they won't perform without the whole group."

"Oh, no!" Darcy exclaimed. "Oh, jeez. And we're only five days away from it, too."

"Exactly. It's short notice, and I don't know what we're going to do."

"I actually might be able to help," Darcy said. "I have a cousin over in Meadowood who's in a band. They mostly do high school dances or weddings, but I can see if they're available for this, if you want?"

Helen looked a little skeptical. "Do you think they could handle something this big? A townwide dance like this?"

Darcy smiled at her friend. "I'm sure it will be fine, Helen. Let me make a call." Darcy went straight to the phone and racked her mind for the number. It had been a long while since she'd said more than hello to Kim. Helen listened in, and slowly her frown was replaced with a smile.

DARCY CALLED Jon after Helen left. He answered his work phone in a clipped professional voice. "This is Detective Tinker, can I help you?"

"It's me, Jon," Darcy told him. "How's it going?"

"Oh, hey Darcy. You need my help, do you?"

"Well, I haven't been kissed in, like, four hours."

He laughed. "That I'd definitely like to help you with but I couldn't even get away from work for lunch. We think we have a lead in this burglary case and we need to check it out."

"Oh, that's too bad. I guess I'll just have to wait." She smiled, always in a good mood when they talked to each other like this. This was definitely what love was. "So, do you think you could get off work by five o'clock?"

"Uh, probably. You want a ride home again? Should we maybe look at getting you your own car?"

"No, no. It's not that. Besides, I'll be able to ride the bicycle again soon. You and I have a dinner date."

"We do?"

"Uh-huh. With Grace and Aaron. At their apartment. She wants us to help her celebrate."

"Oh, well in that case I definitely can," he promised. "I'll have the uniformed guys do some of this. No problem. Unless, you know, the world comes to an end or something."

She tried to laugh at that but couldn't. The way things had gone in their little town of Misty Hollow, the end of the world wasn't that far-fetched.

～

DARCY COULD TELL there was something wrong as soon as they arrived at Grace and Aaron's apartment. She felt it first, a shiver running up her spine as Jon knocked on the door, bottle of carbonated grape juice in one hand. Grace's face as she answered the door was pinched and her eyes were tight. She invited them in, and Jon looked over his shoulder at Darcy. Obviously, he sensed it too.

"What's wrong?" Darcy asked, without waiting for Grace to say anything.

Jon closed the door behind them. Grace shrugged and went straight back into the kitchen. Darcy smelled the risotto on the stove. "I'm sure it's nothing, sis," Grace said. "Nerves. That's all. Pregnant women get emotional, don't we?"

Jon shook his head when Darcy turned to him. He didn't know what to say. Darcy took her coat off and dropped it on the couch as she followed Grace into the kitchen. She put a comforting hand on her sister's shoulder. "You know you can tell us, Grace. What is it?"

Grace sighed and set aside the white plastic spoon she'd been using to stir the contents of the pot. "Aaron was supposed to be home an hour ago and I can't reach him. Not at work or on his cell phone. It's so unlike him. I'm just being silly, right?"

She looked to Darcy for an answer. Darcy didn't know what

to say. She knew she should comfort Grace and tell her it was nothing, that Aaron would be walking through the door at any minute, but she couldn't. She knew her sister was right. Aaron wouldn't be this late without calling her. Especially now that he knew she was pregnant.

Grace suddenly flung herself into Darcy's arms. Darcy wasn't prepared for this level of emotion from her sister. Grace was usually so calm and stable. It had always been Darcy who was the emotional one. Now she held on to Grace as her sister tried not to cry.

Not knowing what else to do, Darcy suggested they go back to making the dinner. She pitched in, stirring the sauce and helping cut up vegetables for the salad. Jon stayed in the living room, and Darcy could hear him on his cell phone out there, calling the station, the chief, and a few other people. She caught his eye at one point. He shook his head. No news.

They ate dinner in silence. What should have been a happy celebration had become solemn and stressful. Aaron's empty chair constantly drew Darcy's attention. Where was he? Darcy had always known Aaron to be a very thoughtful man. To leave his wife worrying like this definitely wasn't like him.

They finished dinner and cleaned away the dishes and still, Aaron didn't come home. Darcy told Grace that she and Jon would stay with her and wait. Grace swallowed and sat down heavily on the couch and shook her head.

"Something terrible has happened to him, Darcy," Grace said. "I just know it."

# CHAPTER 6

*D*arcy woke up slowly, disoriented and stiff. She remembered, then, everything that had happened last night. She and Jon had spent the night at Grace's apartment, trying to be there for her sister. They'd called everyone they could think of, and Jon had even gone outside quietly explaining to Darcy that he was going to call the area hospitals. No one knew anything. Aaron was missing.

She had finally convinced her sister to lay down with her on Grace and Aaron's bed, and Grace had fallen into a fitful sleep sometime after two in the morning. They had both slept in their clothes, and Darcy had never really fallen asleep at all. Her sister was gently snoring now, and Darcy just didn't have the heart to wake her up. Carefully, she slipped off the bed and went down the short hall to the living room.

Jon had slept the night on the couch, but looking at him now it was obvious that he had gotten as little sleep as she had. His clothes were rumpled and there were dark circles around his eyes. He was in the kitchen, cooking scrambled eggs on the stove. He smiled at her weakly, and she went over and wrapped her arms around his waist.

"Good morning," she whispered, leaning her head down onto his chest. He was almost a foot taller than she was, and right now she needed to feel his comforting strength. "He not back yet?"

Jon shook his head as he sprinkled pepper over the eggs. "I'll go into the police station in a little bit and check to see if there have been any accidents reported. I'll call the hospitals again, too, and if I have to I'll call the surrounding police departments. I just wanted to make sure that you guys had breakfast before I left."

"I love you," she said, meaning it deeply. "I'll stay here with her. The bookstore can be closed for a day. Should we file a missing persons report, do you think?"

Darcy started to fiddle with the antique ring on her finger. Her great aunt's ring. Usually it made her feel a little better, made her feel connected to the woman who had been there for her when her own mother was so distant. This morning, though, it wasn't doing anything for her.

"I'll put out a general be-on-the-lookout message for him. He's got to be somewhere."

Darcy nodded. "Sure, but where?"

Jon opened his mouth to say something to her, then stopped, closing his mouth tightly as he took the eggs off the stove and used the spatula to load them onto a serving plate.

"Jon?" she said to him, putting her hands on her hips. "What is it? Come on, you know you can tell me anything."

He didn't look happy about it. "Okay. Look, don't think any less of me when I say this. As a police officer, I tend to look at the facts. We have a man who disappeared after hearing that his wife was pregnant. A lot of men don't take that news well. Some of them even run away to avoid their responsibilities."

Darcy gasped. "Aaron isn't like that!" Wincing at how loud that was she looked down the hallway to the bedroom where Grace was still sleeping. She lowered her voice as she continued, "Grace told me that Aaron was over the moon happy when he heard about the baby. Plus, he isn't the kind of guy to run away from her. This wouldn't be so strange if he was. He's totally devoted to Grace. No. He'd never do this."

Jon put his hands up to show he didn't want to argue. "I trust you, Darcy. I haven't known Aaron as long as you guys have but he doesn't seem like that kind of man to me either. I'm just saying how the facts look."

"Then remember the rest of the facts. Aaron loves Grace. He was happy about her being pregnant. And he would not, ever, run away from her and leave her to worry like this."

Jon nodded. "Okay. I'll go into work right away and get started."

Darcy was relieved that he was taking this seriously. She knew he was only speaking the truth when he said things didn't look good, and she knew he'd do everything he could to find Aaron. He dropped a kiss to her lips and ran his thumb across her cheek, then he grabbed his coat and headed for the door.

Darcy ate a little bit of the eggs along with half a slice of toast before she lost her appetite altogether. She put the rest of the eggs into a plastic bowl and set them in the refrigerator for Grace to have later. She checked her watch and then the clock on the wall and then her watch again. She twisted the ring on her finger over and over, worrying. What had Jon found out? Had he had time to find out anything? Should she call him? Or wait?

When both her watch and the clock agreed that it was ten o'clock Darcy sighed and went down to the bedroom. Her sister was stirring in the bed and her eyes fluttered open. When Darcy got closer, Grace sat bolt upright on the bed rubbing at her eyes. "Aaron? Did Aaron come home?"

Darcy shook her head sadly and watched Grace's face fall. "Jon has been at the police station since it was early. He...he'll figure things out."

"Sure," Grace said with a weak smile. "Of course he will. I've never worked with a smarter cop than Jon. I'm going to get dressed and then I want to go down to the station."

"Grace, you can't go to work today. Not with Aaron, uh, missing."

Grace practically glared at her. "I need to know what Jon has found out. I need to hear it for myself."

Darcy didn't even try to argue. She knew how she'd feel if it were Jon who didn't come home. No one could tell her not to do everything she could to find him again. "Sure, we can go to the police station and see what Jon has found out." She grabbed her coat as Grace did the same. "Okay, sis," she said. "Let's go."

WHEN THEY ARRIVED at the police station they found Jon behind his desk on the phone. Grace tapped her foot impatiently while they waited for him to hang up. Darcy didn't miss the several looks that the other officers in the room were casting their way. Apparently everyone knew what was going on.

Jon cleared his throat and spread his hands apologetically to Grace. "That was the hospital over in Woods Crossing. I've called everywhere I can think of, Grace. There haven't been any accidents. Nobody matching Aaron's description has been taken to any of them, either."

"Okay," Grace said, a determined look on her face. "Then we'll start calling the local police departments."

Jon stood up from his desk, stretching his back. "Grace, I did that already. No one knows anything."

"Well, then we have to put out a BOLO message."

"I did that, too."

Grace clenched her fists. "So why haven't you found him, then?"

"Sis, Jon's doing everything he can," Darcy said, laying a hand on Grace's arm, trying to send calm thoughts her way.

With a slow breath, Grace crossed her arms over her chest and looked away. "I'm sorry, Jon. I'm just upset. I want to know what happened to him."

"It's okay, Grace." Jon hugged her quickly, then settled back to sit against his desk. "It would be helpful if we knew exactly where Aaron had been yesterday."

"I'm not sure. He said that he was going to be running all sorts of errands around town. Out of town, too. He was being very secretive and I just thought he was getting me a Valentine's gift."

Jon gave Darcy a pointed look when Grace said that Aaron was being secretive. Darcy chose to ignore it. She knew what the facts were, no matter how it looked.

"Why don't you keep looking," she said to Jon, with a little kiss on his cheek. "I'll take Grace back to her apartment. We'll look through Aaron's stuff. Who knows. Maybe he left a to-do list or some other clue."

Grace didn't look happy about leaving, but soon they were headed back to her apartment. At least it would give her sister something to do while they waited for word."

DARCY AND GRACE desperately searched for any clues that would give them an idea about what had happened to Aaron. They looked everywhere they could think of, through drawers and through papers and in Aaron's closet. They even turned all of Aaron's clothes pockets inside out.

Darcy went to Aaron's desk tucked into a corner of the back room opposite the bedroom. Surely there would be something in there that would help them out. They'd looked everywhere else.

She went through the desk drawers one at a time. In the bottom drawer on the right of the desk she found his day planner. "Yes!" she said, picking up the little rectangular book. It had a space for notes and a page of phone numbers but all she really cared about was the calendar.

She flipped it open to yesterday's date and could see that Aaron had listed all sorts of different places. Shops. He was doing shopping yesterday. She recognized a few of the names, and a few others had addresses. Most of them seemed to be for places over in Oak Hollow.

She went into the bedroom where Grace was searching under the bed. "I found something." She held up the day planner so that Grace could see. "It's a whole schedule. This would have taken him most of the day. Hopefully this will tell us where Aaron went yesterday."

Grace stopped her searching and hurried over. "Great. Let's go."

"Right now?" Darcy said. Grace nodded and without waiting to see if Darcy followed her she grabbed her car keys and headed out of the door.

GRACE ASKED Darcy to drive them. Darcy knew her sister was upset and nervous, and understandably so. She felt a bit weird behind the wheel, though. It had been almost two years since she'd driven a car. There wasn't really any need for one, living in Misty Hollow. She'd kept her license renewed just in case, and today it had proven to be a good idea.

Driving along the streets of town, Darcy saw tendrils of mist hovering just above the snow. It crept out of the shadows, so faint that anyone else probably would have passed it by without a second thought. Darcy knew better. Misty Hollow got its name from the constant fog and mist that crept through the area. Darcy had come to understand the phenomenon was more paranormal than meteorological. Whenever troubles came to town, the mists appeared.

They drove away from Misty Hollow towards Oak Hollow. Aaron's to-do list included several stores in there. There were no times listed next to the names, so no real telling which place Aaron would have gone to first, but it was as good a place to start as any.

In the middle of the list was an odd name that Darcy took to be a store, even though she'd never heard of a store called "The Bishop." She wondered what they would find when they got there.

She hoped whatever it was got them closer to finding out what had happened to Aaron.

# CHAPTER 7

$\mathcal{I}$t was late afternoon by the time they reached Aaron's first errand marked on his list, the specialty grocery store in Oak Hollow called Nature's Bounty. Oak Hollow was a small city, nearly one hundred miles away from Misty Hollow. Whatever Aaron had wanted here, he must have wanted it badly enough to drive over an hour one way to get it.

Darcy pulled into a parking space in front of the store. The one story building was made of gray stone walls and a wooden shingle roof. Cartoonish pictures of vegetables and fruits were posted up in the front windows. As soon as Darcy put the car into park, Grace was hopping out and marching up to the door.

She was gone before Darcy could stop her or even ask what their plan was. Grace wasn't thinking clearly. Darcy just hoped she didn't do something that got them thrown out of this place. Or worse, got the local police involved in a bad way.

She caught up to her sister as they went inside through the automatic sliding doors. Inside was a brightly lit space of metal shelves and tall glass-fronted coolers. An older man behind the front counter, with thinning black hair that he combed over the top of his skull like a bad toupee, smiled at them as they entered.

He was wearing a green apron with a nametag on it that said, "Hi, my name is Paul."

"What can I do for you two ladies today?" Paul asked them, flashing a smile that showed two missing front teeth.

"You can tell me," Grace said, leaning across the counter to push her cell phone up into the man's face, "why my husband came into your store yesterday."

On the flat screen of Grace's smart phone was a picture of Aaron. Grace kept shoving it toward Paul as he raised his hands and tried to mumble something. Darcy shook her head. The guy looked scared, his eyes wide and his brows lifted. He took a step back from Grace and Darcy figured if she didn't step in, then they would lose any chance at all of having the man talk to them.

The store was dark and filled with shelves of expensive chocolates, bottles of olive oil, wine and various other expensive goods. Darcy filed away those quick impressions as she moved hastily towards her sister.

"Sir," Darcy said in a much calmer voice, "my name is Darcy. This is my sister, Grace. We're trying to find her husband. He's missing. We think he was in your store yesterday. Would you mind looking at her photo to see if you recognize him?"

Grace glared at her, but then her face softened as she must have realized that Darcy was right. If she frightened the poor man into not wanting to say anything, that wouldn't help Aaron.

After an appreciative glance at Darcy, Paul looked closer at Grace's cell phone, squinting and rubbing his chin. "Yup. I do remember him, actually. I'd remember any man that excited about his wife." He smiled at Grace and Darcy saw the tears pool in her eyes.

Paul tapped a finger against the polished wood countertop. "Your husband came into the store yesterday. He called earlier in the day to see if we had this certain vintage of wine from Spain. It's something we specialize in, selling all natural products from small businesses. Your Aaron said he wanted to make a special dinner for Valentine's Day. Uh," Paul scrunched his face up with an apologetic smile, "hope I didn't say too much there."

"That's fine," Darcy assured him. "Do you remember what time that was?"

"Oh, tennish. Thereabouts."

The tears slowly slid down Grace's cheeks. "We went to Spain on our honeymoon. I kept going on about the wine there." She took a moment to calm the tremor out of her voice. "Do you have any idea where Aaron went next? Did he say anything about that?"

The man shook his head. "No. I'm sorry I don't. He paid for the wine and took it with him and that was the last I saw him. Had a line of customers come in after that. Didn't have a lot of time to talk to him." He shrugged and muttered, "sorry," again.

They thanked Paul for talking to them and then left the store. "Do you believe him?" Grace asked Darcy as they got back in the car.

"Of course I believe him, Grace. He's just a store owner that Aaron bought wine from. You need to calm down some, sis. We'll find him. I promise. But we can't charge in full tilt like everybody is a suspect."

"Everybody *is* a suspect," Grace said miserably, hunching down in her seat as she belted in.

"Grace…"

"No. Don't." Grace wiped angrily at more tears. "Just drive."

THE NEXT TWO stops on the list were no help at all. No one remembered Aaron. Darcy didn't lose hope, though. That could mean he hadn't gotten to those places, or it could simply mean that the people at those stores just didn't remember him. She figured it could go either way.

By this time the sun was beginning to set and Grace was in a near panic. They weren't any closer to finding out what had happened Aaron, even as they pieced together the steps he'd taken yesterday. Darcy had called Jon to let him know what they were doing, about finding the to-do list and following its clues. He'd been impressed, and told her to keep at it because unfortunately, he had nothing to report from his end.

Darcy didn't know what to say to calm Grace down. She was also getting very worried about her brother-in-law.

The fourth name on the list was that shop Darcy had noted earlier, "The Bishop." The address printed beside the name was for a lonely street on the edge of the city, where vacant lots sat under thin layers of snow. Grace exchanged a puzzled look with Darcy. "What would Aaron be doing here?"

"I don't know," Darcy answered. What else could she say?

As they pulled up in front of the non-descript building in the middle of the street, Darcy's instincts started to scream at her. The place was a square building made of red bricks. There were no windows and only the one door in the front with no sign or anything other than the street number, Forty Seven. What on earth sort of business did Aaron have in a place like this?

"I don't like the look of this place," Darcy said to Grace. "Um. Maybe we should try the other places on the list first?"

"Are you kidding?" Grace's voice was tight. "Some of those places are all the way back in Misty Hollow. We're here now. I need to know everything Aaron did yesterday. His list says he came here next, and this is where we're going."

"I'm just saying, maybe we should call Jon and have him come with us."

"Sis, I'm a police officer too, remember? And Aaron is still missing. I'm not going to wait here another two hours while Jon drives out to us. Now, come on."

Darcy understood her sister's urgency, but she still knew she'd feel better with Jon by her side. When Grace got out of the car and stalked towards the front door she had no choice but to follow.

The door creaked open on heavy rusty hinges and then closed with a solid thud behind them. Past that, they were stopped by a gate of wrought iron bars, decorative but locked. Darcy recognized the buzzer mechanism that allowed a store owner to open to customers or not as they pleased. It suddenly hit her what kind of store this was.

On the other side of the bars were low display counters cased in glass and plastic to show off the merchandise artfully laid out to catch the light. Diamonds and emeralds and other precious stones shone in gold and silver settings. The place was an expensive, appointment-only jewelry shop. She'd only been in one of these places once before in her life. Everything was white and glittering and no doubt too expensive for Darcy to even be looking at.

A man in an expensive gray silk suit, with an upturned nose and bushy white eyebrows under a bald dome, leaned out over one of the counters to look at them through the bars. "Hello. My name is Richard Bishop, the owner of this fine establishment." He took another moment to look at them doubtfully. "Do you ladies have an appointment?"

"No," Grace explained to him. "We aren't here to buy anything. We're looking for my husband. We think he was here yesterday."

The man's eyebrows knitted together. "I'm sorry, I'm not sure I understand."

Grace held up her phone again with Aaron's picture on it. She pushed the phone through the bars as Mister Bishop came closer to look. "This man. He's, well, we don't know where he is. We haven't heard from him since yesterday and your shop was on his calendar yesterday. Can you please just tell me if he was here?"

Mister Bishop looked up when he caught the tremor in Grace's voice, then his expression softened and he looked at the photo more closely. "No, my dear, I'm sorry. He doesn't look at all familiar."

Darcy could see the struggle Grace was having with herself not to break down in front of the man. She put a hand on her sister's shoulder and took over the conversation. "Are you sure? His name is Aaron Wentworth. We know he was in the city visiting the local shops yesterday."

At the mention of Aaron's full name, Mister Bishop's eyes lit up. "Ah. Now, his picture is definitely not familiar, but I did have an appointment scheduled with a man named Wentworth at four o'clock yesterday afternoon. He never showed up so I just assumed he had changed his mind. A shame, too."

"Why do you say that, Mister Bishop?"

"Well, the man had corresponded with me by e-mail. He had shown me some sample pieces he'd found on the internet, along with some sketches of his own. He had said he wanted something for his wife because she was going to be a first time mother. Well, I told him we handle that sort of thing all the time, but the piece he was asking for would have been quite unique and I'm sure I would have had a great deal of fun creating it for him."

Darcy smiled at Grace. She knew it. She knew Aaron would never just cut and run after finding out Grace was having a baby. Here was more proof of it, as if she or Grace needed it. A man wouldn't ask a specialty jeweler to make something for his wife to celebrate the birth of their child if he didn't want the baby. Not at the prices this place must ask.

"Um, Mister Bishop?" Grace said slowly. "May I see the pictures Aaron sent?"

Mister Bishop pursed his lips. "Oh, I'm afraid I can't do that. Should your husband return and want to commission the piece, I wouldn't want to spoil his surprise. He might take his business elsewhere."

Grace looked angry for a moment before it passed and she nodded. "The appointment he missed was for four, you said?"

"Correct. I'm so sorry you're having trouble. Should I hear from him, I'll be sure to tell him to call home."

With that, the man stepped back, and Darcy understood that was all they were going to get from Mister Bishop. Which was fine, because it was obvious he didn't know anything else.

"Thank you for your time," Darcy said to the man as she gently pulled Grace back outside. At least now they had a time frame for when Aaron had gone missing. He had bought a bottle of wine at ten in the morning, and missed an appointment he had scheduled for four o'clock. Six hours.

What had happened in those six hours?

# CHAPTER 8

$\mathcal{D}$arcy drove them home in thoughtful silence. Full night had come on, and the car's headlights illuminated the road ahead. Grace looked wiped out. Darcy had never seen her sister like this. Ever. Once or twice she tried making small talk, but Grace just kept staring out the window at the night. Finally they pulled into the parking lot of Grace and Aaron's apartment building.

"What are you doing?" Grace nearly snapped at her.

"Grace, you're exhausted. You should get some rest."

But her sister shook her head. "No. I can't rest. I want to check in at the police station."

"Grace…"

"Darcy, I'll walk myself there if I have to."

"Okay, okay. Fine, sis, I'll drive you. Just promise me you'll get some sleep after that."

Grace gave her a non-committal nod that didn't promise anything. With a heavy sigh, Darcy pulled the car back onto the street and drove over to the police station. The night shift should have been on duty, which meant two patrol cars at most, but the parking lot was full.

As they entered the office they walked into a buzz of activity. Officers packed the back room, working at their desks or moving back and forth, papers in hand, phones to their ears. They saw Jon at his desk, discussing something with four other officers, all of whom nodded in turn and walked away to different corners of the room.

The officers around them greeted Grace with short nods or a few words. Now Darcy understood why the parking lot had been full. Every officer in the Misty Hollow Police Department, and some from the Meadowood Police Department that Darcy recognized also, had come into work. Fifteen able bodied men and women and they all wanted to help Grace find Aaron.

Grace barely spoke to anyone. Darcy could see the tremble in her lip. Her big, tough sister was going to cry if she opened her mouth to speak. Darcy was happy to see how everyone had come together for her.

When Jon saw them he waved them over. He stood up and hugged Darcy first, and then Grace. "I've got news. Aaron's car was found in a parking lot in Oak Hollow."

"That's the same town that the jewelry store is in," Darcy said. "We were just there!"

She quickly filled him in on what they had discovered, the time frame they had pieced together by visiting the shops in Oak Hollow. They'd stopped in to the rest of them after leaving Mister Bishop's shop. The florist remembered Aaron, sort of, but only that he had been there in the morning. Not what time specifically. No one else could remember him. That left them with knowing for sure he was seen at ten in the morning and was missing by four o'clock.

"Okay," Jon said as he raised his voice and turned to the room. "Listen up, everyone. We've got a definite time frame now of ten in the morning to four in the afternoon. Work your contacts, contact everyone you know. Davison, how are we with surveillance footage?"

Davison, a younger officer with unruly red hair and freckles, was sitting at a computer across the room. "It would help if I knew a route of travel. And a lot of the places in Oak Hollow don't have exterior cameras, just ones inside."

"Okay," Jon nodded. "Darcy, I'll need you to give Davison a list of the stores from Aaron's calendar. We'll have the Oak Hollow Police follow up and get video surveillance from each one. Hopefully we can find Aaron on there in one or more of the stores, and narrow down the time frame more."

Darcy was impressed to see Jon taking control like this. She knew he'd come from a bigger police department before coming here to live in Misty Hollow, and that experience was serving him well now.

"I'll give him the names," Grace said, obviously happy to be able to do something. "You have someone going to check the car?"

"The Oak Hollow PD already secured it. Their guys will go through it and let us know," Jon told her.

With a nod and a determined look in her eyes, Grace took out Aaron's day planner and went over to Davison.

"How's she holding up?" Jon asked Darcy after Grace was out of ear shot.

Darcy folded herself into his embrace. "About as well as you'd expect. If you ever went missing like this…"

"I know," he said. "I'd be the same if it was you."

"You think the surveillance footage from the stores will show anything?"

"I do. Everything gets recorded nowadays. You did good work today, Darcy."

His compliment warmed her, even as a growing cold feeling spread in her stomach. It had been a whole day with no word from Aaron. She could almost feel the clock on the wall ticking away the seconds, the minutes, the hours. They had to find Aaron.

They had to.

.

# CHAPTER 9

"*Y*ou should stay in bed, Grace."

After spending another hour at the police station, Darcy had finally convinced Grace to go home to get some rest. She would need it if she was going to help Aaron, Darcy told her. Her sister had only agreed to it if Darcy stayed with her again. Jon decided to stay also after going home to get a change of clothes for each of them for the next day.

This morning, Grace had woken up looking green around her face and had raced for the bathroom. Morning sickness had finally caught up to her. The retching passed in a few minutes, and then her sister had laid back down on the bed, curled up into the fetal position around her belly.

"I should," Grace agreed, "but I can't. He needs me."

Darcy didn't need to ask who "he" was. "I know you want to help, Grace, but Jon and I will go and investigate. You need to take care of yourself and the baby. That's what you need to do for Aaron."

"But..."

"No Grace, I insist that you get back into that bed. Jon and I will take care of it. We'll find him for you and bring him home."

Grace closed her eyes tightly and whispered, "You promise?"

Darcy twisted her great aunt's ring fitfully, knowing her sister couldn't see her doing it with her eyes closed. "Yes, I promise," she said, not sure that she'd be able to make that promise come true. She knew she'd do everything in her power to make it happen, though.

With Grace tucked under the covers again, she went out to wake Jon up. He surprised her by coming out of the bathroom clean and freshly shaved, changed into a light blue dress shirt and a new pair of slacks. "Good morning," he said quietly to her. "Is your sister coming with us or is she going to stay here?"

"She's staying." Darcy said. She leaned up and kissed him on the cheek. "Not without an argument, though."

Jon shook his head. "Grace is one of the most stubborn people I've ever worked with."

"Runs in the family."

"Sure does. But it's one of the things I love about you."

Darcy gave him a wink and then tugged him down the hallway into the kitchen. She had already gotten dressed in jeans and a plain green t-shirt. Not very professional attire, she supposed, especially standing next to Jon's tall cop figure. She figured there would be a lot of moving around today, though, and she wanted to be comfortable.

"Did you find out anything?" she asked him. Jon had come home sometime after midnight. She'd heard him come in but hadn't wanted to wake Grace up by getting out of the bed to go and talk to him.

"Not yet. I need to talk to the Oak Hollow PD today, find out about the car and if they found any surveillance footage we can use."

"Well, we're heading there anyway," Darcy said as they both went for their coats. "That can be one of our stops. What did your chief have to say about all this?"

"Just one thing," Jon told her. "He said to do whatever it took to find Aaron."

Jon had Darcy drive so that he could make phone calls on the way. She hadn't driven in years, and here she was doing it twice in two days. Too bad she couldn't enjoy it.

Jon thanked somebody on the other end of the line then disconnected the call and put the cell phone back in his pants pocket. "That was Sergeant Vasquez, my contact over at Oak Hollow PD. He says they left Aaron's car where it was after they processed it last night. There's an officer in a marked unit watching it."

"Did they find anything?" Darcy asked.

"Some fingerprints, but they all seem to be from one person and I'm sure that will turn out to be Aaron. Nothing else out of the ordinary. He gave me the address where they found the car. Let's go over and look for ourselves."

"Sounds good," Darcy said. "Maybe we'll see something they missed."

The parking lot where Aaron's old green Nissan was parked was practically empty of other cars. It was a public parking lot, not really next to anything. Darcy spotted the car right away where it sat next to a black and white Oak Hollow Police Department cruiser, a single officer sitting at the wheel looking bored.

Jon went and spoke to the officer briefly before sending him away, while Darcy went to Aaron's car with the spare set of keys they'd brought with them from Grace.

Everything in the car looked completely normal. His accountant's brief case was on the back seat. Loose change and candy wrappers sat in the center console. Empty trunk. In front of the passenger seat, Darcy found the bag with the bottle of wine in it. Next to it was another bag with an expensive box of chocolate truffles. She put the back of her hand to her mouth and fought back the tears. This was what he had been trying to put together for Grace when something happened.

There wasn't any sign of a struggle. Nothing looked wrong. Jon came over, rubbing his hands together. "See?" she said to him. "There's no bag full of clothes. No bus tickets. Nothing. Aaron wasn't running from anything."

He looked at her funny and then nodded. "I know. I believe you. I mean, I believed you before, but...there's something else. We need to go down the street to the bank. The officer I was just talking to told me there's something going on we need to know about."

She looked at him, full of questions she didn't dare ask.

"I know why Aaron parked his car here," was all he said to her.

THE BANK WAS the Three Twigs Federal Credit Union, a low brick building with narrow windows on it that almost made it look like a fort. They could see officers in dark blue uniforms standing inside, and a big burly man with sergeant's stripes on his jacket's sleeve standing at the front.

Jon hadn't said a word to her for the block and a half they had walked to get here. Darcy had been too afraid to ask. Now that she saw the bank, her hopes lifted a little. "Aaron came in here? Did he need money? Did he make a withdrawal from the ATM? We could get the video surveillance—"

"Darcy," Jon interrupted her, "it's worse than that."

The sergeant at the door eyed them seriously. He had a square jaw a severe buzz cut, and Darcy could see he meant business. "Help you folks?"

Jon took his badge wallet out of his back pocket and showed it to the sergeant. "I'm Jon Tinker, detective with the Misty Hollow Police Department."

The sergeant nodded curtly to him. "Heard you were in town, Detective. Afraid I'm going to have to ask you to leave, though.

Had a robbery here two days ago and we're processing the scene. You understand."

It wasn't a question, and Darcy got the feeling they were being politely asked to get lost without being told anything. She also didn't miss that the burglary happened the same day that Aaron came up missing. Oh no, she thought. Was this what Jon couldn't tell her? "Sergeant," she said quickly, "we're looking for anyone who might have seen my brother-in-law. Is there any way that we can see the security tapes from two days ago?"

"We're going through them now ourselves, Miss," was the tight reply. Then he turned to Jon. "Didn't tell her yet, did you?"

"I was just about to." Jon's face was creased with worry when he looked back at Darcy. "There was a customer in the bank when the robbery happened. He matches Aaron's description. That's what the officer back in the parking lot was telling me. I just didn't know how to tell you."

Darcy felt like she couldn't breathe. "What happened?"

Jon deferred to the sergeant. The man chewed the inside of his lip for a moment then seemed to decide that it would be all right to fill them in. "Can't tell you much. There were three robbers, all wearing black clothes and masks. Looks like from the video they demanded money, but then they left. With the teller. And the man who matches your brother-in-law's description."

Darcy gasped. This was horrible. What would they tell Grace? "Wait," she said, "why didn't you tell us this yesterday? We've been going out of our minds!"

The sergeant held his big hands up, palms out. "We didn't know, miss. Jon here called my Lieutenant last night, from what I understand, and we didn't even know we were supposed to be looking until then. We let you know as soon as we knew. Look, this is an active investigation. Without the okay from my higher-ups, that's all I can tell you on scene."

Darcy fisted her hands and started to scream at the man to tell her everything right then and now, but Jon put a hand around her elbow, stopping her. "Thank you, Sergeant," he said to the man. "We'll leave you guys to it."

Darcy was shocked as Jon led her away, back down towards their car. "What are you doing? We need to know what happened!"

"I know, Darcy, I know. But he literally can't tell us anything else without someone who outranks him telling him to do it. He put himself out on a limb telling us that much."

"So what are we supposed to do?"

They were at their car again now, and Jon smiled at her as he got in behind the wheel. "We're going to go talk to someone who outranks him."

THE OAK HOLLOW POLICE DEPARTMENT was a lot larger than Misty Hollow's. The building they worked out of was three stories high and a line of black and white patrol cars sat out front. Officers going in and out passed Jon and Darcy as they went up to the desk sergeant and introduced themselves.

"We've been expecting you," the desk sergeant said to them. "Go on in."

They were met by a lieutenant, a long-faced man with old eyes in a young face. After going over the same exact information that the sergeant at the scene had given them, the lieutenant led them to a back room where a monitor was hooked up to humming black DVD players.

They sat and watched as the surveillance video from the bank robbery was played for them. It was time stamped, two days ago, 1:43pm. They watched as a tall man with blonde hair wearing a black knee-length coat entered the bank. Darcy recognized him immediately. "That's Aaron."

The lieutenant nodded, taking notes.

As they continued to watch, three men in black coats and

black ski masks rushed in, pointing guns at the teller and at Aaron. One of the robbers went up to the teller, obviously screaming.

"There's no audio?" Jon asked.

"No," the lieutenant said with a shake of his head. "We keep suggesting it to all the banks and businesses in our jurisdiction, but no one listens."

Suddenly the robber screaming at the teller grabbed the poor guy by his arms and dragged him over the counter. They started struggling, but the robber showed his gun again and the teller wisely went still. Then the three men in their black masks took both the teller and Aaron out the back.

The teller had messy red hair and a wide, honest face. Darcy could see the fear in his eyes as the robbers led him away. Or, maybe that was her imagination.

Darcy wasn't sure when she had started to cry, but the tears were hot on her cheeks now. She wiped at them and hung her head and had no idea what to do.

## CHAPTER 10

*I*t was Jon who came up with their next step. Looking through the reports before they left, he caught the name and address of the bank teller from the robbery. Ray Stephenson, 58 Crescent Circle. He didn't tell Darcy what he had done until they had thanked the lieutenant and were back out in Jon's car.

"Why can't we just go with the Oak Hollow PD to talk to his wife?" she asked.

"I don't want to get into a jurisdictional snarl. Plus, you pointed out yourself that this is personal. There's only so much official police procedure will let us do."

Darcy knew what he meant. She'd seen enough police interrogations now, being with Jon, to know his hands were tied by the laws he upheld. Still, she admired him for doing what he did. How did he deal with things like this every day and not come home angry every night?

She loved him more in that moment than she had the moment before, and she figured the next moment would bring something new for her to love.

As Jon pulled up in front of Ray's house in one of the city's residential districts, Darcy could see that the home was small but well kept. It had white painted board siding and little shrubs to the sides of the front steps. A little stone walkway joined the house to the sidewalk. Someone had spent a lot of time on it all. It had a very inviting atmosphere and definitely showed a woman's touches.

Darcy knocked on the door while Jon stood back by silent agreement. A few moments later, the door was opened by a middle-aged woman with graying blonde hair in a slim blue dress. She had a worried look in her eyes and Darcy knew immediately that this was Ray's wife. "Mrs. Stephenson," Darcy said to her with a careful smile. "My name is Darcy Sweet. This is Jon Tinker. Um. My brother-in-law was taken in the robbery. Just like Ray. Do you...could we come in, do you think?"

The woman blinked and seemed to come back to herself. "Oh sorry, yes sure. Please. Come on in." She stood back to let them enter and then guided them into the living room. It was a cozy space, small but brightly decorated with knick knacks and stylish lamps and two plush couches that had floral designs on their cushions. She motioned Darcy and Jon to one of these. "Please sit down. I'm...I'm so sorry about your brother-in-law, Darcy."

She started to cry, but then caught herself and sat down on the couch across from them. "Now. What can I do for you?"

"Mrs. Stephenson—" Darcy began.

"Please call me Heather," the woman said with a weary smile.

Darcy nodded. "Heather. Could you tell me more about Ray? Anything that might help us understand what happened to Aaron?"

"Aaron? Is that your brother-in-law?"

Darcy nodded. "Yes. We're very worried about him. Just like you are for Ray. Maybe we can help each other. Can you think of any reason why the robbers would take Ray hostage?"

Heather's eyes widened. "I never thought of...no. There's no reason for it. Ray wasn't into anything dangerous. He didn't gamble. He didn't even go out to drink! What are you saying? Are you saying that this is my Ray's fault?"

Darcy knew she had offended Heather with her question even though she hadn't meant to. Jon leaned forward to take over. "We know it wasn't Ray's fault, Heather. We're just trying to figure out anything we can. Aaron is a good man, too. He has a baby on the way and his wife is worried sick."

"Oh my," Heather said, putting her hands to her mouth. "I didn't know. Ray...Ray was my whole world. Without him, I don't know what I'm going to do." She couldn't hold the tears back anymore, and they started falling down her cheeks.

As Jon continued to ask questions, getting little or no answer, Darcy stood up and quietly began walking around the living room. There were several photographs hung on the wall, and she recognized Ray in several of them. He smiled in most of them, his green eyes a good match for his red hair. He seemed so happy. A good man caught in a bad situation. On a corner table where one of the lamps stood, there was a little bowl full of loose change and other things. Among them, a plastic nametag with Ray's name on it.

Checking quickly over her shoulder to make sure Heather wasn't watching, Darcy palmed the nametag and stuffed it into her pocket.

Jon looked up at her as she came back to the couch. With a look, Darcy told him it was time to go. He smiled back at her, catching on. "Well, thank you for talking with us, Heather. Really. We have to go, but we'll keep in touch. Can we get your phone number? Maybe we can call each other if we hear anything?"

Heather was only too happy to do so. Darcy was glad when they were finally walking out of Heather's house and getting back into Jon's car. The stolen nametag with its little pin on the back was burning a hole in her pocket. She hated stealing it from Heather, especially when the woman was going through the same grief that she and Grace were, but she needed something personal of Ray's.

Her abilities worked in very specific ways, and she had the feeling she was going to need them if they were going to find Aaron.

THE CAR RIDE back to Misty Hollow was miserable for both of them. They had decided not to call ahead to Grace. This was the kind of news that you had to tell someone in person.

Everything had hit Darcy at once as they drove away from Heather's house. All of the emotion she had worked so hard to keep hidden for Grace's sake filled her now like lead in a balloon. She felt weighed down and useless.

"I don't get it," she said as they neared the town limits. "If Aaron is still with the bank robbers, why are they holding on to him? If they let him go, then where is he? Why hasn't he called?" She wiped a hand over her face and stared out the car window.

"Everything will be all right," Jon said to her after a moment.

Darcy wished she could believe it. "You don't know that."

"Okay," he admitted. "I don't know that for sure. But Grace is a strong woman. Aaron's a good man. You and I have solved harder things than this."

The tears were threatening to come again. "Sure. But this one is personal." She thought of the cases that she had helped Jon with, the murders and the deceits involved in them, and she thought too about how they'd had to get past his accepting her abilities. He was right when he said they'd solved harder things before. They would work together on this one, and she wouldn't stop until they'd solved it.

"We will get Aaron back," he said to her, as if he could read her mind.

She reached over and took his hand in hers while he worked

the wheel one-handed. She knew they would do everything they could together to solve the mystery of what had happened to Aaron.

And she would do everything she could. Her abilities had helped her in the past. They had to help her now.

*D*arcy and Jon headed straight for Grace and Aaron's apartment when they got back to Misty Hollow. The skies had darkened as they travelled home and a few flakes of snow had fallen. The air was very chilled. On the cold breeze that blew through town, wisps of mist floated. They were thicker and heavier than they had been even this morning.

Grace met them at the door and the look of hope in her eyes nearly did Darcy in. When they sat her down and gave her the news about Aaron being kidnapped there was a horrible moment when Darcy saw her sister break down completely. She cried hysterically, clinging to Darcy, while the two sisters held each other in silent support.

When Grace could pull herself together again she sat up straight and rubbed angrily at her eyes. "So what are we doing? What are we doing to get him back?"

Jon looked at Darcy. They'd been expecting that question. "Grace," Jon said to her, "we're going to let the boys over in Oak Hollow do their job. They know the players over there like we never could. We'd be in the way."

"I can't accept that!" Grace yelled. "I will not sit here and do nothing while my husband is in the hands of those…those…!"

Darcy felt Grace trembling with anger. "We aren't going to just sit here. I promise. I know what I'm about to say is a long shot, but I'm going to try to track Ray and Aaron. I stole something personal from Ray Stephenson's house. We've got plenty of Aaron's stuff here. I'll find them. I'll find Aaron."

Grace looked terrified. Darcy knew how much stress this was putting on her sister, and that couldn't be good for the baby. "Darcy, you can't find them. They'd have to be dead. Aaron is not dead, you hear me. He isn't!"

"I know, I know," Darcy said quickly. "I don't think that Aaron's dead. I promise. I just have to try, though. I'll push myself as far as I can. I'll make it work, somehow."

Grace looked at her then with dull eyes, all the fight gone out of her. "You just try anything that you think will work, Darcy."

Smudge came running to greet her when Darcy got back to her house. Jon had let her borrow his car, even though she could have walked home in under an hour. They didn't want to waste any time. Besides, it was getting colder out. Winter wasn't done with them yet.

Closing the door behind her, she bent down to rub Smudge behind his black and white ears. "I'm going to need your help," she told him. "We're going to try something a little different this time."

Smudge meowed back at her. He sounded a little doubtful.

It didn't take her long to gather together the things that she needed from around the house. She brought them to the living room, where she would have a wide and comfortable space of floor to sit on, then she stood there, wondering. Twisting the ring on her finger and chewing her lip, she wished now that she'd let

Jon come with her like he wanted to. She'd asked him to stay with Grace, though. It was more important that her sister had someone with her. Darcy had done this before. It shouldn't be any problem.

She hoped.

Darcy went around and closed all the curtains tight across the windows in the living room, casting it into darkness. She arranged the six thick, white candles in a circle on the floor and lit them in order, one at a time. Then she lit two incense sticks and placed them in their burner on the coffee table. The incense didn't really do anything for her purposes. She just liked the smell. It relaxed her.

She picked up the two objects she had brought with her. Ray's nametag from work, and Aaron's favorite book. She'd never read "The Bell Broke," but she'd seen Aaron reading it through more than once. That would be more than good enough to make a connection with him. She grimaced as she thought that. She didn't want her brother-in-law to be dead. At the same time, she didn't know if she could make a connection strong enough to find him still alive.

Smudge raced over to her and climbed into her lap and made himself comfortable. "Thanks, Smudge," she said to him, gently stroking his fur until she was calm enough to proceed.

She started with Aaron first. She held the book tightly in her two hands, and concentrated. In her mind, she pictured the mists of the town. She let them swirl and twist, trying to make a connection through them. Time passed. She didn't know how long she sat like that, but finally she popped her eyes open and took a deep breath and admitted to herself there was no connection to be made to Aaron.

It almost made her smile. That was good news. Right? It meant Aaron was still alive.

She hoped.

Next, Darcy picked up Ray's nametag. She concentrated

again, on picturing Ray's face among the mists in her mental picture. She stroked Smudge's fur idly, unable to disconnect fully from the world around her. She could always delve deep into the world of the other side when there was someone to contact.

She guessed that was good news, too. Ray Stephenson was still alive.

It was hopeless. She couldn't feel him in any way. Gently nudging her faithful cat off her lap she stood up and blew out the candles. She racked her brain for anything else she could do. Nothing was coming to her and she was getting more and more frustrated.

As she was putting the candles away the phone rang. Darcy's skin crawled with icy prickles, and she had the feeling that something wasn't right. Rushing to the phone she answered it to hear Jon's voice. "Grace is in a lot of pain. The ambulance will be here any minute. We'll be going to the hospital over in Meadowood. Meet us there, okay?"

The baby, Darcy thought to herself as she ran to get her coat and the keys to Jon's car. She was in a near panic as she gunned the accelerator, making the car fishtail out to the road. Grace could not lose this baby. It would just be too much.

# CHAPTER 12

*D*arcy had risked more than a few traffic tickets on her way to Meadowood. Rushing through the doors of the hospital Darcy headed for the information desk. "Can you tell me where they took Grace Wentworth, please," she asked the woman at the front desk.

The woman, short and squat with dark hair and a perpetual frown, looked up at her. "That depends, honey. Are you a relative?"

"I'm her sister. Darcy Sweet."

The woman nodded, her eyes turning kinder. "They told me to expect you. Hold on, now." She tapped a few keys on the computer in front of her. "Yes, still in the Emergency Department. Go through them doors right there, okay? I'll buzz you through."

The swinging doors opened to her as the woman unlocked them with a touch of a button, and Darcy hurried through into a brightly lit space dominated by a rectangular desk. Behind that desk, doctors and nurses in different colored scrubs and white coats stared at computer screens or scribbled out orders. Doors leading to different rooms stood lined up along three sides of the

Emergency Department, all of the doors closed to protect patient privacy.

Jon was standing outside of room six, and he held his arms out to Darcy as she rushed over to him. "It's okay, everything is going to be all right. The doctors say it's likely just stress. There's going to be a few more tests, but they aren't worried. Grace is more embarrassed than anything else."

Darcy was so relieved that she practically collapsed into his arms. She started to cry and hugged him tightly, not wanting to let go. "Everything is so overwhelming right now, Jon. What are we going to do?"

Jon hugged her back and kissed the top of her head. "It's okay, I'm going to make sure that everything works out." He kissed her again.

She wanted to believe him. She just wanted to be held and protected right now. She knew that must be all that Grace wanted, too. "Thank you for being here for me," Darcy said to him as she stood up on her toes to kiss him full on the lips. She didn't care who was watching.

He palmed her cheek and smiled at her. "I will always be here for you."

She hugged him one more time and then stepped back. "Can I see Grace?"

"Not yet. The doctor is in there with her. He said we can go in as soon as he comes out to get us."

THEY WENT out to the hospital waiting room and Jon got them both cups of coffee from the vending machine. It was lukewarm and disgusting. Darcy hardly tasted it as she sipped at it, worrying about Grace, and Aaron, and their baby. As they sat side by side in plastic chairs, Darcy felt the same icy tingles crawling across her skin that she had felt when Jon had called to say Grace was going to the hospital.

She sat up straighter and looked around. Something felt off to her again. She couldn't place what. "Do you feel anything?" she asked Jon.

"No. Like what?"

Instead of answering him Darcy stood up and said, "I'll be right back." He gave her a look with raised eyebrows but didn't try to stop her. He was used to her odd little behaviors now. He didn't even find them that strange anymore. Or, at least that's what he told her.

She felt herself being pulled in a certain direction. The tingling along her skin drew her down the hallway into the hospital, to the right and up a set of stairs to the second floor. It was all patient rooms up here. The nurses at their station smiled at Darcy politely, then ignored her.

She walked down a line of numbered doors, some open, some closed, most of them with patients lying in their beds. At room number two-fifteen, she stopped. Her skin practically shivered and she knew she was supposed to see who was in this room.

She entered slowly, carefully stepping closer to the sleeping form of a man on the hospital gurney. His leg was in a cast and held up by a sling suspended from the ceiling. Machines beeped as they monitored his condition.

His face was turned away from Darcy. One step at a time, she walked around the bed, closer to the room's window, to look at him from the other side.

Darcy stopped still, not even daring to breathe. The wide face had a bruise around the right eye. His messy red hair was even more mussed now from lying in bed.

There was no mistaking it. This was Ray Stephenson.

## CHAPTER 13

ack down the stairs Darcy raced. In the waiting room she scanned for Jon. He wasn't there. The same hospital worker at her desk caught Darcy's eye and nodded her head toward the Emergency Department door. "He went in there, honey," she said to Darcy. "Your sister's awake now. Go on in."

In her room, Grace was sitting up, her eyes sad and her smile weak. "Hey, Darcy. Guess I really did myself in there, didn't I?"

"It's not that bad," Jon said for her. He was sitting on the edge of Grace's bed, one leg folded up over the other. "You just need to rest and get your strength back. I have to tell you, I wouldn't be doing any better in your spot."

Darcy grabbed Jon's arm. "I found Ray Stephenson."

"You...wait, what?" Jon stood up, searching her face. "You mean with, uh, your abilities?"

"No, no not that. He's here. He's here in the hospital, Jon!"

Grace was watching them intently. "You mean, that teller who got taken with Aaron? He's in the hospital? We need to go question him. Right now!"

She struggled to get out of from under the sheet on her bed. It was obvious how hard it was for her. Jon reached over and easily put her back down. Grace was furious, and she slapped at Jon's arm, but she didn't have the strength to fight him. "Jon, stop it!"

"Grace. Let me and Darcy take care of this, okay? You need to rest. For the baby. And for Aaron, too."

Grace looked like she wanted to murder Jon where he sat, but she nodded and laid her head back down, staring fixedly at the ceiling.

Jon motioned Darcy out into the hallway and when the door to Grace's room was closed behind them, he asked her, "What did you see?"

Darcy filled him in on what she had found upstairs in room two-fifteen. "I don't understand," Jon said when she was done. "How come nobody told us about this? We put out the message to all the local hospitals that first night."

"You put out the information about Aaron," Darcy reminded him. "We didn't know anything about Ray Stephenson until today."

"Yesterday, you mean," Jon corrected her. "It's after midnight now."

"Well, I'm not waiting another day to find out what's going on," she said to him. "Let's find somebody who can tell us what's going on."

They went up to the work station in the center of the Emergency Department. Behind the rectangular outline of the desk were three nurses and a doctor chatting quietly.

"Excuse me, doctor?" Jon said. He displayed his badge to them. Darcy could tell it got their attention. "My name is Detective Jon Tinker. I'm with the Misty Hollow Police Department. I need to talk to you about one of your patients. There's a man in room two-fifteen who we believe was kidnapped during a robbery in Oak Hollow."

The doctor, an older man with thick wire-rimmed glasses,

blinked repeatedly and scratched at his ear. "Ah yes," he said. "I'm familiar with that patient. I saw him when he came in yesterday. John Doe. Could barely speak. Mild concussion, broken leg. Suffering from amnesia and unable to tell us anything including his name. You know him?"

"We're sure his name is Ray Stephenson. The city police in Oak Hollow should have sent you out a message by now."

The doctor looked at one of the nurses, who shrugged. "I'm not sure."

"Doctor, we need to guard this man. When can we interview him?"

"Well, you can interview him in the morning, I'm sure, but I can't guarantee what he'll be able to tell you. Is there some urgency?"

Instead of answering that question Jon asked to use the phone behind the desk so he could contact the Meadwood PD to provide protection for Ray, and then he promised Darcy he would call Ray's wife to let her know where he was.

"I'm also going to have to call the Oak Hollow PD. The robbery took place in their city. I'm sure they'll want to send some people over to speak to Ray in the morning."

Darcy hugged him briefly. "You're going to be busy. Can I borrow your car again? I need to go back to Misty Hollow for something."

He looked puzzled but just nodded and handed her his keys. "I'm guessing you'll explain it to me later?"

"Of course," she said with a smile. Things were finally looking up. They knew where Ray Stephenson was. That was a start. The smile faded quickly, though, when she remembered that Aaron was still out there, somewhere, missing and possibly still in the hands of three men in ski masks.

WHEN DARCY ARRIVED BACK in Misty Hollow she headed straight for her book store. Turning the lights on inside, she went to the back office. She had tried using her gift to contact Aaron and Ray, and for obvious reasons it hadn't worked. Ray was still alive. Aaron must be still alive as well. That didn't mean she didn't have other resources to try.

"Millie, I need your help," she called out.

From the shelf above the desk in the office, her great aunt's journal fell. It thumped against the desk, popping open to lay on its spine. As Darcy watched, the pages turned, as if a strong wind had caught them. She knew better. It was her aunt's hands turning the pages to find the passage Darcy needed. The passage she had suddenly remembered at the hospital when the doctor was talking about how Ray Stephenson couldn't remember anything.

When the pages stopped, Darcy sat and scanned the neatly written paragraphs. It was instructions for helping ghosts who were too old to remember the lives they had lived before their deaths. If a ghost remained on this earth for too long without passing over, their connection to who they were became so weak that their memories actually faded.

Not unlike what had happened to Ray Stephenson.

If it worked for the ghosts, Darcy reasoned, then it might actually work for Ray too, even though he was still alive.

She read through the whole thing twice. The actual technique didn't sound that difficult. It involved settling her mind into a peaceful state, reaching out to the ghost, and then carefully remembering the details of her own life. The act of visualizing her own memories was supposed to help the ghost remember how to do the same thing for themselves.

Could it work for the living? She didn't see why not. The essence, or spirit, or whatever one chose to call the spark of life inside a person was released with death. Darcy could commune with those spirits because of her gift. But a living person held that spirit within them still. She should be able to reach out to it in much the same way.

Closing the journal she put it back up on the shelf. "Thank you, Millie," she whispered. On her way out she turned the store's lights off again, leaving darkness in her wake.

*B*ack at the hospital in Meadowood Darcy went back into the Emergency Department. Grace was asleep now. Jon was in the room with her, in a chair in the corner. He put a finger to his lips meaningfully and waved her over to him. Curling up into his lap felt good. She was beginning to feel very tired, and the night wasn't over yet.

"Did you find what you were looking for?" Jon asked her quietly.

"I hope so. I'm going to go up and talk to Ray now. I might be able to help him pull his memories back up. Did you get in touch with the local police?"

He nodded, his hands gently rubbing her back. It felt good. "They've sent two officers over to guard Ray's door until the Oak Hollow boys can get here. I'll come up with you and let the officers know it's okay for you to talk to Ray."

She nodded. "Um. Can you keep them out of the room while I do this?"

"I'm sure I can. This is going to be one of those kinds of conversations?"

"Yes," she said, and she left it at that.

The officers at Ray's door talked it over with Jon but ultimately they deferred to him, since it was more his case than theirs anyway. So Darcy found herself inside Ray's room, alone with the sound of the beeping machines and Ray's gentle snoring.

She shook his arm gently until his eyes popped open. "Oh, hello," he said to her. "Are you a doctor?"

"My name is Darcy Sweet," she explained. "I'm actually working with the police. I guess you'd say I'm a consultant. I understand that you have a touch of amnesia. If you're willing, I think I can help you get your memory back."

Ray's green eyes widened, and he nodded enthusiastically. "I can't explain how it feels to not know...anything. I'm willing to try whatever you want if you think it will help. There was a robbery, the cops said? At a bank? I just don't remember."

"That's okay," she said to him with a reassuring smile. "I'm going to help."

Darcy sat down carefully on the bed beside him, making sure not to bump his injured leg, and took both of his hands in hers. "I need you to close your eyes, take deep breaths and focus on your breathing. Concentrate. This, uh, might feel a little weird."

He looked skeptical but then he did as she asked and closed his eyes. Darcy took some deep breaths of her own and slipped into her meditative state. In her mind, she focused on images of mist, swirling and twisting, a neutral gray color that washed away her worry and anxiety. When she felt at peace she began to recall her own memories. She watched her childhood unfold, like images cast by an old time movie projector onto the wall of the mists. The scenes were a little distorted but with effort they became clear and crisp.

Childhood became her teenage years, and then adulthood. Her failed marriage, Millie's death, the bookstore and finding Jon and her sister and Aaron. Her memories turned to the last few days, with Aaron's disappearance and the robbery and—

"I remember!" Ray suddenly gasped. "Oh, dear God I remember. Ray. My name is Ray Stephenson. I work at the Three Twigs Federal Credit Union in Oak Hollow and there was a robbery and they took me." He suddenly looked very frightened. "They took me and this other man…"

Darcy leaned forward, anxiety gripping her again. This was it. This was what they had needed. "Jon!" she called out. "Jon, come in here!"

He came through the door in a rush, looking from Ray to Darcy. "What is it?"

"He remembers," Darcy told him in a rush. "Ray, tell us. Tell us what you remember."

Ray screwed up his face and then said, "There was just the one customer, you know? Tall guy. Blonde. Anyway, three men in black clothes and masks came bursting into the bank. They had guns. They were yelling at me to give them money. I tried to tell them I only kept three hundred dollars in my drawer. It made them angry. They pulled me into the back where the vault was, and made me open it. They took nearly everything in there."

Jon had pulled out a notebook from a pocket and was hastily writing down notes. "What happened then, Mister Stephenson?"

"They took me and the other guy to a car they had waiting out in back of the bank. They stuffed us both in the backseat and had guns pointed at us and then somewhere they tossed me out and I landed so hard and then…well, the next thing I remember is waking up here."

Darcy felt her lip quivering as she asked her next question. "The man who the robbers took with you. His name is Aaron, and he's my brother-in-law. Do you know what happened to him?"

Ray sadly shook his head. "No. I'm sorry, but I don't know. He was still in the car when they tossed me out."

She nodded. That was more than they had known an hour ago.

"Mister Stephenson," Jon asked him, stepping closer. "Is there anything about the robbers you can remember that might help us? Did they use any names, did they have an accent? Did you see any of their faces?"

"No, they never took their masks off. I didn't notice anything about their voices. I think at least one of them was white, though, from what I could see through the eye holes. Oh, right. The guy who pulled me over the counter, he had two different colored eyes. One was blue, one was brown. It was kind of creepy. Then there was…" He stopped, turning his eyes away and looking a little embarrassed. "There was a smell though. A sweet smell. Almost sickeningly sweet. I don't know that I've ever smelled anything like that before."

Jon looked at Darcy. He smiled at her in that way that let her know he was proud of her. "Good work," he mouthed to her silently.

She hoped it was good enough to help them find Aaron.

# CHAPTER 15

"It's actually good news," Jon was telling Grace as they drove her home a few hours later. It had been three days now since Aaron's disappearance. Good news was something they definitely needed. "If the robbers dumped Ray out of the car it means they aren't interested in hostages, and they aren't interested in hurting anyone. That's cause for optimism."

"Let's go straight to the police station when we get back to Misty Hollow," was all Grace said in response.

Darcy and Jon exchanged a look.

"Honestly, you two, I feel fine now." Grace sat up a little straighter in the front passenger seat to prove her point. "I don't need to be in bed any more. I won't rest until we find Aaron. Just take me to the police station when we hit town."

"Okay, whatever you say," Jon said to her.

Darcy wasn't convinced that it was the right thing for Grace to do but she also knew she couldn't argue with her sister. It was exactly what Darcy would do if Jon was missing.

They were pulling into the police department parking lot when Jon said, "I'm not sure what the sweet smell would be that Ray remembered, but a robber with two different colored eyes? If he's been arrested for anything before, that should stand out. Not too many guys with different colored eyes."

Darcy had to agree and she hoped that would be the clue that would lead them to Aaron's abductors. She got out of the car and then leaned through the driver's side window to give Jon a quick kiss. "I need to go home and change. And shower. And maybe eat something. Make sure Grace takes it easy, will you?"

"Hey," Grace said to her, "I'm right here, you know that, right?"

"Just take care of yourself, sis."

Grace rolled her eyes, but Darcy could see the little wisp of a smile on her sister's face.

As Darcy left the police station parking lot to start walking home, she looked over at the town square being transformed for the Valentine's Day dance the next day. Everyone was hustling about, stringing red streamers and hanging heart shaped lights.

"Darcy, Darcy!"

Darcy looked back to see Helen running up to her. "Where have you been?" Helen asked in a panicked voice. "I've been running around trying to get everything organized and I couldn't find you anywhere!"

Darcy realized that she hadn't done any of the things that she promised to do for the dance. "Helen, I'm so sorry. There's just been so much going on with Aaron's disappearance and Grace taking ill and—"

"Wait," Helen said, putting a hand on Darcy's arm. "Aaron's missing? I heard something about that but I thought it was just silly rumors. Oh, Darcy, I'm so sorry. How's Grace?"

"As good as can be expected, I suppose. We're working on finding Aaron now and we think we're close. Are you set for the dance?"

"Well, sort of. That cousin of yours has been a godsend. She and her band are all set for tomorrow. At least something's going right!"

Helen looked a little embarrassed as she said it, as though she shouldn't be happy about a dance when Grace's husband was missing.

"Don't worry about it, Helen," Darcy reassured her friend. "I know that if you can do anything for us you will. I'll let you know what happens, all right?"

The two women hugged and then Helen rushed off giving instructions to someone with a box full of roses.

Darcy turned away from the busy scene, wishing that all she had to think about was getting ready for a Valentine's Day dance. It wasn't long before she had made it home. A grateful Smudge rubbed up against her legs until she opened a can of cat food for him and set it next to a saucer of milk. "Sorry, boy," she said to him as she scratched behind his ears and let him scarf down his food. "I know I haven't been here much. I'll make it up to you, I promise."

She quickly showered and changed. While she was showering, the idea of what she should get Jon for Valentine's Day finally popped into her head. She knew it was such a low priority right now, and she wished her brain could just turn off, but she finally knew what she would give him. She hoped that he would like it. One less thing on her mind, she finished getting dressed and quickly headed back to the police department.

She had hoped that in the time she was gone, Jon and Grace and everyone else crowding the desks at the police department would have figured out who the robbers were. Jon scowled when she came in, though, and shook his head.

"Not a single criminal in all the databases we can access has two different colored eyes." He smacked his palm down on his desk. "I really thought that would give us something."

Grace sat miserably at her desk next to Jon's. Her hands kept playing with the papers on her desk like she didn't quite know what to do with them. Darcy watched her write something out, then shake the pen as it ran dry, and then angrily throw it away and continue writing with a different pen. The colors of the ink didn't match. The first pen had been black, and this one was blue…

A thought occurred to her. "You know, Jon, I used to love watching reruns of Columbo on television with my aunt Millie. Did you know Peter Falk had a glass eye? He hid it pretty well, but one eye was fake."

Light dawned in Jon's eyes. "Of course! We're not looking for a criminal with two different colored eyes."

Grace finished his thought for him. "We're looking for a criminal with a fake eye!"

"Do they keep records of things like that?" Darcy asked.

"Sometimes," Jon said, already typing away furiously at his computer. "If the arresting officer is smart enough to make a note of it…"

It was several minutes later when Jon looked up with a smile. "Got him. Howard Manning. Arrested three times on counts of robbery, one conviction. Spent five years in state prison, where he was arrested again on an assault charge. Seems he lost his left eye in a fight with another inmate. Cost him another two years. Out now and according to his parole record…"

He turned his computer screen so Grace and Darcy could read it.

"Living in Meadowood," Grace read out loud.

Jon picked up his phone and dialled the Meadowood PD.

# CHAPTER 16

"Are we ready?" Jon spoke into his handheld radio.

Darcy sat in the front seat of the car with him. Grace sat in the back. They were parked just down the street from the address they had for Howard Manning. They were within sight of the three story brick building on the corner of Second Street and Thackwood Drive. No one would notice them, though, in Jon's personal car.

"Almost in position, Detective Tinker," the officer's voice came back to him over the radio. "Stand by."

A joint operation of the Meadowood Police and Oak Hollow's PD was about to swarm the building to arrest Manning. Earlier, an undercover officer from Oak Hollow had gone inside and came back out again to confirm Manning was inside. He was considered armed and dangerous, so no one was moving in until everyone was ready.

"Jon," Darcy said to him. "You noticed what else is in that building, didn't you?"

"Yes. It explains what Ray smelled, doesn't it?"

The upper two stories of the building were apartments, and one of the three apartments on the second floor is where

Manning lived. The first floor of the place, though, was a chocolate shop. Open and busy for Valentine's Day, the store was doing a brisk business.

A sweet smell, Ray had said. Almost too sweet. The store made their own chocolates here, or so the sign in the window said. Darcy imagined the smell from living over a place like that would soak into your skin and your clothes both. The building looked like it was old, and she figured the apartments were probably cheap...

Darcy yawned. Jon looked over at her with a raised eyebrow. "Sorry," she said. It was the same day they had brought Grace home from the hospital, just a few hours ago. Everything had been put together quickly but it meant none of them had gotten any rest.

Grace yawned after her, loudly. With a little smile Darcy and Jon both looked back at her.

"What?" Grace said, good naturedly. "I'm pregnant with Aaron's baby. What's your excuse?"

Darcy stole a glance at Jon. They hadn't really had a discussion about whether or not he wanted children. This horrible ordeal with Aaron and Grace had taken up their every waking moment over the past few days. She wondered, when they ever got down to talking about it, what his answer would be.

Right now she turned her attention back to Grace. Reaching back, she held her sister's hand briefly. "We will find him, Grace. We will."

"We don't even know for sure this is the guy who did the robbery," Grace pointed out.

Darcy couldn't argue. All they had was an answer for the smell Ray had mentioned and a known criminal with a glass eye. That didn't mean he was the same one at the bank where Aaron had been taken. But Darcy knew. The way her skin crawled whenever she looked at the building on the corner. She knew.

"When we go in," Jon said to Grace, "I want you to stay here.

We'll get Manning, we'll make him talk. But you stay here, okay? You're too close to this."

Grace nodded. Darcy was surprised. It was a mark of how worried her sister was that she didn't even try to argue.

"We're go, Detective," the voice came back over the radio to Jon.

He handed the small radio with its stubby antenna to Darcy. "I'll radio you when we know more," he said, and kissed her lightly on her cheek. Then he turned to Grace and squeezed her arm. There was nothing he could say, though, so he silently left the car and raced to join the dozen or more uniformed police officers swarming up to the chocolate shop with its upper floors of apartments.

Darcy still had hold of Grace's hand. Together, the two sisters watched as the officers quickly and quietly cleared everyone out of the chocolate shop. Of course, people being people, most of them just went half a block, turned around, and watched the scene unfolding. Darcy had communicated with any number of ghosts whose only crime in life had been curiosity. It didn't just kill cats.

"I hate this," Grace said after a few minutes had passed with no word. "I should be in there."

"Jon is right," Darcy said to her. "You're too close to this one. You wouldn't be any good to Aaron if you got yourself hurt now. We'll know more any minute."

Tense moments passed as they waited. Darcy held onto Grace, and Grace kept mumbling under her breath, "Come on, come on, please…" Darcy felt so helpless. All of their work had brought them to this moment. If Manning turned out not to be the guy they were looking for, she didn't know what they would do then.

On the second floor, a window suddenly broke and a man tried to climb out onto a fire escape only to be grabbed from behind and roughly pulled back out.

"Well," Grace said. "I guess he was the right guy after all."

Darcy had to fight the urge to run from the car and race up the apartment steps and demand to know what was happening. She could only imagine how hard this was for Grace as they waited for someone to tell them something.

When Jon's voice finally came over the radio in her hand Darcy jumped. "We got him! We got him!" He was excited, Darcy could hear it in his voice.

"Give me that," Grace said to Darcy. She took the radio and pressed the talk button with a thumb. "Jon, is it him? You've got Manning?"

"What?" he said back to them. "Oh. Yes, we've got Manning. That's not who I mean, though."

Darcy knew what he was about to say, and tears of joy filled her eyes.

"We found Aaron," Jon said to them. "He's fine."

# CHAPTER 17

'Fine' might have been a bit of an overstatement, but no one was complaining.

At the hospital in Meadowood again, in a room just two doors down from where Grace had spent the previous night, Aaron lay in a bed. His right arm was in a cast and there was a yellowish bruise on the left side of his face. He couldn't keep the big grin off his face though, and Grace would not let go of his left hand. She wouldn't move from his bedside, either. They had found him, and he was alive, and that was enough to make all of them smile.

"Other than the broken arm and some bruising, you're in pretty good shape, Mister Wentworth." It was a different doctor than last night. This man was short and had a young face. "You're going to need to stay overnight for observation, but other than that you should be able to go home tomorrow."

"Just in time for Valentine's Day," Aaron said, turning to Grace. "Thanks, Doctor."

"Don't thank me, I just work here." The man seemed to think that was the funniest thing ever, and left the room laughing after shaking hands with Jon and Darcy.

"I had all these plans," Aaron started to say. They could tell he was still weak from his ordeal, from being held by three men in a small apartment for days on end. "I'm so sorry, Grace."

"Shh," she said to him. "Stop it. You just rest. I'm staying here with you tonight and Darcy can come back in the morning and pick us up and then we can go home. Trust me, being with you is going to be the best Valentine's Day gift ever."

"Sounds good to me," Aaron agreed.

They leaned into each other, gently kissing and touching. Without taking her eyes off her husband Grace said, "Don't you think you two should leave? You've been here too long now anyway."

Jon and Darcy looked at each other. "Okay, sis. We can take a hint," said Darcy.

"We were leaving anyway," Jon said. "I have to go back to the Meadowood station and help question Howard Manning. They caught the other two men also, Grace. Just so you know."

"Good," she said. "I hope they rot in jail. Now, seriously. Get out."

Jon chuckled as he led Darcy out of the room and to the hospital exit. "Good to know he's okay, isn't it?"

"Yes," Darcy agreed. "Now let's go nail these guys."

AT THE MEADOWOOD police station Darcy watched from behind one-way glass as Jon and a Meadowood detective sat down across from Howard Manning. They had let her stay as a courtesy, at Jon's request. The voices from the room came through the speaker on the wall. She wasn't the only one watching. This had turned into one of the biggest cases that Meadowood had seen in a long time.

"You've been advised of your rights," Jon reminded Manning. "You've waived your right to an attorney. I have a few questions."

Howard Manning looked bigger in real life than Darcy had

imagined him. His skin was blotchy and pale, and his mousy brown hair was chopped short. He fiddled with the edge of the table nervously as he nodded.

"You're sure you don't want an attorney?" the detective from Meadowood asked.

"Yeah I'm sure." Manning's voice was gruff and pinched. "You guys are gonna give the deal to the first guy what talks, and that's gonna be me. I know how this works. I've been through it before."

"More than once," Jon said. "We've seen your record. All right. You tell us what happened, you sign off on it, and agree to testify against your partners. That's the deal."

"And I get what?" Manning asked gruffly.

Darcy saw Jon's fist clench and then relax. Anyone else probably would have missed it. Jon was holding back a lot of anger right now. "What you get, Mister Manning," he said, "is us talking to the District Attorney on your behalf. Don't forget that we found a man bound and gagged in your apartment. Don't forget you tried to run from us when we executed our arrest warrant. Don't forget that you've been seen spending money from the bank heist. It's not like you're going to skate on this."

"All right, all right," Manning said, obviously understanding how bad his position was. "What d'you want to know?"

"These other men," the Meadowood detective said, referring to his notes, "Harry Floson and Douglas Merceaux. They were your accomplices?"

"Yeah, yeah. You know that already. We went into that bank, held the teller at gun point and made him give us the money. He wasn't gonna do it at first. Can you believe that? I remember a time when bank tellers was eager to give up the cash so they wouldn't get hurt."

Darcy shook her head. She understood the dead a lot better than she would ever understand some of the living.

"So why take the two men?" Jon asked. "You had the money. What good were they to you?"

Manning sat back and folded his arms. "Simple. That teller man was trying to run. Couldn't have that. We needed to get away first. So we took both of them. Hadn't planned on hostages, but we figured we needed to keep them quiet until we got away."

Jon waited for the other detective to get all that down before he continued his questions. "But then you let Ray Stephenson go."

"That a question?" Manning asked.

Jon's hand clenched again. "The question is this. You let one guy go, you held the other man. Why?"

Manning shrugged. "Two hostages was too much trouble. We'd already gotten away by then. Or so we thought," he grumbled. "Anyway. We could only keep one of them, so we tossed the little redheaded teller out of the car and left him. The other guy turned out to be some kind of accountant or something. Thought maybe we could get a ransom for him. Never got around to that, though, before you guys found us. How'd you do that, anyway?"

Jon pointed to his own eye, then to Manning's. "You should maybe get an eye that matches your color, if you want to keep committing crimes."

Manning grimaced. "Knew it. Had to get it cheap, though, 'cause I didn't have money. Was going to order me a real nice one with the take from the bank."

Darcy blinked away tears as she listened to the man prattle on about what he would have done with all that money. Dumb luck. It had just been dumb luck that the robbers kept Aaron and not Ray. If they'd tossed Aaron out first, then it would have been Ray they would have kept in Manning's apartment. Darcy and Grace and Jon never would have gotten involved. Manning might never have gotten caught. Things would have turned out very differently.

Not that she would ever want Aaron to go through what he had, but she was happy with the results. Ray Stephenson was safe and sound. Aaron, too. Manning and his buddies were going to prison. It made her smile to think about.

Her life always took her in strange directions, but she'd learned to accept that she often ended up where she needed to be, whether she wanted to be there or not.

"You know," Manning was saying, "that guy was getting way annoying. Wouldn't stop going on about how he had to get home to his wife. She was having a baby, he said. She needed him, he said. Gah. Good thing I kept that gag on him. I couldn't stand it."

Jon stood up, and for just a moment Darcy was sure he was going to punch Manning in the face. She leaned forward, willing him to do it. Instead, he just turned to the Meadowood detective. "You can take it from here?"

When the other officer nodded to him, Jon quietly left the room.

JON AND DARCY slept through the rest of the day after they got home. Going straight up to their bed, They managed to kick off shoes and socks and coats and then fell down on top of the covers in each other's arms. They didn't wake up until noon the next day, both of them starving. They fixed huge sandwiches and hot bowls of soup and ate in silence. They were sitting next to each other at the table, and somehow her hand touched his. Then his fingers caught hers, and then his bare foot rubbed over hers, and the next thing they knew they were headed back up to bed, most of their meal forgotten.

Darcy didn't remember falling asleep again. She just knew it was dark when they woke up. They didn't wake up again until the next morning. Valentine's Day, Darcy realized. And close to time for the dance.

"Happy Valentine's Day," she said to Jon, curling into him tightly, kissing his lips. "I love you."

"I love you too, Darcy Sweet. Happy Valentine's Day."

Smudge pounced on both of them and meowed loudly. Laughing, Darcy reached over and scratched his neck vigorously. "Happy Valentine's Day to you too, Smudge."

"We should get changed for the dance, don't you think?" Jon asked her.

Showering and dressing, they talked to each other about Grace and Aaron and what might happen to the three thugs who had caused so much grief to so many people. Darcy was feeling better than she had in a long time, and she smiled and hummed happily on their drive back into town.

The mists had receded, as they always did after a crisis passed by Misty Hollow. Most of the snow had managed to melt as well, and the decorated square was alive with lights and music. Stars shined brightly in a clear sky. "Look!" Darcy said. "There's my cousin's band. Oh, don't they sound wonderful?"

"I agree. Care to dance?"

Darcy was mildly surprised. "Dancing in public? Well, I never thought I'd hear those words coming from Jon Tinker's mouth. Yes, I'd love to!"

Darcy was very relaxed as she swayed to the music. Her head was resting on Jon's chest as they danced a slow dance around the makeshift dance area in the town square. Several other couples were doing the same thing.

"I'm so happy that everything worked out," Jon said to her. "You know in all of this craziness I didn't have time to wrap your gift." He stopped dancing and pulled a book out of his coat pocket.

"You know, I felt that there," she said to him coyly.

He laughed with her and handed her the book. Her eyes got a little wider. It was a rare edition of the Canterbury Tales, one of Darcy's favorite reads.

"Oh, Jon. This is wonderful. Thank you, I love it." She wrapped her arms around him and leaned up to give him a quick kiss. "I have something for you, too. It took me forever to figure out what to get you I hope you like it." She pulled a card from her own coat pocket and handed it to him.

He looked at her with a smile in his eyes and then quickly ripped the envelope open to pull out the card. Opening it up he read the words inside. She was worried until the smile touched his lips as well. "Darcy. Perfect. Just what we needed. A long weekend away together at our favorite cabin."

"I figured, you know, with everything that just happened, we could use some alone time together."

"Just what I wanted," he told her, drawing her into his arms. "I love you."

"I love you, too," she said as they both began to move to the music again.

The dance continued on through the night, and Darcy had never felt more happy, or more loved.

### -The End-

# BOOK 6 – HIDING FROM DEATH

# CHAPTER 1

*D*arcy Sweet smiled as her boyfriend Jon drove them, finally, back home. It had been a good weekend for the two of them, away from everything, just enjoying each other's company. She had gotten the getaway at their favorite cabin for Jon as a Valentine's Day gift. He'd gotten her a rare copy of The Canterbury Tales by Chaucer. It was one of her favorite books of all time, just the way the prose was written and the fact that it had such an influence on the way books had been written ever since.

She leaned across the center console of Jon's car and rested her head against his shoulder. When he put his arm around her, she smiled. She loved books, but she'd brought the edition of Canterbury Tales with her on their weekend away and never opened it up once. That was how much attention they had paid to each other. It felt good, to finally spend that kind of time on each other.

As they entered the town limits of Misty Hollow, every building, every sight brought back memories. Their little sleepy town had been host to secrets and murders that had kept Jon, and Darcy, too busy to slow down. Then there was her sister's husband, Aaron, who had been kidnapped during a bank robbery over in Oak Hollow. It seemed like everyone she cared about was getting caught up in some trouble.

It was the middle of February now but already the snows had melted away from the lawns and streets of Misty Hollow. Winter never really lingered here. Not like it did in the mountains up north. It would be chilly still well into March, of course, and she was grateful for the warmth of the car's heater and her snugly zipped jacket.

"What time is it?" she asked Jon. The clock on his dash had been wrong for months and she could never remember if it was too fast or too slow.

"Just after one o'clock in the afternoon," Jon told her, consulting his wrist watch. "We made good time."

"You didn't have any trouble getting today off?" Today was Monday, and both of them should have been at work. Jon as a Detective with the Misty Hollow police force, and her at the Sweet Read bookstore here in town.

Jon winked at her. "Nope. I told them there was some very pressing, very urgent business I had to attend to out of town."

Darcy felt herself blush. She knew what they had done all weekend. There had been a certain urgency to it, she supposed. She looked up at him now, with his short dark hair and stunning blue eyes, and that face that she had memorized so well. "I love you," she whispered to him, twining a finger into her own long dark tresses.

He held her closer, steering expertly with one hand, and whispered back, "I love you, too."

They turned out of town again on the road that led to her house. It had been her Aunt Millie's house, actually, but just like the bookstore it had become hers when her aunt passed away. It was a big house sitting among tall pine trees, two stories, with white painted siding that was going to need some serious attention come spring. She was glad she had Jon to share it with her now. Her black and white cat, Smudge, didn't quite feel the same way.

Darcy smiled. Smudge would warm up to Jon. Eventually.

On their way to her house they passed by where her friend Anna Louis had lived. Until she had been murdered. Darcy shivered to remember it and was rewarded by a squeeze from Jon. The house was smaller than Darcy's, just a bottom floor and an overglorified attic that passed as a second story. The bank had done some renovations to the place since Anna's death in an attempt to sell it, but a legacy like that was hard for a house to overcome. No one had lived in it since.

Until now, apparently.

"Jon, look at that."

"Hmm?" He turned to look at Anna's house. "Hey, look at that. The lights are on. I guess they finally sold it."

"That can't be true," Darcy said, her mind immediately thinking of trespassers and worse.

"No, really," Jon said. "Look at the sign."

Darcy did. The sign he meant was the For Sale sign out front. On top of it had been placed a little red rectangle that exclaimed "Sold!" Darcy slumped back in her seat. Somehow, the idea that someone had been illegally trespassing had sat better with her than knowing that someone had bought Anna's house and was now living in it.

"Are you okay?" Jon asked, picking up on her mood immediately. "You miss Anna, don't you?"

"Every day," she admitted, as they pulled into the driveway of their home.

As they walked inside the house, Jon grabbed her by her hand and twirled her into a spin. He caught her again as she laughed, and began swaying with her back and forth, their luggage forgotten.

"Jon, what are you doing?"

"I'm dancing with you, Darcy Sweet."

"Oh, for Pete's sake. There's no music."

He smiled at her as they danced their way into the kitchen. "I don't need music when I'm dancing with you."

They laughed together at his corny remark, and everything was right with the world again.

Just past the dining room table he stumbled and fell backward into the wall. Smudge scooted out from under his feet, a streak of black and white fur. He zipped to the nearest doorway and then sat there looking at Darcy. She could almost read his thoughts in those feline eyes. "You brought him here," he was saying. "He's your problem."

"Are you all right?" she asked him, still smiling, offering a hand that he gladly took. "Did Smudge do that to you?"

"No, no it wasn't him," Jon said, a little embarrassed. "I tripped over these boxes. Why do we have these boxes here?"

Darcy looked down at the two cardboard boxes piled one on the other. On the side in black marker was written, "Kitchen."

Darcy put a hand on her hip and teasingly screwed her face up at him. "Because, Mister Tinker, you moved into my house but have yet to put all of your stuff away."

"Oh. Is that it?" He bent to his knees and opened the top box. "Oh, hey, this is my good cooking stuff. No problem, we'll just replace all of your older stuff."

"What!" Darcy knelt next to him and began closing the box again. He would open it, she would close it, and it became a game that had Darcy in tears she was laughing so hard. "You will not replace my stuff with these cheap knock offs!"

"Cheap!" Jon laughed with her. "I'll have you know I spent almost twenty dollars on all five of those frying pans! Your stuff is old. Let's keep mine."

"It might be old but at least I know it won't burn up the first time I try to fry bacon!"

"Mmm," he said, rubbing his stomach, still holding the frying pan in his hand. "Sounds good. Here. Use this pan and go make us some."

"Jon!" she exclaimed, tackling him from behind and trying to tickle him, the one weakness she knew he had. Somehow, he turned it back into their dance and soon they were turning circles around the kitchen, Jon holding her in his arm and the frying pan in his hand.

When he stopped, he grabbed her frying pan from its hook over the stove. She had to admit it was older, with the scorch marks on the bottom to prove it, but it was obviously sturdier as he held them up side by side and made a show of comparing them critically, one eye scrunched up.

Her stomach hurt at this point, she was laughing so much. "You know what?" she finally said to him. "Let's just keep both. The more food, the better."

"Deal!" he said at once, hooking both pans above the stove this time. "I'll even share the responsibility of washing the dishes."

She leaned up against his chest, her hands resting lightly on his shoulders. "Sounds good to me. You're a great guy, you know that?"

"I do. It's on my business cards, actually."

She slapped his arm lightly. "You know what I mean. You make me happy."

Tilting her chin up he kissed her lips. It was a long, slow kiss. When he pulled back from her he looked her deep in her green eyes. "If I make you happy, then I'm doing something right. Come on, let's finish unpacking those boxes before I trip and kill myself."

They put pots and pans and cooking utensils away, sometimes cramming them in where there wasn't any space for them. When they were done, Jon threw the boxes out the back door ceremoniously. "There," he proclaimed. "I am officially moved in."

From his doorway, Smudge mewled and Darcy would have sworn he rolled his eyes.

Jon looked at the cat skeptically. "Do you think he'll ever accept me taking up so much of your life?"

"Give him time," she told him. "Smudge is used to being the only man in my life."

THE NEXT MORNING, Darcy woke up to the sunlight slanting into their bedroom window. Smudge stirred and stretched between her legs, comfortably curled up on the blankets. Jon's arm was across her belly. The clock told her it was still an hour before she actually had to get up, but she decided to make an early day of it.

After a shower with the water turned up really hot Darcy went downstairs to make herself some eggs. Smiling, she plucked down Jon's cheap frying pan and mixed scrambled eggs with milk and chopped green pepper and a few other ingredients. The fragrant smell of cooking filled the air.

Jon came down just as she was dividing the eggs onto two plates. She had planned on keeping his wrapped in the microwave but she smiled as she saw him. This was much better.

"Good morning," he said to her, scrubbing a hand through his hair and coming over to kiss her lightly on the cheek. "That smelled so good I just had to come see." He peeked over her shoulder and raised a knowing eyebrow seeing his frying pan there on the stove.

They ate at the kitchen table, talking about this and that, about the weekend at the cabin, about what they had to do at work today. It was a leisurely meal with plenty of time for both of them to wake up. It was a rare thing for both of them. Soon enough, though, it was time to finish getting ready.

Jon drove them into town. Usually Darcy walked or in better weather would ride her bicycle. It wasn't that far into town from their place. Jon needed the car today for work, though.

They drove by Anna Louis' old place, and Darcy again

thought about who could have possibly moved in there. "How could someone have bought the house so quickly?" she wondered out loud. "We were only gone for a weekend."

He drove on in silence for a moment, then reached out and took her hand. "I can see this is bothering you. Do you want me to look into it today? Everything should be public record."

Darcy didn't want to be one of those people. She usually hated gossip. But it bothered her, knowing that someone new was living in Anna's house. Someone she didn't know.

Plus, when she stared at the front door, a cold feeling slithered up her spine. That was never a good thing. She'd learned, over the years, to trust feelings like that. She had been born with a gift, an ability that made her sensitive to the other side. The messages she got were usually unclear, but she knew better than to ignore them.

"Yes," she said to Jon. "I'd like to know who's living there. Thank you, Jon."

# CHAPTER 2

*J*on dropped her off on Main Street. He had to go one way to the police station and she had just a short walk down the street to get to the Sweet Read bookstore. They exchanged a quick kiss and a promise to try to meet for lunch so Jon could tell her if he found anything.

The morning was crisp and clear and the breeze had just a hint of warmth in it. Spring might come early this year.

She passed by a few of her friends. Linda waved on her way to open the library. Blake Underwood was headed to the post office. He smiled at her on his way, obviously in a hurry. She had to admit, it felt good to be home.

The bookstore was already open, even though it was before nine in the morning. The sign on the door proudly read "OPEN a good book today." Sue must already be here.

Stepping through the door Darcy unzipped her coat and looked around. The stacks of books were nice and neat and in order. Two boxes of books, a new delivery, sat just inside to the right. Seeing them, Darcy had to sigh. When she first took over the bookstore she was taking in new shipments of books every week. Now, it was only a few boxes a month. Misty Hollow was a small town and even with the customers she took in from Oak Hollow and Meadowood and other nearby places, her income was way down. The surge in electronic media hadn't helped the small bookstores in the least.

She set that concern aside for another time and hung her jacket on a wall hook over the boxes of new books. "Sue?" she called out. "Where are you?"

"In the back!" she heard Sue call back to her from the office.

Sue Fisher was a twenty year old college student and Darcy's only employee. She came out of the office now with a wide smile. "Oh, I'm so glad you're back. I don't mind running the store when you're away on vacation but there's so much I don't know how to do!" She laughed, and Darcy thought it was a little forced.

Darcy hugged her friend. She could tell right away that something was wrong. They'd worked so closely together for so long that they knew each other that well. She wanted to let Sue come out with it herself, but all she did was sweep back her long blonde hair and walk over to one of the already neat stacks of books and begin rearranging books that were in perfect order. She didn't even ask how Darcy's weekend had been.

"Sue?" Darcy said. "What is it? Are you okay?"

"Oh sure," Sue answered. "Everything's great." She shuffled the same books she had just reshelved. "No. That's actually not true. Everything's not great. It's terrible."

Darcy was worried now. "You know you can tell me anything, right Sue? Is it Zach?"

Sue had started dating a boy named Zach just before Valentine's Day. She had been completely head over heels with the guy but her taste in men hadn't always been the best.

"No, it's not him." Sue put the last book back in its place again and then shrugged. "Well, it's sort of that. Look, I have some exciting news. I'm just not sure how you're going to take it."

"Sue, you know I only want what's best for you."

"I know that. Well." She took a deep breath and then everything came out of her in a rush. "Zach and I have been talking. We, uh, want to spend more time together. And there's this new curriculum at school, an advanced degree in literature. It's what I've always wanted to do and I've been waiting for weeks to get on the waiting list. Now there's an opening and if I don't take this chance now I'll miss out."

She stopped, out of words, looking at Darcy, uncertainly biting her lower lip.

"Sue, that's wonderful news!" Darcy hugged her friend, honestly happy for her. "Why would you ever think I'd be upset over that?"

"Because, it means I won't be able to work at the bookstore. Not for a while, anyway. This is a pretty intense course."

Darcy nodded. She hadn't thought of that. "Well, of course I'll miss you," she said. "But like you said this is an incredible opportunity and I don't want you to miss out. I've been lucky to have you fit in your job here inbetween your school courses as it is. I've always known that."

They hugged again, and Sue told Darcy more about the course work she would have to do, and about her boyfriend Zach. As they worked, Darcy listened to every word but her attention was split between that and the store. Would she have to hire someone new to take Sue's place? Considering how sales had slumped this winter, she probably could handle it by herself.

Movement over in the corner of the store caught her eye. Great Aunt Millie stood there, transparent to the rest of the world, a shade of her former self. Millie had never moved on from the bookstore. Darcy had never asked why, respecting her aunt's privacy. She figured when Millie was ready to leave, she'd let Darcy know.

Now Millie looked slowly around the store, passing through book shelves even as she ran her finger along the spines of various books. This place had meant a lot to Millie. Her aunt had poured her heart and soul into it, almost literally. Looking at her specter now, Darcy thought it looked like Millie was asking the same question that she was.

Would they have to close the bookstore?

FOR LUNCH, Darcy took herself out to the La Di Da Deli. A quick phone call to Jon let her know that he wasn't going to be able to join her so she was on her own. He had been very rushed with her on the phone. "The town has been busy while we were gone, sweet baby," he said, using her pet nickname for her. "I'll talk to you later, okay? I love you."

"I love you, too," she said to him, and then he hung up. She grabbed her coat to leave feeling a little disappointed.

She could have gone over to her friend Helen's bakery, but the Bean There Bakery and Café was always so busy during the lunch hour. Helen was the mayor in town as well, and had hired some new help for her store. She was suddenly reminded that Helen had met a man, a baker who she'd hired for the store. Darcy could tell there was a lot more to it than that, though, and she promised herself to catch up with Helen soon to see how that was going for her.

Helen Nelson was one of the people who had been caught up in the mysteries and secrets Misty Hollow had hidden so well for so long. Her husband Steve had been sent to jail for the murder of her friend Anna, and Darcy had been a big part of that. Helen didn't like to talk about it anymore. She'd put that part of her life behind her, and Darcy couldn't blame her one bit.

Of course, that brought her thoughts back to the question of who was living in Anna's house. She sighed as she walked through the town center. She supposed the easiest thing to do would be to just go up to the door of her new neighbor and knock. She'd have to ask Jon if he found anything out yet, of course, but saying hello was something neighbors did.

Still arguing with herself she went inside the Deli and up to the counter. A young girl who Darcy recognized as one of the town's young teenagers took her order. Victoria, she thought the girl's name was. She smiled as she took Darcy's money and made change, the transparent plastic braces on her teeth barely noticeable.

She was burning with curiosity about what Jon had found out. It would just have to wait, though. Or maybe she could get Jon a sandwich and use it as an excuse to drop in on him? It was a sneaky thought. Not that she hadn't ever done it before. He really had seemed busy, though.

As she stood there pondering that idea she overheard a conversation between two other customers at a nearby table. There were a few round tables in the deli set out for customers to eat inside if they chose, even though most of the town got their food to go. Darcy recognized the two women sitting at this table. Cora Morton and Evelyn Casey were both members of her book club. They hadn't met recently, what with everyone's busy schedules, but Darcy knew these two had a handle on all the gossip in Misty Hollow.

"Have you heard?" Cora was asking. "Someone moved into Anna's house!"

"Oh, yes," Evelyn replied, taking a sip of her tea, "it's nice to know that someone will be taking care of the place again.

Both of the women were elderly, with very proper clothing and nearly matching pearl necklaces and gray hair done up in buns. Darcy took a few steps closer, trying to make it look like she was reading the menu board above the deli counter. She almost felt bad about eavesdropping. It had to do with Anna's house, though, and Cora and Evelyn weren't exactly being quiet about what they were saying.

"Well that may be," Cora said to Evelyn's remark, "but she doesn't have to be that rude about it, now does she?"

"Oh, now how would you know that, you old coot?" Evelyn teased gently.

"Well, I went to see her, now didn't I?" Cora humphed. "Brought her a nice basket of muffins, too. She just slammed the door in my face."

"She did not!"

Evelyn sounded horrified, and Darcy had to keep herself from giggling at the way the two women were carrying on about this bit of juicy gossip. She didn't want to give herself away.

"Oh yes she did!" Cora insisted. "I heard she did it to some other people in town, too."

"How terrible. I hope it was no one I know," Evelyn said from behind her tea cup, making it perfectly plain that she actually hoped it was someone she knew.

But Cora shook her head. "No. This woman is from out of town. I'm not sure where. Laura Lannis is her name."

"Lannis? Well, that's certainly not a local name." Evelyn sounded disappointed that she wouldn't be able to spread gossip about anyone from town. "Who is her husband?"

Cora frowned. "Well, that I don't know. She's living there by herself, at least for now. Oh, there's a son. Someone told me his name is Max, I think."

"Older boy, is he? I have a niece who needs to settle down."

"No. Eight years old. Much too young for your niece," Cora joked with a smile.

"Oh, my dear," Evelyn said with a wave of her hand, "where Kendra is concerned I'm not being choosy!"

The two women laughed together and the conversation turned to the failed love life of Evelyn's niece. Darcy wanted to sit down with them and ask more questions about this Laura Lannis who had moved into Anna's house but she got the feeling Cora and Evelyn didn't actually know anything else. The girl at the counter had her order ready then, anyway, all sealed up in a paper to-go bag with the Deli's name on the front.

"How strange," Darcy thought to herself as she stepped out onto the sidewalk again. "Why would she be so rude to people just trying to welcome her to town?"

She knew some people valued their privacy, but if this woman was going to make a home for her son here in Misty Hollow, she would need to meet the people here. Darcy found it very curious that anyone would come to a new town and not want to try to blend in and make new friends.

She'd just have to wait and hear what Jon had found out.

BACK AT THE BOOKSTORE, Sue met her with an uncertain smile. "Are you sure you're not mad at me?"

Darcy had almost forgotten how upset Sue was over her news. "No, Sue, I'm certainly not mad at you. I'm happy for you that you're going to have this opportunity. Who knows? Maybe someday I'll have one of your books on these shelves."

Sue laughed at the thought of that and seemed to feel better, even more so after Darcy gave her a quick hug. "Why don't you take your lunch break now, okay?" she told Sue. "When you come back you can give me all the details about when you'll have to leave."

Sue nodded, grabbing her coat and promising not to be long as she swept out of the door, making the little bell ring.

Darcy twisted the delicate antique ring on the finger of her right hand over and over. It was a habit she had whenever she was nervous or worried about something. As happy as she was for Sue, her leaving for more schooling had really brought the situation of her bookstore to the front of her mind. She actually owned the building, but the business license payment to the town was a monthly expense she was just making now.

"Millie, what am I going to do?" she asked out loud. She knew her great aunt was here. She always was. She just didn't always answer.

From the office, Darcy heard a thump. She rolled her eyes. A book had fallen off the high shelf above the desk, by the sound of it. "You can't just come out and tell me?" she asked with a hint of irritation.

Marching to the office, she found one of the leather bound history books she had picked up at a rare bookstore fallen onto the desk. She and Jon had gotten those on one of their first trips together. She remembered wanting them for the histories they had of the local towns, including Misty Hollow.

Sitting at the desk with the book now, she opened it to the section she had marked. "Misty Hollow," it read, "Established 1853." There was a rich history to this town, even if the modern day buildings and paved streets didn't always show it.

She turned through the pages, skimming through the paragraphs and glancing at the photographs of how life used to be. Horse drawn carriages, men holding double-handled saws to cut down trees, children in school using slate boards and chalk to do their lessons. How different life was, she mused. Things change so quickly, and it's hard sometimes to keep up with the changes...

She sat bolt upright in the chair. That was it! That was the answer. It would be a big change for her little bookstore, but it felt like the right thing to do. She shook her head with a smile and looked around her at the empty room. "Thanks again, Millie," she whispered.

The bell over the door rang. Sue was back. "Darcy!" she called out. "I got a sandwich to go. I thought we could eat together, if you haven't finished yours already."

Darcy had actually forgotten all about lunch. Excitedly she walked out of the office to meet Sue with a smile. "I have one last job for you to tackle for the store before I can let you go," she said.

∼

THAT NIGHT on her walk home, Darcy couldn't help but be in a good mood. She whistled as she went, watching the sun paint the clouds in different colors as it began sinking towards the horizon.

Off Main Street she turned, following the path that led her home. Her good mood faltered a little as she passed by Anna Louis' old house. Now it belonged to Laura Lannis, she supposed. Darcy stopped and stared at the windows with their lights burning brightly behind them. She thought she saw shadows move inside a couple of times.

What was Laura's story? Why had she moved to Misty Hollow? Where had she come from, for that matter, and why was she being so unfriendly? There were any number of questions that burned in Darcy's mind. That was the kind of person she was, after all. It had always gotten her into trouble, but even the trouble she got into ended up making good things happen. Usually.

A chill went up Darcy's spine as she stood there looking at the house. She shivered, but she knew it wasn't from the cold. She knew the difference. There was something wrong with this situation. Her instincts always let her know. Clenching her teeth she decided to go over to meet Laura Lannis tomorrow morning. She felt a responsibility to know what was going on in there, since it had belonged to her friend.

She was sure Jon wouldn't approve her decision, but he had become accustomed to her following her instincts, or her gut feelings as he called it. He was still a little nervous about the way she could sense things or talk to people who had passed over. Even though he'd seen her do it any number of times, she knew it still made him a little uncomfortable.

She huddled into her coat to ward off the cold tendrils that still lingered like icy fingers down her back and started walking toward her own house again. Like it or not, this was something she was determined to do.

In the fading sunlight, mist rose from the ground along the path, collecting at the foot of the trees she passed, making the coming night seem even colder.

$\mathcal{D}$arcy spooned out balls of cookie dough onto the greased pan. The oven was set and she figured she'd have at least three dozen homemade chocolate chip cookies from this one batch.

Smudge curled around her legs, meowing up at her. "Sorry, my friend," Darcy said to him. "Chocolate isn't good for cats. Be a good boy and I'll give you a little milk before bed."

Smudge made a snorting sound that Darcy understood perfectly well.

She was just setting the timer on the first batch of cookies when Jon came home, whisking through the door with a smile and humming some song that she thought might be Bon Jovi. "Hey, beautiful," he said when he saw her, sweeping her into a spin and dancing with her as he hummed some more.

Darcy smiled and squealed as he twirled her around and held her from behind. He kissed her ear and it sent shivers down her back. "Something smells good," he said.

"Is it me, or the cookies?" Darcy asked.

"Definitely you." He hugged her once more and then let her go. "So who are the cookies for?"

"I wanted to bring them over to Laura tomorrow. Kind of a welcome to the neighborhood gift." She stirred the rest of the cookie batter with a wooden spoon. "I heard Cora and Evelyn talking in the Deli today, though. Seems other people have tried to welcome her to Misty Hollow and she's actually shut the door in their faces."

Jon took his jacket off and set it over the back of one of the kitchen chairs. "You know, I heard that today, too. The desk sergeant actually took three or four calls from people saying how they had tried to talk to this Laura Lannis and she wouldn't give them the time of day. Can you believe people in this town? They want us to go investigate her because she's acting suspicious."

He reached around Darcy to pick up a teaspoon and then tried to steal some of the batter. She slapped his hand. "Don't you dare. So. What did you find out about Laura, anyway?"

He shrugged and made another stab for the dough. "There's not much to learn, apparently. Laura Lannis, age thirty-nine, moved into Anna's house with her eight year old son Alex while you and I were away at the cabin. Apparently the sale was made in cash, which I have to admit is a little strange, but not unheard of." He shrugged. "No criminal record that I could find. She's just another neighbor."

"Another neighbor, in Anna's house," she added.

"I know, Darcy, but Anna wouldn't want her house to be empty forever. Right?" He kissed her cheek and as she was smiling at his little gesture he moved swiftly past her to scoop out a spoonful of the raw batter and pop it into his mouth.

"Hey!" she laughed. "You're as bad as Smudge."

He smiled at her with the spoon in his mouth, humming and dancing around the kitchen again. Darcy rolled her eyes at him. "Oh, for Pete's sake. I give up. Go upstairs and change, Detective Tinker. I'll make you a snack if you promise not to eat any more of my cookie dough!"

~

AFTER JON HAD LEFT for work the next morning Darcy put all of the cookies into a yellow plastic container with a lid. Jon had offered to wait and drive her into town as well but she had told him she didn't know how long she would be and there was no sense in the both of them being late. He'd kissed her, taking his time, and then wished her luck.

The temperature had gone back down again overnight. Putting her winter jacket on over her heavy sweater and stepping into her insulated boots Darcy took the cookies with her and walked across the meadow between her house and Anna's.

She frowned. It was Laura's house now. She guessed she'd have to get used to that. Right.

The grass was covered with frost and crunched under her boots with each step. It wasn't a long walk between houses. As she got closer to her new neighbors, she could see lights on in the windows and thought she could even hear a woman's voice calling to someone.

The other thing she noticed was the mist that trailed along the ground at her feet.

Walking up the steps to the front door, she took a deep breath. Raising her hand she knocked three times, and then waited. The door was suddenly pulled wide open in front of her and a woman with long, jet black hair stood there in a purple robe, a scowl on her face.

"You must be Laura," Darcy said cheerfully, lifting the container of cookies up as if to explain why she was disturbing them. "Hi. I'm Darcy Sweet. I live in the next house over. I wanted to bring you something to welcome you to town."

"That's very nice of you," the woman said quickly, already shutting the door, "but this isn't a good time. I'm sorry."

"Wait," Darcy said, hoping to draw this woman out somehow. "At least take these. They're homemade chocolate chip."

Just then, a child that must be Laura's son Alex came up to Laura, attaching himself to her side and looking up at the container of cookies the way that every eight year old looks at chocolate. He had a pixie face and short, straight brown hair that went down just to the top of his ears. His pajamas had pictures of sharks all over them.

Laura put a protective hand around her son and practically glared at Darcy. It was less intimidating than it should have been because of the way the woman slouched, hunching her shoulders. It was then that Darcy noticed how much makeup Laura wore, far too much to be pretty. Her hair was unnaturally dark, too, and was probably dyed. Laura couldn't help but wonder who the woman was trying to impress.

"We have things to do," Laura snapped. "Please leave. Alex, get inside."

"Mama?" Laura's son asked, his eyes pleading. "I like chocolate chip."

Laura's face softened as she looked down at him. When she turned back to Darcy there was less hostility in her voice, but just as much caution. "Thank you," she said. She took the cookie container from her. "I'll get it back to you. Now, please just go."

Without letting Darcy say another word, Laura shut the door. Darcy had just enough time to see a smile on Alex's face before she did.

"Well," Darcy muttered as she went back down the steps, "that could have gone better." Maybe Cora and Evelyn and the other people in town were right. Maybe Laura was just an unfriendly person. She'd have a hard time making it in Misty Hollow if this was the way she was going to treat everyone. At least she had accepted the cookies. Darcy supposed that was a start.

Darcy made it to work just after Sue had opened the shop. When she came inside and took her jacket off, Sue was helping a mother pick out a book for her little daughter. "Something with fairies?" the mother asked hopefully. "Sophie won't read anything else."

Sue nodded with a smile. "Those used to be some of my favorite books, too. Let's see. I remember there was a series I used to love..."

Darcy left them to it and went into the office instead. She was still upset over her encounter with Laura Lannis. There had to be some way to draw the woman out, didn't there? She sighed and sat down at the desk. Maybe it was none of her concern whether Laura wanted to be part of the neighborhood. It bothered her, though, and she couldn't decide why.

Sue swept in just then. "Hi, Darcy! First sale of the day. She bought the first two books in the series and promised to come back for more if her daughter likes them."

"That's great, Sue. I sure will miss you when you leave."

Sue's smile turned a little sad. "Yes. Me too. Is everything all right? You seem a little down."

Darcy twisted the ring on her finger. "I'm upset over my new neighbor, actually. You heard that someone moved into Anna's house?"

"I heard the gossip around town," Sue told her. "Have you met them?"

"I did, just this morning. The mother's name is Laura Lannis. She shut the door in my face."

"Oh no!" Sue said. "How terrible. Everyone in town is talking about how rude she is. I don't know if she'll be able to make much of a life for herself here if she keeps acting like that."

"See that's what I thought, too," Darcy said. She drummed her fingers on the desk. "I don't know. I want to go and try to talk to her again but maybe I should just let her be. Maybe she has a good reason for being so private."

"Like what?" Sue wondered. "This is such a great town full of such nice people. I know I've made so many great friends here. Maybe she just needs to know how to meet people."

The bell over the door jingled as someone else came in the shop. Sue looked over her shoulder. "Oh, that's Dawn Wagner. Probably looking for another Harlequin Romance."

"Are there any she hasn't read yet?" Darcy joked.

"Not many." Sue answered. "I'll help her find something good. Look, Darcy, I know you're going to keep trying to make friends with your new neighbor. It's the kind of person you are. You'll think of something." Then she went out into the store and left Darcy alone with her thoughts.

The books on the shelf above her shifted suddenly and she looked up in time to see Great Aunt Millie's journal slide forward off the edge and fall toward her. She caught it, smiling. "You think I should keep trying too, don't you Millie?"

She flipped through her aunt's journal, looking for inspiration. It had helped her out any number of times before. She read a few of her aunt's passages, talking about life in Misty Hollow, about friends she had known and things she had done. There were pictures, too. Several of them showed Millie in front of the bookstore or working the shelves. Millie had always loved books.

A thought came to Darcy slowly. Books were a way to bring people together. Like Sue and that young girl earlier, both of whom loved books about fairies. People who had read the same book could always talk to each other, no matter how different they were. Maybe she could do something similar with Laura and her son.

Feeling good about her idea, Darcy closed her aunt's journal and set it back up on the shelf. "Thanks Millie," she said, knowing her aunt was somewhere nearby to hear. "You always know the right thing to say."

Out in the bookshop she smiled at Sue and Dawn, perusing the romance section. That was actually one of their more popular sections in town, paperback books that got churned out by the industry every few weeks. Darcy had never gotten into the romance books. They always seemed a little too much the same to her. Like love was easy and real life didn't matter so long as you had a man to hold you in his arms. She smirked. Jon was a real man, and he held her in his arms plenty, but he also made sure that real problems in their lives had real solutions.

Walking through the children's section, she picked out a short stack of books that she thought a young boy like Alex might like. She didn't know him or what his interests were, but she remembered that his pajamas had sharks on them. She picked out a story about a shark who goes to school, and a National Geographic book all about sharks. From the front of the store she picked up the two locally-authored books on Misty Hollow to add to the group. There. That should do it.

Sue finished ringing Dawn's purchase up, two paperback books with strapping, shirtless men on the front. Dawn was a short woman well into her retirement years. She smiled sweetly up at Darcy and waved goodbye as she left the shop.

"What are those?" Sue asked, pointing to the books in Darcy's hands.

"I figured I'd try a different kind of housewarming gift for Laura."

"Hey, that's a great idea," Sue agreed. "I knew you'd think of something."

"Hey," Darcy said, "speaking of such things, did you look into our other idea yet?"

Sue beamed at Darcy. "I sure did. I'm going to write up everything for you so you can see what we'll need to do. There's going to be a little bit of an initial cost but we should make it back pretty quick, I think."

Darcy set her hand on Sue's arm and gave it a squeeze. "I knew I could count on you. Why don't you get started on it. I trust you. I want to bring this over to Laura now."

Darcy walked back out of town down the street that led to her house and before that, Laura Lannis' house. She had the books in a tote from the store, the "Sweet Read Bookstore" logo on the front of the blue nylon bag. She disturbed tendrils of mist as she went, fog that the rising sun hadn't burned away. Darcy knitted her brows together in thought, wondering what problem the town sensed now.

Stepping up to the front door of Anna's old house again she knocked without hesitation, an uncertain smile on her face. Just like before, the door opened almost immediately. It was like Laura had been watching outside to make sure no one was creeping up on the house.

Laura Lannis stared hard at Darcy. Her dark black hair was pulled forward across part of her face. She was wearing the same purple robe as earlier. She crossed her arms and leaned in the doorway. "Why are you here again?"

Darcy held out the bag. "I don't remember if I told you earlier, but I operate a bookstore in town. I know I already brought you the cookies this morning but I thought maybe this would be a better way to welcome you. There's some books in there for Alex that I thought a young boy might like. Even a couple about sharks. I also put in some books about our town, so you can learn the history of Misty Hollow. History is very important, don't you think?"

Laura stared at her, narrowing her eyes as if trying to decide if Darcy was for real. "I don't need any books. Thank you. Now again, please, just leave us alone."

Darcy wouldn't be put off that quickly. "Please. We're a very friendly town here, if you take the time to get to know us."

She held the bag out, waiting for Laura to decide either to take the gift or slam the door in her face again. Laura shifted from foot to foot, looking inside the house, then back to Darcy.

For just a moment it appeared she would shut the door without another word but then she sighed. "You people around here are certainly insistent."

Darcy smiled as Laura reached out to take the tote bag of books from her hand.

When their fingers touched, it was like an electric shock zapped through her. Her vision blurred into bright white light. Sound buzzed in her ears, an incoherent rushing that she gradually recognized as her own intense breathing as she ran so hard that her lungs burned.

Darcy didn't know where she was. She only knew that she was running for her life and if she stopped she'd be a dead woman. A house. She was racing out the back door of a house that she knew was hers even though she didn't recognize it at all. In her arms, she held a child, trembling in terror as they fled.

Somewhere in the back of her mind she understood that this was a vision. She had been thrown into it so violently, though, that she hadn't had time to prepare, and now everything the woman in her vision saw and experienced felt real, like it was happening to Darcy herself.

Darcy turned around as she made it out the door. She had to know that she and her child were safe. She saw the inside of the house, dark now that the hall lamp had been smashed. A man was laying in the hall, holding his hand to his head like he'd been hurt. "You can't run forever!" the man yelled after her. "I will find you!"

She couldn't make out much of the man. The woman in her vision knew him, knew his name and what he was doing in the house, but Darcy didn't have the time to figure it out. She had to get away. He was a large man, with greasy dark hair. That was all she could see before she was out of the house and away from there.

The man didn't follow, but still Darcy ran. She had to keep running. The woman in the vision didn't dare stop. She would never stop, because she believed the man's threat.

Darcy believed it, too.

As she ran she passed a white church with a tall spiraling bell tower. There were houses, and then she was running past a store. The name of the store and the town's name were printed on the window in stick-on letters. Darcy turned, trying to see the name better, to learn where she was at least.

Her reflection stared back at her. She was Laura Lannis.

The shock of what she just saw threw Darcy from the vision. She stumbled back from Laura, and the bag of books dropped to the porch with a thud.

"What's wrong with you?" Laura asked. It wasn't concern in her voice. It was some of the same fear that Darcy had felt in her vision just now.

"Mom?" a small voice said. Disoriented, Darcy looked down to see Alex clinging to Laura's leg. The child she had seen in her vision. It had been Alex.

Laura gently pushed Alex back. "I home school him," she explained even though Darcy hadn't asked. "Besides, it's winter break. Now, you've given us your gifts and I'm going to ask you to leave. Goodbye."

She shut the door before Darcy could say anything more, leaving her nothing else to do but turn and walk away. Feeling dizzy, she went up the path to her house. She replayed her vision in her mind as she went.

In the store window of her vision, Laura had looked differently than she had now. Her hair had been blonde, and she had been pretty without so much makeup. Her eyes had held the same fear they did now. Each time Darcy had come to Laura's door she'd seen that look, like she was being hunted.

She went into her own house, closing the door tightly behind her. Smudge came running immediately, meowing happily that Darcy had come home so early.

"I'm not here for long, Smudge," she said. "I just need to catch my breath and, uh, orient myself."

"Meow?" Smudge asked her.

Laughing, she bent down to pick the big black and white tomcat up. "It's okay if you don't understand. Cats shouldn't have to worry about things like this."

She scratched between his ears. People shouldn't have to worry about things like what she saw in her vision, either. Who had Laura been running from? What was she hiding from? Was that why she'd come to Misty Hollow and why she was hiding out in Anna Louis' old house?

Darcy didn't know. She only knew she had to find out. Giving Smudge one last good ear scratching she set him down and got her coat back on again. She had to tell Jon what she'd learned.

# CHAPTER 4

*D*arcy checked in with Sue at the bookstore before heading over to the police station. She was online checking on their new project, and promised that she could keep an eye on the store until Darcy got back. She went straight from there to the police station.

Jon and Grace were both at their desks. Everyone else was out on patrol except for the desk sergeant who had let her in. Darcy hadn't seen Grace since getting back from vacation the past weekend. They'd called each other, though, and Grace had told Darcy about how bad her morning sickness had gotten. Her sister waved to Darcy from her desk where she'd been put on light duty.

Darcy smiled to see how grumpy her sister was. Desk duty wasn't Grace's idea of police work, but she and her husband Aaron had just lived through a nasty experience when Aaron had gotten into the middle of a botched robbery. They were being a little overcautious with the baby now, maybe, but Darcy understood how they felt. There was only so much tragedy anyone could handle in their life.

Grace ran her hands back through her short black hair and leaned back in her chair. "I am so bored, sis. Please tell me you came to take me to lunch or something."

Darcy leaned over Jon's desk to trade kisses with him. "Yes," he said, "please take her to lunch. She'd driving me nuts."

Grace stuck her tongue out at him. "Whatever. Next time Aaron gets to have the baby."

"Just think, sis," Darcy said to her as she sat down in the chair in front of Jon's desk, "you'll be the first one in the family to have a baby of their own."

Jon shifted in his chair. Darcy noticed but didn't say anything. They had never finished their discussion on whether it was time for them to start their own family yet. She was really curious how he felt about it, but now was not the time.

"Well," Darcy said, "it's a little early for lunch but I do have something that might keep you busy. You too, Jon. I went to see Laura Lannis again this morning."

Jon rolled his eyes at her. "I knew you would. She already turned you away once, didn't she?"

"Yes, but I think she may have had a reason." Darcy described the vision she had when Laura's hand touched hers. She put in as many of the details that she could remember. The dark man, the house, the church with the spiral bell tower. She mentioned holding the child in her arms and then how Laura had looked in the reflection in the window. "It was obviously her, but without the dyed black hair and heavy makeup."

Jon leaned his elbows on his desk. "It definitely sounds like she's trying to hide something. Definitely explains why she won't talk to anyone in town. She's scared."

Neither of them argued that Darcy was wrong or mistaken in what she'd seen. They both knew about her abilities, so they knew that what Darcy was describing was real in some way, even if they didn't fully understand what Darcy could do. Jon had watched Darcy contact spirits before, and her abilities had helped solve more than one of his cases.

"So the question is," Jon was saying, "what do we do now? If she doesn't want to come forward with this problem there isn't much we can do as police officers."

"We can still look into it, though," Grace argued. "And I think we should. I mean, if she's on the run from some guy, it could affect the whole town. Plus, she'll need help whether she's willing to ask for it or not. You know, Darcy, that church that you described in your vision sounds very familiar to me."

"I know, right?" Darcy said. "I thought the same thing. I've been trying to place it but I just can't put my finger on it. I'm sure I've seen it somewhere before, though."

"You think it's a place in one of the towns around here?" Jon asked. He had moved to Misty Hollow not even a year ago, just before he and Darcy had started dating, so he wasn't as familiar with the area as Darcy and Grace were. They'd lived here most of their lives.

"It might be," Darcy admitted, "but I just don't know."

"I tell you what," Grace said. "I'll look into that. I'll also try to find any reports of missing women that might match Laura's case."

"Women with a son," Jon reminded her. "That should definitely narrow it down."

"Are you sure you have the time?" Darcy asked her sister.

Grace made a little snorting sound. "It sure beats checking other officer's paperwork or whatever other job they can think to give me. I hate light duty."

Jon laughed at her. "Well, like you said, next time Aaron can be the one to get pregnant."

Darcy had a good feeling about this. All they had to do was find that church, and maybe they could find out what kind of trouble Laura was in. Then they could help her. If she'd let them.

~

JON CAME HOME LATE that night, but with no good news. Grace had spent hours trying to track down any active missing persons reports, and had checked with every police agency in the state just in case. As near as Grace and Jon could determine there were no reports of a missing mother and son to be had.

After a restless night's sleep Darcy allowed Jon to drive her into work again. She didn't want to be alone, didn't want to pass by Anna's house knowing there was something weird and dangerous going on there. He kissed her goodbye and held her hand at the door to the bookstore, knowing how upset she was.

It was more than just the intensity of the vision. More than the fact that this woman was now living in Anna's house. It was the incredible sense of fear that she had felt through Laura in the vision. Whatever she was running from with her son had her terrified.

In the bookstore Darcy kept herself busy all morning by rearranging the shelves, clearing out a space near the front. That led to her clearing off several shelves, dusting them down, and then restocking them.

Sue had the morning off. She had several last minute things to take care of before she went back to school again, and it was almost her last day of work already. Darcy began to wonder if she should throw some kind of party for Sue. A going away party. The more she thought about it, the more she liked the idea. Yes. A party with all of Sue's friends here in Misty Hollow. They could hold it right here in the store.

Darcy drew her hand back, a tingling cold sensation jittering across her fingers. Several books fell to the floor at her feet. When they did, the strange sensation disappeared.

She stared at her fingers, and then at the mess of books down at her feet. She sighed. "Millie, I'm not in the mood for jokes." Her aunt was always playing jokes like this. She'd lost track of how many people had been in the shop when books had gone flying across the room or fallen on their toes. Today just wasn't the day for it.

She put the books back on the shelf one at a time, stacking them left to right. Until the tingling crept into her fingers again. She didn't pull away this time. Instead, she pulled that particular book back off the shelf and looked at it closer. It was a picture book, one of several books Darcy carried in the shop that featured the local history. There were a few that dealt with haunted places near Misty Hollow, some that were real and some that she'd found to be fake. There were half a dozen about the role Misty Hollow and Meadowood had played in the war.

This book was a history of architecture in the surrounding towns. A picture book of buildings. Including churches.

Darcy couldn't believe it. She'd forgotten that this book was in her shop. Now she rushed over to one of the reading tables and set the book down, quickly flipping through the pages. The first buildings were from the early 1800s, made of wood or thick square stone. Nothing like what she'd seen in Laura's vision. She kept looking, gradually going forward in time.

Then she found it. A white church with a steepled roof that led up to a spiraling bell tower. She ran her fingers over the picture, remembering little details from her vision now that she had barely noticed as Laura had made her mad dash to get away from the dark man. Details like that stained glass window in front, or the way the top of the front door was round.

The paragraph under the photo told about how the church had been rebuilt in 1956 after a fire that had claimed several buildings in Cider Hill.

Darcy snapped her fingers. Of course! Cider Hill was a town about five hours away from Misty Hollow. Grace and Darcy had gone there once with their mother for a town fair. She remembered there had been pony rides, and someone making up kids' faces like clowns and butterflies, and marching bands in a parade. And over in the church, there had been an ice cream social.

That's where she remembered the church from. In her mind, she replayed the vision again. Now that she knew where the church was, other details became clearer as well. Laura had run away from the dark man past a store. Darcy hadn't been able to make out the letters in the window before, but now she knew what they said. "Cider Hill Hardware."

Slapping the book closed again she went for her coat. It was still the middle of the morning but even so she put out the sign telling people she'd be back in fifteen minutes. She actually didn't know how long she'd be, but she had to let Jon and Grace know about this new information.

JON WAS TALKING with a uniformed officer, Johnson, when he saw Darcy come in. He handed a file to Johnson and then came over to give her a quick hug. "You know if you keep coming here they're going to give you a desk and a caseload of your own. I've already spoken to the chief about it."

She laughed but she didn't feel like she had time to joke around with him. "Jon, I figured something out. I found that church I saw." His eyes widened as she explained what she had seen in the book.

He looked at her intently and she felt herself blush a little looking into his eyes like this. "So," he said. "This is going to be another one of those kinds of cases?"

She didn't have to ask him what he meant. Jon knowing about her abilities was one thing. He still didn't quite understand them, not completely. They were working on it, though, and he never made her feel like she was doing something bad for using a special power that she had been born with. She loved him for that.

"It looks like it will be," she said to him. First the vision, now this. She wouldn't tell him about the mists around the town. She didn't think he was quite ready for that level of weird yet.

He nodded with a sigh. "I love you, Darcy Sweet. You certainly keep my life interesting."

She hugged him again. "So what do we do now?"

"I'll reach out to the police over in Cider Hill. If they even have a police force there. Maybe they know something that we can connect to Laura."

"She needs our help, Jon." Darcy had never been more sure of anything.

"I know. I mean, I believe you. Do you want to wait here while I figure this out? I sent Grace out for some coffee to give her something to do. She should be back in a few minutes."

Darcy gave Jon a knowing smile. "She's starting to get on your nerves, isn't she?"

"Let's just say your sister isn't the kind of person who can just sit. She needs to be constantly doing something."

"Well when the baby gets here she and Aaron will have plenty to do." Darcy couldn't wait to see her new niece or nephew. How strange it was going to be to have a baby in the family. "I think I'll go back to the store for now. I'm all hyped up and I'm not sure if I could just sit here, either."

"I'll call you there, then, if I hear anything," he promised her. "I have a few other things I'm supposed to be doing, though, so if you don't hear from me just head home. I'll meet you there."

They kissed each other goodbye, and Darcy left. She hoped Jon would find something soon. She had the feeling that time wasn't on Laura's side.

~

DARCY CALLED to the police station before going home from work. It was Grace who answered her call. Jon was out of the office, she said, taking a call about a stolen car. Darcy thought she actually sounded jealous of him.

"You want me to have him call you when he gets back, sis?"

"No," Darcy said. "I'll wait for him at home. Hopefully he won't be too long."

Darcy waited for Jon until well after dark. Whatever case he was working was definitely keeping him busy, she supposed, because he hadn't even called by the time she had changed into her pajamas ready to head for bed. Smudge kept her company as the minutes rolled by. She watched the red numbers change on the bedside clock, and still no Jon.

Still wide awake at almost midnight, she heard Jon come in downstairs. She listened to him set his keys down and put his coat away and then heard his footsteps creaking on the stairs. She had turned the light off in the bedroom when she came to bed. Carefully, he opened their door and slipped in. She watched him, there in the shadows, stripping out of his slacks and his shirt. The light from the hallway fell over the muscles of his upper body and she couldn't help but smile. She knew she should tell him that she was still awake, but she was enjoying this.

After slipping into some blue cotton pajama bottoms he stood very still, hands on his hips. His breathing was the only sound in the room. What was he doing?

When he jumped onto the bed, she squeaked and tried to roll out of the way. He landed across her legs, pretending that he couldn't get up again. Both of them ended up laughing uncontrollably as she pushed at him and he flopped around and Smudge hissed at them both and dashed off.

"Stop it!" she scolded playfully. "Oh, I was trying to act like I was asleep. How did you know?"

He rolled over onto his side, laying next to her, and took her hand to kiss her knuckles. "I always know. You have this way of breathing when you're asleep. Plus I caught you watching me."

She was glad of the dark so he wouldn't see her blush. "You're home so late. Is everything okay?"

"Hm? Oh, yeah, everything is fine. I just needed to help some of the officers look into this stolen car case. A car that had been reported stolen from Meadowood showed up in Johnson Chase's driveway this afternoon. It was a whole big thing, with us working with a couple of Meadowood detectives to process the car for evidence. Even the Chief showed up."

"Oh? Was it a sports car or something?"

"Nope." He kissed her knuckles again. "Just some guy's little red two-door. Nothing special." His look turned coy, with his eyes in shadow and his lip curled. "You're special, though."

"I am?" she cozied into him. "How am I special?"

"Well, for one, you're smart."

"I was kind of hoping for pretty, but I'll take smart."

Jon stroked her long hair and tickled the side of her neck. "You are pretty. But also, smart. That church was in Cider Hill just like you said."

She popped her head up, suddenly excited. "What did you find out?"

He helped her sit up with him, holding her hands. "It took me a while, especially with that stolen car taking up most of my night. There is no local police force in Cider Hill. They use the State Police. I spoke with one of their sergeants, and he says hardly anything ever happens there."

Darcy's heart sank a little. "So there was nothing to it?"

"He said hardly ever. There was one thing that he remembered, an incident from last year. A man was murdered there. No body, but a lot of blood. Chip was his name. Charles McIntosh. The main suspect, the only suspect, was his wife."

Darcy felt chills running up her back. A murder. That would

be their luck. "So what happened to the wife?" she asked. "Did they arrest her?"

"No. She ran away. Along with her young daughter. She's been on the run ever since and there's an outstanding warrant for her. They're pretty sure she's the one who killed Chip. Her running only made her look more guilty."

The vision Darcy had seen with Laura running away from the dark man came back to her. *"You can't run forever!"* the man had said. "Do you think the wife was Laura?" she asked Jon.

Jon twisted his lip up as he thought. "No, I don't think so. The woman in the report from the State Police was named Isabelle McIntosh. The sergeant said everyone around there called her Izzy."

"Sure, but Izzy might have changed her name to Laura," Darcy pointed out.

"I thought of that, but Izzy's child was a girl. A daughter. About the same age as Laura's son, but a girl."

Darcy nodded. She'd seen Alex in Laura's house. A young boy in shark themed pajamas. "So maybe Laura isn't Izzy. Maybe she's someone else, and she's running for a different reason and if we don't help her Jon then—"

Jon cleared his throat. Darcy focused her eyes on him again. "Sorry," she said. "I know I'm getting carried away, but I really feel like Laura is in danger. What I felt in that vision, it was so terrifying. There has to be something I can do for her."

"You're going to go ask her about this, aren't you?" Before she could even try to explain what she was thinking he let go of her hands to cup the sides of her face. "I know you, Darcy. I know you won't let this go no matter what the State Police say. I'll get them to fax me a copy of Izzy's photo. Her daughter's too. That will give us more to go on. Just, promise me you'll be safe, okay?"

"What was the daughter's name?" Darcy asked him, loving the way his warm hands felt on her skin.

"Lilly," he answered. "Darcy, promise me you'll be safe."

"I promise," she said.

He didn't look like he believed her, but the words apparently satisfied him for now. They laid down under the blankets, his feet playing with hers. There would be time enough tomorrow to figure out the mystery of Izzy McIntosh.

# CHAPTER 5

The next morning Jon woke up before Darcy and left a note for her on the table. He promised to call her as soon as he had the photographs from the State Police, and left a very personal message about last night that had Darcy blushing again.

The walk into town was a brisk one, with the temperature dropping back down overnight. Winter was supposed to be gone. In Misty Hollow, it was settling back in.

Laura Lannis' house was dark as Darcy passed by. She didn't want to go there again until she knew more about what had happened in Cider Hill. She didn't want to spook Laura...or whoever she may be.

Darcy had skipped breakfast at home so she could have it at the Bean There Bakery and Café instead. A coffee and a muffin from Helen's café was one of her favorite treats. She saw her sister Grace inside through the window, already at the counter to order something. Helen was working there this morning, her graying hair up in a ponytail that made her seem younger than she was.

The warmth inside the café was definitely welcome. Darcy

unzipped her coat as she went up to stand next to Grace. "Hi Grace. Good morning, Helen."

"What's good about it?" Grace snapped at her. There was a scowl on her face. "We've got stolen cars and all sorts of crime taking place in this town and the best I can do is get coffee and muffins!"

Darcy was surprised at her sister's tone but Helen just smiled at Darcy and winked. "Your sister is feeling out of sorts this morning, Darcy. Not uncommon, I think, in women with her, um, condition."

Grace put a hand to her belly and sighed, rolling her eyes. "I'm sorry, Darcy. I've been irritable all morning. I'm not even sure why. Poor Aaron probably thinks I hate him."

From behind the counter Helen produced a folded paper bag and a styrofoam cup with steam coming out the little hole in its plastic lid. "I'm sure Aaron understands, Grace. Men have tolerated their wives during pregnancy since the beginning of time, because they know you're giving them the greatest gift. Don't worry about him. Kiss him when you go home tonight, tell him you love him, and you'll see."

Darcy saw the way Helen smiled as she wiped her hands on her white apron and turned to look back over her shoulder at the double swinging doors that led to the kitchen area. Darcy smiled, too. There was a new man in Helen's life, a man she had hired to work here as a cook. It was obvious there was a lot more to it than that, and Darcy was happy for Helen that she had found love again.

Helen saw Darcy looking at her and her cheeks colored just a little. "Well. What can I get you today, Darcy?"

"Just a coffee and a blueberry muffin, please. Grace, do you have time to sit down and have breakfast with me here?"

Grace shrugged. "Why not? It's not like I have anything to do back at the office except shuffle papers."

The way she said it made Darcy laugh, and then Grace was

laughing with her, telling her to stop it this was serious, but laughing still. They sat with their muffins and talked for a while, and it felt good to have that time together.

Just before they got up to leave the conversation turned to Laura Lannis and the murder in Cider Hill. "Jon told me what he found out," Grace said. "You know, I remember that place now. That fair always seemed so big to me when I was a little girl. It was always so much fun. Hard to believe something like this murder happened there. Are you thinking Laura is this Izzy woman?"

Darcy didn't want to believe it. She didn't know what Laura was running from, but she didn't think it was murder. There was something else going on, and whatever it was had terrified Laura in her vision. "I'm not sure."

"Just promise me you won't go running off and getting into trouble, okay sis?"

"Would I do a thing like that?" Darcy asked with false seriousness.

Her sister laughed again. "Fine. Just be careful."

THE BOOKSTORE SEEMED empty without Sue around. She wasn't gone, not yet anyway, but she was out again this morning on their big project. It was really hitting Darcy that she would be alone in the store by herself all day once Sue went back to college.

Across the bookstore from where Darcy sat at one of the reading tables, the door to the office closed. She smiled. Well, she wouldn't be completely alone. Great Aunt Millie would always be around. "Why are you still here?" Darcy wondered out loud, not really expecting an answer. "I've helped dozens of spirits move on from this realm, Millie, and in my opinion if anyone deserves a peaceful afterlife it's you."

Just like she'd expected, the only answer she got was silence. Maybe Millie would get around to answering that question for her one of these days.

The jingling noise the bell over the front door made was so unexpected Darcy actually jumped up from her chair. Jon came in, a paper bag in one hand and a smile on his face. "Hi, sweet baby," he said to her. "I thought I'd bring us lunch."

She laughed and sat back down again. "It's a little early for lunch, isn't it?"

Jon frowned and checked his watch. "Nearly eleven o'clock now. That's close enough. Besides. I brought you a gift."

"Oh, really? What is it?"

He put the sack from Helen's deli down on the table next to her, the smell of freshly baked sandwiches and coffee smelling so good, and slipped out of his coat. His blue tie had managed to get tangled around a shoulder of his dress shirt and he took a moment to smooth it out before pulling out a folded piece of paper from his back pocket.

Darcy raised an eyebrow at him as she took the paper. "I prefer flowers, for future reference."

Leaning down, he kissed the top of her head, then opened the bag to take out the carefully stacked coffee cups and two foil-wrapped sandwiches. "There's going to be lots of flowers in your future, I promise. In the meantime, I thought you might like this better."

Darcy opened the folds of the page to find a police bulletin, the word "WANTED" written in big black letters at the top. There was a picture of a woman in the middle of the page, a close-up taken from some photograph where the woman was smiling and laughing.

Darcy gasped. The page was a faxed copy, and the quality wasn't the greatest, but there was no mistaking it. This was the same woman she'd seen in her vision. Laura Lannis, only with blonde hair and a smile instead of that scowl she always seemed to have on her face now.

"Jon, that's her," Darcy said. "That's Laura Lannis!"

Jon finished unwrapping his ham and cheese melt and then reached over to tap the bulletin. "This," he said, "is Izzy McIntosh. Wanted for murder."

Darcy unwrapped her own sandwich, a turkey and swiss, toasted and steaming. She took a bite of it and chewed as she thought. "Mmm," she said. "Honey mustard. You always know."

"Yeah, I'm a great boyfriend." His smile slipped as he chewed. "But, I'm also a police officer. If the woman living next door to us in Anna's old house really is Izzy McIntosh, I have to tell the State Police. The sergeant I spoke to was very interested in knowing if I had found her."

Darcy's heart skipped a beat. "What did you tell him?"

"I told him the truth. We didn't have anyone in town named McIntosh, but if I found her, I'd let him know first."

Darcy could breathe again. She hugged him quickly as he held his sandwich out of the way. "You really are the best boyfriend ever."

"I'll take that. Darcy, you have to understand, I can stall this, but I can't stop it. I know you're worried about her, and you think she's in danger, and you want to help her. If Laura really is Izzy—"

"I know she is, Jon," Darcy said firmly. "I know she's hiding from something, too."

"You know because of a face in a vision. That's not anything I can take to court." He brushed his hands together to clean off some crumbs from his fingers and then sat back. "Now, if I go to Laura's house with this photo and find out for myself that it's her, I won't have a choice but to arrest her. So, it's a good thing that I haven't had the time to go check on this yet, don't you think?"

Darcy nodded, knowing what Jon was saying. He was putting

himself in a tricky spot and he was doing it for her. She had never loved him more than she did in that moment.

"Plus, there's the whole question about Izzy's daughter. Laura has a son, right? Alex?"

Darcy had a few thoughts on that, but she nodded her head. What else could she say?

"So there you go. Reasonable doubt. At least for me. There's obviously a lot more to find out before we do anything. You should eat your sandwich," he said to her. "Then maybe you have some errands to do? Like just outside of town?"

Darcy pushed the sandwich aside and got up from her chair. Sitting down on Jon's lap, wrapping her arms around his shoulders, she flipped her hair back over a shoulder and locked her eyes on his. "I do have several errands to run. Starting with kissing you."

"Well," he said with a happy grin. "You'd better get started, then."

DARCY HOPED no one came to the bookstore while she was gone. She really would have to hire someone when Sue left. She couldn't keep putting up the be-right-back sign and then leaving, even for something this important.

Rushing down the path that led to her house and the one Laura had moved into, Darcy made quick time. She rushed up the steps of the porch and knocked on the door before she could lose her nerve. There was no answer. She knocked again with the same result.

Finding a window on the front that didn't have the curtain pulled completely closed, Darcy peeked inside. She couldn't see anyone. Her heart beat loudly in her ears. Should she try going in? Logic told her no. It was dangerous. It was illegal. It was wrong.

And she was going to do it anyway.

After Anna's death, Darcy had found the house key that Anna had given her. As neighbors, they had checked on each other's houses any number of times. Darcy had put the key on her ring and kept it there, partly for the sake of having something of Anna's to hang onto, partly because she had thought it might come in handy someday. It looked like today was that day.

She fit the key to the front door lock, hoping Laura or the realtor for the house hadn't ever changed the locks. It fit, and the handle turned quietly, and the door swung open without any alarm. Darcy breathed a sigh of relief.

She stepped inside quickly and then shut the door behind her. Around her, the house was silent and still. She remembered the whole layout, downstairs and upstairs, every room, every door. The furniture, even, was still Anna's. She took a moment to remember her dear friend, then got started on what she was here for. There was no way of knowing where Laura was or when she'd be back.

Darcy didn't know what she was even looking for. She just started looking. Papers on the kitchen table were all about the sale of the house, and all of it was in the name of Laura Lannis. There was nothing in any of the kitchen drawers but some silverware. There weren't any photos or pictures stuck to the refrigerator. All in all, there was hardly anything in the house at all to show people lived here.

Laura, or rather Izzy, was travelling light.

The living room was the same, without even a photograph on the wall. The downstairs bathroom had two toothbrushes and a tube of paste and handsoap and other things, but no personal items. In the garbage, she found a discarded box of hair dye, dark black like Laura's was now.

Frowning, feeling like a thief, Darcy went upstairs to the bedrooms.

The first one she went into looked like it was being used by both Laura and her son. A second bed had been set up, crammed in where there really wasn't space for it. That was odd, she thought. It was like Laura didn't want to let Alex out of her sight even when he was sleeping.

There weren't many clothes hanging in Laura's closet. A few jeans, some shirts, and that was it. Darcy bit her lip, embarrassed, but went through the dresser drawers anyway, telling herself she was trying to help Laura and she needed to be sure. In the top drawer there was an opened pack of underwear, some socks, and a couple of bras. Nothing else. The other drawers were empty.

As she was about to shut the dresser up again she stopped. The open pack of underwear was a plastic set of six like you might find from a department store. There were two or three pair taken out, but the others were still there. They caught her eye. They were covered in cartoon fish.

Not really something a grown woman would wear, Darcy thought to herself. She picked the package up to look closer at it. They were cotton panties and the picture on the front showed a smiling little girl. They were sized for a child.

Alex. Laura's little boy was really Izzy's little girl. What had Jon said her name was? Lilly. Lilly McIntosh.

Darcy put the panties back. There was no doubt in her mind anymore but she couldn't very well bring a pack of opened underwear to Jon and call it proof. Especially since she wasn't supposed to be in their house in the first place.

Even more so because she wasn't trying to get Laura arrested. She was trying to find something that would let her help.

Putting everything back where she'd found it, Darcy tried to decide what she should do next. It was obvious that Laura hadn't left a note lying around that said, "My name is Izzy McIntosh and I need help." There had to be some other way to find out what was really going on with her. Izzy McIntosh was supposed to have killed her husband. Darcy didn't believe it. It didn't fit what she had seen in her vision. Not to her mind, anyway, but Jon was right. She needed some way to prove it.

"Oh," she said, as a thought suddenly occurred to her. If Izzy's husband was dead, Darcy could probably reach out to him on the other side and ask him how he died. All she would need was something personal of his to guide her through the murky pathways of the afterlife.

Maybe there would be something downstairs, something she missed. Izzy must have kept some personal items from her past. Even someone on the run must have something that reminded them of who they used to be.

She started back down the hallway to the stairs. That's when she heard a woman scream.

It was followed by the sound of the front door swinging wide and slamming into the wall, and the muffled voice of a man swearing. "Stop it, you're hurting me!" she heard Laura yelling. Alex—Lilly—was screaming, too. "Don't hurt my mommy! Don't hurt my mommy!"

Darcy didn't think. She ran down the stairs as quietly as she could and then snuck along the wall until she could see into the kitchen where Izzy had been thrown to the floor. Two plastic bags of groceries had spilled around her, oranges and boxes of kids' cereal and a broken jar of spaghetti sauce. A man stood over her, tall and dark, wearing a long dark coat and a baseball cap pulled low over his eyes.

Darcy knew him. The man from her vision. She was sure of it.

Lilly threw her eight year old body over her mother, crying hysterically and still pleading for the man not to hurt her mommy.

The man raised a gun.

"Everyone, he's in here!" Darcy shouted as loud as she could, making sure to bang into the wall and push an end table over and make as much racket as possible. "Call the police!"

It was probably one of the stupidest things she had ever done in her life, she thought to herself. Even so, it worked. The man's head jerked up at the commotion and then he spun around and raced out the front door. He was gone.

Darcy rushed into the kitchen. "Izzy, are you all right?" she asked.

Izzy's eyes grew wider. "What did you call me?"

"It's all right," Darcy said to her. "Yes, I know who you are. I'm not going to tell anyone. Um. Well. Other than my boyfriend. He knows." She turned to the little girl disguised as a boy, still hugging tightly to her mother. "Hello, Lilly."

Lilly didn't smile, but she sniffed her tears away a little and whispered, "H-hello."

Izzy stood up, picking Lilly up with her. "I can't believe this. Oh, I can't believe this. First he finds me, then you! We're not safe here. We're not safe anywhere!"

Darcy went to the phone hanging on the wall. When she picked it up and started dialing, Izzy rounded on her. "What do you think you're doing?"

"We need to call the police. That guy might not be fooled by my trick for very long."

"Trick? What trick? Where are the other people you were talking to?"

Darcy listened to the phone ring on the other end. "That was the trick. There's nobody here but me."

"You can't call the police!" Izzy insisted. "I can't let them know who I am!"

"Don't worry," Darcy said. "This one already does. He's my boyfriend."

597

# CHAPTER 6

$\mathcal{D}$arcy and Izzy and Lilly sat at the kitchen table, drinking tea that Izzy had freshly brewed. Darcy had helped them clean up the ruined groceries, after making sure the doors were all securely locked, and in the mess of things Izzy had bought was a box of green tea bags. When Darcy had said she'd love a cup of tea, Izzy had looked almost grateful to have something to do that would keep her mind off, well, everything else.

Now, they sat and waited for Jon. He had been out on another stolen car case. This time, the car had been stolen from someone living in Misty Hollow. He promised to be there as soon as he could. "You know what this means, right Darcy?" he had asked.

She did. There was a very good chance that Jon would have to arrest Izzy. Unless he had a very good reason not to.

"I'm still not sure I should talk to you," Izzy said to her, turning her tea cup around and around. The ceramic mug was actually meant for coffee, but they were the only cups she had in the house.

Darcy tried to look Izzy in the eye but the other woman kept looking away. "It's all right," Darcy said. "I promise, I'm here to help you. I know I may not look like much, but I actually help people all the time. I have this gift that allows me to see things that other people can't. That's what happened to me yesterday on your porch. I had a vision. A vision of you running away from a man."

Darcy went on to describe the whole scene perfectly to Izzy. Her mouth fell open when Darcy was done. "How can you know that?"

"I told you," Darcy insisted. "I had a vision."

Ordinarily, Darcy would never tell anyone about her gift. People either thought she was crazy or they laughed at her or they tried to get Darcy to contact long dead relatives who hadn't wanted anything to do with the people when they'd been alive, much less now when they were dead. She had to convince Izzy that she could help, though, and the truth seemed to be the only way to do it.

"Mommy?" Lilly said slowly. She sat in a chair pulled right up next to her mother and did her best to attach herself to Izzy's side. Lilly stretched up to whisper in Izzy's ear, "I think we can trust her."

Darcy smiled at Lilly. "Thank you, Lilly."

Lilly's face turned pink and she went silent again. What she had said seemed to tip the scales for Izzy, and she visibly relaxed, like a weight had just been taken off her shoulders. "All right, Darcy. I'll tell you the story."

"I know some of it." The clock on the wall chimed the hour. Darcy looked at it, surprised to find it was only two in the afternoon. "You went on the run with your daughter and went into hiding, right? That's why you've kept yourself shut up in this house."

Izzy nodded, staring down into her tea. "I couldn't let them take Lilly away. If I'd turned myself in…"

Darcy knew the part that Izzy was leaving unsaid. She was wanted for the murder of her husband. Lilly's father. If she'd been arrested, then her daughter would have been taken away and put in state custody or something. No mother would want that.

Looking down at her daughter with a sad smile, Izzy ruffled Lilly's short hair. "I had to make Lilly dress like a boy and call herself Alex. I figured we'd be harder to find if we were travelling as a mother and her son."

Lilly stuck her lower lip out. "I didn't like it. Boys have stupid clothes."

"Yes," Darcy said with a laugh. "They really do."

"My brave little girl," Izzy said. "Her daddy and I were having a fight. Mommy saw him with another woman and it started a fight."

Darcy nodded, understanding that Izzy didn't want to say too much in front of Lilly. The girl was too young to hear that her father had been cheating on her mother, or that Izzy had caught him doing it.

"So her daddy and I went away for a weekend," Izzy continued. "We were supposed to fix what was wrong, have time to talk and just figure things out. There's a nice motel just outside of Cider Hill, where we lived. Private cabins set back in the woods. It was very nice. The first night we stayed there, well, Chip and I argued a little but we talked it out and things seemed to be going good. We went to bed, and I felt better."

A single tear fell down Izzy's cheek and she wiped it away quickly before Lilly could see. "The next morning I woke up, and Chip was gone. I don't remember what happened. I slept like a rock, and when I woke up he was gone and there was all this...all this..."

Blood, Darcy knew she meant. There was all this blood. It had been enough for the police to assume Chip was dead, and that Izzy had killed him. Poor woman, Darcy thought.

Unless, of course, she really did kill her husband.

"So I ran," Izzy said with a shrug. "I went back for Lilly and grabbed a few of our things and we haven't stopped running since last year. I thought I could buy this house and hide out here."

"You paid in cash?" Darcy asked. "That must have been a lot of money."

"It was the only way I wouldn't have to prove who I was," Izzy explained. "Things had been bad between me and Chip for a long time. I had put a lot of money aside, just in case, and I managed to cash in my savings bonds before everyone in Cider Hill knew I was a fugitive. We've had enough to live on, but my money's just about run out. The trip to the grocery store we just took almost broke me."

"I can't imagine what you've been through," Darcy said to Izzy. She had begun twisting the ring on her finger, wondering how deep this mystery ran. "I want to help you, if I can."

"How can you help?" Izzy was obviously frustrated. "I tried to hide us, keep us safe. I changed our looks and moved us here to the middle of nowhere and it didn't do any good. He still found us."

The man who had attacked them here in the house, Darcy realized. "Who was he, Izzy? Who was that man?"

Izzy froze, her hands tightening around her mug of tea. "I don't know."

Darcy waited for her to say more, but Izzy sat quietly and very still. There was a lot more being left unsaid but Darcy decided it wouldn't do her any good to press the matter. No doubt that the man she had seen here in the house with the gun was the same dark man from her vision. There had to be a connection to what had happened to Izzy and who this man was. Maybe if she showed Izzy she really could help then she'd feel safe enough to—

A loud knocking on the door made all three of them jump. Lilly clung to her mother's side. Darcy stood up from the table, ready to reach for the phone again or run them all upstairs or maybe even grab the nearest heavy object to defend them. The teakettle looked promising.

"Darcy?" a voice said through the door. "It's me."

Jon. It was Jon. Darcy felt a wave of relief wash over her. Izzy hugged Lilly to her still and glared daggers at the door. "It's all right," Darcy said to her. It's my boyfriend. Remember I told you about him? He can help us."

"He's the police," Izzy said, unconvinced. "He'll turn me in."

Darcy knew the spot she had put everyone in when she'd called Jon but she really hadn't had any other choice. "I'll tell him what you told me," she said to Izzy. "Jon is a good man. He won't let anything happen to you or your daughter."

Izzy still looked unconvinced but she allowed Darcy to go and open the door. Jon rushed through, pulling Darcy into a tight embrace. "Are you all right?"

"I'm fine, Jon. Thanks for getting here."

"I would have been quicker but this case with the stolen cars has us all running in circles." He looked past her then and saw Izzy sitting at the kitchen table with her little daughter. "Isabelle McIntosh, I presume?"

The woman frowned at him. "I suppose you should just call me Izzy, now that you know. Everyone else calls me that."

There was a moment of awkward silence then, and in that silence Darcy could almost hear the gears turning in Jon's head. He closed the door behind him, careful to lock it again, and whispered to Darcy. "Can I talk to you in the living room?"

She told Izzy they would be right back. Izzy didn't look happy about it, and Darcy worried that the woman would bolt with her daughter through the front door as soon as she and Jon stepped around the corner. On second thought, she realized that probably wouldn't happen. Izzy had told Darcy about how she was almost out of money. Not to mention that she had changed her name and her looks and moved several towns over and none of it had kept her out of danger. Right now, this was the safest place for Izzy and Lilly. Darcy hoped the woman could see that.

In the living room, Jon folded his arms across his chest and made sure to keep his voice down low. "Darcy, you know I have to turn her in. I can't hide this anymore."

"Jon," Darcy said in a whisper that matched his, "I think there's more going on here than what it looks like."

"What are you saying? You don't think she killed her husband?"

Darcy told Jon everything that Izzy had told her, not leaving anything out. "Now, I know the State Police have a warrant out for her arrest, but something doesn't add up. Where is Chip's body? Why would some guy be after her? He broke in here with a gun and was going to shoot her, Jon. What does that mean?"

He lowered his head in thought. "I admit there's a lot going on with her case. More than the State Police are aware of, obviously. That doesn't mean we can just ignore the fact that there's a warrant for her arrest."

Darcy put a hand to his chest. She could feel his heart beating. "Please, Jon. Don't turn her in. Not yet. There has to be something we can do for her. I don't think she did this thing. I can feel it. Have I ever steered you wrong before?"

He blinked at her. "Uh, yes. I'm pretty sure I arrested Helen Nelson, future mayor of Misty Hollow, because you were positive she was a murderer. And let's not forget how we arrested your own brother-in-law in that same caper. Or how about the time—"

"Okay, okay, I get it." Darcy was annoyed that he could bring up all of those different mistakes of hers by memory. "I'm not perfect, Jon, but don't forget that my gift has helped you solve cases before, too. Right?"

He shifted from foot to foot. "Yes it has. I don't understand it, not completely, but I can't deny how it's helped us in the past." He took a deep breath, then let it out slowly. "You really think she's innocent?"

"I don't know yet. Yes. I think so, but I need to do a few things first. What's more important right now, I think, is that she's in danger. We need to help her."

"Help her how?" Jon asked, his eyes narrowing suspiciously.

This was the part that she was worried about. If Jon said no... "We need to bring Izzy and Lilly over to our house. Kind of protective custody for them."

"Are you insane?" The words burst out of him and he suddenly realized how loud his voice had gotten. He shot a look back toward the kitchen, then took them a few steps further into the living room, lowering his voice back to a whisper. "Darcy, I can't harbor a fugitive in my home! I'll lose my job!"

"Only if someone finds out," Darcy argued. "Plus, if you solve the larger case here, who would say anything?"

"The Chief would, that's who." He paced back and forth, quick and short steps that led him back to her. "No. We have to turn her in."

"Jon, we can't turn an innocent woman over to be arrested for something she didn't do."

He pushed his hands back through his jet black hair as he clenched his jaw. Darcy knew she'd asked a lot of him in the past, and this was more than she'd ever asked, but she felt very strongly about this. Helping Izzy and her daughter was the right thing to do.

She took his hands in his and waited for him to look at her again. "What if I can prove her husband is still alive?"

His expression didn't change, but the lines around his eyes softened. "Then that would give me something to go to the State Police with, at least. Darcy...I love you and I trust you. But I can't just ignore my duty."

"Does anyone know you're here?" Darcy asked. "Do they know who Izzy is?"

"No, they don't. You called my cell phone when you scared that guy off and I didn't want to tell anyone where I was going, because...well, you know why."

"Okay," she said, "then that gives us a little time. Just let me try something, all right?" She pushed up on her toes and kissed him gently on his forehead. "Just keep an open mind."

She could tell he was worried, both about his job and about what they were getting themselves into. He didn't say a word as they went back into the kitchen. Darcy sat down across from Izzy, her tea now cold and forgotten. "I need to try something, Izzy. I told you that I have a gift. I can see things, and I can communicate with people," she hesitated, looking over at Lilly's wide eyes. "People who aren't with us anymore," she decided to say.

From the corner of her eye she saw Jon's eyebrows shoot up. She hadn't told him about her letting Izzy in on her secret.

Izzy shook her head. Her eyes hadn't left Jon and they were full of mistrust. "I don't trust psychics. I don't need my fortune read."

"It's not like that. Look, I don't need you to believe, but Jon here has seen me do it. He knows."

She looked over at Jon for confirmation. He pressed his lips together, but nodded his head.

Izzy didn't know what to say. She stuttered and stopped and then blew out a breath. "Fine. At this point, I'll try anything. What is it you want to do?"

"It's very simple," Darcy said. "I want to contact Chip."

## CHAPTER 7

*J*on agreed to get the things that she needed. She kept her supplies in the downstairs closet now so that she had the candles and matches and incense altogether in one place. When it had been just her in the house, then it hadn't mattered where she put her things. With Jon's stuff mixing in with her own she had to be more organized.

Now she sat in the middle of Izzy's living room floor, cross legged, in a circle of five thick, white candles. Their flames flickered and raised small tendrils of smoke. Outside of the circle, a stick of incense burned in its holder, lending a nutty, earthy smell to the room.

In her hands Darcy held a set of keys. They had been Chip's set, the set he'd used to drive him and Izzy to their motel room where he was killed. Izzy had taken them to get out of there, had kept them with her even though they didn't do her any good now. Attached to the ring was a little tag with a pro football team's logo on it. Darcy didn't know enough about football to know what team it was. It didn't matter, though. All that mattered was that it was important to Chip.

Darcy cleared her mind, breathing slowly and deeply, blocking out the room around her.

Lilly's whispering broke her concentration. "Mommy, what's she doing?"

With a smile, Darcy went back to what she was doing. Breathe in, breathe out. Clearing her mind, she pictured the mist, the same mist that slinked through the town. It billowed and swirled in her mind and gave her the blank screen she needed to project her thoughts onto. Concentrating on the feel of the keys in her hand, on the person who had owned them, she cast outward, looking to talk to the soul of Charles McIntosh.

When nothing happened, she centered herself and tried again. This wasn't anything unusual. Sometimes the spirit of the person she was calling on didn't want to be contacted. Sometimes she almost had to force the departed person to have a conversation with her.

Breathe in, breathe out.

She called out to him in her mind. Chip? Are you there? Searching, waiting, she concentrated harder on the mist. In a corner of her mind the billowing shapes darkened and almost formed into something but then they folded in and around themselves and spilled away.

Nothing.

Breathe in, breathe out.

After a long time, she gasped and opened her eyes. Her mouth was dry and pasty. Her muscles ached. With an effort, she unfolded one leg and held it out straight to work out a cramp that had settled into it. "I couldn't do it," she said to Jon and Izzy. "I couldn't contact Chip."

Jon held his hand down to her and helped her up. "Doesn't that mean…?"

Darcy nodded as she settled her weight onto that one foot. "He's not dead."

"He's not...?" Izzy looked like she was about to faint. "What do you mean? Of course he's dead. I saw his blood."

"Momma?" Lilly asked, unshed tears in her voice.

"Shh, baby," Izzy said to her daughter. "I'm sorry, I didn't mean to scare you. But Darcy, I saw it. I know what happened."

"But you don't, do you? Can you remember anything from that night?"

Izzy shook her head miserably. "I've tried to remember. I've tried and tried. All I can remember is waking up with him gone and covered in his blood."

"The State Police forensics team checked the blood on the bed, too," Jon said to Darcy. "It was definitely his."

Frowning, licking her lips to get some moisture back in them, Darcy frowned. "I don't understand it, either, but I can tell you without a doubt that Chip is not dead. Izzy, can I get a glass of water, please?"

Jon was still looking at her in that conflicted, sort of angry way. "I believe you, Darcy. I want you to know that. But I can't just not do my job because you had a vision."

"Jon, it's more than that. She's an innocent woman. Isn't part of your job to protect the innocent?"

"Darcy you know it's not that simple. She's wanted for murder."

"A murder she didn't commit."

From over by the sink, Izzy cleared her throat. She held out the glass of water to Darcy. "If you two could stop arguing for a minute, maybe you could ask me what I want to do?"

Jon shook his head as Darcy took the water. "I'm sorry Izzy. I know we're not making this any easier on you. I don't think you get a say in it, though."

Darcy looked at him sharply. He shrugged, and then sighed. "I tell you what. Let's get them over to our house, and then we can talk more. You haven't told us anything that can really help you."

"She said Chip isn't dead," Izzy said, pointing to Darcy. "If you believe her then why would you want to turn me in?"

"How did you wake up with blood on you?" Jon asked. "Where is Chip? What happened in the cabin? Can you answer any of that?"

Izzy folded her arms around herself. "No. I can't. You think I don't want to?"

"But there is something you're keeping from us, isn't there?" Darcy said to her. "I can feel it."

When Izzy didn't answer Darcy touched Jon lightly on his shoulder. "Let's get her over to our house, before whoever that was comes looking for her again. Okay? Then maybe we can all talk more."

Absolutely no one looked happy with that idea. So Darcy figured it must be the right thing to do.

OVER ON HER OWN PORCH, Darcy pulled out the keys and unlocked the front door. The smoky tendrils of mist had thickened in the late afternoon sun. It swirled around the front steps, disturbed by their footsteps.

"Let's get inside quick," Jon said, scanning all around them. "We don't know if that guy is still out here."

Darcy pushed the door open and let Izzy and Lilly go in first. Reaching around for the light switch she turned it on and stepped in after them, Jon coming in close behind her. "The living room is through there," she said. "Why don't you and Lilly sit down and get comfortable?"

She dropped her keys on the table and was taking off her coat when the lights went out again.

Behind her Jon grunted loudly. A loud thump scared her just before something large and heavy bumped into her and knocked her down. She was on the floor, looking up at everything from an angle. In the weak daylight coming through the windows Darcy saw a large man in a dark coat rush into the living room.

"Where is the money? Where did he hide it?" The man was yelling. Darcy knew it was the same man who had attacked Izzy before. He'd followed them to her house.

"Please, I don't know anything!" she heard Izzy say.

Disoriented, Darcy tried to get up, to get to Izzy and help them. Jon was faster. He was already racing past her, shouting at the top of his lungs. "Police officer! Stay where you are or I'll shoot!"

There was the sounds of a scuffle and then Darcy heard the lamp topple over and something else that might have been the endtable crashing over onto its side. She got into the living room just in time to see Jon falling backward over the couch as the dark man ran for the back of the house. Jon was up and after him a moment later.

Darcy went to Izzy where she huddled in a corner with Lilly. "Are you two all right?" she asked.

Lilly nodded and sniffed, her little eyes wide. Izzy rocked her daughter back on her lap. "We're okay, Darcy. Thank you. I'm... I'm sorry I brought this into your house."

Darcy sat down next to them. "I told you we would help you and I meant it. You need to tell us everything, though. I know you're trying to keep something back but I don't think that's going to do anyone any good. Do you?"

Slowly, Izzy shook her head. "You're right. I've just been running for so long that I don't know how to trust people any more. I'm sorry."

When Jon came back in, out of breath, his gun out and in his hand, Darcy had Izzy and Lilly sitting back on the couch again. "He's gone," Jon told them. "I couldn't see where he went. He broke in our back door, Darcy, and it looks like he cut the power on the outside of the house. Pretty gutsy. A person can get electrocuted that way."

He put his gun back in its holster, looking from Darcy to Izzy and back again. "What's going on?"

"You should sit down for this," Darcy told him. "Izzy has something she wants to tell us."

Jon gave her a puzzled look, an expression that she was getting used to seeing on his face, and sat down next to her. They faced Izzy and waited, not rushing her, letting her get it out in her own time.

"My husband was an accountant. He made good money at it, too, giving us enough to live on and then some. That's how come I had as much in my savings as I did when I went on the run. Well. I thought Chip was making his money honestly, anyway." She took a shaky breath before continuing. "It turned out, he was making some shady deals with some people from the city. Very rich, very powerful people."

"The mafia?" Jon guessed.

Izzy shrugged. "The mafia, drug dealers, I'm not really sure. Chip referred to them as 'The Hand' once. I just know it was illegal. A few weeks before he…disappeared, some men came to the house. They were not nice people. One had a scar on his face, the other looked at me in a way that made my skin crawl. They went into my husband's private office but I could hear them yelling at him. They threatened his life if he went to the police. They said he had to keep making their books, or bad things would happen to him. And to us."

Darcy thought again of the man from her vision, the man who had attacked them twice now. "That man today, he was one of the men who came to your house that day, wasn't he Izzy?"

She nodded, wiping at the moisture that was collecting in the corners of her eyes. "The one with the scar under his eye. Yes. I don't know how he found me."

In halting sentences, Izzy went on to explain that even before she found out about Chip cheating on her, this trouble with "The Hand" was breaking their marriage apart. She had every intention of leaving Chip, but then he begged her to go to the motel with her, to try to fix things. She'd believed he was honestly trying to save their marriage. Now, she wasn't so sure.

"If he's not dead, then where is he?" she asked. "How could he just abandon me and his daughter like this?"

"I don't know," Darcy said. There was no way her gift could find someone who was still alive. As much as it had helped her and others over the years, sometimes it felt like it was just a burden. "We will help you, somehow. I promise you that."

Darcy turned to Jon, who nodded, his face carefully neutral. She could tell he was still mad at her for making him choose between her and his job. She just hoped he could forgive her. Soon.

"One thing's for sure," Jon said, standing up. "We can't stay here. I'll call someone to fix the power line, but it's obviously not safe here. Let's see if we can get Grace to meet us at the station. I'm sure she won't mind staying a little later if it means doing some real police work. I think we're going to need all of the help we can get."

Grace stood up from behind her desk as Darcy and Jon with Izzy and Lilly came in. Darcy hugged her sister. "Wow, Grace. You can really feel the baby bump now."

"You should feel it from my side." She grumbled when she said it, but Darcy saw the smile on her face. "So. I got as much information on this Hand group as I could while I was waiting for you. It turns out they're known for racketeering and money laundering. They're on every known gang list in the state. Loosely associated with the mafia, but independently run. I found a list of known members from the State Police. Here."

She turned her computer screen around for the others to see.

On it were a series of photos, with names and vital statistics listed for each person.

"You've been busy," Jon said to her.

"I'm pregnant, not permanently disabled," she snapped at him. "I keep telling you guys I can do more than shuffle papers."

Jon raised his hands in a mock indication of surrender. "Okay, okay. I believe you. You tell the Chief about this?"

"Not yet." Darcy sat back down, carefully balancing herself on the chair. "I didn't know what you had, or what you wanted me to tell him."

She looked meaningfully at Izzy and Lilly, then back to Jon. "Maybe you should tell him something? Soon?"

"My next phone call," Jon promised. "There's just been a lot going on—"

"That's him!" Izzy exclaimed, pointing at one picture among dozens on Grace's computer screen. "That's the man!"

They all crowded around the computer. The picture Izzy had indicated was of a muscular white man with thinning black hair and piercing gray eyes. A crescent shaped scar curved out along his cheek under his left eye. "Adolphos Carino," the name read, along with his age and his height and his weight.

When Darcy looked at the photograph, her vision of the night Izzy ran away from Cider Hill flashed through her mind. She saw the dark man again, yelling after Izzy. *"You can't run forever!"*

"Well." Jon rubbed at his jaw. "That gives us a name to put to our attacker. I have an idea I know who's been stealing cars in town, too."

"You think it was our friend Adolphos here?" Grace asked him.

"I do. It makes sense. The first car was stolen from Meadowood, and then dumped here, where another one was stolen from Garret Hobbs driveway. We'll have to tell our patrols out looking for that car to be careful. If this Adolphos has it, then there's no telling what he'll do if he's stopped."

"Right," Grace said, writing notes on a yellow pad of paper. "I'll take care of that with the desk Sergeant. What do we do about it in the meantime?"

"We need someplace for Izzy and Lilly to stay where they'll be safe. I can't exactly call the State Police yet, unless the Chief orders me to. Now that we know a little bit more about everything it's clear that Izzy is a victim. She needs to be protected."

Darcy smiled brightly at Jon. She was so proud of him for making that decision. She knew it hadn't been easy. He saw her looking at him and leaned over to kiss her cheek. "I'm sorry if I was a jerk."

"I'm sorry if I was, too."

"Very cute, you two," Grace said to them. "It doesn't solve our problem, though. How about they come stay with me and Aaron for now?"

"With you?" Darcy asked. "Are you sure?"

Grace spread her hands. "It makes sense. We live in an apartment off the ground floor. No easy access. If anyone comes looking for them all we have to do is keep the door closed and locked and call someone."

Darcy had to admit that it did make sense. She just hated how, once again, a mystery had swept into town and put all of her family and friends in danger. She had to wonder if she was some kind of magnet for trouble. Maybe her connection to the other side attracted people in danger to her for her to help.

If that was the case, then she and the universe needed to have a long conversation when this was over.

"Darcy, there's one other thing," Grace said. She took her sister by the hand and led her over to the other side of the empty officer's room. "I, uh, was going to have you and Jon over for dinner some night soon and ask you this, but it doesn't look like we're going to have a day without tons of excitement in it for the next little while. So. I wanted to ask you…"

Darcy didn't know what her sister was getting at. "Grace, what is it? Is something wrong?"

"No, no nothing like that," she said quickly. "Everything's fine. You know that Aaron and I are excited for our first child and we want everything to be just right and we were talking, and, um, we want to know if you'll be the baby's godparent?"

"Me?" Darcy thought her voice squeaked, she was so excited to hear Grace ask that. "Of course I would! I can't think of anything that would make me happier."

They hugged again, and Darcy practically bounced on her heels as they did.

# CHAPTER 8

$\mathcal{D}$arcy woke with a crick in her neck and Jon's arm across her waist. Grace's pull-out couch wasn't exactly a comfortable way to spend a night. She could feel every spring under her back. When she shifted to a more comfortable position, Jon's eyes popped open. With a yawn and a stretch he ended up folding his body across hers. "Good morning," he said to her with a smile.

"Mmph," she said back. "Next time we find a four star hotel to hide in."

"Deal. Settle for making breakfast with me?"

He looked so cute with his hair mussed up and his eyelids all droopy. They had both slept in their clothes for lack of pajamas, and his shirt hung all wrinkled down his front. She kissed him on the forehead. "Breakfast. Then maybe a shower?"

"Together?" he teased.

She laughed. "You make the pancakes. I'll see if there's any bacon in the freezer."

While they were starting everything, getting pans and bowls out as quietly as possible so they wouldn't wake any of the others especially Izzy and Lilly, Jon became very quiet.

"What are you thinking about?" Darcy asked him.

He looked sheepish. "Is it that obvious?"

"I just know you that well," she said with a smile.

"Actually, I was thinking about this whole situation. I think I have a way to catch our visiting bad guy, this Adolphos character. The only drawback is it's going to mean putting Izzy in harm's way again."

Darcy thought she might know what he was getting at. "We'd better wait for her to wake up and ask her what she thinks."

"I agree." He put another pancake on the stack he had already cooked and then turned to her. "There's something else."

"Oh?" She wasn't sure she liked the way he had said that.

He wiped his hands on a dish towel before encircling her waist and pulling her to him. "You need to know I'm still a little angry about the spot you put me in with Izzy and Lilly. That whole mess could have cost me my job. Or worse, got me charged as an accessory."

"But, Jon, you talked to the Chief and explained the whole thing to him, right? He said to do whatever you had to?"

Jon nodded, his eyes studying the lines of her face. "Yes, but he wasn't happy about it. Luckily by that point we had all of the proof we needed to show reasonable doubt about Izzy killing her husband. Otherwise...well, let's not dwell on the otherwise. So, here's what I need to say to you."

Bracing herself, Darcy tensed up in his arms. She bit at her lower lip to keep it from trembling.

"Darcy Sweet, you were right," he said at last, his lips curling into a weak smile. "What we're doing is exactly the right thing. Thank you for making me do it, because on my own I would have just arrested her and let the State Police figure it out. You make me a better person."

She didn't know what to think. It was probably the sweetest thing Jon had ever said to her. Warmth spread through her body and turned her cheeks pink. "I love you, Jon Tinker."

"I love you, Darcy Sweet."

"Aw," they heard Grace say from the hallway leading down to the bedrooms. "You guys are so sweet you make me just want to brush my teeth. You made breakfast?"

Later when they were all eating breakfast, with Izzy and Lilly sitting at the kitchen table with Aaron and Grace and Jon and Darcy eating from their plates over the countertop, Jon laid out his plan to them.

Grace mopped up maple syrup with a forkful of pancake. "Are you sure that's a smart idea? We don't know what this Adolphos is capable of. Or more correctly, we know exactly what he's capable of. He's dangerous."

Jon nodded, placing his empty plate in the sink. "I know. And there's a lot of risk to this. Izzy, if you don't want to try this, we can do something else. I just can't think of what that would be, other than turning you over to the State Police. We've all agreed we don't want to do that if we can avoid it."

Izzy had hardly touched her breakfast. She looked down at her daughter, who was making her way through her second pancake after munching a pile of crunchy bacon. Finally she nodded. "I'll do it. My daughter deserves to be able to live without being afraid all the time. I'll do it. For her."

Darcy found Jon's hand and gave it a squeeze. Now they had a plan.

LATER THAT DAY, Jon sat with Darcy in the second floor hallway of Izzy's house. They had been there for hours now, waiting for something to happen. Izzy was downstairs, sitting at the kitchen table with the curtains wide open so anyone could easily see her from outside.

"Are you sure he's going to come?" Darcy asked Jon.

"I'm sure," he answered. "It's just going to take time. Grace tailed Izzy while she walked all around town for nearly an hour. There's no way that Adolphos didn't see her. Then she came right here. It won't be long."

Darcy tugged at the neck of the bulletproof vest she was wearing. Jon had made both her and Izzy wear them, just like he was. Adolphos was a killer, and he'd come at Izzy with a gun twice already. They weren't worried about him shooting Izzy through the window, or even bursting through the door shooting. He thought Izzy had information that he wanted.

Izzy's husband had been involved in money laundering and worse. It wasn't a big leap from that fact to know what Adolphos had been asking about yesterday. *"Where is it?"* he'd asked. What he meant, was that Chip McIntosh had been skimming money from the criminal organization The Hand. Adolphos wanted that money.

The problem, as Izzy had pointed out to Jon, was that Izzy had no idea where the money was.

So now Jon and Darcy waited for Adolphos to take the bait and make an appearance. He'd told her several times that he wanted her to stay at the station or with Grace, but Darcy had insisted on coming. She thought maybe her sixth sense might be of some help. Plus, she had started this whole thing, and she wanted to see it through to the end. Grace and two uniformed officers had taken up positions in a car parked behind Jon and Darcy's house, ready to swoop in when needed.

Which apparently wasn't going to be anytime soon.

"You know," Darcy said, talking just to pass the time, "Sue's leaving for college. She won't be able to work at the shop anymore."

"Really? Hmm. That's too bad. When's she have to go?"

"Next week, I think." The reality of it rushed in for Darcy. "I got to thinking about running the bookstore by myself. It's too much."

"You could always hire someone else." His eyes were on the

stairs as he spoke to her, and she could tell his ears were pricked for any sound. "Or maybe cut back on the hours?"

"Well, I know the shop hasn't been doing as much business as it used to, but Sue and I are working on a plan to change that."

"Oh, yeah? You should tell me about... Shh," he raised a hand up, motioning for her to be silent.

Darcy felt a chill go up her spine at the same time that Jon went very still. Someone was coming. Someone with bad intentions.

They heard the door slam open downstairs and Izzy cried out. Then the voice of the dark man, shouting. "It's just you and me now. You tell me where he hid the money or you'll never see your daughter again!"

Jon was already halfway down the stairs. Darcy followed him to the wall separating the living room from the kitchen. He motioned for her to stay back, then crouched down to give himself leverage, and jumped out at Adolphos.

Darcy heard the scuffle start and when she came around after Jon, he was on the floor with the intruder, struggling to get the gun away from him. Izzy had backed away into the corner by the sink. Adolphos' face was scrunched up and the cords in his neck stood out as he wrestled with Jon. Both men were tall and strong but Darcy could see that Adolphos had the size advantage. She had to help.

Picking up the teakettle from the stove she carefully circled the two men until she had an opening, fully aware of where the gun was being pointed the whole time. When she saw her chance she smashed the kettle down as hard as she could on Adolphos' head. It was a heavy green metal thing, and it made a hollow thunk against the man's skull.

The strike dazed Adolphos long enough for Jon to wrestle the gun away from him and toss it aside.

"You're coming down to the station," Jon said, panting as he pinned Adolphos down on his stomach, handcuffing him behind his back. "We all need to have a long talk."

Darcy went to Izzy and held her, feeling the way she trembled. "It's all right, we got him."

"Thanks to your assist," Jon said to Darcy. "Maybe they should issue us teakettles instead of pistols."

GRACE and the uniformed officers drove Adolphos into town to the police station. It had been a long couple of days, and Darcy was glad to see they were close to finding an end to it all. She and Izzy watched through the two-way glass of the interview room as Jon sat down across from Adolphos, hit man for The Hand.

Dressed in black pants and a nice black silk shirt, Adolphos was every bit as scary as his photograph. The crescent scar under his left eye was puckered in a ruddy face that glared daggers at Jon. His hands were still cuffed, and the cuffs were chained to a ring on his side of the metal interview table.

Jon tapped a pen against the yellow pages of his notebook. He was recording the entire interview, but Darcy knew that he liked to make his own notes as well. Through the speakers, she and Izzy could hear every word that was said. "You've been advised of your right to remain silent, remember," Jon told Adolphos.

"I know my rights better than you do," the man sneered. "No doubt you've seen my rap sheet. I've been arrested on any number of crimes. Each time, I walked. I'll walk this time, too."

Jon raised an eyebrow. "What makes you so sure of that? You've attacked Isabelle McIntosh twice now in my jurisdiction. We know you're working for a group that calls themselves The Hand. We know you're after money that was stolen from the group by Isabelle's husband, Charles McIntosh, also known as Chip."

"You know a lot for a dumb cop." Adolphos shifted in his

chair, somehow managing to look comfortable in spite of his circumstances. "So you must know how this is going to work. I'm going to offer to give you information on certain...activities that are related to organized crime that your little rinky dink agency here will be much more interested in. As will the State Police, and I should think the FBI as well. Call Agent Dominie at the capitol office. I'll give you the number."

"Where's Chip McIntosh?" Jon asked, seeing the conversation wasn't going anywhere.

Adolphos shrugged. "Don't know. We know he's still alive, of course, but we haven't been able to find him. You're the smart guy. You figure it out."

Jon kept at it for a half hour longer or more before finally giving up. He closed his notepad and walked out, coming around to where Darcy and Izzy were. "We're not going to get anything more out of him. We'll charge him, of course, but unfortunately he's right. With what he knows he'll buy himself a reduced sentence."

"You think he'll really walk away free?" Izzy asked, her face horrified.

"No," Jon said. "Not completely. He'll serve a sentence in a nice cushy Federal Prison, most likely. What we need to worry about right now is finding your husband. You thought he was dead all this time. Now, you know he's not. So, think now. Where would he go to hide?"

Izzy bent her head in thought. When she looked up again her eyes were wide. "His brother has a summer home a few hours away from here. He hasn't used it in three years. Chip took it over. No one goes up there anymore."

She gave them the address and Jon went to grab his coat. Darcy followed tight on his heels. Jon stopped her with a hand on her arm. "Not this time. Not that I wouldn't mind you backing me up with a teakettle again but let me and the uniformed guys handle this one." He kissed her on her cheek. "I'll be back."

DARCY SPUN the antique ring on her finger fitfully as she sat with Izzy in the Bean There Bakery and Café. Lilly was still being watched by Aaron. They had agreed it was best to leave her there until they found out if Jon would find Chip. There was no sense in confusing the poor girl any more than she already was. In spite of her concern for Jon, Darcy's stomach had reminded her she hadn't eaten all day, so they had decided to go for sandwiches and coffee.

Helen came over to their table after waiting on some of the other customers, and sat down with a smile. "Well, Darcy, it's good to see you've gotten our new neighbor to come out of her shell. Hello there, I'm Helen Nelson, mayor of Misty Hollow."

Izzy smiled uncertainly and made small talk for a few moments. Darcy reminded herself that most of the town had no idea of the drama unfolding around them. In a lot of ways it was a nice change of pace. Usually the troubles that came to Misty Hollow caught everyone up in their webs.

"Oh, Helen," Darcy said, suddenly remembering. "I wanted to ask you something. You know that Sue is leaving, right? I wanted to do a going away party for her. Two days from now, maybe? Could you possibly bake a few dozen cookies for it? I'm going to invite the book club and Linda from the library and some others."

"That's a wonderful idea," Helen agreed. "I'll do some other appetizers, too. We sure will miss Sue."

After they finished their sandwiches they made their way back over to the police station. "Izzy, that's Jon's police car," Darcy said, seeing the dark sedan parked out front.

They went inside, buzzed through by the desk sergeant on duty, to find the inside of the police station humming with activity. Grace sat at her desk, directing several uniformed officers to tasks that had them all scurrying. At Jon's desk, a man sat with his hands cuffed in his lap, miserably hunched over. His shirt was torn along the left sleeve and his pants were filthy. A healed over scar along his left forearm showed Darcy where he must have cut himself to leave his blood behind and frame his wife for his murder.

As if he knew she was there, Chip turned and locked eyes with Izzy. His blonde hair was cut short and choppy, and his face was covered with stubble. Izzy put a hand to her mouth to muffle a gasp. "Chip…"

Jon nodded to Darcy, and she understood. "Izzy, let's go into the waiting room."

"No!" Izzy suddenly ran up to where Chip was sitting and slapped him across the face. "How could you do this? How could you do this to me? To our daughter? How dare you!"

He shrugged. "I had to go into hiding."

It was the only explanation they would ever get from him.

# CHAPTER 9

*T*wo days later, Jon and Darcy were putting the last touches around the bookstore for Sue's going away party. Streamers were strung along the bookshelves. Balloons were tied and floating from the chairs. Next to the front counter, the big surprise was covered with a large blue tablecloth.

Grace, Aaron, and Izzy were all helping. Lilly ran among the bookstacks, taking children's books down off the shelves, flipping through their pages and putting them back, over and over. Darcy smiled to see it. She'd been so worried when Izzy had told her daughter about her daddy still being alive and going to jail. Lilly had thought about it, then looking straight at her mom she'd asked, "I guess we'll have to send him Christmas cards at the jail, huh?"

Darcy looked over at Jon, smiling and laughing at something that Aaron had said. Someday, they'd have their own little daughter or son. She couldn't wait to talk about it with him.

Jon had told them about turning Chip over to the State Police, and how the warrant for Izzy had been rescinded given the circumstances. She would still have to make several statements and testify at any number of hearings, but for the moment she was free.

Helen arrived with trays of cookies and muffins and little finger sandwiches. Not long after, the store was full of people from town, eating, laughing, and dancing to music.

Great Aunt Millie was there too. At one point, a single balloon untied itself from a chair and came floating over to hang in front of Lilly until the little girl grabbed its string. Millie always had loved children. It's such a shame that she'd never had any of her own.

Sue was late in arriving to her own party. When she got there, the whole place erupted in cheers and applause, causing the young woman to blush fiercely. Beside her, a young man with a kind face broke into a wide smile and leaned over and whispered in Sue's ear, making her blush even harder. Darcy recognized Zach, Sue's boyfriend.

The two of them came over to where Darcy and Izzy were standing. "Hi Sue!" Darcy said. "Like your party?"

"You shouldn't have done all this, Darcy!" Sue was laughing, holding Zach's hand tightly. "This is too much."

"It's not even close to enough to show my appreciation for everything you've done here. Everyone in town is going to miss you. Oh, this is Izzy McIntosh. Izzy, this is Sue and her boyfriend Zach."

"Nice to finally meet you," Sue said. They talked for a while and then Helen came to pull Sue off to some other people.

After Sue walked away Darcy turned to Izzy. "You know, with Sue leaving I'm going to need someone to help me here at the store. And if I remember, you kind of need a job."

"Boy, do I ever," Izzy sighed. "I have no idea what state my finances are in. I have to have Chip declared alive again, and see if I'm entitled to any of his money or if it all has to go to pay back what he stole, and it just keeps getting worse the more I think about it. A job would definitely help."

"Then why don't you come work for me?"

Izzy looked mildly surprised. "That's so generous of you. Are you sure?"

"Well, it's actually kind of selfish on my part. I'm going to need someone to help me with the surprise Sue and I put together. Jon!" She called across to him and he looked over, his mouth full of a muffin he had just bitten into. He came over to her, kissing her with crumbs still on his mouth. "Silly man," she said. "Can you stay with Izzy for a few minutes? I need to do something."

Leaving Izzy with him, she rounded Sue back up from the crowd again. "Are you ready to show everyone?"

Sue nodded, too excited to speak. They went over to the cash register, to the object covered over by the counter, and Darcy called for everyone's attention. With the music still playing in the background everyone quieted down and waited for what the big announcement was.

"I'm so glad that everyone made it for Sue's going away party," Darcy said loudly. She looked out and saw so many faces she recognized. Clara Barstow, Blake Underwood and Evelyn Casey, Linda and her boss Marla and all the others. "This town has always been a place where good people come together to help each other. We're losing a good friend as Sue goes off to fulfil her dream." Applause rippled around the room and Darcy had to pause to let it die down.

"We're also going to welcome a new friend today," Darcy went on. "Can we all say hello to Izzy McIntosh, and her daughter Lilly?"

There were murmured hellos and whispered questions among everyone, and a few people came over to introduce themselves personally to an obviously flustered Izzy.

"Before Sue leaves, we want to show you what we've been working on." Everyone's attention was back on Darcy again. She nodded to Sue, and Sue nodded back, and both of them took a corner of the tablecloth to lift it up and over with a little flourish.

Underneath was a stand-up display made from heavy duty yellow cardboard. Across the top of the display were tall red letters. "A Library in Your Hands," it read. In the display itself were three rows of neatly stacked e-readers, all in brand new boxes.

Approving murmurs rippled through the room. "I am proud to announce," Darcy said, "that the Sweet Read Bookstore is now offering e-readers for sale, along with a slew of your favorite books in electronic format to purchase or rent."

Darcy smiled over at Sue. "Thank you," she whispered. "You did a great job on this."

The young woman, one of Darcy's best friends, came over and hugged Darcy tightly. "I'll miss you," she said.

"I'll miss you, too." Darcy was surprised to feel tears in her eyes. A mix of emotions swept through her. She had spent so much of her life being the oddball, but in moments like these she could see how truly loved she was, and how many friends she had.

Misty Hollow was truly a wonderful place to live. Fate had led Izzy and Lilly to just the place they needed to be when they were in trouble.

Of course, trouble always found Darcy Sweet. She knew another mystery would come to town soon enough. They always did.

**-The End-**

# ABOUT THE AUTHOR

**Kathrine Emrick writing as K.J. Emrick is the author of the popular Darcy Sweet Cozy Mystery series and Pine Lake Inn Cozy Mystery series.**

Strongly influenced by authors like James Patterson, Dick Francis, and Nora Roberts, Kathrine Emrick dreamed of being an author for the majority of her life.

She never quite gave up on the idea of being a published author and at the age of 51, thanks to the self publishing explosion,, she finally realized her dream. Her maturity allows her to bring a variety of experiences and observations to her writing.

She lives in beautiful South Australia with her family, including several animals. Kathrine can always be found jotting down daily notes in a journal and like many authors, she loves to be surrounded by books and is a voracious reader. In her spare time, she enjoys spending time with her family and volunteering at the local library.

Her goal is to regularly produce entertaining and noteworthy content and engaging in a community of readers and writers.

**To find out more please visit the Kathrine's website at kathrineemrick.com**

Printed in Great Britain
by Amazon